LITTLE PORTIA

ff

LITTLE PORTIA

Simon Gray

faber and faber
LONDON · BOSTON

First published in 1967 by
Faber and Faber Limited
3 Queen Square London WC1N 3AU

This paperback edition first published in 1986

Photoset by Parker Typesetting Service, Leicester
Printed in Great Britain by
Redwood Burn Ltd Trowbridge Wiltshire
All rights reserved

ISBN 0 571 14598 1

' "Issues from the hand of God, the simple soul" '
'Issues from the hand of time the simple soul'

For my parents

Checking inside the book, I see that Faber and Faber published *Little Portia* in 1967. In those days it took over a year to move a book from typescript into the bookshops, and I have an idea – though I can't be sure of this – that it took me about two-and-a-half years to write it. There were certainly long hiatuses at Cambridge when drink and poker became desperate alternatives to the typewriter, and I got married and moved to London, where I'd managed to land a lectureship at Queen Mary College, down the Mile End Road, between drafts. I can't say between which drafts, as there were so many. Boxes full, in fact. I wish I had them now, to serve as an *aide-mémoire* on a grand scale, but they've long gone. About a year after the novel was published someone at the University of Boston – I assumed the librarian – wrote asking if he could have any material I possessed connected with it. This seemed a perfect solution to an increasingly pressing problem. My study was small, I'd already started stockpiling drafts of something else I was working on, and yet I couldn't quite bring myself just to chuck out the visible history of *Little Portia* with the other rubbish. I wrote back to the University of Boston, agreeing to allow them to help order my life on condition that I took no part in the arrangements. One day a couple of men arrived, surveyed without surprise (they weren't literary critics, after all – although one of them had a mildly rapacious smile) the mountains of labour out of which *Little Portia* had been born, packed them neatly into crates, and went off with them. So now, short of flying to Boston and foraging in the warehouses, I have nothing but the published novel to help me recall the writing of it. Which is why all I'm absolutely sure of is that I began it in Cambridge, and finished it in London, between 1961 and 1963, and that it was the move to London – as a suddenly fully employed and married man, with a child on the way – that finally unblocked me and made finishing it possible. And yet it remains for me not simply a novel mainly about and set in Cambridge, but a Cambridge novel – in its tone, its attitude towards its characters, and its pervasive atmosphere. Well then, if not a *Cambridge* novel, then a novel that had its seeds in my sense of Cambridge.

I spent six of the nine years I was there passing myself off as a research student at Trinity, while in reality editing a small literary magazine called *Delta* and completing two novels – *Colmain* and *Simple People* – both also published by Faber and Faber. My non-working hours were spent, as I've already hinted, playing poker, drinking whisky, and trying to have affairs. It was, of course, a life of suppurating loneliness from which circumstances, mainly in the form of my wife, rescued me. As I've already described all that in an essay called 'My Cambridge'*, I've no intention of going into it again but I suppose I have, rather grudgingly, and at last, to put on record one central fact about my time at Cambridge. Whatever I felt about it while I was there, and have continued to feel about it during the two decades since I left, it provided what for want of a better word I'll have to call material for two of my novels, *Simple People* and *Little Portia*, and for three of my plays, *Close of Play*, *Quartermaine's Terms* and *The Common Pursuit*, the last two of which were written during the last five years. The eponymous hero of another of my plays, *Butley*, was educated at

*First published in *My Cambridge* (Robson Books 1977) and re-published in *An Unnatural Pursuit* (Faber 1985).

Cambridge, and I have no doubt that there are references to Cambridge scattered through the rest of my work. So somehow it would seem that I'm still at Cambridge. Or that Cambridge is still at me. I made an attempt to cross-institutionalize myself in two early plays, *Otherwise Engaged* and *Dog Days*, by giving almost all the characters in them an Oxford education, but renegade references to Cambridge, faintly pejorative, faintly wistful, nevertheless insist on turning up even there. But of all the things I've written *Little Portia* is the one most deeply rooted in Cambridge, to the point almost of having about it the whiff of autobiography. And yet of my plays, the one that is closest to it in content is *Quartermaine's Terms*, and there is nothing autobiographical, as far as *I* can determine, in that. But then *Quartermaine's Terms* wasn't set in the university milieu, except geographically. It is set in an English language school for foreigners, and is glimpsed at various moments in its early history, from shortly after its inception through the beginnings of a happily brief decline, on to the death of one of its two principals and the beginning of what might turn out to be a permanent resurgence. Its central character is St John Quartermaine. He is a bachelor from another age, although he's in fact quite young. Somewhere in his early forties at the most, I'd imagine. All the other characters revolve around him without making contact with his real nature, which is nevertheless (though accidentally) on display to theatre audiences – at least I like to think so. In my conception at least, Quartermaine is both there in his decency, unfailing courtesy and active but incoherently expressed kindness, and not quite ever there completely because, I suppose, the pulse of life doesn't beat quite strongly enough in him, except when quickened – in the last scene of the play – by intense and unexpected pain. He is sacked from the school, the only world in which he feels at home, by Henry Windscape, the new principal. Windscape is a perfectly fair-minded and honourable man. He is also Quartermaine's friend, for whom Quartermaine has performed various services (among them, baby-sitting), who nevertheless realizes that the days of Quartermaine and his ilk (if there ever was such an ilk) are over. Quartermaine, for all his unconscious moral virtues, is an inept teacher – how then can he give value to his employers, discharge his responsibility to his students? I set the play in the sixties, during the period in which I wrote *Little Portia*, because I've subsequently come to believe there was some date there, that I can't localize, when a courtly tolerance passed out of English life for ever. It passed, I believe, virtually unnoticed, certainly unmarked by any large public event, in a number of inconsequential deaths, like Quartermaine's, that were the result of reluctantly administered executions by the likes of genial old Henry Windscape, who had himself suffered more than any chap should have to suffer, in the death of a beloved daughter.

But this is probably the retrospective ordering of a nostalgic, even sentimental, mind – of a mind become nostalgic and sentimental. I was forty-five when I wrote *Quartermaine's Terms*, which is set in the period when, at the age of twenty-eight and twenty-nine, I was actually writing *Little Portia*, the last section of which is concerned with a language school in Cambridge. In fact the unseen principal of the school in *Quartermaine's Terms* has the same name as the highly visible principal of the school in *Little Portia*, an act of unconscious reminiscence – at least, I was quite unaware of it until I read the novel through a few days ago, for the purposes of this introduction. Both the play and the novel also share a character called Meadle. The two Meadles have quite a lot in common; a North Country background, a thrusting ambition, and an innate tendency to disaster. Where they are different is in the author's attitude to them, I think. In *Quartermaine's Terms* I'm clearly a fan of Meadle's, suffering a little as he suffers, and prepared to celebrate, along with him, his occasional triumphs. I also allow him an off-stage girlfriend (Daphne, afflicted with a speech impediment) and a complicated emotional life. The Meadle in the novel, however, never quite escapes his role of dynamic but peripheral joke. Although he seethes desperately away in his pursuit of promotion, he appears to have no life at all outside the classroom and staff room. What should be his moment of greatest triumph is in fact a major disaster, and is celebrated as such by both the author and the novel's central character, Grahame Thwaite.

Nevertheless, the 'source' of *Quartermaine's Terms* is quite evidently the last section of *Little Portia*. And the 'source' of the last section of *Little Portia* was my own experience as a teacher in language schools in Cambridge. Significantly enough, this was part of my time at Cambridge that holds no horrors for me in memory, seems really rather friendly, as if it were separate from my life first as an undergraduate and then as a postgraduate, although in reality the two were not only continuous but intertwined. I taught in one school or another almost every vacation until my last few years at Cambridge when I taught part-time throughout the year at the grandest of the schools – the model for the school in the novel, and so, of course, for the school in the play.

My first school was the Davis School of English. I started teaching there in the summer before I became an undergraduate. I'd been an *assistant* at the Collège-Technique of Clermont-Ferrand, had applied from there to do research at Cambridge on Henry James and, once admitted, had switched to undergraduate status. It was 1958 and I was twenty-one. I had a suspect (in England anyway) degree in English from Dalhousie University, Halifax, Nova Scotia, and as I had gone there straight from an English public school – my father had emigrated, or rather re-emigrated to

xiii

Canada – I felt that my three years in Halifax had really just been an interruption in my education proper, my personal equivalent of the National Service that had interrupted the education of almost all my school friends. Also, although my research outline – which amounted to a few sentences culled from Leavis's essay in *The Great Tradition* inflated into five pages or so about James's 'ultimate failure' as both man and artist – had been accepted by whatever board scrutinized such things, I knew that to spend five years or so pretending to inflate my five pages or so of bogus and impertinent moralizing into three hundred pages or so of impertinent and bogus moralizing would tax even my gift – explored at second-hand in *Little Portia* – for sustained fraud. But getting into Cambridge as a research student had the great advantage of facilitating my getting into it as an undergraduate. Instead of taking exams, being interviewed, etc., and so facing possible rejection, I merely wrote to Trinity humbly offering to take a few steps down the ladder, to where I wanted to be, and that – I discovered almost by return of post – was that. So when the academic year ended at Clermont – I'd got the job through the French Consul in Halifax, by the way, sight unseen – I faced a summer between myself and my postponed career as a Cambridge undergraduate, with no money to get through it. A friend, a graduate of Cambridge in French and at that time *lecteur* at the university of Clermont, wrote to a friend of his in Cambridge, who taught at the Davis School. My friend's friend spoke to the principal. The principal wrote offering me a job, sight unseen, and again that was that. I go into all this as a way of explaining how things, some things anyway, still worked in the late fifties, when the back door was not only wider than the front door, but usually on the latch. Grahame Thwaite, the hero of *Little Portia*, gets his job at his language school, sight unseen, because his sister recommends him to the principal.

The hours were long at the Davis School. I had to teach from 9.30 to 5.30, with an hour off for lunch, Monday to Friday. The pay was £13 and some shillings a week. I add this information as a way of explaining how other things, some other things anyway, still worked in the late fifties. If nowadays one couldn't get such a job in such circumstances, one wouldn't anyway accept it – be *allowed* to accept it – on such terms.

The teaching methods would now be thought primitive. There were no language laboratories, for instance, no technology at all, in fact, apart from a large and cumbersome tape recorder with two enormous, whirring spools of tape that either unravelled or tangled themselves into knots before snapping. When I could get it to work I made the students read passages of Shakespeare into it, so that I could point out defects in their accents. I then read out the same passages myself, so that they could hear not only how it should be done *qua accent*, but how it should be done *qua drama*. I believe my readings confused them somewhat, as I now clipped sharply away like Olivier, now rumbled eccentrically from side to side of a phrase like Richardson – in fact, spoke in an accent both unlike my own, and any other that they'd ever heard. The true work was done from books. There was a grammar textbook, a work of sheer genius, in which I discovered such forms as the future perfect conditional for the first time in my life. In other words, in order to teach English as a foreign language I had also to learn it as if it were a foreign language. The result was that I didn't so much pass on long digested information, as relay excited bulletins from the grammatical front.

The students were mainly middle-class boys and girls of between seventeen and twenty-five, from the Scandinavian countries, and from France, Italy, Spain, Holland and Germany. There were a few exotics from such countries as

Turkey and Japan, and one or two whey-faced, steel-spectacled drabs from the Eastern bloc. I only recall two of them distinctly. Most vividly, a large, twenty-five-year-old Swiss called Ferdinand Boller. He wore a baggy suit with knife-edge creases in unexpected places, down one sleeve for instance, and across the bulge of his rump. I imagine he ironed these deliberately but inadvertently himself, as he was the most maladroit man I'd ever met. His voyage across a room was marked by the clatter of falling chairs, the tumbling of books, the scattering of papers. It was also marked by grunts and stoopings, gesticulations of apology, and strange eruptive laughter. Herr Boller's attitude towards himself during these misadventures appeared to be one of self-reproachful bewilderment. On one occasion he broke a window with his elbow, by standing up in front of it and taking an unnecessary step back. On another I found him alone in the classroom, with his hands locked around the neck of a standard lamp, as if attempting to strangle it – although I suppose he was merely setting it upright after knocking it over. He was an exceptionally sweet man, hard-working, with a love of all things English, but he brought to the study of our language the same uncomprehending proneness to accident that he brought to the physical world. When asked his opinion of *Lady Windermere's Fan* – one of our set texts – he furrowed his brow and folded his hands on the table, in a lumpish impersonation of a literary critic, before pronouncing that 'This Oscar Vilde, I tink he is an bit off an humbugger, yes?' I did my best to insert this *trouvaille* into many of the drafts of *Little Portia*, but finally had to drop it on the grounds that it was too obviously contrived. It finally bobbed up in a play I wrote years later, called *Dog Days* – the heroine of which also taught in a language school, as did the wife in *Otherwise Engaged* – and as I hadn't known it was going to until I saw it on the page after I'd written it down, I decided to let it be. Herr Boller himself bobbed up in *Quartermaine's Terms*, in the form of an off-stage presence who sends Quartermaine postcards in almost unrecitable English – the only student, as the Principal observes, 'ever to think he'd got something out of St John's classes'. In one draft I had him enter just before the final curtain, just after Quartermaine's sacking, togged up in lederhosen, an effulgent parody of a yodelling Swiss, to salue the despairing and freshly exiled Quartermaine as his happiest memory of England. I wish now that I'd found room for him in *Little Portia* as well. Ferdinand Boller's spirit might have gone some small way towards shaping the unheroic Grahame Thwaite's for the better.

As it turned out, it was the other student I still remember that was to have most influence in the authorial shaping of *Little Portia*. She was Norwegian, already spoke almost perfect English when she arrived at the school, was tall and blonde, exceptionally pretty, and had something rather odd going on in her small, blue eyes. It might have been an ophthalmic complaint that made them flick and swivel so much. On the other hand, it might have been lust. She used to walk me home after classes. I refrained from inviting her in until one afternoon she simply followed me through the door, made tea, put on one of my records (Bach) and held out her arms. Instead of gliding into them I remained seated on my bed, hands folded into my lap, in a posture reminiscent of Herr Ferdinand Boller lumpishly confronting Oscar Wilde, thus forcing her into an exhibition of solo dance. She floated around the room, brushing against me, swaying away, her eyes rolling, swivelling, flicking, sometimes even closing. And there on the bed I sat, throbbing away with lustful self-hatred, from which I attempted to rescue myself with reminders that I mustn't on any account betray the trust placed in me by the Principal of the Davis School, who doubtless only took me, sight unseen, on the tacit understanding that I didn't misbehave myself with the female

xvii

students. And the male ones too, I expect. After she'd danced, she drank her tea and left. A few days later she fell into the hands of a notorious Turkish student called Ali, for which I blamed myself almost entirely, though from her expression, as she sat beside him in class, I could see that she found the arrangement perfectly satisfactory, even when sporting a black eye. But then that's how things – the more delicate things – also worked back in the late fifties. Anyway, how they worked if you'd just come from a provincial French town, by way of a provincial Canadian town, by way of an English public school, by way of a Montreal childhood, by way of Hayling Island, Hampshire, as your birthplace, with Barbara Mary Cecilia Gray (*née* Holliday, half-Welsh, half-English) as your mother, and James Davidson Gray (wholly Scots) as your father. And so, inevitably, that's how they worked for Grahame Thwaite in *Little Portia* when he went up to Cambridge, even though he'd never been to either Clermont-Ferrand or Halifax, Nova Scotia, and was an orphan.

But I know for a certainty that Grahame Thwaite and I weren't entirely on our own. One of my closest friends as an undergraduate was the son of a prominent London psychiatrist, had done his National Service (which, as the autobiographical novels of the time established, was really one long sexual encounter) and was universally acknowledged to be among the most sophisticated of the university's young men. Among his many talents was an easy way with women. When walking with them he invariably took their arm, whatever their age, however beautiful, and talked to them in a low, confidential voice, smirkingly. He entertained them in style, with drinks in his room followed by dinner in town, then drinks back in his room, etc. What the etcetera amounted to became clear one evening when I dropped in for a drink. He was looking both insouciant and tense, like a world-class sprinter in his blocks. 'What's up?' I asked, as I shifted my buttocks around on the cushion of a chair that I'd never previously found uncomfortable. He explained that he was taking Samantha out for dinner. 'It's going to be rather a special evening, in point of fact.' I tugged a towel out from under the cushion, and wondered what it had been doing there. 'I've got them everywhere. Under the sofa cushions too. Over there.' He pointed to the window seat. 'And in the bedroom. Two. Under the pillow. I've even got one in the bathroom.' This was clearly intended to be a joke. 'You see, I've finally decided the time has come to go all the way.' I went from being amazed to not being surprised to being deeply comforted in a matter of seconds. If Anthony, who had all the social graces, *and* actually liked the company of women, *and* whose father was a famous shrink – why then, how many others were also as backward as me? Under the circumstances, I didn't mind exposing my ignorance. I said I still didn't understand about the towels. 'Well, as far as I can make out, she's never been all the way either. And I gather that, well, some of them bleed a lot, you see. And I don't know where it's going to happen, do I? I want it to be spontaneous.' His eyes clocked the possible locations, including the window seat where my imagination, inflamed though it was, couldn't quite follow. And indeed it didn't happen on the window seat, as I discovered the next morning, when I hurtled around for a cup of coffee. Nor on the sofa. Nor in the chair. Nor in the bed. Nor anywhere at all. After drinks, dinner, drinks, it had been the same old etcetera, i.e. French kisses and a ration of nipple sucking until he'd made his move, which Samantha had checked with evidently professional aplomb, and then made the subject of a long, untherapeutic, indeed headache-inducing discussion about the meaning of their relationship and precisely how far she was prepared to go without going all the way. Unlike Anthony, though, she could confess that she'd already been there once or twice, which gave her both a conversational

xix

and a moral edge. She knew what she was talking about when she said she didn't want to go there again, at least with Anthony, at least until they knew each other much better. So forth. Then he'd walked her back to Newnham or Girton, presumably taking her arm as they went, and talking confidently and smirkingly into her ear.

It wasn't Anthony's experience with Samantha that I was 'using' when writing of Grahame Thwaite's almost identical, if more exhaustingly prolonged defeat by Sylvie Wasserman in *Little Portia*, but my own with a girl whose name I can still recall with a tender loathing from time to time. Perhaps tussles with resolutely knickered girls (who'd invariably taken them off for someone else) followed by meaningful discussions, headaches, and a broken spirit were a kind of rite of passage for men of my generation. Or perhaps I got it all wrong, and the coincidence of an Anthony and his Samantha has led me into a self-mollifying generalization. Much of this is, I suppose, quite incomprehensible to the generations that came after, when the young men appear to have learnt about sex in their mothers' laps. So to speak.

So, given the possibility of thousands of deknickered Samanthas and Sylvies, triumphantly bestridden by hundreds of Antonios and Alis, back there in 1958 or so, I'm not going to claim that in *Little Portia* I was speaking out for all the public school and university-educated Englishmen of my age. When it comes to it I wasn't even speaking out for Anthony, who probably saw his own situation in a quite different light from the one in which I saw mine, or Grahame Thwaite saw Grahame Thwaite's, or I saw Grahame Thwaite's. In the end I could only claim to speak out for that hot and lumpish figure sitting on his bed in Cambridge over a quarter of a century ago, quite unable to clutch what he urgently wanted, however long it danced around him. That figure – the hot and lumpish one, not the dancing one – could serve as the controlling image of my first three novels

(I wrote four, the last a sex-thriller under a pseudonym) and an expression of what was possibly their only source of inspiration. In *Colmain* (published in 1963), and *Simple People* (published in 1965), the two central characters, one a lieutenant governor of a fictional Canadian province (Nova Scotia, of course), the other a young man born in England but brought up in Nova Scotia, are both of them simultaneously driven by their sexual needs and imprisoned by their fear of the consequences of sex. In the end, both are seduced into a darker imprisonment. The lieutenant governor is conducted into an unwanted marriage, the hero of *Simple People* corrupted from suspicious Nova Scotian innocence into a baffled European cynicism. From an academic point of view it could be said, I suppose, that I found a way of writing my post-graduate thesis on Henry James after all, albeit as fiction.

I don't mean to imply that there is any Jamesian theological theme to *Colmain* and *Simple People*. The two novels were described by reviewers of their day as comedies of manners, which seems to be about right. I feel fairly confident that neither would seem to whatever readers they ever had as the slightest bit autobiographical – except in the sense that all fiction is autobiography, as surely as all autobiography (and biography, come to that) is fiction. And yet they would almost certainly not have been written if I hadn't needed to transform the ghastly comedy of my early (early!?) sexual life into something neatly distanced and done with.

In *Little Portia*, on the other hand, I set out to present the ghastly comedy quite untransformed. In my account of Grahame Thwaite's childhood I introduce the sadistic pederast, Mr Brownlow, whose name is only one syllable longer than that of a sadistic pederast who made my own life at ten years old an exhilarating misery. In my account of Grahame Thwaite's adolescence I have him fall in and out of – but mainly in – love with a boy who died, only a few years younger than a boy to whom I was very attached at school. At Cambridge there is Sylvie Wasserman, whose origins in my own experience I've already touched on. And so on, to Grahame's botched affair with the perfectly inappropriate, completely desirable Janice, to his final settling down at the language school that bears such a close resemblance to the one I ended up teaching in. The differences – that I had two brothers and two parents, while Grahame has no parents and an older sister on whom he grudgingly depends – in fact, the novel could be described as being about *their* relationship, with every other of Grahame's relationships a testing of it and a fruitless struggle to be free from it – are either radical or irrelevant, depending on the disposition of the reader. My own disposition as a reader of it twenty years after being the writer of it encourages me to believe that I wanted the novel to be a bold description of everything I'd so far understood about sexuality, frustration, loneliness, the bondage of attachments – bondage, in one form or another, is the recurrent *motif* I'd find myself pointing out to students, if I were unfortunate to be teaching the book as a set text. I know, too, that I deliberately set out to escape from the tone – which I thought of as fastidiously ironic, though it might in actuality have been merely politely jeering – of *Colmain* and *Simple People*. In other words, in *Little Portia* I was after the *truth* of being *me* – a hopeless quest, even for the world's only expert. Each of the many drafts were written in the first person, including the one finally submitted to and accepted by Faber and Faber. It was only after it had been with them some weeks, and I'd failed to settle into that state of dozy self-congratulation that should follow work successfully completed, that I found myself back at the typewriter, rewriting from beginning to end, in the third person. I can't recall any of the arguments or insights that led to this complete reversal of my original intention, but I do remember the passionate conviction with which I re-addressed myself to the central character, my determination to find for him a focus from a considerable distance. I can only suppose that I lost my nerve at the prospect of going about in the world unclothed. Or at any rate undisguised.

Whether this fundamental revision made for a better or worse novel I'm in no position to judge, but I have an idea that the intervening authorial voice gives a confidence to the passages I most liked on my recent re-reading – the childhood and public school scenes, and particularly the Christmas party at the language school; while over-controlling other passages – the middle stretch during the undergraduate years, for instance, when I longed for the yelps of pain to be less muffled, and for Grahame to be set free to brood on his own destiny. If I had some of the early drafts to hand I'd be better able to assess the gains and losses, but as I reported at the beginning, these were delivered years ago to Boston University. It's odd, now I come to think of it, that though the recipient has sent me a birthday card and a Christmas card every year for the last twenty years or so, he's never come back for more. Possibly he's afraid that a man who had to write so copiously to produce a comparatively brief novel, would eventually take up more space than his work warranted or the University of Boston could furnish. His name, by the way, is Gottlieb. Dr Howard Gottlieb. Until writing it down here I've always assumed that Howard is a Ph.D. and the university librarian, but I suddenly realize that he could be a medical doctor, a psychiatrist, for instance, doing research into various kinds of obsession.

BOOK ONE

CHAPTER ONE

In Portsmouth they were much in demand among couples ten or fifteen years younger than themselves. For one thing they brought such expertise to social occasions. They knew how to make drinks out of surgical alcohol and a dose of nutmeg, they knew how to keep a party going after the surgical alcohol had run out, and they knew all the little places that stayed open, against war regulations, when the party had begun to fade. They were also good dancers, good tennis-players, and excellent poker players. They won trophies in the mixed-doubles competitions, and they finished most card evenings a few pounds up, with all their friends intact. They had charm.

Of course, Gordon was rumoured to have had trifling affairs with nurses in the hospital, and Yvonne went in for secret lunches with young naval officers in Southsea. But such adventures merely added to their lustre, for who could imagine Gordon without Yvonne, Yvonne without Gordon? They went so well together, Gordon, with his fine figure, his sensual features, and his jovial blue eyes. There was a most striking contradiction about him, too, for if he looked smooth, soft and strokey, like a well-knit baby, he could nevertheless assume a most commanding manner, just right for a naval officer, just right for a doctor. Yvonne, on the satisfactory other hand, was frail and dark, her skin always slightly and mysteriously tanned. She had green, serious eyes, a languid manner, and was thought clever. Her drawled jokes had a sting in them, and

3

her analyses of character could be devastating. Gordon liked everyone he met, and said so. Yvonne despised everyone she met, including the young officers with whom she later sneaked lunch, and said so. Together and apart they made many people happy, and helped relieve the tensions of war.

They had two children, a little boy and a little girl, whom they carelessly and publicly adored. They perhaps adored the little boy more, because he was round faced, open-natured, and seemed to share the general enthusiasm for his parents. Yvonne loved to hold him in her slender brown arms and to smother him with kisses in the evening. Then late at night or early in the morning, while Gordon was driving the baby-sitter home, she would pick him up again just for the pleasure of sniffing at his sleeping flesh. The little girl was different—pale and thin, with a very serious expression for four years old. Her mother's scent didn't cling to her in quite the same way—she was a bit spare and dry for a child. But she too was probably, though rather secretively, delighted with her parents, and had a sweet, gravely protective attitude to her little brother.

By and large the Thwaites were a magnificent example of the English middle class family, and had they been used on propaganda posters, might well have contributed to the demoralization of the enemy.

The only shadow on the horizon was an inevitable one. What would Gordon do when the war ended? He would be older than when it had started—he could see that for himself—and he couldn't linger on in the navy for ever. The navy had a habit of retiring people, and he would need capital to settle into practice, to settle down generally.

'But we *are* settled down,' Yvonne would say, glancing sardonically towards the children's bedroom. 'Could we be more so?'

'Well, there'll be a future, you know,' Gordon replied, in

4

his most authoritative manner. 'The war's as good as won.'

'Is it?' she smiled at him. 'Well, Bunny, we'd better hope for a late rally from Jerry.'

This sort of conversation, though frequent, did little to solve the problem. They were in the habit of spending too much money, originally on the romantic premise that their time might be short, and life must therefore be gay; then because they were used to it. The clubs cost a great deal; so did the indispensables, like the woman who cleaned the flat, and the baby-sitters. Nothing was provided for, and they were getting on.

Even so they celebrated peace as if it meant safety for ever. Yvonne wept a little over Grahame's cuddly little body. His flushed face, his plump limbs, his sweet smell, had never been so precious to her. 'The world', she informed him in a trembling voice, 'is won for you, my darling.'

'And for you, dear,' she whispered, blowing a kiss at the blonde head of her daughter and hurrying through the door.

'It's the end of a way of life,' Gordon said, as he swung the car out of the drive with a masterful rearranging of gears.

Yvonne checked her make-up in the mirror. 'Then we must celebrate it properly. It may be our last real party.'

It was. They were demolished by an oncoming lorry on the way back from the yacht club at four the next morning. At the inquest the lorry driver was cleared of all blame. He was able to prove that the Alvis had swung right into his path, without signals or reason. In the instant before impact he had had the fleeting impression that no one had been driving, but this, as the coroner pointed out, was quite impossible. Someone must have been driving, though very eccentrically. 'The evidence indicates, indeed,' he said, in a troubled summing-up, 'the possibility that both the deceased were driving.'

'The Thwaites! Gordon and Yvonne!' They were talked of as if they had been among the last victims of the war. 'They had everything to live for,' someone said. 'They were so full of *life*. They danced long after everyone else. They always do.'

'But they were quarrelling,' someone else said—a newcomer whose first experience of the Thwaites had been his last. 'I heard them when they were getting into their car.' There was a pause, and then, almost in a chorus, 'Oh, that was just their manner. It's a tragedy.'

'An absolute tragedy', the solicitor insisted to the young couple who had taken Grahame and Dianah in, 'that everything should have been left in such a muddle. I've no doubt he was a fine man, a fine naval man and a fine medical man, but . . .'; he shook his head.

The woman, pregnant with her first, looked apprehensively at her husband. 'What about the children, though?'

Aunt Mary had her own version of the tragedy. She described it to Colonel Rones as if it had been engineered by a simple moral being that her niece had driven to its wit's end. 'If people lead silly, silly lives,' she said, 'something silly happens to them. It's a law, and quite a satisfactory one.'

Colonel Rones hinted that it might be less satisfactory for the survivors, especially when they were under five years of age; to which Aunt Mary replied that the great thing with children was to make sure they grew up healthy. Morton, she added, with an uncharacteristically diffident smile, was excellent for that. Wasn't it?

The Colonel stared about him in astonishment, and spoke at length. If his sentences were inconclusive and embarrassed, their meaning was plain. Aunt Mary's answer was equally plain, her sentences quite conclusive, and she succeeded in embarrassing the Colonel into a hasty agreement.

The dialogue had followed a pattern familiar to both, although on a more serious topic than usual. 'Legally', Aunt Mary pointed out for the third time, 'the children are mine. They have no one else.'

It was quite consistent with her notorious nature that she should accept the children so matter of factly, and should pretend to complete confidence about bringing them up. On their first day, when they sat dismally on the sofa in her living-room, staring away from her in terror, she assumed her most commanding tone, and lectured them on their long-term development, each stage of which she had mastered in advance. The children grasped few of the details, but they reverberated to the essential fact. The demonstrative mother they yearned for had gone. They were in the clutches of a usurper.

But Aunt Mary, who seemed to the children such a simple, finished horror, had had her complexities, and her soft dreams. Her parents had been retired army, Indian, and had given birth to her late—in the summer of 1891—either as an afterthought or from an oversight. They had been in middle age while she was growing up, and growing old while she was still in her young womanhood. Her adolescent ambition was to qualify as a children's nurse, and for a time, during her parents' amazingly long and selfish twilight, she had been able to practise as one. When they had died at last, leaving her Mallows and an annuity, she had lost all chance of a career. Fortunately Colonel Rones's brother, Rex, had made an unexpected offer of marriage. He was an unambitious solicitor unambitiously in search of a wife. 'Mary,' he had said in his lifeless tones, 'we are right for each other.' She didn't agree with this preposterous assumption, but she refrained from retorting as she was tempted to; and, for the sake of fulfilment, accepted his proposal. Three months after the engagement was announced Rex had come to Mallows with some talk of duty and patriotic delays, and then plodded off to the war that would end in a few weeks. He died a year later of a perforated intestine in a hospital outside Brighton. Aunt Mary, who had stoically expected him to be among the thousands ticked off with little white crosses on a continental battlefield, had never understood what he had been doing in Brighton. But after a time she ceased to wonder. She had her own life to lead.

And its course had been plain. It was too late to hope for another proposal (Colonel Rones was winning medals in France, and was therefore unavailable), too late to train into one of the few occupations open to women of her class. So for the next twenty-five years she sat on Morton's committees, helped run Morton's charity bazaars, harried the authorities in Portsmouth, and in numerous other ways made herself the most loathed spinster in Morton. The people she knew she had known for years. They were retired services, or elderly residents with private incomes and enough ill health to justify an idle life of sea air. The only people she saw regularly were her co-workers on the charities, and Colonel Rones, who had settled in a bungalow on the far side of the island. Her life lacked nothing except a few odds and ends.

But it was precisely this trifling lack that had prevented her from selling Mallows and moving into a bungalow, as Colonel Rones had frequently advised her to do. She clung to the house, she said, because she was used to it. But she had seen it sometimes, as she approached it from the Shore Road on her way back from the village, as if it were full of diminutive odds, helpless ends. The arrival of the little Thwaites had thus been merely the vindication of her foresight. If Morton was the best place in which to bring children up, then Mallows was one of the best houses in the best place. From the outside, with its sham gables and Victorian bricks, it seemed to be yet another of the island's

8

architectural jokes. But inside, with the sun streaming through the french windows in summer, or with a log fire crackling in the enormous grates in winter, it gave off an effect both of comfort and of space. With Bella, her cook-general, to slave about the house; with a governess at the beginning, a tutor followed by the local Slocum school in the middle, and proper educational establishments at the end, why should she not bring up the children as well as anyone else—better perhaps, than the frivolous Yvonne and her baby-faced husband? She might almost have arranged the whole thing herself.

The progress of the children was very satisfactory. They moved in respectable stages, had the proper illnesses, and grew taller. Dianah, it was true, continued to be thin and pale, but then, as the governess explained, she was a *thin* person, and pale by circulation. Grahame, more conventionally, was plump, and here Miss Hagler was able to draw on her experience to assure Miss Medway that he would finish up powerful—perfectly normal, if that was the way you thought about boys. Their behaviour was impeccable. They were both quiet and well-mannered. Dianah never took advantage of her superior wisdom, nor Grahame of his developing strength.

'They're very good with each other,' Miss Hagler said. 'I've known children to go at each other all the time.'

'Why?' asked Aunt Mary, who really didn't know.

Miss Hagler covered her small mouth with her large hand, in a gesture of self-censorship. 'From jealousy.'

'Jealousy? Jealousy of what?' She had a sudden, conceited suspicion. 'Not of me, I hope.'

'Oh, no, Miss Medway. Certainly not. Of each other.'

'Why?'

'Because it's only natural.'

There was a little pause. Then, 'If it's only natural, why aren't these two jealous?'

'Because they are good,' Miss Hagler said, as she walked smoothly out of the room, 'and happy with each other.'

But as it turned out, they too had their normal darknesses, although they took a form almost directly contrary to the ones Miss Hagler was used to dealing with.

'Together in one bed.' She courageously held her hand away from her mouth. 'Together, Miss Medway.'

'I see.' Aunt Mary rose from her desk. 'Grahame's crying,' she said, in the tone of one who registered details, but was not of course surprised by them.

'He's crying, yes. Because he knows it's wrong. Because he knows it's happened before. Yes, he's crying.'

'Happened before? Why didn't you tell me?'

'Because I've only just caught them.'

'I see.' She took a step toward the children. 'Why do they do it?'

Miss Hagler's tilted head indicated that there were reasons; and that only professionals like herself dared guess at them.

'You're not to do it,' Aunt Mary said, to a spot precisely between the blonde, smiling girl; the dark, weeping boy. 'Ever again.' She glanced at Miss Hagler, who nodded twice, revolved slowly on nurse's feet, and then drew the children behind her, down the dark corridor that led to the stairs that led to their rooms. As Aunt Mary stared after them, she wondered momentarily which child had been found in which bed. But clearly the question was irrelevant, or Miss Hagler would have told her. So she closed the door and returned to her desk, which was more like a wooden machine than a piece of furniture, and attended for the next few hours to adult matters.

But what Aunt Mary could dismiss, Miss Hagler, in the

line of duty, was forced to confront. From that evening on she put herself morally on the alert. She was not shocked by the incident (although she rather hoped her employer was) for she had had ample experience of worse behaviour. It merely came as a reminder, just when she had come to think of her two charges as quite angelic, that even she never knew for certain what went on in infantile bodies, however thin and virtuous, however round and healthy. She considered Grahame's misdemeanour to be natural; she considered most misdemeanours to be natural (she had been brought up a Calvinist in Gosport, and been jilted twice in her twenties). People began as babies, which was most natural, most improper. But as they thrust themselves upwards a trained hand stripped their natural, improper selves from them. Such, in a chaotic way, was Miss Hagler's professional code, and almost her whole theology. For the immediate circumstances it was reduced to the working maxim—'Control the boy.' No doubt she would have made appropriate emendations if she had known that Grahame was only in his sister's room, in his sister's bed, at his sister's express invitation.

She controlled him easily. She told him what it was he mustn't fondle in the bath or fiddle with on the lavatory, and she fastened the fly of his pyjamas with a safety pin when tucking him in for the night. She reminded him that any little boy found in the halls of Mallows after 7 p.m. would end up explaining himself to his aunt, whose bite was worse than her bark. And she told him a simple fable that she herself had learnt at her mother's knee, about a child with filthy habits who was eaten, bones and blood and toe-nails too, by a cleansing angel. She worked on these remedies for a couple of weeks, and then tapered them off. She was sure that they would be successful, she had never known them to fail. And the exaggerated manner with which he sat in his bath with his hands on his knees, the speed with which he performed his functions in the lavatory, and the expression on his face when she clipped on the pin while bringing her little tale to its frenzied conclusion, confirmed her diagnosis. His behaviour subsequently was model—as, of course, was the girl's. If sometimes they seemed more demonstrative with each other than any of her previous charges, she put it down to the girl's refined but maternal spirit, the boy's chastened and dependent nature. After all, they *were* orphans. Miss Hagler, a great professional, knew that there were some emotions that even she couldn't provide.

Colonel Rones sat on the edge of the sofa with a tea-cup on his knees and a plate of buttered scones beside him. The sun shone through the french windows and from the back of the garden, behind the shed, there came the throaty noises of the chickens. Colonel Rones no longer confused these cries with the mewlings of children, for he understood now that his friend's wards never cried. He had also noticed for himself that both children seemed healthy, one thinly so, one plumply so. Thus, in general terms, there was no real point he could make. Aunt Mary, sitting opposite him on a hard-backed chair, surely knew it. She surely also knew that the Colonel's mind had strayed past the general terms, into territories so foreign that she would find them ridiculous.

He cleared his throat. 'I'm glad', he said, 'that they're happy.'

'Why shouldn't they be?' She bit off a piece of ginger-nut. 'Hagler's good for them. They like her.'

The Colonel admitted that that seemed to be the case, and added that there was a lot of talk these days, but that he himself was in favour of genuinely trained women. Always had been. Always would be. Raised by one himself. Rex, too. He fingered his long chin, knuckled his thin white moustache, and hunched his shoulders. All of which showed that he was getting up his nerve.

'Only thing', he picked up his teacup and put it down, 'they've, I suppose, got to know.'

'Know? Know what?'

'Why—about their parents.' He leaned forward part by part, as if on hinges. 'It's been worrying me. Frankly.'

'Worrying *you*?'

'Occurred to me they might be wondering. Or have forgotten.'

She took off her horn-rimmed spectacles and laughed at him. This was her favourite method of refuting him, when in a good humour. 'Of course they've forgotten. Children have short memories, as Hagler says.'

'But is it', he creaked backwards, 'quite fair?'

'Fair?' She laughed at him again. 'If they're well and happy, and have forgotten?'

'I meant to the, actually, parents?'

She watched closely, ready to detect on either face the signs of an anguished consciousness. But there was no anguish in Dianah's polite smile, in Grahame's rosy frown. They sat in their special chairs, side by side and with their backs to the nursery windows. They were as tranquil as judges.

'Do you think', she asked at last, in a voice that was only rough because the feeling was tender, 'that you understand, my——" she shook her spectacles at them in substitution for an endearment.

'They're dead and buried,' Dianah summarized, 'and not coming back.'

Aunt Mary, prepared by Miss Hagler for poignant confusions rather than for pungent precis, stiffened. 'They're resting. As we *all* must rest in the end.'

Dianah's smile intensified, presumably in agreement;

13

while her brother indicated his feelings about the matter by lowering his head and releasing a few sounds that were suspiciously like laughs.

'They took it', she told Miss Hagler, 'without emotion.'

'Did they, Miss Medway? Oh, yes?' And it was perhaps to rectify this—for Miss Hagler felt that orphans must know what it is to be orphans, or where would be the gratitude?—that she hurried straight into the nursery. She had, on certain subjects, the tongue of prophets. Even so, it took her at least an hour to break through the girl's insistent smile, to silence the boy's weird chuckling; and so to elicit from both the expressions appropriate to the information she was imparting. 'Oh, yes,' she concluded, 'they *might* have gone to Heaven, but it's not usual.' As soon as she had abandoned the theme, however, the girl's smile returned, and the boy quickly found something else to laugh at. Neither child had ever shown a tendency towards comic interpretation before, and for once Miss Hagler was almost baffled. She took up the thread again, with some remembered Calvinist images, and finally she succeeded in arousing Grahame to such a vision that she had to spend another hour soothing it away.

That evening Aunt Mary completed the painful process of disaffection by taking them through a few old photographs that had been part of the Thwaites' irresponsible legacy. She herself had never studied them properly before, and they seemed to her, as she held them up, to be of exceedingly poor quality and in doubtful taste. Both Gordon and Yvonne, such very physical presences, had always chosen to set themselves against very animated backgrounds. The surrounding and accidental life had resulted in a shrinkage of the intended subjects. They had lost their features—especially their eyes and their noses—and worst of all, they had lost whatever social distinction they had possessed. Gordon, in his naval uniform, looked like a cinema usher, and Yvonne, who had had a penchant for lace at her throat, somehow suggested a waitress on her day off. Fortunately the children had little time for the blurred and featureless midgets at whom Aunt Mary pointed a heroic finger. Their interest focused entirely on the details—a giraffe at Whipsnade, a W.A.A.F. in a paper hat being carried piggy-back across a crowded restaurant. As a result, Aunt Mary was strengthened in her newly acquired belief that only adults had memories, and locked the pile back in the desk drawer with a clear conscience. The next afternoon she was grimly playful with the Colonel for making a display of scruples where scruples were unnecessary. 'There was', she said, 'no problem, Basil.'

And for her there really wasn't, in any department. Even their elementary education had been meticulously planned. To begin with there were carefully selected children's books with Miss Hagler after lunch, and disciplined lessons in reading from Aunt Mary herself after tea. Then, as they advanced in age and understanding, they were graduated to more sophisticated authors. Miss Hagler, for one, was only too pleased to abandon the simple but tedious tales of fairies and goblins in favour of the decent fantasies she brought back from her weekly visits to the island's Boot's. She was discreet about these literary experiments, for she wasn't sure that Miss Medway's taste would coincide with her own. But she knew that the children never vouchsafed information unasked, and she also knew that Miss Medway, who took as evidence only what was on show, never asked any but the obvious questions. The children's books continued to lie on the nursery table, the Boot's books to repose in her own bedroom closet. Every evening before they went to bed she read passages from here and there, and then filled in, as she put the blankets around them, on the intervening chapters. The fact that they enjoyed the stories so much was a tribute to their authors' virtue—if

15

any tribute, other than her own censorious addiction, was needed. Besides she was alive to the hidden dangers—it was one of her qualifications that she could turn even a forbidden paragraph to moral advantage.

'That Greg is a very wicked man.' And she skipped five pages.

'Why, Miss Hagler?'

'Why, Dianah? Well, even your brother knows it's wrong for people, men and women, boys and girls, to be undressed together. Remember how raging your aunt was when I found him in your bed? And he's only kept from it because I've eyes all over me. Even when I'm off in my bed with a cold. Grahame, are you laughing?'

Miss Hagler was off in her bed with a cold, Aunt Mary was giving tea and a lecture to Colonel Rones in the living-room, and the children were in the garden. The french windows were open, so that an eye, one of Colonel Rones's piercing blue ones, one of Aunt Mary's alert, unseeing brown ones, could be kept on them.

'You're to stay in sight,' Aunt Mary called, and took the order for the fact.

'I warn you,' Miss Hagler had frequently said, 'you so much as look at the marsh behind the hens, and you'll be swallowed.'

And the marsh *looked* greedy, darkened by the bushes that ran in a tangle around its edges, with the water seeping up.

'Ah ha,' Miss Hagler had said, 'green and lush, yes. But it will suck you down.'

As from a great distance, through the sun in the garden, came the voices of Aunt Mary and Colonel Rones. A spatter of Colonel Rones, either laughing or coughing, and very distinctly Aunt Mary asking him what was the matter, Basil? Miss Hagler's eyes were scuttling along the roof of

16

Mallows; her voice was whispering that during the war rats had come out of the marsh, to rip the hens and munch the eggs. Among the bushes they could see the ripples of darkness, where the rats watched.

The plank was firm under Grahame's sandals, although slippery. He had to move with his arms stretched out, slowly, as if he were blind. From the instant he had stepped on to the plank he was frightened, and wanted to go back. But he went inching forward to the centre of the marsh. Even when the plank began to slide away under him, with the green mud lapping at its edges, he went on delicately, until the mud was over his sandals, and Dianah screamed.

He had been waiting for the scream. It had been in the still of the marsh since they'd come. He threw up his arms to it, the plank skidded away, and he fell. The smell clogged him and sucked him down. He heard Miss Hagler's voice as he was gobbled up.

He scrambled to the bank where Dianah bent forward, holding out a clean hand.

He could hear the voices again, and whenever there was a silence he knew that he would be discovered. He sat huddled into himself, naked, until Dianah came back. She scrubbed at him, at his chest, his legs, his arms. She took the underpants he'd pulled off, and polished his stomach. He only wanted to be clean, free from the filth and the damp, to be into normal clothes again and back on the other side of the coop. He tried to keep out of his mind the terror of the call from the living-room, or Miss Hagler staring down from above, but Dianah's fingers circled busily between his legs, and gradually he forgot his fear and lay back, smiling pleasantly, his legs crooked.

Afterwards they wrapped the clothes into a bundle and hid them among the weeds. They came back to the hen-coop just as Colonel Rones called from the living-room. They slipped around the side of the coop and went towards

17

the apple tree, and Colonel Rones came towards them across the grass. Behind him, standing outside the french windows, was Aunt Mary.

There was something wrong with the trousers Dianah had fetched for him. The wrong shade, the wrong length, whatever it was would be seen instantly by Colonel Rones, who would tell Aunt Mary. Colonel Rones's face was full of knowledge, but he said nothing, letting them go past him towards the living-room, where Aunt Mary, her face expressionless, her spectacles in her hand, was now sitting at her desk. She slid one of the drawers, and it came open with three little clicks. She put a paper into it, and shut it, with three more clicks.

'The sofa, children.'

They sat down on the sofa.

'Colonel Rones will speak to you.'

'You look very well.' Colonel Rones stooped, his hands on his knees. 'You have been behaving?' He crouched farther forward, until his face filled Grahame's whole vision, and his moustache, which had always seemed completely white from below, now revealed itself as yellow. The eyes, blue and sharp, had little threads of red in them.

'Little boys', Colonel Rones said, baring the teeth under his yellow and damp moustache, blinking his red eyes, 'must speak when they're spoken to.'

'Speak to the Colonel, Grahame,' Aunt Mary said. 'Speak to him.'

'Ah!' The Colonel straightened. 'Ah!'

'He's shy this afternoon. What's the matter, Grahame?'

'He's got a very queer smell to him.' The Colonel turned to Dianah. 'What have you been up to?'

'Up to?' She sat with her hands in her lap, smiling. 'Playing under the apple tree, Uncle Basil.'

'Ah! Under the apple tree.'

'And by the hen coop.'

18

'Ah! The hen coop. That's why your brother has that smell to him.'

Aunt Mary rose and came towards him. She sniffed at him as she sometimes sniffed at Bella's cooking. 'He smells,' and he sat there, red and still, whiffing out at her the odours of the marsh. 'Dirty.'

The Colonel laughed. 'Little boys always smell dirty.'

Grahame grinned up at him. It was deliberate, and therefore difficult.

'The little fellow,' the Colonel said, 'the little fellow.'

'Grahame, are you laughing?'

'No, Miss Hagler.' He tried to stop the swelling within him by shifting his eyes to his sister, who was waiting for the reading to continue.

'You still haven't explained about those trousers that are missing. I'm sure I don't know where they are. So you stop your laughing, or do you know where they are?'

He shook his head, perhaps in down-payment on the tears, apologies and confessions that usually followed a bout of mirth, but Miss Hagler, who was pursuing another forbidden passage with swift eyes, took his expression as a symptom of his general spiritual condition, and murmured that she hoped he *was* sorry, for all the trouble he caused: *and* grateful, for all the kindness he received. She had already plotted to lay the responsibility for the missing trousers at Bella's door. Bella was notorious for her carelessness, and so vulgar in her speech that Miss Hagler and Miss Medway made sure that she had as little contact with the children as possible.

Which meant that they could only visit Bella by means of a trick. Every afternoon they would go out into the garden and then slip around the side, to the back door, which

19

Bella opened for them with smiles and winks. Bella was fat, had white, frothy hair and round blue eyes, and treated the children with such easy friendship that they might have been *her* nephew and niece. 'All right then,' she whispered, as she bustled them in. 'But keep a sharp.'

The kitchen was large, with a stove and a rocking chair at one end, and the sink and the oven at the other. There was a long wooden table for preparing the food, a pantry which contained the provisions for the house and a large box for Bella's most personal possessions—photographs of herself when a young dancer in Plumstead, photographs of her son, who had been destroyed by the war and was currently in a home as a prisoner, seven or eight pairs of shoes, and a pair of gentleman's dancing pumps, the sight of which brought tears to her eyes. There was also a brown envelope which held a knobbly object, like three sugar cubes stuck together, that the children were permitted to feel, but which Bella couldn't show them for fear that their Aunt Mary would slay her dead.

Bella was evidently very fond of Grahame, and would make him sit on her great round knees, in the hump of her lap, and tickle him under the arms and in the ribs until he squirmed, desperate to escape and delirious for more. 'Quite a little laydee,' Bella sang, 'is your sister Din Din.' She would chuckle towards the girl's averted face. 'Oh, you're two little orphings. That's what's so gruesome.'

'What's an orphing?' he asked her. He knew the word, naturally, but he enjoyed Bella's explanation, which gave him a strange, fresh sense of himself.

'An orphing is when you've got no one. No dad. No one like my Eric.'

'But Eric hasn't got a dad.'

'Yes. Oh, yes, my Eric has.' Although quite often she said Eric hadn't.

20

'But why is it gruesome?'

'Because you've got no friends, neither, that's why. Only me.' And she stuffed his head into her stomach and rolled her legs and made him almost seasick with warm, smelly movement.

When they were old enough Aunt Mary read them samplings from *Pickwick Papers* and then from *Great Expectations*, which was her favourite novel. She was particularly partial to the last passage, and when she read of Pip and Estella going down the years to their happiness, her voice would turn so husky that she failed to hear the odd, supplicating noises that erupted through Grahame's throat and nose, or notice the stiff, patient smile on Dianah's neat face.

'Upstairs now,' she would say, pretending to inspect the binding of the book, 'to Miss Hagler.'

Who waited, inevitably, with her Boot's book open, and other couples going down the years to their happiness. But Miss Hagler's renderings never provoked Grahame to anything more than an occasional, desperately repressed snort, or Dianah to anything more than a slight, formal widening of the lips.

'I'm off,' Miss Hagler said, 'on the dot.'

Grahame looked at Dianah, who made a few lines with her pencil and asked, without looking up, where Miss Hagler was off to.

'Never you mind.' She was holding a sausage-shaped black bag, was wearing her best hat, which was covered with false cherries and had a pink veil. Her downy lips were trembling. 'I'm off to Brighton for my health.'

'Where's Brighton?'

'It's where some people go when they're not wanted.'

His own lip began to tremble. 'Why?'

'Because the time has come for you to do without.'

'Because of me?' Miss Hagler had frequently warned him that he would make her ill, and be her death.

'Off,' she merely repeated, as he crouched at her feet, staring up and ready to offer tears. And tears were, clearly, the correct response, because suddenly Miss Hagler's face went into a spasm so horrible that her upper lip and her nose almost met, and then with a noise like the lavatory after it had flushed, she fell on top of him. Her arms went around him. 'Oh, what will become of me, what will become of me.' She scrambled on her knees to Dianah, who bent forward and placed a kiss against her veil.

Miss Hagler rose and crashed from the room, hiccoughing.

'Is she really going, Din?'

'I expect so.'

'What will become of her?'

'She'll find some more orphans. It's her job, Dodie. Anyway, she'll be back in a minute, because she's forgotten her bag.'

Miss Hagler was back in a minute—swept into the room on a new wave of uncontrollable feeling; and discovered one of her abandoned charges rolling about the floor in a positive sickness of laughter; the other beaming at him with pallid complacence. It was a sight that was to haunt her for the remainder of her professional career.

There was nothing sentimental about Mrs. Holydrake. She was a stout woman with grey hair, a Roman nose, and a perpetual black dress. Her husband had been the headmaster of a preparatory school in Portsmouth, where she herself had frequently taken a hand in the teaching; but now, ten years a widow, she was settled comfortably in Morton on the royalties of Mr. Holydrake's Latin primer. She had, however, never lost her passion for education, and was very glad to do it again fifteen hours a week, however small the . . .

'. . . emolument. I should warn you that I'm a slave-driver, Miss Medway.'

'I'm very glad,' said Miss Medway, who thought seven pounds a week a preposterous sum, and would tell Mrs. Holydrake as much when the time came. 'The children want to work.'

It was so. During her career as a school teacher Mrs. Holydrake had come across many excellent pupils, but the speed with which Aunt Mary's niece could do sums amazed her, and the ferocity with which Miss Medway's nephew went at essays almost alarmed her. She wasn't given to what she called 'prying', but she began to suspect that there might be a connection between the orphan state and the desire to improve oneself. The children had their faults, of course, but these would easily be corrected by discipline. She checked the boy's tendency to fiddle and stoop by threatening to stop his reading, and she rationed his essay space and made him spend extra time on his maths and grammar. 'A guard against excess', she said, 'is a guarantee of success. Make that your favourite motto, Grahame.' The girl, on the other hand (who never fiddled or stooped), was encouraged to spread herself imaginatively, so that she would make up through practice in the one department in which she was deficient. With the boys her methods were successful, but the girl's literary development continued to be disappointing. Her essays, although twice their previous length, continued to possess only the same amount of interest. Eventually she was forced to conclude that they were gifted in different directions, and would therefore do her credit in different ways.

'Grahame's essays are full of fancy.'

'I see.' Aunt Mary's tone was defensive; her gaze on the point of becoming aggressive.

'I'm pleased with him.'

'Ah!' With an adroit shift of expression. 'Yes, he's an imaginative child.'

'And Dianah has a good little head for maths.'

There was no ambiguity here, and Aunt Mary could register her pleasure freely. 'She gets it from my side of the family. We have always been good arithmeticians.' As many a Morton tradesman had, with an expletive or two, admitted.

'They will do well.'

'I know.'

She knew. She watched them maturing intellectually under the guidance of Mrs. Holydrake, and had no fears for their future. They seemed to her in every respect well provided for. They had been weak and dependent; she had provided health and Miss Hagler; they had been innocently unlettered; she had provided books and Mrs. Holydrake. Other complications had been as easily resolved. When they were subject to illnesses, she provided young Dr. Blander (although she despised him. She despised all doctors just as she admired all nurses) and when they appeared strange—Grahame was still given to inexplicable bouts of a noise that sounded like laughter; Dianah sometimes sat smiling with meaningless courtesy for hours, as if under hypnosis—she asked them questions that instantly drove their little troubles away. Even in her superbly practical master plan she had made allowances for childish eccentricities. Sudden laughter, prolonged silences, what were these but individual symptoms of growing up? And they were remarkably polite. All her co-workers on the charities, who met every Tuesday afternoon at Mallows, said so. They were extremely fit. All her co-workers said that, too. They needed nothing because they had everything.

'The little boy's a splendid specimen,' the Admiral had whispered to her at one of the bazaars. 'We enjoyed having them to tea. Enjoyed it enormously.'

24

'Thank you,' Aunt Mary replied. 'And we enjoyed having your grandchildren.' Although she couldn't remember whether they had been splendid specimens or not.

After tea they went out into the garden and stood under the apple tree, silent. Finally the boy spoke. He was tall, with blond hair, a long upper lip and a loud voice. He also wore long trousers and a blazer, and from Grahame's point of view had only one flaw. He was too superb.

'What school do you go to?'

'We're going to the Slocums' next year,' Dianah said.

'It's a bad school.'

'Is it?'

'Very bad school,' the girl said. She was plump and dark, and wore a red frock with a bow at its back. 'Very bad.'

'Grandpa says it's a scandal,' the boy said.

'I go to a school in London,' the girl said. 'Don't we, Greg.'

'We both go to a school in London.'

'Is that a bad school, too?'

'A very good school. It's good for Common Entrance. Everyone says that. Our headmaster's called Birchie, and there's a boy there called Jeeples. Jeeples was coached by Walker.'

'At my school', the girl said to Dianah, 'we have sewing. Can you sew?'

Dianah pointed to Bella, stupefied at the kitchen window. 'She's our servant. She does all the sewing.'

The boy took Grahame aside, down to the chicken coop, and told him more. By the time he had finished Grahame had found some gods at last—Walker, and Jeeples, who the boy said was tops. But really he knew that the boy himself was tops. Once he looked across the garden to Dianah. She was listening politely to the girl, but her eyes were on him.

'Girls,' the boy said. 'All they know is sewing. And play-

C 25

ing hospitals.' He laughed benevolently. 'Playing hospitals.'

'And houses.'

They laughed together and swaggered around the chicken coop, and had a look at the marsh.

'Lots of times', Grahame said, 'I hunt the rats, you see.'

'I like hunting rats. When I've got time.'

The afternoon was a great success. They heard Aunt Mary screaming so, from the door, to the Admiral's wife, in the car. The girl sat beside the Admiral's wife, and Tops sat in the back, lazily saluting his young friend in the garden. He had granted the young friend an invitation for a round of golf on the Admiral's putting green. Followed by a cup of tea and a cake with the Admiral himself.

Dianah was carrying a brown paper bag full of apples for the Admiral, and was wearing a red bow in her hair. Grahame walked beside her in his first grey, and in a white shirt and brown shoes. The Morton Side was blowing directly from the sea, throwing the sand up and whirling bits of dead grass from the banks around their ankles, so he kept glancing down at his shoes, to make them hold their polish. He also made sure that the buckle of his belt was exactly centred, and constantly he fingered the knot in his striped tie.

They crossed the road with the tactical cunning Colonel Rones had instructed them in, Dianah staring to the left, Grahame to the right. Then they went up the long, winding drive that led to the Admiral's garden. It was three times the size of the back garden at Mallows, with rose bushes and shrubberies and banks of flowers. The putting green was in the centre of the lawn, and their hosts were already playing on it. The boy had a club in his hand. The girl was arranging the ball at his feet.

Grahame noted the casual way the boy strutted about the

26

grass, noted the authority of his gestures to the girl. Every movement of the tall body, every utterance of the piping voice, was full of mystery.

'I don't see why we have to have them here.'

'Because Grandpa says so.'

'But he's wet.'

'And so's she. She doesn't say anything.'

'Well, he's worse than—hello, hello, jolly glad you could come, aren't we, Jill, we wondered if you would find the way. Would you like a go.' He held out the club and smiled, and his smile was dreadful.

The Admiral's house was the largest in Morton. The living-room was the largest and the french windows opening on to the putting green were the largest. There were flowers everywhere, in large bowls. Only the Admiral and his wife, sitting on the sofa, were on the small side. But there was a large tea laid out on a table opposite the sofa, and four chairs placed next to each other, and all size is relative. The Admiral and his wife were not diminished by the space around them. They commanded it.

'We like to see children eat,' the Admiral's wife said. She was as plump as Bella, with white hair like Bella's and large blue eyes like Bella's. But she was different from Bella in an essential or two. Although she smiled and clicked her teeth in a friendly fashion, there was something watchful about her face, as if even so large and bright a room, or four such polite children, held dangers. She did not look at the Admiral beside her, but she gave the impression that she could see everything he did.

'Your aunt's apples', she said, taking them from Dianah, 'are the best in Morton.'

The Admiral scanned them emptily. 'I expect', he whispered, 'you've dug up my course.'

'No, Grandpa.'

27

'I'm glad to hear it,' the Admiral whispered. 'But I expect you have all the same.'

The Admiral's wife poured lemonade out of a jug into four glasses, and said in a voice to end the conversation, 'Gregory would tell you if he had.'

'Of course he would,' the Admiral agreed, raising his hands from his knees and then replacing them. 'No son of my son is a liar.'

'No, Grandpa.'

'And, anyway,' Dianah smiled at the Admiral, 'it was only just a little bit.'

Grahame stared down at his plate, but not quickly enough to avoid seeing that the Admiral was twisting brutally at his knee-caps; and that the Admiral's wife was no longer clicking, was now in fact clacking, her teeth.

'What was just a little bit?' the Admiral whispered.

'Sandwiches.' She got to her feet and moved around the table. 'In my day, Alfred, children wanted cakes.'

The Admiral held up a hand. It was a small mahogany-coloured hand, with one finger shrouded in leather. 'You lied to me did you, Greg?'

'*He* did it, Grandpa.'

'I'm sorry.' Grahame stared at the Admiral's coffined finger. 'I'm sorry.'

The Admiral's wife stood at the side of the table with the jug in one hand and a bowl of sugar in the other. She laughed around and clicked her teeth and pointed her eyes at Mary Medway's nephew, and said she was sure that the children wouldn't do it again. 'It's all over now, Alfred.'

No, excuse me, my dear, it was not all over now. He had never believed, by God, that anyone in his family, a son of his son, my dear, by God, could tell lies; could tell tales. There were only two honest people in the room, by God, my dear, apart from their two selves and their granddaughter, my dear, and they, by God, were the Medway orphans. Which left, you see, my dear, by God, the son of his son.

Who began to cry.

'Don't blubber, you rat,' the Admiral whispered. 'I hate blubberers.'

The Admiral had confessed to this prejudice in the nick of time; one of the honest Medway orphans had been on the point of blubbering himself.

'A liar,' the Admiral listed, for he had a methodical mind. 'A tell-tale. A blubberer.'

The girl began to cry.

'Oh, but oh don't weep, my darling,' the Admiral said, with the most astonishing change of tone—into a kind of throbbing huskiness—the honest Medway orphan had ever heard. 'It's not your fault your brother is a vicious rat. Oh, oh, my princess mustn't weep.'

The girl put her hands to her face.

'Now look what you've done,' the Admiral's wife said, as she leant past the pale and smiling Dianah, past the pale and staring Grahame, to offer the Admiral an iced cake in the shape of a dog.

The Admiral refused the cake by shaking his leathered finger at it. 'If the boy's a——'

'Stop it, Alfred,' she screamed.

The Admiral screamed something back at her, and stopped it.

'It's all over and done with.' She picked up a knife and ran it through the dog. 'I love to see children eat.'

'So do I,' the Admiral said, and gave his guests a friendly nod.

After tea the boy and girl accompanied them to the bottom of the drive. The boy's eyes were pink from weeping, and the girl, touching her nose daintily with a large blue handkerchief (a gift outright, from her grandfather), kept

29

fixing a bright stare, now on Grahame, now on Dianah. The first of whom clumped forward as if in a state of shock; the second of whom walked neatly along, humming.

When they reached the Shore Road the boy spoke at last. 'You're wet. And I'm glad you're going to that school, and that your aunt is the worst bitch in Morton, Grandpa says.'

'Come on, Dodie. We don't want to talk to him because he's a liar and a sneak and a blubberer, the Admiral said.'

But no, he had to explain to the boy that he understood why he hated him. He could not suffer the humiliated redness of the boy's face, the splotched misery of it. He was sorry, sorry. He struck him in the face.

'You've killed him,' the girl said. 'He's dead.'

He ran off across the road, with Dianah behind him, and then along the sand banks, to safety. Afterwards they sat on a bench about a quarter of a mile from the Admiral's house. He was shaking from the blow he had delivered, and from seeing himself examined and destroyed by the whispering Admiral. The boy was dead, and he knew what that meant.

'He won't say anything, Dodie.'

'Won't he, Din?'

'No, because it would be more tales.' She undid the ribbon and wound it round his wrist as if it were a bandage; she fastened the loose end around her own wrist. They sat on the bench for a long time, Dianah with her hair falling to her shoulders, her face serious as she analysed the afternoon and helped him to his vision.

'*He* was wet,' he cried, at last. 'Wasn't he, Din?'

But he hadn't wanted him to be wet. He had wanted him to be Tops, just as he had wanted to be in his world, which had seemed to stretch far outside Mrs. Holydrake, far beyond Mallows and Aunt Mary, and most of all far, far beyond his sister's understanding. He had thought that he

30

was going to find out something at last from the Admiral's grandson, but all that he had found out was that there was always Din and only Din. Through her he learnt the manner that helped, the politeness that distracted, and gradually he came to accept her as a kind of intermediary between his anxieties and the expectations of Mallows. But he never doubted for a second that he was enough for her, just as he never doubted that she wasn't nearly enough for him. He drifted to sleep at night in new personalities that she couldn't have imagined, but however great the distance he travelled then, whatever company he kept, *she* was there in the morning as his reality.

So Aunt Mary proved, day by day, that she knew as much about motherhood as any mother. Naturally she sometimes wondered what went on in their differently shaped heads, but they had only to speak and to act and she was sure that all was laid bare. There was, as far as she could see, and she saw everything that was visible, nothing to worry about.

But Colonel Rones, the born worrier, had a reservation. It took him half an hour to get it out.

What did they do, he pondered aloud and as if to himself, about company, eh?

Company was one of the things she hadn't had to provide. They had each other, my dear Basil, for company.

But company, in that sense, was not quite what the Colonel had in mind. It took her another ten minutes to work out the sense in which he did have it in mind. 'Society, Basil?'

This was a different commodity, as she was forced to admit. At that time Morton was still an untouched part of the South Coast. It could only be reached from London by a difficult train journey that involved a delay at Havant, or by a tedious drive and a ferry. It was too remote for casual trippers, seaside prospectors, or long-distance commuters. The miles of rippling sand—Butlin's gold of the future— were deserted even in high summer, except at the village end where the tradesmen's children played. For those who had settled for professional reasons—the two doctors, the two solicitors and the seven dentists—or for those who crossed to Havant and Portsmouth every morning and returned every evening, there was a golf club with a huge, gruelling course. The real social life, as Aunt Mary understood the term, went on in the living-rooms and gardens of the retired. But some sort of social life, she reluctantly supposed, also went on in the golf club; of which she was not, of course, a member. Nor was Colonel Rones, although he could yearn towards the dipping greens from the window of his bungalow.

'I am not', she said, in answer to his ridiculous hint, 'going to swing a golf stick in order to find friends for the children. I don't like the young set. I haven't even met them. Except for Blander, and he's incompetent.'

'He's also a bachelor.'

'Exactly.' She nodded at him as if she had proved something or other; and he nodded ambiguously back, because he was too polite to explain that she hadn't.

'They went to tea with the Admiral's grandchildren. Besides they'll have all the society they want at the Slocums'.'

The Colonel nodded again, less ambiguously because he thought her even more in the wrong on this particular point. 'The Slocum pupils will certainly', he agreed, 'be different. Less, er, well-mannered?'

'My dear Basil, they're not going to Slocums' to *meet* people. They're going there to *learn*.' Which certainly involved her in a contradiction somewhere.

'Just thought', he apologized, 'it might be bad for them to spend all their time with each other.'

'Nonsense.'

32

Clusters of insects hopped around her thick brown shoes and a solitary gull wheeled in the clear sky above her white umbrella, but she sat stiffly on her camp-stool, as indifferent to the frivolities of nature as if she had been working late in her bed, with her writing board at her side. In the lap of her grey skirt there was a neat pile of forms, the top one of which related to a local undertaking on behalf of the blind. It was a hot afternoon in mid-September, with only a faint breeze to ruffle the white hollows of the sand banks, to stroke the water trapped between the hard ridges close to the sea, and there was consequently nothing in the setting to attract the attention of an active-minded spinster who had been familiar with it for nearly sixty Septembers. She put on her tortoise-shell spectacles, took her fountain-pen out of her wicker basket, and began to work. She was quite right to do so, for there was even less to note now that the children had disappeared.

They had climbed into an alcove of the bank about a hundred yards down the beach, and were providing each other with society in a fashion that had become increasingly characteristic. Dianah was sitting against one of the sloping, sanded walls, her narrow head resting against her clasped hands. She was smiling, as she always did in public, and her small grey eyes were full of tears, as they frequently were in private. Grahame was sitting cramped opposite her, his hands locked around his chubby knees and his dark head pushed forward. His voice boomed around the small, dangerous chamber and brought rivulets of sand trickling down upon his head.

When he had come to a stop, from lack of breath, Dianah made a gesture, as if to touch a burning object, and then moved gawkily towards the opening. She lowered herself to the ground and walked in a wavering line away from the alcove and the face now thrust belligerently out of it.

33

Two minutes later they were together again. The girl had sunk to her knees and tears were coursing down her cheeks. But although her shoulders trembled, her expression as she stared at her brother was politely negative.

'I'm sorry, Din.' He knelt compassionately beside her. 'I don't really think you're wet, honestly, Din.'

She smiled through her tears and put an arm around his waist, and tacitly encouraged him into further apologies of the same order. They stayed there together until they saw their aunt rise from her camping stool, and then they walked behind her, back to Mallows. Dianah's expression was that of a particularly sophisticated child, one who was prepared to acknowledge passing adults in an adult manner; and the boy, his head lowered, was making those rough sounds that approximated to laughs.

'They are very happy with each other,' Aunt Mary told the Colonel at the next opportunity. 'There was no need for fuss. None at all. They'll be perfectly all right at the Slocums'.'

And the Colonel, who had made his stand, was glad to climb down. 'After all,' he agreed, 'they'll be coming home for lunch.'

When Mr. Slocum had first been approached about taking on the Medway wards, he had had doubts similar to Colonel Rones's. The school itself was flourishing financially, and was impressive to look at. There were two houses set side by side, one for the girls, one for the boys—in large grounds of lawns, trees and shrubberies; there was a long drive, two fine white fences, three great oaks; and on the practical side, more room for children than there were children in Morton to fill it. Over the whole estate there hung an atmosphere of pastoral graciousness that was enhanced, on a still day, by the distant lapping of the waves. Only the pupils, red-faced and thick of thought, contri-

34

buted an alien note, and Mr. Slocum, who loved nine-teenth-century poetry, felt it deeply. He was sure that the Thwaite orphans, with their well-bred accents and their Mallows backgrounds, would be as out of place in his class-room as the rest of his pupils would be in Miss Medway's living-rooms (he assumed she had several). During his first panic at the prospect of social and academic humiliation, he had almost claimed that the school was full. But the gleam in Miss Medway's eye, and an accompanying vision of Mrs. Slocum, led him into a different boldness. He informed Miss Medway that he would be delighted to take on the children—providing, of course, that they were up to stan-dard. Miss Medway, with a chilling laugh, referred him to Mrs. Holydrake, who [informed him, also chillingly, that both children were highly educated and remarkably intelli-gent. There was nothing to do, therefore, but to accept them. They would only be there for three years and then would pass on to those institutions for which they had been designed by nature. And after they had gone, as Mrs. Slocum reminded him, there would be some credit for the little school in Morton that had despatched them there. A Slocum boy at Windhoven; a Slocum girl at St. Anne's.

Mr. Slocum had always been short-staffed, and for some years had been planning to find a new man to help him with the younger boys, but it wasn't until his conversation with Mrs. Holydrake that he at last put an advertisement in *The Times Educational Supplement*. The advertisement received one answer, from a man who had some years' experience in fashionable London prep schools behind him, and although still at the height of his powers, had been forced by ill health into semi-retirement. He was so superior on paper to what had been anticipated that Mr. Slocum's first reaction was a nervous recoil; but Mrs. Slocum, with sud-den dreams of reputation, had insisted that he be snapped up. 'He's worth having', she said, 'on any conditions.' They were quite stiff, for it was the applicant who laid them down. He would only come if he were given complete charge of the senior boys' class, which meant that Mr. Slocum would have to give up poetry with the faintly more receptive pupils. On the other hand the problem of the Medway boy—described by Mrs. Holydrake as a pheno-menon—would be solved.

With, that is, an added precaution. Mrs. Slocum advised him to meet judgment with judgment. The only way to squelch arrogance in children was to show them, from your greater height, that you loathed it deeply. Thus on the first morning of the term Mr. Slocum positioned himself on the porch and glared towards the drive. As soon as he detected the Thwaites's faces—as polite and as superior as he had feared—he sauntered forth to confront them. He took up a negligently dignified position at the gate, and beckoned them over. He was a tall man, with floppy grey hair, a jacket stuffed with papers, and a worn-out tie. He had large front teeth and spectacles, smelt strongly of nico-tine, and was altogether incapable of looking dangerous. But he frequently looked extremely nervous, and he looked extremely nervous now as he tried to meet the four critical eyes and announced that he wanted a little word. Which, boomed out across the sunny grass, echoing among the high oaks, was almost as long as it was incomprehensible. His expression as he spoke indicated that he knew the situation was desperate unless the children were merciful, but the way in which the boy and the girl nodded and said, 'Yes, sir,' as if they frankly agreed that there was some-thing in them that would have to be watched, secretly reassured him. They seemed modest little people, with no sense at all of their own importance. And what was best of all, they bore no resemblance, either physically or in man-ners, to that old bitch their guardian. In fact, the new man had been a needless extravagance, especially as he had cabled to say that a recurrence of his illness would prevent him from taking up his new duties for a month or so.

It was in the juvenescence of the year, then, when the Morton grass was stirring along the banks, when the winds from the sea were softening and the marsh behind Mallows was liberated from the grip of ice, that he came.

Mr. Burnlow stood at the end of the aisle, his hands in his pockets, his short legs spread. His eyes under their heavy lids moved tenderly.

'I think you will play Portia for me.'

'Sir.'

'By which time, you'll know.' He made a painful noise in his chest and came slowly down the line of desks. He paused. He looked down. He smiled. 'Or do you know now, in your private self?'

There was a long silence, during which Mr. Burnlow's breathing filled his ears, and Mr. Burnlow's perfumes, musky and sweet, filled his nostrils. He shook his head. 'Sir.'

'And there's no way', Mr. Burnlow murmured, stooping, 'that I can make you know? Between the secret two of us?'

'Sir.'

Mr. Burnlow walked away, back up the aisle. 'Don't worry.' He rested a hand on the shoulder of Harkness—a boy with the mind of a walnut and the physique of a wrestler—and squeezed it to check its twitchings. 'Down, Harkness. Down, boy. Don't worry, Portia. I shall find a way.'

'Who?'

'Mr. Burnlove.'

'All right.' He turned a page to conceal that his heart had slipped. 'Anyhow it's Burnlow. Low. Burnlow.'

'Burnlow?' She ran her pencil down the column, and

wrote in a number. 'He looks funny to me, like a penguin, Dodie.'

'He's not.'

'In what way?'

'In what way what?'

'In what way'—she erased a digit—'isn't he?'

'Isn't he what?'

'Funny.'

'He's not. That's why.'

'Well, what is he, then?'

'He's all right.' He turned another page, scanned it rapidly, and turned another. 'He knows a lot, for one thing. Much more than Mrs. Holydrake.'

'I suppose people can know more than Mrs. Holydrake and still look like penguins.' She wrote in a new figure, put her pencil down, and sang a few bars of Linden Lee. He glanced quickly and blankly over the top of his book, to counter her smile of satisfaction. But as their eyes met he could see that she wasn't satisfied. At least not quite. He had hoped that by not mentioning Mr. Burnlow's name, he could keep him out of her mind. But really he had always known that she would touch on the vital place at last.

Mr. Burnlow walked to the window. He patted his white forehead with a black and scented handkerchief, and gazed out. 'You're afraid,' he said to the pale circle of his own face, that was reflected in the upper pane. 'Did you think I was going to punish you?'

'Sir.' He knotted his fingers behind his back, and shook his head.

'Do you think I'm going to spank you?'

'No, sir.' He shook his head. 'No, sir.'

'Ah.' He eased himself gently around and mopped a soft cheek, that was lightly dusted with powders. 'Ah, and really not?'

'No, sir.' By shifting his gaze past Mr. Burnlow's shoulder, he could see Din anxiously waiting for him on the porch. He wagged his fingers slightly, and then as Mr. Burnlow turned back to the window, he waggled them frantically. He didn't know what he meant by these signals. Whether she was to go away and stop snooping about; or whether she was to wait at all costs, in case he needed her.

Mr. Burnlow's shoulders gave a hiccoughing jump. He lowered his head and blew hoarsely into his hand. 'Is that your sister, out there? Is it your sister?'

'Yes, sir.'

Mr. Burnlow walked with his slow, rolling gait, out of the room.

As soon as the door had closed he leapt forward and rapped on the glass. But there was only a second to stare into her worried eyes before Mr. Burnlow, moving slowly past the panes, was between them again. When Dianah stepped away Mr. Burnlow moved laughingly after her, and when she turned sideways, to keep in her brother's vision, he circled around her and blocked her off. Then he bent over her in a low bow, and straightened away from her with his short arms spread, and finally, sweeping playfully at her, he ushered her down the steps of the porch and on to the lawn. Then he turned. His footsteps echoed along the wood, down the uncarpeted hall, across the classroom, towards the boy who waited at his desk.

'Your sister', he raised an arm to his mouth, 'is a very faithful little person.' His hand, small and white and plump, hovered in front of his face, as if about to catch an invisible butterfly; it cupped itself and drifted forward. 'Faithfulness is a great virtue. Are *you* faithful to her.' And his fingers made the trapped face nod slightly.

'Will you be faithful to everyone you care about?' and his fingers made the trapped face nod, emphatically.

'Ah!' His dark eyes dreamed down. 'Ah! To everyone,

40

Little Portia?' And his fingers made the head wag sideways. 'Little Portia?'

'Sir?' He gazed up into the veiled and dreaming eyes. 'Sir?' And knew his life had changed. Mr. Burnlow was Tops.

He spooned into his boiled egg and waited for the third voice and the difficulties.

'What will he do about tea, please, Aunt Mary?'

'I suppose he can have it when he comes back, Dianah. Mr. Burnlow will only keep him an hour.'

'Can I have mine when he does, Aunt Mary?'

'We'll both have it when he does, Dianah.'

'Thank you, Aunt Mary.'

And from the habit of imitating his sister's politeness, he too thanked his aunt. But for the rest of the evening he eyed Dianah coldly. He knew that an advantage was being taken, and that her singing and smiling concealed prying intentions.

The desk was always pushed back at a certain point in their lesson, so that there should be no disturbance from the porch, so that alien faces couldn't intrude. They were cut off from the world. Mr. Burnlow said, so that they would be more visible to each other. They could be intimate. They could be *free*. Little Portia.

At first, brought to a heightened consciousness of himself by Mr. Burnlow's lapping closeness, he failed to understand much of what was said to him. But gradually he sensed the meanings from the accompanying glances, and knew by instinct when to look puzzled and when to smile. Most important of all he learnt to suppress his fear that Mr. Burnlow would talk of him as he frequently talked of Ron Harkness. 'Ah, Ronnie, Ronnie. In the pursuit of intricate beings, Little Portia, there is no time, there is no

D
41

time for the Ronnies of the world, the brute virgins. Alas!'
But this was what the soft tone, the expressive eyes, the
gentle hands, truly and magically conveyed—that they
were in pursuit of an intricate being. The phrase associated
itself with the richness of perfume, the swelling waistcoat,
the pink, smiling lips. It reverberated between them during
the early lessons in history and essay writing, it hung in
the atmosphere as they studied a geometrical problem or
investigated the riddles of algebra.

'You are clever, Grahame. But I make you brilliant.'

'Yes, sir.'

'Because I'm your conjurer, Little Portia. I wave my
wand over you and wisdom gushes from your sacred fount.
Gushes.'

'Yes, sir.'

'Gushes.'

It was true. With Mrs. Holydrake he had either known
or not known, and had thus either answered or confessed.
But with Mr. Burnlow he always felt that he did know,
obscurely, in some little part of himself, and that Mr. Burnlow's hand, resting on his arm, or Mr. Burnlow's eyes, resting on his face, would bring it all free. But there were times
when the conjurer or his magic failed. If this happened
during their private hour then Mr. Burnlow, sighing and
smiling, would tease him into understanding. But if it
happened during class, in front of the others, Mr. Burnlow
would turn away from him, disdainfully, and in despair he
would look through the window, and try to see past the
porch and across the lawn into the room where Mrs.
Slocum would be teaching the girls. On certain afternoons
he could make out Din's head bent over a book, or Din on
her feet, reading aloud; or Din with her hand up. But the
prospect of a sister so composed in her studies did nothing
to lessen his own sense of failure. Nor did the ridiculous
ignorance of Giveller, Dodds or Harkness. He could

hardly enjoy turning a contemptuous inner face on them because they had failed to give the simple present of *donner* when Mr. Burnlow had turned an outwardly contemptuous face on him, for failing to give its simple past subjunctive.

'You were dismal this morning, Grahame. Exhibitionist, narcissistic, lovely of course. Of course. But so dismal. So dismal.'

'I couldn't remember.' He lowered his eyes. 'I tried, sir.'

'Ah, yes. You always try. You try too hard, Little Portia. But be a little secret. Don't spread yourself over everything as if you were a tube of paint. You're at your best when you keep a mystery back.'

'Yes, sir.'

'An intricate being.'

He whispered the words to himself again and again, they throbbed softly within him at night, they repeated themselves in thrilled whispers during the day; so that the series of soft and fluid movements with which one afternoon he was drawn against the waistcoat, into the very heart of the perfume, seemed merely the natural outcome that had been anticipated so often. Mr. Burnlow had caught his intricate being. He laid his mouth against his Little Portia's ear, and told him so.

After that he was always afraid that the moment wouldn't come; and nearly as afraid when it did. It wasn't the lap itself, with its sudden stirrings; not the hands, that held him close and explored him delicately; not certainly, the buttons on the waistcoat that rose and fell against his cheek. It was something that he could not see or feel—an intuition that the eyes in the hanging face would show an incomprehensible expression; that the mouth that nibbled his neck would wear an incomprehensible smile. It was, perhaps, an intuition that all the pieces of himself that Mr. Burnlow enjoyed—the back of his legs, his thighs, particularly the

43

skin under his trousers—were too interesting to Mr. Burnlow for Mr. Burnlow to be interested in *him*, apart from these things. And then when he was pushed off at last, his anxiety would be replaced by a strange watchfulness. He would stand by the chair as Mr. Burnlow shuffled his books and papers together, and he would note the white softness of Mr. Burnlow's neck, the ridge of skin that folded over the cream collar; the shininess of the hair that was thin at one side of the scalp and seemed to grow across it, net-like and rootless. He noted, too, that Mr. Burnlow's cheeks were wet, that his round shoulders shuddered, and that mixed in with the lemony sweetness of his perfume there was another smell, that was like the Mallows's hen-coop, or even the marsh behind it. He stood coldly close to Mr. Burnlow, and amazed himself by investigating him as if he were a toad.

'What do you see, Portia? What do you see?'

But what he saw then were the eyes that ruled him and the face that he adored.

She would be either waiting for him on the Shore Road or would appear slowly and thoughtfully from behind a bank. There was no way he could attack her for these accidents without also explaining that Mr. Burnlow had made him wonderful; while *she*, she made him ordinary, merely himself again. So they walked in silence until the effect of the lesson had faded, and he was prepared to tolerate her a little. And at least she never asked him questions. The very name on her lips would have made him finish her with a phrase or two, or even a blow; and she seemed to know it. But she listened closely to Aunt Mary and Colonel Rones when they were interrogating him.

'Very well, thank you, Aunt Mary.'

'He's a good teacher, Grahame.'

'Yes, Aunt Mary.'

44

'And a kind one, Grahame. I hope you remember to say thank you. *Every time*.'

'Yes, Aunt Mary.'

'I've spoken to him,' said Colonel Rones. He strode across the room and took up a position with his back to the windows. 'Sickly.'

'He has asthma, according to Mrs. Slocum.'

'Something like that,' the Colonel agreed. 'Something.'

'What, Basil?'

'Well, only—certainly never had chaps like that when *I* was at school.'

'No one took an interest in you?'

'Oh, yes.' He nodded. 'Most certainly they did.'

Of course he found it difficult to bear these conversations between Aunt Mary and Colonel Rones, both of whom seemed to think that Mr. Burnlow was only a person, like themselves. Particularly he couldn't bear them because of Din's uninterested smile, that camouflaged her wiggling ears. He hated her at this time. He hated everyone except Mr. Burnlow. He wouldn't even go to the kitchen, for fear that Bella would drag him on to her lap, and force some of the old games upon him.

But he had other, secret satisfactions. He was beginning to use something of Mr. Burnlow's tone, something of his manner. If it was true that he hardly ever knew the meaning of the jokes Mr. Burnlow made him make, it was also true that he always knew when he was making a joke. He could be witty, it seemed, about Aunt Mary's way of snapping at the Colonel, and once or twice, in seizures of wisdom that had their source in Mr. Burnlow's questions, he talked of Din's habit of nosing into his affairs.

'You're two repressed waifs', Mr. Burnlow said, 'who will murder each other with love. When she's just a little older she will bleed for you, Grahame. All over you.'

'Yes,' he had profoundly replied. 'But she likes me.'

It was strange, then, that when he returned to Mallows in the evening he would be unable to sustain his power unless he was by himself. Aunt Mary's severe eyes reduced him at once, and Colonel Rones's bristling height held him at his five foot two, psychologically speaking. He would even find himself talking to Din with warmth and excitement, to make up for having talked about her with so much penetration. He needed Mr. Burnlow's presence to keep a complete hold on Mr. Burnlow's personality, which meant that Mr. Burnlow was to some extent always with him. He thought about him at night, and thought about him at week-ends. Before the first class of the day he sat tensely at his desk, waiting. If any of the others mentioned the name, his stomach jarred; and when the door finally opened, and Mr. Burnlow came in, he would have for a second the sensation of unconsciousness. Until Mr. Burnlow looked at him and smiled, and he caught from the front of the room the first faint whiffs of the familiar perfume. From then on he was himself again. His eyes would flick from one dismal face to another, to observe the coarse details that confirmed his superiority over every living being, except his proper master.

The weeks passed into months, the months into terms; and Mr. Burnlow, who took him privately during the holidays as well, passed from the upper insides of his legs into his trousers, and from there to his buttocks. And by similar degrees he got used to Mr. Burnlow's habits, and vain as a consequence. He became very intimate with him, cocky and teasing. He called him (on invitation) by his first name, which was Lindsay, and asked him about the ring on his finger and the clip on the back of his bow tie. He began serious discussions about the books Mr. Burnlow used to slip into the bottom of his satchel, as a treat.

'It's wet,' he said, 'Lindsay. And dismal.'

'Ah!' Mr. Burnlow's arms cuddled him closer. 'But is it immoral, Little Portia?'

'Immoral?' For some reason he thought of Colonel Rones. 'Immoral, Lindsay?'

'When Uncle Stephen and the boy sleep in the same bed, that wild, storm-tossed evening. That evening of lightning and miracles. Immoral? Amoral? Unmoral? Which is it, Little Portia? I've explained the difference. Is it *im*?'

'Why is it immoral, Lindsay?'

'Oh, I'm glad you know it isn't, Little Portia? His fingers scuttled up, under the rims of the knickers. They caught at something, tweaked it, and scuttled swiftly down. 'Now is that *im*, *a*, *un*, Little Portia my dear? Do you mind my doing that?'

He stared sightlessly across the room. 'Doing what, Lindsay?' he chirruped.

'Ah! It doesn't matter now. You'd better go now.'

'Go?' He strained obediently against the arms, that folded him down into a deep embrace. 'Yes, Lindsay.' But the waistcoat was pressed against his mouth, and muffled him.

'Please go now, Little Portia,' Mr Burnlow commanded huskily. 'I insist.' And his arms leapt away from the struggling body as if an invisible force had wrenched them apart. 'Go, Portia,' he shouted. 'Go.'

He went. But he looked back from the door, just a glance; and carried to Mallows and into his bed that night an image of Mr. Burnlow lying forward across the desk, his arms hanging down by his side, and his face, brightly damp, supported under the chin by a book.

'So you don't enjoy the pagan Ron as Caesar?'

'Well, I would, Lindsay, yes, if Harkness could read.'

'Do you think, Little P., that he has the figure for it? Or the face?'

'I don't really, Lindsay, no.'

47

'But you see, Little P., I rather fancy myself as Caesar's wife.'

'Ronnie Harkness's wife?'

'Oh, good heavens, above suspicions, I mean.'

'Above suspicion.' He nodded, in the hope that he would nod his ignorance away.

'Above suspicion.' Mr. Burnlow's hand slid abstractedly up a slim young calf, and then absently rolled the grey woollen socks down to the neat young ankles. 'Which is why, my darling, you're not above punishment. You realize that, of course.'

He nodded again, and for the same reason. For he knew that when Mr. Burnlow spoke in class, there was silence; and when Mr. Burnlow smiled, there was stillness. Mr. Burnlow, with his scorpion's tongue, with the menace of his magic eyes, contained them easily. Even Ronnie Harkness, who had once challenged Mr. Slocum to a fight only seconds after Mr. Slocum had left the room, was paralysed by Mr. Burnlow. In Mr. Burnlow's class, then, there was no punishment; inasmuch as Grahame understood the word.

Until the next morning, when Mr. Burnlow met his stare with a shift of his eyes to George Dodds, and ignored his smiles, and refused to acknowledge his waving hand during the questions. He knew eventually that there was danger, great danger. All his mute appeals were received with the same shallow gaze, and an instant smile for elsewhere, and although he tried to decipher each sentence as if it concealed a personal message, he knew that there was really nothing for him to understand; except, of course, that he had been forsaken for ever. Mr. Burnlow was consigning him back to himself, and Mallows, and Din. So in desperation he looked out of the window to the other building, searching for the blonde head that was the old link with his feelings. And immediately the voice sounded for him.

But the eyes that stared were not for him, and the mouth that smiled was not for him. Mr. Burnlow stood at the end of the aisle, his hands in his pockets, and his short legs spread.

'Is there something there more important than anything here?" He rattled some change in his pockets. 'Thwaite?'

The noises that came from his mouth were made by Giveller, Harkness, Dodds, when Mr. Burnlow was playing with them for their idiocies. He did not make such noises, with his Lindsay. But his heart thrilled within him. Even in his fear he knew that a different adventure was about to begin. Mr. Burnlow, after an hour of rejecting him, was recognizing him again.

Which Mr. Burnlow did by ordering him to his feet; and then ordering him to stand at his desk, with his head up and his arms to his side. That this was the extent of the recognition he showed by turning to Harkness's exercise book—spludged and foul; and whispering into Harkness's ear—doubtless in the same condition.

He stood stiffly, his head held rigid, his heart still throbbing. He could feel their eyes upon him, from every part of the room, their grins and grimaces. It was as if he were tied to Mr. Burnlow, who wouldn't look at him, by the others, who did. Mr. Burnlow moved about the room, pausing at a desk here and a desk there, talking sometimes with his back to the class, moving slowly and coldly down the aisle towards his little captive, and then slowly and warmly veering off towards one of the free. But everything he did was somehow for his captive's sake. The tingling body, the jumping senses, were in his control. He studied Dodds and Giveller, and murmured to Harkness; but through them he fondled the knots and made them secure. And soon he would come again, and with a special and wonderful look, release him. His Lindsay would sense his yearning, his fear, his excitement, and come.

49

But all that came, when he could no longer bear the hurt of his neck and the stiffness of his legs, when his exalted spirit hung limp again, were tears.

'Ah, Little Portia.' The voice was husky and from a dream, 'Ah, Portia. Would you prefer a private punishment? On your naked bottom. Here. Here. Where my finger on your naked bummy. Bum. Bum.'

'Lindsay?' But the perfume clogged his nostrils, and the waistcoat stopped his mouth, and suddenly it was like the early times when he had investigated the neck and collar and scalp, without feeling the magic or the love. There were the details now, playing with him and suffocating him, but there was no Lindsay, to make him his special self again. He was afraid.

After that there were many punishments that were variations on the first. He was made to stand at the front of the class, with his hands behind his back; he was made to stand in the corner, with his eyes shut; he was made to sit at his desk, during the break, with his arms raised above his head. And eventually he accepted it as part of his life with Mr. Burnlow, and whenever he was addressed in a particular way his whole being would leap in response. He realized that he was talked about by the others, and this too was an excitement. For if, previously, he had been privately distinguished by little smiles and personal stares, he was now publicly distinguished, by the punishments. Behind *their* heavy smiles was a dull version of what he himself felt whenever Mr. Burnlow had a low word with Harkness, or a passing pat for Dodds.

'You have no mother, my darling,' Mr. Burnlow explained, as his fingers brushed within him and made him rear. 'That is why I punish you. I have a mother who used to punish me. Once she tied me to a chair for an afternoon, and had other little boys, and a pretty little girl, to tea, so that they would see me there. And she would gag me, too, for being difficult, and for the quickness of my wit. You have no mother to love you, and do that to you, my Little Portia, so I must take her place. I must punish you, but only because I adore you. My mother has a teashop in Pimlico. You and I will visit her, because she wants to meet you, Little P., as if you were my, oh, my God, oh Jesus, oh Holy Jesus,' and his fingers darted up again, his ring scraping the flesh of thigh; and his arms looped about, bindingly.

The hands that owned him dug deeper, and the halting breath became a menacing and wordless choke, and for the first time he thrashed and tried to scream out against the blocking waistcoat; jerking his legs in the air and pounding his hands against the soft back, until there was a crash, another scream that was not his, and he had rolled free. He crouched away from the desk and stared up.

Mr. Burnlow sat with his arms hanging down, his stomach heaving, his eyes fixed on the door. He swayed to his feet. His fingers fiddled with the wings of his polka-dot bow tie, and water trickled out of his mouth. 'Madame, oh, Madame, my pleasure.'

'Grahame. Go home at once.'

He caught a glimpse, as he ran out, of a small face, white and bony, and a pointing finger. Then the door slammed behind him, and the voices were cut off. It opened again to a piercing cry. In a distant part of the school, where the Slocums dwelt, another door opened. Feet clattered, cheeks were slapped, there were fearful sounds that he identified as the sounds of Mr. Burnlow, begging.

He ran down the drive to the Shore Road. He ran and ran, along the undulating banks, across the road, into the garden, towards the open French windows of the living-room. He would have run out again, through the opposite windows although there weren't any, if he hadn't been caught in a steely circle of arm, and forced to his knees. A pair of remote blue eyes blinked down at him from above the yellow tips of a distinguished moustache. Then he was carried to a sofa.

Colonel Rones sat facing him on a hard-backed chair, his arms spread out to cut off flight. Once, very slowly, he shook his head and murmured, 'Old chap.'

He saw obscurely, as through many shadows, the out-stretched arms of Colonel Rones. Then he fell away, within himself, peacefully. Nothing had happened. He was asleep, and would never awake, except to Din and the noises in the garden. He was free.

But they came towards him almost at once, Aunt Mary's face more insistently there, each small wrinkle, both glittering lenses. Colonel Rones, leaning forward with his hands on his knees, was showing a smile.

'Grahame, please answer me, child. Are you all right?'

He let his head nod forward; feebly.

'Has he ever done anything nasty to you, Grahame?'

'Anything, old boy?'

He tilted his head back.

'What?'

The room filled with the other presence, stronger by far than the two crouching figures, their probing eyes. Then Aunt Mary put her hand on his. 'Anything worse, dear, than he was doing this afternoon?'

He nodded.

'Why didn't you tell me, dear?'

He mumbled ambiguously; in fear that her worry would go away.

'Said', the Colonel quickly and incorrectly interpreted, 'that he was afraid of the beggar.'

'I see.'

They went over to the desk and began a conversation in low voices, while he sat dangling his head, with his hands twisted into his lap. Quite alert, though, to the droppings of their talk. 'Child harm.' 'Man jailed.' 'That creature.' 'Fuss and scandal.'

'Grahame. Grahame my dear?'

He looked at her from streaming eyes. Her small face, blurred and wrinkled out of focus, was like a bespectacled apple.

'You're not to think about this, dear.'

'No,' he whispered.

'It's all in the past.'

He let out a sob of agreement.

'The Colonel will deal with him. He'll never bother you again.'

'Thank you, Aunt Mary.'

Colonel Rones saluted him and strode out of the room.

'Now you may go upstairs, if you like, and see Dianah.'

He went upstairs, moving his feet as if they were chained. He knew that although he wasn't to think about it any more, he mustn't immediately show that he wasn't thinking about it. So he shuffled weakly down the hall, and into the bathroom. He wiped away his tears in the mirror, so that he could inspect his face properly, but he left his cheeks a trifle damp. Then he shuffled weakly out, and hesitated in front of the nursery door. He coughed. He turned the knob. He shuffled weakly in.

She was sitting at the table, with her hands clasped in front of her, frowning. She stared at him for a second and then she rose and put an arm around his shoulder. 'Dodie. Poor Dodie.'

He allowed himself to be soothed and petted for a while, and then he sat down. 'Why did *she* come, Din?'

'I don't know, Dodie. I don't know. I just said that Mr.

Burnlow was very fond of you, and she said he seems to be, and I said yes he likes to put you on his lap and cuddle you as if you were his son even, Dodie, and she said——'

'But how did you know, Din?'

'Oh, well only because I saw you through the keyhole, because I left my satchel behind, and I just peeped to find if you were nearly finished, and that's all. I could *see* him being nice to you.'

There was a long silence between them. She stood beside him, staring down into his face, and then she moved away and hovered behind him. But he had found the truth in her eyes.

'So I don't know why she's angry, Dodie. Do you? I mean, she telephoned the Colonel and ran out of the house. Why should she be so angry?'

He shook his head.

'It's funny though, isn't it? Isn't it, Dodie?'

In a faltering, courageous voice he explained that perhaps it was because Mr. Burnlow had wrestled him and hurt him and thrown him to the floor in a temper.

'Oh. But he was usually nice to you, wasn't he?'

'No.' He shook his head. 'No, he wasn't. He was always punishing me. He was always hurting me.'

'No, no, Grahame. Let *me* get down.' Mr. Slocum squatted on the porch. 'You've had a most unhappy experience. Most unhappy.'

The tears rose swiftly and surely, but he blinked them back as suddenly, and to his horror, Mr. Slocum became merely rumples and blotches and large teeth. His cheeks began to tighten, his chest to hurt.

'I'd prefer you to think he meant you no harm. Did he harm you, Grahame?'

'Sir, he wrestled me about and threw me to the floor, sir.'

A paw fell on his shoulder; a shaggy head, smelly with

54

nicotine and burnt matches, was thrust close to his. 'But you must forget about it. You will be all right, Grahame, if you forget all about it. What does my favourite poet say?'

'Oh, for the touch of a vanished hand, sir. The sound of a voice that is still, sir.'

Mr. Slocum made a weird woofing noise. 'He also says, "Bear bravely, Grahame, bear well, for all things pass." '

'Yes, sir.' And mercifully the dog rose and transformed itself back into Mr. Slocum before the laughter came.

'He was ill, Grahame, ill.' And Mr. Slocum stared down at him so sadly that he wondered for an instant whether there should be tears for Mr. Burnlow, as well. But tears in general seemed to do.

He was to forget the matter. Everyone said so. It wasn't to be mentioned again. It wasn't even to be thought of. But what exactly was he to forget, and how exactly was he to set about it? For a long time a particular smell, sweet and suffocating and a little lemony, would make his senses reel with shame, and the certainty of impending disaster. Phrases in books revived the memory of phrases whispered which revived the memory of being smiled at, and teased, and understood. Then the smiles became caresses, and the caresses were evil, and the smell returned, and his senses reeled. He could not easily forget how he had used to speak to Mr. Burnlow, and had called him Lindsay, and had stored up jokes and imitations for him; but he did his best to forget the glimpse of the white face and the pointing finger, the tone of *her* voice. It was months before the incidents became vague, and the judgments satisfactorily confused, until finally he could remember only what he had been to Mr. Burnlow, and had forgotten what Mr. Burnlow had been to him.

In a sense Mr. Burnlow's questions about immorality, amorality and unmorality had been answered at last. All

of them came from doing things that led to a finger pointing at you, as a finger had pointed at Mr. Burnlow. They
came from feeling strange things about someone else and
being found out and despised. And the way to avoid *that*
was to watch yourself, work very hard, and be as safe as if
you were with Mrs. Holydrake.

He worked very hard, until he and his sister knew too
much for the Slocums even to pretend that they were teaching them anything. They stayed on there, nevertheless—
there was nowhere else for them to go—attending the
classes like visitors who were interested in local methods of
education. Their real lessons came in the evening from a
young man who taught at a grammar school in Portsmouth. He was a slight, quiet, industrious little person,
with a wife and three children to support, and like Mrs.
Holydrake he believed in education, although for different
reasons. Education had brought him from a slum in Gosport to a bungalow close to the Colonel's in Morton, just as
education would take his pupil from the Slocums' to a
school like Windhoven. Mr. Victor knew very little about
Windhoven, except that it was almost famous, and therefore that he was against it on political grounds. But he was
convinced that its academic standard was high, and would
present a challenge to his own system. He liked the idea of
conquering it from the side-lines, so to speak, and set
about teaching Grahame first to master the Common Entrance, then the Scholarship exam.

'They're very well prepared, Miss Medway,' he said, at
the end of his second year. 'Grahame's particularly well
prepared.'

'I'm sure he is.'

The light of a small ambition shone from Mr. Victor's
eye. 'He could get a scholarship, Miss Medway.'

'Scholarship boys are odd,' Aunt Mary pronounced, for

56

she had heard people say it when she was a girl. 'They try too hard and fizzle out.'

'Perhaps they do,' Mr. Victor agreed after a moment, with a sad and wasted irony. 'Perhaps they do.'

Of course it never occurred to Mr. Victor that there might be areas in which Grahame was unprepared. He saw that the boy would never do at his own grammar school—he was too formal, too stiffly good-mannered—but these qualities would be what the public schools were after; what indeed they were all about. He got on well with the boy *personally*, he told his Portsmouth colleagues, but he disliked the idea of him almost as much as he disliked the idea of Windhoven. Both embodied a part of what was hateful in the social organization of the country. So after his conversation with Miss Medway the two disapprovals merged into the conclusion that the boy and the school were just right for each other, and his interest in his pupil became exclusively academic, rather as if he were working on a controlled educational experiment.

Colonel Rones had some doubts, though; which he naturally hesitated to express. His mumbles and evasions were endured for two consecutive teas, and then he was brought sharply to the point.

'Just', he said, 'that it will be a jump. Going from private lessons and Mallows to a school like Windhoven. It's not at all like Slocums'.'

'I should hope it isn't.'

'The standards, you see.'

'Little Victor says he's brilliant, Basil.'

'I was thinking of the——'

'Social life, Basil?' For it had become her pet joke.

'Something like that.' In fact he had stopped thinking at all. He was listening to the voices of Old Windhovens who had fallen on unremembered battlefields; he was being surrounded by spectral walls, and harried, far within his being, towards the Great Gates which had never opened for him. Ancient needs reasserted themselves and withered terrors bloomed again. He had entered Windhoven fifty-six years before, but he saw it all as he had seen it then. He had been a victim.

'Grahame', she said crisply into his dazed old face, 'will get the best out of it. He'll soon make friends and all that sort of—Basil, whatever's the matter with you?'

He clutched with both hands at his teacup, pressed his knees together, and said in an odd, piping voice, 'It will make a man of him. It will do him good.'

'Of course it will. That's why he's going there.'

And she actually believed it would. Since the unpleasant business with Mr. Burnlow she had decided that almost everything did children good. The boy had put the unfortunate and ugly incident behind him, and gone, under her remote command, from strength to strength. He was excellently mannered, extremely studious, as fit as a fiddle —in a word, splendid. And if Mr. Burnlow, that most corrupt of individuals, could do no harm; then how could the most normal institution in the country do anything but good.

'Have a ginger-nut,' she said, passing the Colonel the plate and watching him reassemble himself. 'You've been neglecting your exercises again. I can tell by your colour.' Which, she was pleased to note, was returning rapidly to his cheeks.

'Thank you, Mary,' he barked. 'Yes, Windhoven will make a man of him. There'll be nothing like the Burnlow affair at Windhoven.'

The Colonel came to a halt on another compliment, cleared his throat, and switched his gaze about half an inch to the other side of Grahame's face. Then, with a jerk of his pointed knees, he began again. He used short sentences, sharp, each one separated from the rest by a distinct pause, rather as if he needed time to reload and aim. But if there was much emphasis, there was so little variety that Grahame could understand the whole without listening to any of the parts. He gazed down at his hands and twisted them into each other and nodded his head, and let the little pellets strike off the surface of himself. As with Clipson, as with House Master, he would just wait for the end.

Which came when Aunt Mary coughed outside the door, entered briskly, and announced that it was time. For tea. The Colonel, caught in the middle of an awkward clause to do with self-respect, clamped his lips together, touched his chin, and decided that he had done. 'We've had our little——" he said, rising to his feet, 'man to man'. And now he really must be getting back.

'Stay to tea, Basil.'

'Must be getting back.'

'I have made the tea,' she said and led him to the door. A second later she thrust her head in, directed her gaze at the fire-place, and decided that the whole matter was closed.

She opened it again the next morning after breakfast. 'If people don't like you,' she said quickly and not necessarily to her nephew, 'they probably have a good reason. If anyone dislikes you for a bad reason, then you must ignore them.'

'Yes,' he said.

'The Colonel has kindly explained the situation if they're right.'

'Yes,' he said.

'But if they're wrong, you must ignore them.'

'Yes,' he said.

'Then *they* will ignore you.'

But during the course of their one interview together, House Master had made it plain that he ignored no one and nothing. Rather, that it was his specific and noble function to bring everything, however shameful, to the light. Grahame tried again, as he had tried a thousand times already, to understand what it was that House Master had understood about him, had advised him against, and finally had forgiven him. But all he could manage were the accidental associations that clouded his mind and prevented him from understanding anything but his own helplessness.

There had been a strange smell in the room, of something brown and sweet and cavernous, that had seemed at first to come from the desk, and then from the floor, and then from the stooping form of House Master himself. He had stared up at the long, pale face and had tried not to notice the smell, in fact tried not to notice anything but the face, and the sentences that were coming from it. House Master was telling him not to worry, nothing was going to happen to him, this was just a little chin-chin. But he would have preferred one of his encounters with Clipson to chin-chins with House Master. At least interviews with Clipson, developing through terror and humiliation, by way of Clipson's increasingly noisy breathing, to pain, were logical. But House Master, with his soft voice, his frowning smile and his dark smell, was entirely mystery.

'Mmmmm.' House Master took from his pocket a thick, square pipe and a small yellow bag. Hs long fingers stroked into the bag, twisted shreds of tobacco into a ball, and smoothed the ball into the bowl of the pipe. His eyes stared wisely down, his head nodded with revelations. 'Mmmmm, now, old chap,' he took from his trouser pocket a box of matches, rose from behind his desk, and lit the pipe. 'Mmmm.' His eyes widened, his chest sucked with excitement, his fingers shook the lighted match as if it were alive and biting. 'Mmmmm.' A cloud of smoke enveloped his face, and the smell in the room was at last given a visible form. 'Old chap. Mmmm. That's better.' He popped his lips and smiled. 'How's the footers?'

'Not in a team, sir,' he said, in a voice he made loud from a fear of whispering.

'Mmmm.' House Master sat on the edge of the desk and bent forward. 'And your friend, Jacobs?'

'No, sir.'

'No?'

'Not in a team, sir. Either.'

'I see. Mmmm. Mmmm.' House Master straightened, blew smoke through dark narrow nostrils and shook his head. 'Tell me about your friends, old chap.'

'Jacobs, sir.'

'Is Jacobs your *only* friend?'

'Sir.'

'What about all the other fellows in Dorm?'

'Sir.'

'You like them, do you?'

'Sir.'

Yes he did, extremely. But he had learnt very early in Arnold's House that his liking fellows made no difference to whether fellows liked him. One fellow, Aprilson, had had a grandfather, a father, two uncles and a brother in Arnold's, in the same dorm, and thus gave the impression

61

that he himself was not so much a young Windhoven as a number of Old Windhovens gathered together and shrunk down to one small one, for the mere pleasure of doing it all again. Aprilson had blond hair and very frank blue eyes, and from the first day was accepted as dorm leader. There were only two boys whom Aprilson refused to lead. One was Jacobs, who had bent legs, curly black hair, and eyes so small that their colour was irrelevant.

'Look here, Hendy,' Aprilson had said, 'that's race prejudice. That's not Arnold's.'

'Yes,' Jacobs said. 'That's not Arnold's, Henders.'

'Clam, Jacobs,' Aprilson said. 'And grease off. Not because you're a Jew, but because *you're* not Arnold's, either.'

So he had admired Aprilson, and despised Jacobs. So he had stood apologetically on the edge of Aprilson's group, a little behind Henders, in the hope that he would be drawn in amongst them without being noticed. So Jacobs had spotted him as an outsider like himself, and stuck close to him until they were told to grease and clam jointly. So he was the other fellow Aprilson refused to lead.

'Well,' House Master stubbed his thumb into the bowl of his pipe, jerked it away with a small cry, stared evenly down into his eyes, and asked him what he did at night. 'Don't be ashamed, don't be ashamed.' There seemed to be a connection between the answer he was meant to give, and the smile on House Master's face and the smoke from House Master's mouth. House Master knew what he did at night.

'Go to sleep, sir?' he suggested in a voice that trembled as much as it boomed.

The smile altered slightly, the pipe was held away; to suggest that this was wrong.

'Lie there awake, sir?' he boomed.

The smile altered again, in a different way; the pipe

62

shuddered to show that this was more like it but that he was to try again.

'Thinking, sir.' Although he knew he was right to shout like this—Clipson had often added an extra stroke for mumbling—he wished that his voice didn't sound to his own ears as if it were coming from someone much larger than himself, standing behind him.

'Mmmm.' House Master indicated that he was warm, very warm, and wondered aloud what he thought about.

About the red walls that closed him in, and the dark green fields that stretched beyond them. About the incomprehensible services in chapel, with the hymns he could never find in his book, and the psalms that rolled with such sweet ease from the throats of all real Windhovens. And of course he also thought about Aprilson and Henders and Matthews and Tanner and Budd and Gard, who whispered of School Trumples and House Milders, in fact of all the activities that he and Jacobs were beaten for missing, because they could never find out what they were, or where they took place. And when he could no longer bear to think about all these things, he thought about Morton and Mallows, and above all Din, who wrote to say that she liked St. Anne's because it was nice. Sometimes he could actually make her narrow face appear behind the lids of his eyes, and when he had done that he could usually manage to sleep, at last. But he couldn't tell House Master all that. Even though House Master, fanning the air and smiling, knew without being told; and was leading him, step by step, towards the telling.

'Boys?'

'Sir?'

'About boys, old chap? Jacobs?'

'No, sir.'

'Girls?'

'Sir?'

'Girls, old chap?' A cloud of blue and a pop of lips. 'From books, say?'

He shook his head. 'Sir.'

House Master shook his own head and explained that it was one or the other.

He stared into his lap for ever and ever, and mumbled, in a voice no longer booming, that it was girls, sir. He made an effort to pronounce Din's name, but couldn't.

House Master crossed his legs and smiled in so kindly a way that he felt obliged to smile back. It felt very odd to be sitting in the deep leather armchair smiling up at House Master, but it felt odder when House Master stopped smiling, and for a confusing second looked angry. But when he himself stopped smiling—which he did instantly—House Master smiled once more. And told him, from behind a new fog, to listen carefully.

The fighter pilots had had a short time to live. They had been lonely. They did things to themselves.

Fighter pilots were men. The bravest men that had ever flown in planes.

Because they did things to themselves did not mean that they were not brave.

They had been lonely.

Boys, too, did things to themselves.

Grahame did things to himself.

Grahame was the bravest man that had ever flown in planes. He had a short time to live. That was why he did things to himself.

'Do you understand me, old chap?'

'Sir.'

'And you won't do it any more?'

' No, sir.'

'Mmmm. Mmmm.' The pipe stabbed towards him. 'But I don't forbid, do I?'

'No, sir.'

'I advise, don't I?'

'Yes, sir.'

'And there's nothing you want to tell me about Jacobs?'

'No, sir.'

'So.' And House Master put his hand on his shoulder and led him to the door. 'I'll tell Clipson we've had a chin-chin, and got to the bottom of it all.'

He lay curled in his bed, his eyes shut, trying to drift away on forbidden memories. Around him he could hear the creaking, the rustling, the soft talk. He knew that Jacobs would be lying with his little eyes open, waiting to find out what House Master had said. But that night, with House Master's speech about fighter pilots and doing things to himself still in his mind, he could not talk to Jacobs. He was afraid that Jacobs would understand what it was he had been doing and flinch away from him. He clenched his arms around his chest and pressed his face into the pillow, to keep House Master's talk out, and to keep Jacobs's questions out, and gradually, slowly, through the darkness Din hovered towards him. She was not exact, there was a blur around her face, her long hair fanned, but there was an atmosphere of her worry and care, an atmosphere of her safety and the slipping away of himself to sleep, and the sound of the sea rolling, and footsteps, Aunt Mary's, clacking, quick, clack, to clear the haze.

He was sprung into the light.

He lay rigid, his arms down to his side, his feet together, at attention.

The worst thing was not being able to adopt his usual position—head lowered, eyes on the ground. The worst thing was having to lie rigid, gazing up into the red, throbbing face and noticing that one of Clipson's front teeth was dirty. He saw Clipson noticing his noticing; and becoming more throbbing because of it.

65

House Master had let him off too easily.

He was disgusting. Disgusting. Disgusting.

Quick, clack, the footsteps went away.

The darkness came back.

They stood around him, drumming the name that described his nature. He was a wanker. And screeney. He was screeney, because he was a wanker. One voice was louder than the rest, although the face was at first separated from the rest. But gradually, with a series of shuffling side-steps that carried him out of a patch of moonlight into the dense and chanting mass of shadows, Jacobs found his place and came jubilantly under Aprilson's leadership.

After that he spent all his free time in the Colluns, a room off the library, with another exile called Cranton. The Colluns was small and had high windows so tiny that the light scarcely reached either of the two wooden armchairs; but it was quiet, with ancient reading lamps and a musty smell of seclusion. Cranton was always there in Free Time because he was too ill to be anywhere else, except possibly in the Infirm. He had had an operation the previous year, the effects of which still showed in his wide, slightly staring eyes, his white cheeks, and the careful way he moved his long, thin body.

'I don't have to do anything,' he said once, staring intensely at Grahame, 'except go to class. And I probably wouldn't have to do that. They wouldn't make a fuss.'

'Why not?'

'Well, I ate some ground glass in my soup last year and they know it's their fault.'

Most of the time Cranton was absorbed in a book; or wrote into a large, red file; or translated articles from Spanish magazines about bullfighting. He accepted Grahame's presence with eager sympathy.

'I expect you hate it here?'

'Well, no, of course not. No.' Clipson had frequently put

66

the same question to him, although in a different tone, and he knew the answer.

'But you probably wish you weren't here?'

'No. Why?'

'Well, you come here to get away from your House, don't you?'

'Do *you*?'

'Oh, no, I like it here. It's the best place in the school.'

And this was the problem. Cranton went to Colluns to read and write because those were the things he most wanted to do. Grahame went there to read and write because he couldn't do any of the things that everyone else did, however much he wanted to. He was always expecting to be found by an Arnold's, and ordered away.

'I'm a bit like Shelley,' Cranton explained. 'They would hound *me* out of Windhoven, except they don't care. My stomach might collapse again.' He wanted to be a bull-fighter when he left, and would illustrate the death of Manolete, flinging his head back against the wooden chair, sucking in his cheeks, and whispering in Spanish. Sometimes he fell sideways into Keats's eternal slumber. 'A matador de toros *and* a poet,' he forecast. In the small, high, dim room, with his face drawn and his lids sealed under the pool from the lamp, he could achieve an effect of eerie yet tranquil doom.

'People should have very quick lives and early deaths,' he explained. With, of course, a few last words whenever possible.

But Cranton was also a listener. He enjoyed hearing Grahame's accounts of Clipson's beatings, and what had happened in the dorm, and was on several occasions kind enough to compare *him* to Shelley. Thus for a short time Grahame's experience would be tinged by nobility, and a powerful flame burned in his chest. But once back in the dorm, with Aprilson staring coldly past him, or Jacobs telling him to grease, he would see the weaknesses in Cranton's methods, and almost hate him for them. He knew what Aprilson would make of Cranton (screeney) and what Clipson would to to him, if *he'd* been in Arnold's.

As for himself in Arnold's, he found he could shrink so far away that he ultimately disappeared altogether. To everyone who looked at him he was merely an object, without sense or intelligence, and thus he could move amongst them virtually unnoticed. He went past Clipson and the other monitors with lowered head; he sat at the end of Junior Diners, and never ate more or less than was put before him; he undressed discreetly, managed to wash a few minutes early, and feigned modest sleep. When he couldn't go to Colluns he would sit in a corner of the Junior Common, cut off by a block of lockers, where he could hunch over one of Cranton's books and almost ignore Jacobs's grinning inspections.

At least he was safe. And he had a friend.

But there must have been a strong element of doubt about Cranton, or he would have mentioned him to Din during their long walks. He told her everything else— about Clipson, about House Master, about Jacobs; and he talked in general terms of his difference and his failure. Together they covered every mile of the windswept beach, from the golf-course at one end to Laker's Dip at the other; they spent hours huddled into a newly discovered and larger alcove, which was where, in the privacy and the physical intimacy, he found that he could make his most lucid accusations against himself. And all the time, with Din patiently listening, calmly asking questions, always beside him, he moved towards his ultimate definition. It was a large definition, that included every possible Windhoven judgement. 'People don't like me', he said, 'because there's something wrong with me. Even if I don't do the things they say, they *expect* me to.'

'If you're polite, Dodie, they can't do anything.'

'Yes,' he said, 'they can.' And told her how. But as his description of his predicament became more absolute and despairing, the predicament itself became more remote. Clipson, House Master, Jacobs, Aprilson, were all transformed into unreality, as if they were figures that he and Din had made up between them. His fears themselves vanished with repetition. Their talks, their walks, her sympathy and suggestions, were more important than the phantoms that caused them.

Then the weeks away from Windhoven became the days towards it, and as the First of term approached the phantoms took substance again, with their particular powers, their own voices and gestures. He was no longer in control. He spent the last night at Mallows staring up from his pillow.

But he was still in possession of his technique. In class he, who worked hardest, and came first, was the least questioned. In the dorm he, who was the most despised, was the least noticed. He had dwindled into a little speck where he could not be reached, and he only expanded into himself again during the hours that he spent in the Colluns, with the one person who had no wish to harm him and was actually anxious to see him.

But the football field presented a more serious problem, for here insignificance was a prime offence. The problem was to be both active and modest, energetic and yet undistinguished. He therefore looked determined, ran everywhere, and stayed away from the ball. He enjoyed the running, for it kept him warm; and there were accidental, furtive pleasures—hearing Jacobs reprimanded for not trying, when he knew that Jacobs tried very hard; hearing Jacobs ridiculed for being clumsy, when he knew that Jacobs was only clumsy *because* he tried very hard. He himself looked a trier, and he could hardly be clumsy if he had nothing to be clumsy with. Afterwards, of course, there were the changing rooms, with the naked bodies flying around him, the rough and tumble into the pool, the casual violence that had at all costs to be avoided. He never bathed in the pool, but showered quickly, dressed behind the lockers, and ran back across the fields to the library and the Colluns. He had made a life for himself, and was neglected and safe.

Or would have been, if the Junior Colts master hadn't come over to the 'C' one afternoon. He was a small, burly man with black hair and nimble feet, and he was always, he told the twenty-two incompetents who were assembled on the grass before him, *always* on the look-out for laddies who could be promoted into the 'B' or even the 'A'. During the game he ran up and down the touch-line to keep pace with the rhapsodic movement, and his attention finally fixed on a conspicuous figure who raced everywhere, tried very hard and might actually have done something if only he had been lucky enough to receive the ball.

'There's *one* laddie on the field,' he said at half-time, as he danced towards the reassembled twenty-two, '*one*.' His eyes roved to one side, then to the other; they peered over the tops of heads, and penetrated through the clustered bodies. 'Yes, laddie, you. Now this half I want you to go in after the ball. You won't get it from this lot.'

After the game he showered and changed, and fled to the Colluns. He tried to put the Junior Colts' master's encouraging smile and eager voice out of his mind. They represented a threat to his achieved anonymity, although he could not see how.

He saw next Footers. He had been removed from his usual game to the 'A', and Aprilson was his captain. He knew that Aprilson would think his promotion an impertinence (as he did himself), but he could only apologize for it by running harder than ever, and staying even farther away from the ball. It was difficult, though. When he raced into the open spaces the ball magically followed, accompanied by cries from the Junior Colts' master to 'Use it, laddie, oh, use it.' He didn't know how to use it, and was forced to dispatch it immediately, to whomever was nearest. At half-time he was congratulated on the neatness of his passing, but warned to have a go by himself, to be a little selfish, to burst through on his own.

He had no intention of being a little selfish, having a go by himself, bursting through on his own. He knew he would be bad at it, and disgraced. At the same time there was something in him that wanted the disgrace to come, so that he would be sent back to where there was no interest in him. The two desires—to pass successfully through the next half-hour into his former safety; to fail dramatically, and so be relieved of the tension that was the fear of failing dramatically—struggled within him. And there came a moment which brought the conflict to its crisis. He had the ball, and there was no one to tap it to. He ran forward a few paces and stopped. A defender slithered impotently past and fell to the ground, the ball was still somewhere near his toes, and from behind there was Aprilson's voice, encouraging him by name. He took a few jerky steps forward, and felt the ball slide out of his control. He hoped to be knocked over; knocked out; destroyed past accusation. But the ball stuck in front of him, and all obscurity was gone for ever. He lashed a desperate foot and reeled backwards.

Aprilson cantered beside him, back to the half-way line. 'Good shot,' he said. 'Well done.'

For the rest of the game every move he made was followed carefully, and every move he made was awkward, and every move he made was a success. The hand of a hideous fortune was on him. When he stumbled with the ball, he had dodged a tackle; when he prodded the ball away from him it was a pass; and finally, running purposelessly as the ball bounced across the goal-mouth, he glanced it gauchely into the net. He knew then that if failure and disgrace were to come, they weren't to come that afternoon. He ran back to the centre, beside Aprilson and the other forwards, his arms swinging modestly at his sides, his boots rising and falling crisply, and enjoyed more of Aprilson's smiles and congratulations. He was the man of the match.

He showered and changed by himself, as usual, but when he had finished, his hair plastered back and his shorts and singlet under his arm, he loitered for a moment in the locker-room and pretended to search for his boots. Aprilson tossed the ball to him, and he managed to catch it and toss it back with a mumbled 'Aprils'. That evening, as he walked to the library, he re-lived his two goals, the first as a sliding and acrobatic kick, the second as a crafty negotiation of the knee. He remembered his dodges and dribbles, his neat passing. He had had his afternoon and could go back to it in his imagination for ever. But of course he went forward, to the afternoon when he could flick his towel at Aprilson's bum, and was always the man of the match.

Cranton was in his usual chair, a pile of bullfighting photographs on his lap, and more out of things than ever. 'Have a nice time?' he asked. Grahame's having to play football was one of his favourite jokes.

'I got a goal.'

Cranton threw up his arms, closed his eyes, and pretended to swoon. 'My Christ. A goal. Gratters, old chap.'

'Two actually,' and hurried to explain them in details that made them ludicrous (but were the truth) before Cranton could perform this service for him.

The next afternoon he was on the Junior Colts' practice

list. As soon as he saw his name he knew that his success had been a trap. For a moment he thought of not going, but suddenly Aprilson was beside him at the notice-board, and was pointing to his name, and saying, 'Gratters, Thwaite.' So he went, of course. And after the training, which involved nothing more dangerous than a run around the pitch and some dribbling and passing, he slipped into the quiet end of the pool, bathed himself, and changed a few feet from the lockers. He was the first into the pool, the first out, the first changed; but he had done it as they were doing it. He hung about a good five minutes, bouncing the ball off the walls and throwing it to passing peers, and from the door Aprilson, in a normal voice, asked him if he were coming. He went back to the House with Aprilson and two other Arnold's, and afterwards he went up to the Colluns and talked of bullfighting with Cranton. But during their conversation he felt a power in himself that led him to contradict Cranton a few times, and float above him. And that night, when Aprilson in his bed called good night across the dorm, and Henders followed suit, and Jacobs stared uneasily at him from the shower door, he nursed a small hope, and let it bloom. He had an appreciation of a fact vital to his future—that he was strong and quick, as physically capable of playing football as the next Windhoven. Morton winds and Mallows diet had brought him, as Aunt Mary had always known they would, to physical perfection. And the essential lessons taught by both Mrs. Holydrake and Mr. Victor were about to achieve practical demonstration. Hard work made people better than anyone else.

By the end of the term he was a leading member of the locker room. He hurled the ball about as he had dreamed of doing; he leapt into the bath; he flicked at passing bums with his towel; and was in a word, and especially to Aprilson, 'Thwaitey'. Almost the embarrassments of the first term had vanished from memory. Aprilson was a good friend—his sense of Windhoven life, his decency and young authority were acquirable characteristics after all. Once they were beaten together for ragging in the showers—an event that raised the whole tone of beatings in the dorm— and another time Clipson congratulated them together for winning their Junior Colours. It was evident in advance that if Colonel Rones were to be summoned to Mallows because of his report, it would only be to congratulate him on it. A few afternoons on the pitch had transformed him from the House leper into everyone's familiar—except, of course, for Jacobs. Whenever Jacobs sidled up he shouted, 'Grease off, Jacobs!' and whenever Jacobs spoke he shouted, 'Clam, Jacobs, oh clam, Jacobs.' And Jacobs, perhaps recognizing something different from the automatic insults he was used to acknowledging with a grin, would grease and clam. But eventually his treatment of Jacobs became a habit, and Jacobs was allowed to stay, and speak a flattering word or two.

He still went to the Colluns for a short time every evening. Probably Cranton was also a habit, although he sometimes wondered what he was doing there when he could be in the Common with Aprilson or shouting 'Grease' and 'Clam' at Jacobs. And although Cranton continued to mesmerize him with his renderings of doomed lives and lovely deaths, he would go cold with the embarrassed memory of them when back in Arnold's. Aprilson had confessed that he had disliked him at first because he thought he was screeney and only did things to attract attention—'Although I didn't believe you did, you know, what Clippers said you did. Because we would have found out first.'— and in that perspective Cranton's soft moans, his dark, brilliant death-glances, his sudden collapses were—as he had already suspected—screeney.

Cranton's attitude to football was another irritation.

74

'But, my Christ, you don't want to play, do you?'

'Of course not,' he said at once. It was Cranton's worst trick, that he could make him say the things he wanted him to say. 'But I've got to.'

'But you don't have to be good at it.'

'Yes,' he said, in a sudden burst of insight. 'I do.' For it had occurred to him that although Cranton knew a great deal and read a great deal and was the person he liked best at Windhoven, he still had to spend all his time in the Colluns. While he, Grahame, could go where he liked, and was Thwaitey.

He assumed a jolly indifference. He almost swaggered down the platform towards her, his bags in his hand. He joked about the trip, asked her how she was, and paid no attention to her answer. He was a thousand boys returning to their sisters from a hundred schools. He kept her at a distance all day, and all the next, by talking mainly of his football, and sheltered behind Aunt Mary's brisk acceptance of his change. But he knew the revelation was bound to come, and dreaded it. She followed him everywhere with her eyes and her worried smile.

'We could go for a walk, Dodie,' she said, on his third morning.

'All right.' He rose reluctantly from the sofa, and they went together to the beach. He decided that the best method of limiting her interest in him was to develop a curiosity about her, but she replied so simply that nothing seemed to lead on to anything else. For a time they walked in silence.

'Do you like it, then?' she asked, in just the tone he had been gritting his teeth against.

He felt himself flush, all the same. 'It's better now that I'm in the team.'

'Does that mean they leave you alone?'

'Yes,' he said, and to bring the conversation to a halt he ran ahead, and with the sea crashing in his ears and the gulls swooping above him, took a few practice kicks at an imaginary ball.

The next day he bought a shiny football from Mipps and took it down to the beach. Din sat watching on a nearby bank, but he made it clear, from the way he danced on his toes, swung a subtle feint over the top of the ball, and then powered some shots between ghostly posts, that for him the sand was only a horde of menacing backs. Whom he defeated one after another with his body swerves, his deft feet, his courage. Occasionally he emerged from his rapture and glanced at where she sat, pale and solemn, studying him with cold eyes.

'Ron Harkness and Georgie Dodds do that,' she said, as they made their way back to Mallows for lunch. 'I saw them the other morning. *They* like to kick balls about.'

So the next morning he went far past their usual stretch, to Laker's Dip, where he found Dodds and Harkness with an inferior rubber toy. He hung back for a moment and then with a stiffening of his shoulders, approached with his ball extended.

'It's funny', she commented, when he got back, 'that you never liked them at Slocums'.'

'I didn't know them then.'

'And are you getting to know them now?'

'Yes,' he said, although he wasn't. He simply preferred their company to hers, to her way of looking at him, to her forlorn, unhappy smile. She made him feel that he had done her harm by being happy at Windhoven, and a success. But he refused to take the blame. He wasn't *going* to let her remind him of his first term, and of how he had been with her during those holidays.

Cricket came less easily to him than soccer, but there was no need to prove himself over. By the end of the first month he was batting number five in the 'A' and was the established player under Aprilson. He rose, not by talent—there were at least two other laddies with more feeling for the game—but by a kind of natural law that controlled the careers of well-co-ordinated boys who tried hard and seemed happy. It was as if he had always been in a team, had always understood the proper Windhoven responses.

He would have understood them even more properly if it hadn't been for Cranton who, in his odd way, could still cause difficulties.

There was, for instance, the case of Fairwell. He was a thin, slight boy who had arrived two terms late because his parents had been in India. He was a few months older than the others in the Dorm, and he had an air of superior self-involvement and a detached critical smile that separated him from them. He was courteous and remote, and was treated with respect. But Fairwell, thin and slight and a little foreign, had a boldly disgusting nature. He showed it first by smiling at the dorm's junior sporting hero as if there were secrets between them; he revealed it further by always contriving to wash or shower at the same time as the dorm's junior sporting hero, and in the adjoining sink or stall; and finally he wrote a letter, and slipped it into the sleeve of the dorm's junior sporting hero's pyjamas.

As he spread the note on his knee and read it through, he was attacked by an odd sensation, quite unconnected—a smell, heavy and sweet and a little lemony, that was probably the smell of Fairwell's special Indian soap. When he managed at last to raise his eyes to the far bed, Fairwell was straightening out blankets that were already drum-tight. He moved in self-absorption, with his customary remoteness, but something in the inclination of his head and the way he kept his body bent indicated that he knew he was being watched. Then he stood away from the bed and glanced around. His glance went everywhere, from Jacobs sitting cross-legged with his feet on his pillow, to Henders writing a letter, to Aprilson, the dorm's senior sporting hero, studding his cricket boots; to Matthews and Gard and Tanner and Budd—towards everyone except the boy he most wanted to see.

Who thus knew, through the confusion and fear and the lemony-sweet smell, exactly what to do. He strode directly up to Fairwell, and tore the letter into many pieces. He scattered the fragments over Fairwell's bed, put his hands on his hips, and told Fairwell how he stood in the eyes of Arnold's. He turned to Aprilson, who was on one side of him; to Jacobs, on the other. He included the rest, who were closing in around them. He called Fairwell a wanker. A screeney wanker.

Fairwell stood quite still, his wash-bag and his towel hanging from his hand. Although his smile was offensively superior, his eyes, moving from the hand now placed against his chest to the face now thrust close to his, were blank. Once he shook his head and made a convulsive movement backwards, as if he were trying to walk himself into the wall. But the iron edge of the bed trapped the backs of his knees, and stopped him.

'He's obscene.' Which was one of the new words Cranton had brought back from the hols. He transferred his grip, slowly and calmly, to Fairwell's wrist, while Jacobs and Aprilson, Henders and Matthews, Budd and Tanner and Gard took hold of Fairwell in pieces and places, by the arm, by the collar of his pyjamas, by the cord of his dressing-gown. Together, moved by a spontaneous morality that required no explication, they carried him to the showers. Fairwell hung among them, inert except for his feet, which moved with quick, Chinese steps as if hurrying themselves to an exciting appointment. They pulled the dressing-gown from him, and rolled his pyjama bottoms

78

down his legs, and peeled the tops from his arms; and Fairwell's limbs twitched and jerked in a depraved dance of assistance. His body was bony white, except for a livid scar across his abdomen, but he seemed unconscious of his nudity, of his white buttocks and of his exposed penis, small and thin, that stuck impudently out from a cluster of blonde hair. When he was cuffed under the shower he sagged to the ground, his blonde head placed precisely under the nozzle; and settled there as some skinny animal might settle for sleep. Only once did he raise his head, to fix his emptied eyes on Grahame's face.

He came back after the lights had been switched out. He slipped through the door between the beds. Grahame, waiting in the darkness, caught the noises and saw the thin shape falter past. He reared up and hissed 'Screeney wanker' three times, as if ridding his system of the phrase for ever. Then he sank back into a deep sleep.

'But he was horrible.'

'He was in love with you, that's all.'

'In love with me?'

'Yes.'

'Well, isn't that—I mean, that's why—we didn't hurt him, really. He's all right.'

'Is he?'

'He was obscene.'

'Like Shelley? Anyway, obscene's my word. Find your own word when you do things like that.'

'Fairwell like Shelley!' But he couldn't find a way of explaining. He only knew that if Cranton had seen Fairwell naked and terrified, he would have felt and done the same. And then, the second after, he understood that Cranton wouldn't have. 'We didn't *mean* to hurt him.'

'Don't apologize to me. Apologize to him.'

79

'I'm not apologizing.'

'Then shut up.' And opening his folder, he ignored him for the rest of their hour together.

That evening Jacobs lurched against Fairwell in Common and sent him spinning against a locker, and Grahame and Aprilson went over to Jacobs and told him to leave Fairwell alone or they'd put *him* under the showers. 'Fairwell's had his punishment,' Aprilson said.

'Yes,' Grahame said. 'We're going to forget about it.'

'I don't call *that* an apology,' Cranton said, when Grahame had told him.

'He looked jolly pleased.'

'Did he? Well, you only hurt *him* because of what *they* did to you, so I expect you feel better now.'

'Of course I didn't,' he said firmly, as he sat in his usual nodding and listening devotion, glad that everything was all right between them again.

He spent the summer touring with the Junior Colts as the vice-captain under Aprilson. He didn't score many, although he always felt he could have done better. His batting had improved from constant practice at the nets, but once out on the strip and encircled by hostile players he would be overcome by nerves. The ball zipped up at him from odd angles, changed its shape in mid-flight, and twisted out of his desperate vision on to the stumps. Time after time he put himself out of his misery with a foolish stroke, but back in the pavilion, or sitting with the other players on the boundary, he loathed his safety and the treacherous coward who had chosen it.

His fortnight at home was just enough to show Din how definitively he had changed. He was gay and easy with her, full of news of his cricket tour; he was buoyant, protective and agreeable. He took her to Morton's one cinema, accompanied her on walks along the shore, and read with her sometimes in their old study. He was everything that he should be, as he was sure all brothers were, and Aunt Mary, studying him sometimes with triumphant eyes, could see nothing wrong with him anywhere.

'A fine-looking chap,' the Colonel agreed. 'Does the school proud.'

He was happy in Morton, with some books lent to him by Cranton and with a sister who could accuse him of nothing, and only impatient a little to be back in Arnold's, and for the football term to begin; and only uneasy a little when he thought of Fairwell.

But Fairwell had left. The extra bed in the Second Year dorm remained against the wall, and it was as if he had been a ghost, who had left behind him a slight chill. The incident passed easily into anecdote, and after a time was forgotten.

He and Aprilson were promoted through the Middle Common to the Inner Common a year ahead of the others. They were in the Colts together, then in the Senior Colts, for cricket and soccer. Each season Aprilson was captain of both teams, and Grahame was vice-captain. They were known throughout the school (but not by Cranton) as the Arnold's twins, although the advantage was always slightly with Aprilson, to whom authority granted authority as generously as nature had granted talent. By such standards it was no consolation to Grahame that he was always first in class.

But in their sixteenth year Grahame's football talent achieved a new dimension and their positions were suddenly reversed. He discovered in himself an extraordinary gift for finding openings. He found them by instinct, deliberately not planning in order to keep his luck with him. He would race forward, swerve into a position, slow down and wait for the passes. He loved the suspended sensation as he hovered in front of the backs, with his eyes inoffensively on the area between them. If he kept his mind off the ball, and lingered there in innocence, it always came to him in the end; and often a goal as a result.

In the end he outdistanced Aprilson and got into the First ahead of him. Of course Aprilson was the second person (after the captain) to congratulate him on his selection, and always came to the matches when the Senior Colts weren't playing. And of course they shared a senior dorm together, and were close friends. But Aprilson wasn't in the First, and there was a small but distinct distance between them suddenly.

For the masters themselves treated the First with respect. Windhoven had contact with schools like Eton, Winchester and Charterhouse only on the playing fields, in matches that were written up in *The Times* and the *Telegraph* and the respectable Sunday papers. Who would have heard of Windhoven, who had not heard of the First? Thus when Grahame thought about his team-mates it was always as an atmosphere and place—the steamy baths, and the lockers with W XI on each door; the smell of mud and fatigue and triumph after a victory; the special path that only they were allowed to use, across fields to school in the evenings. They called each other by their Christian names, used the same slang, and had the same jokes about Don Haler the coach. In the same way it was unlikely that Grahame had any separate being to the other ten—except of course that he was known to be a friend of Cranton, the Scholar, and the cleverest boy in the school. But a Windhoven First with a gift for finding the openings could afford an eccentricity. The goalkeeper, for instance, was in the habit of scaling the walls and cycling ten miles merely to see a film, and the left-half appeared to derive pleasure from chamber music. The First was the First, and Thwaitey was famous.

But there was an agent of destruction. He was chunky,

fast, and the Repton right back. During the first twenty minutes of the game Grahame persuaded him he wasn't there, and nearly scored a goal. But this sudden emergence attracted the Reptonian's attention, and from then on he dogged him everywhere, with a contemptuous patience. He hung beside him for the pass that was bound to come, and when it did he obtruded his chunky body and dribbled invulnerably off. He had many knees, many shoulders and protruding hips, and as he tackled and displaced he would murmur, 'Hard cheese,' more to himself than to Grahame, and inflict a mild injury.

He should have strayed out to one of the wings, and brought the right back trailing after him; or he could have retreated to the half-line and worked his passage there. But his whole genius was being challenged, and a kind of fatalism held him to where he was used to playing. He was determined to win the ball again, at least one last time, although secretly he knew he never would. As soon as it was slipped through there came the thud of the indestructible body, the 'hard cheese', and a blow to his ribs or his ankles. He was up against an embodiment of a force which gave him no chance; which would never give him a chance. When he was robbed for the fifth time he swerved around, cut in front, and threw himself sideways. There was a glimpse, before he blacked out from the pain, of the stubborn head bent forward; and a sighing in his ears of 'hard cheese' that he carried with him into the spangled dark. Then the Windhoven inside-right, the youngest player by a year and marked out as a future captain, was carried to the side with a sprained ankle.

It was monstrous to watch Aprilson playing in his place, more monstrous of Aprilson to play well, most monstrous to have to congratulate Aprilson afterwards. He limped into the pavilion after the Charterhouse match, and

83

though he was received as a familiar figure, the First was still the eleven that had won. Aprilson sat on the bench, muddy and damp, surrounded by the others as if he had been absorbed into them and imaged forth again. The tinge of the First was on it: now. He smiled with just a little too much anxiety on Grahame's behalf, too much modesty on his own, and every word he said was really his own decent version of 'hard cheese'. So Grahame limped away again. He couldn't bring himself to stay to tea. He wanted no talk of Windhoven triumphs until they were his triumphs too.

Even so he would have gone to Fields the next Footers if Aprilson hadn't run past him in the school yard, his boots swinging over his shoulder, his W shirt trailing carelessly from his hand. 'See you there, Thwaitey.' And seemed to put on a special and fluid spurt, towards destiny.

Which left the Colluns and his old refuge.

'You'll be able to read a few books for a change. That's the best thing for you.'

'But football's just as much me.' He raised his leg and eyed the throbbing ankle, bandaged to deformity. 'It's a main part.'

'Have some Gide.' Cranton selected two books from the pile he had arranged on the table. 'Or some Genet. They'll tell you about yourself.'

'But they're in French.' He lowered his leg with a wince, and tried to keep his mind off Aprilson carving through the backs and winning his colours. 'I hope we win.'

'*You* won't win, though; will you, Thwaitey?'

He read a few books. He had always tried, from a long way in the rear, to follow in Cranton's intellectual footsteps, but his class work and his football had cut him off from everything but a passing acquaintance with the names, and the habit of nodding knowingly through Cranton's haunting precis. But now he was convinced that if he read as much as Cranton read he would eventually see as Cranton saw, feel as Cranton felt, be as Cranton was. It would at least do until he was W XI again, and had displaced April-son definitively. So he waded uncomprehendingly through Sartre and Joyce, laboured into Kafka, and noticed, with every doggedly turned page, that radical changes were taking place within.

'You see,' Cranton elucidated, 'it's because you're an orphan that you want to be a Windhoven hero.' He himself was half an orphan, which he said was worse than being a whole one. 'I get so much love that I don't want to try at anything. That's why I'm more interesting than you.'

'Dianah wants to possess me, too.'

'Oh, Christ, don't be so competitive. You're not at footers now, Thwaitey.'

'I'm not competitive. You are. You're always boasting about being more feeble than me.'

'I didn't say I was feeble. In fact, I'm very strong—certainly much stronger than you. All I'm saying is that my mother doesn't give me a chance, and that's why I hate her.'

'Hate her?' As usual Cranton had gone seven steps farther than he could have dared imagine. 'Do you really?'

'When I'm at home, anyway. She's starting an aquarium, and after that it'll be little dogs and cats and budgies. She wants to make me a case history, you see. I expect *she* got the glass into my soup somehow. And your sister's the same, only not as clever.'

'No, she isn't. I know she's not very bright, but she's gentle.'

'That's what I mean.' It was one of Cranton's entrancing characteristics, to give his pale smile, to half-close his dark eyes, and say that one of Grahame's contradictions was what he meant. 'Anyway you should like Gide. He'll tell you all about yourself.'

'At Windhoven?'

Cranton laughed. 'Everywhere.' And looked mysterious.

It was as if their friendship were begun all over again, under circumstances that inevitably made them different towards each other. He had always known that Cranton knew more than he, but he had equally known that he, as the Windhoven First, was the generous giver of attention, and Cranton merely the entertaining outcast that he enjoyed cultivating. Cranton's knowledge, after all, had nothing to do with what really mattered, and whenever he had been made to feel foolish by it he had been able to walk smilingly away. But now, hobbled by his foot, he tried to perfect himself in Cranton's strange language. He read novels and poems, and developed in sophistications. They discussed sex a great deal, and what it meant to be like Rimbaud. They agreed that it was better on the whole to be different and in exile. Occasionally during these prolonged periods together he would glance at the thin, sickly figure in the chair opposite with something of his old, physical confidence, but in reality he almost forgot the football fields and the tribute he owed them.

He was greeted back with loud shouts and a generous use of his Christian name. He roared through the first half, and if he made little contact with the ball, he was everywhere in pursuit of it. During the second half he got the ball more often, but the foreignness of possession made him clumsy. It would take him a while, Don Haler said, before he found his feet again.

But his shooting was wild, his passes went astray, and he had lost his gift for finding the openings. In the first match of his return he missed an easy goal, and later, throwing himself into blind attack, he deflected a scoring shot with

86

his elbow. The half who marked him ruled him, and the violence of his tackling, which might have led to injuries, produced two free kicks and an unpleasant reprimand.

'Are you coming to tea?'

Aprilson flushed. 'Oh, there's not much point.'

'Come on. Come in to tea.'

Aprilson came. He sat humbly at the end of the table with the official reserves and had a cup. He was talked to on all sides, and smiled a great deal.

'Yes, well a little time yet, laddie,' Don Haler said, putting a hand on Grahame's shoulder, and communicating his disappointment through a tender squeeze. 'It'll come back.'

It didn't. The harder he tried, the clumsier he was. The changing room after the match was a place of humiliation —the averted glances, the analyses that had to be suspended while he was by. The Windhoven First had dwindled to ten with an eye on Aprilson, and a pariah. He stayed after practice and trained by himself.

'You've outgrown it,' Cranton said, 'and don't care any more.'

'It's not for *my* sake. It's for them.'

'Them? Who are *they*?'

'Them. The others.'

In fact he hadn't missed them until he was amongst them again as a hindrance. But suddenly he needed to be back to his triumphs, and his normal, victorious life, before it was too late. So he trained and trained; he ran and ran; all through the matches he ran; until like an escalator he ran himself down into the Second, and Aprilson back up into the First.

'Just for the time,' Don Haler said. 'Until you come good as they say.' And shifted his apologetic eye away from Grahame's motified one.

'I don't think they should have dropped you,' April-

87

son said that night. 'They haven't really given you a chance.'

'But I was holding them back.' He took a practice kick at an imaginary ball, and missed Aprilson's knee by a whisker. 'Gosh, sorry. Anyway, I always said you ought to be in the First.'

And in fact the need for him to conceal his desperation brought him close to Aprilson for a week. Then Aprilson was the Arnold's who walked along the special path from Fields, and spoke the language and knew the jokes. He was called Christopher by Don Haler, and from embarrassment, or something that was as much like embarrassment as it was like triumph, he avoided talking football. Which meant that, apart from Arnold's matters, they stopped talking about anything. They were the best of friends in that way.

'Well, if you haven't outgrown it, then you should have. So shut up.'

Eventually, as if under orders, he gave up trying. He went to the Second matches casually, played his part casually, and scarcely noticed whether Windhoven won or lost. As a consequence he scored a few goals, but he avoided making a tackle or chasing the ball hard. In the end he stopped going to practice, not because he meant to, but because it slipped his mind. He would go into the Colluns after school, Cranton would be there, and Footers had gone by.

'Things are difficult for you at the moment, laddie?'

'Yes, sir.'

Don Haler pondered. 'Well, what's the matter, do you think?'

He stared intensely into Don Haler's eyes, as Cranton had told him he should. 'At the moment, sir, I can't do anything right with the ball. I think, sir,' he lowered his gaze, 'I'm trying too hard.'

88

The sports master pondered again. 'Well, don't be afraid to come to me when you think you *are* ready, laddie. We're still counting on you for next year.'

'Sir, I'll come when I'm ready then, sir. Thank you very much, sir.'

'They don't need you any more,' Cranton explained. 'You're not the type they want, any more.'

It was true. His name disappeared from the second eleven lists without further comment, and he was never again called to account. He tried to pretend to himself that he was pleased, but at first the memory of Don Haler's ready acquiescence was a torment to him. He suspected that if he hadn't broken the news to Don Haler, Don Haler would have eventually broken it to him. But at least Cranton and he were together every evening, and for the three Footers afternoons as well.

But it never occurred to him that he was in love. His feelings had developed with such rapidity, but through so much concentrated habit, that he was never conscious of them, although he was acutely conscious of attendant anxieties. If Cranton were so ill that he had to spend the day in Infirm, he would brood in the Colluns as if bereft. And if in the evenings, during their most intense talks, he suddenly found Cranton's hand on his, his heart would leap and his cheeks would flush. Later, isolated by the ordinariness of the faces around him, imprisoned in the dorm with Aprilson and his victories, the echo of a word or the re-feeling of an accidental touch became everything. What the day moved toward, what the night stole from him. Yet it never occurred to him that he was in love until Cranton, with a distanced smile, asked him directly. And then he was so astonished that he found himself gazing around the room with eyes that were suddenly and unaccountably blinking.

'You're blushing, so you must be in love.'

He shrugged his shoulders with Gide sophistication, and wondered whether Cranton was in love, then?

'Well, I'm not blushing, am I?'

'But are you?'

'No,' Cranton said. 'I'm not. At least with you.'

'Nor am I with you,' he said immediately.

'So glad. Now let me see that poem.'

He extracted it from his jacket pocket and held it out with a hand that trembled. It was his first venture into verse, and was a biography of Rimbaud. So far it was thirty-two lines long, and was the creation of a kind of ecstasy. He did not think highly of it, although he knew it was one of the most extraordinary poems ever written, possibly the product of genius, and that Cranton would say so.

Cranton read the lines quickly, laughed loudly, and tore the page, with flourishing sweeps of his hands, into pieces. These pieces he scattered across the floor with more flourishes. Then he left the room.

Grahame watched him go with stupefied eyes. Then, making little sounds through his nose, he picked the pieces up and put them in his pocket. He walked to the door, with no idea of going anywhere except, hopefully, to his death.

Cranton stepped into his path at the foot of the library steps. 'I did it to see if you would pick the pieces up. Did you pick the pieces up? You would pick them up. *Did* you?' He was grinning, and his dark eyes were brilliant. 'I expect you hate me now. Do you?'

'Why did you do it?' His voice shook with the effort of insouciance.

'Oh, because it was a filthy, boring poem.' Cranton took his hand and squeezed it. 'Because you make me sick, you see.' He squeezed again. 'Because you try so hard.' He gave one last squeeze, then turned back up the steps, towards the Colluns. 'Because', he added over his high, bony shoulder, 'I wish you'd go away and leave me alone.'

He walked slowly out into the yard. Figures were standing in postures made weird by his misted eyes. Someone seemed to call to him, but he walked on, through the yard and into the cloisters. He walked around the cloisters many times before he went back, up the stairs, to the Colluns. He hovered at the door, drifted farther in, stood doggishly before the occupied chair.

But Cranton was deaf and blind to his supplicating presence. He wrote briskly into a file, and when he raised his eyes it was only to draw from the deprived face some inspiration that drove his pen more swiftly across the paper.

So at last he went away again, down to the cloisters again. He stood in the half-light and understood that the end of his life had come. He had no sense of himself at all, although he was crying a little.

Later he returned to the library. He walked deliberately to the table to collect his books and file and to finish with Cranton for ever.

'Where have you been?'

Where had he been? He had been far away from himself, to solve all his problems in negation. He had brought himself to an end.

'For a walk.'

'Christ, I've been waiting. I've got something to read to you. *About* people like you. It's very funny.'

He spent a good part of the remaining weeks of term in the cloisters, rooted to a spot somewhere between the squat chapel at one end and the open yard at the other; bringing himself to an end.

'You're not Rimbaud,' Cranton said. 'But you can kiss me if you like. If you can.' It was the evening of the last full

91

day of term and they were alone in the darkening cloisters. There were no sounds but the echoes of their own footsteps, the throb of their own voices. 'Of course, I know you want to,' Cranton said, as he walked indifferently on, 'but you're probably too ashamed. Are you ashamed?'

'No.'

'You do want to kiss me?'

'I don't know.' His hands were sunk into his pocket, and he kept his face pointing directly ahead. He knew that the crisis had come at last, that he both dreaded and wanted. The game of rejection and torment had reached its final phase, and was about to be transcended. 'Of course I don't understand you,' he explained suavely. 'I don't suppose I ever will.'

'Well, you can kiss people without understanding them, can't you. Try and be a little Gide.'

'Of course.' He turned towards the thin shape, the pale elongation of face. He closed his eyes and stepped forward in a kind of crouch, as when he kissed Aunt Mary at the end of the hols. 'There,' he said coolly, when his lips had grazed the proffered cheek.

They walked on for a little, in silence.

'We're going to the bench in the small cloisters, I suppose?' Cranton wondered eventually. 'Sin at close quarters, in ecclesiastical surroundings. Isn't that what we're after?'

'I suppose so,' he agreed. 'As long as God's watching.'

Their footsteps rang with astonishing loudness on the stone corridors, and the bench was an amazing distance away, and yet there seemed to be no transition at all from clapping through the cold dusk to standing in front of the cold slab in the little niche, where they bandied wisdoms about sensuality. Then there was some arranging to be done, before the abandonments could begin.

'It's more appropriate,' Cranton said, cramming himself between the two walls, 'for you to lie on top of me. Because you're the footballer and the hero, physically speaking.'

He knew that Cranton was somewhere in the bogus red caverns on Chapel Side, and once he thought he heard him sliding towards him, through the darkness, laughing. In the yard at the end of the passage he saw figures moving, in the fading sunlight. Don Haler and Aprilson were framed against the mouth of brightness, eternally, and Jacobs's voice, hoarse and offensive, reached his ears. Then Don Haler pounced off in gym shoes, and Aprilson followed, to where the green fields rippled; and Jacobs clammed, and probably greased as well.

As he became calmer he saw clearly what had to be done. In the end he rose and walked until he could speak again, and had worked out the things he was going to say, that would cancel the past and make him free, fit for Don Haler and Jacobs, fit for Aprilson especially. Then he went to the Colluns.

Cranton's folder was on the chair, with the little blue pencil beside it, and there was the kind of tension that always came from his short, busy absences.

He stood by the table, ready; and as soon as the side door opened, he spoke.

'I see.' Cranton walked in an uncertain line towards his chair. He bent to pick up the folder, let a few pages slip between the flaps to the floor, stooped awkwardly to retrieve them, and dropped his pencil. He turned. 'All right.' He sat down, put his hands on the wooden armrests and stared around the room. There was a tight smile on his face that marked his digestive agonies. 'All right.' Then he reached down and picked up his pencil and folder, and shuffled the loose pages in.

'Is that quite plain?'

'Quite plain, Thwaitey.' And when he raised his face

93

again it was calm, and his smile was relaxed. 'Thanks.' He opened the file and arranged his fingers carefully around the stub of pencil. He began to write, slowly.

'No. No, it's not plain.'

Cranton looked up. 'I thought you wanted me to forget it.'

'Yes.'

'Well,' he looked down again, 'I'm forgetting it.'

'No.' He made a sound, shook his head, and made another sound.

'You'd better go', Cranton said mildly, 'and leave me alone.'

'Go?' He hung forward, forlorn. 'Go?'

'Well, that's what you want, isn't it?'

He shook his head. 'I can't help it,' he whispered. 'I can't help it.'

'But you said you didn't want to see me again. And I'm perfectly ready not to be seen again.' He laughed. 'By you.'

'But I don't mean it. Honestly. Honestly.' He raised an arm and wiped his forehead.

'Oh, Christ.' Cranton stood up, gathered his things together, and turned off the ancient lamp. He paid no attention at all to the streaming eyes and wheedling words that followed him. The door closed behind him, clickingly.

He saw occasional forms at the upper windows of School House, and knew them to be Cranton. He heard doors slam and voices raised within, and knew them to be Cranton. He raced to the library because Cranton would be there. Then he ran down to the cloisters, where a solitary boy walked, that must surely and at last be Cranton.

He imagined Cranton slipping out of School House, going rapidly in a taxi to the station. Or imagined him hiding behind the Upper Common curtains, and peering down with smiles. Cranton acquired friends suddenly, and sent them out as spies, to make sure that he had gone. So he hung about School House, at the foot of the stairs, reading casually in the rain until he was sent away by Cranton's House Master. He went back to the Colluns but the small reading lamps had been turned off, the windows had been closed, and the holidays had begun.

The footstep outside the door was Cranton's.

'Thwaite?'

'Sir?'

'What are you doing, Thwaite?'

'Nothing, sir.'

'What time is your train?' The librarian was a small, balding man with spectacles, so attentive to the books that he was believed to be deaf and a German. 'Are you packed?'

'Yes, sir.'

'What *are* you doing here, then?'

'Looking for someone, sir?'

'But who?'

'Oh, well, actually just Aprilson, sir.'

'Aprilson? Who is Aprilson? I've never seen him here.'

'And Cranton, too, sir.'

'Cranton's gone. He returned his books this morning.'

But he saw the lie in the small face, the malice in the German eyes. 'Gone, sir?'

'Yes. Are you all right, Thwaite?'

'Sir.'

'Sure?'

'Sir.'

'You look ill.'

'No, sir.'

'Still, you should see Matron.'

'Sir.'

But he didn't see Matron. Instead he collected his trunks and waited outside the Great Gates for the last school bus.

The landscape of three different counties rolled past the

95

windows of his carriage, and the rain fell on their green fields. An old lady did *The Times* crossword puzzle beside him, and a young man with curly hair smiled at him constantly and smoked cigarettes. But he paid no attention to the earth and sky, or to the human activities around him. He was gathering himself into a long letter that he would write from Mallows, in which he would confess his cowardice, beg forgiveness, and admit at last that he was in love.

In fact he wrote eight letters.

'Do you think he'd mind if I came too?'

'She said he could have only one friend at a time.'

'Who said?'

'His mother.'

'Did she write to you, then?'

He glanced out of the window at a passing motor-bike. 'I 'phoned up the other day.'

'Why did you 'phone?' She swung her blonde hair out of her eyes and smiled. 'Did you know he was ill?'

'No. He was going to write to me about something, actually the history club, and didn't. So I 'phoned to remind him.'

'Oh.' She settled back into some speculative humming— she was President of the St. Anne's Glee Club—and a moment later interrupted herself in the middle of *Hunting Hearts, Oh*, to wonder whether he'd said he *had* 'phoned from Mallows? And then to wonder why he'd gone all the way to the Morton post office when he *could* have 'phoned from Mallows? And finally to guess at the illness.

'Appendicitis is it, Dodie?'

He swung around and attempted to glare her into silence. 'It's only a perforated intestine.'

The Colonel lifted his head and honked his horn. 'Perforated, old chap?'

'Yes.'

'Is that very serious, Uncle Basil?'

'Well, Dianah.' He put his foot down and forced the Morris into one of its rare bursts of speed. He was a cautious driver, given to the horn and the brake, but he dressed in flowing scarves and great gauntlets, as if for danger. 'Well, it depends on the state of the chap that has it. I'm sure,' he slowed down, to edge in sixty yards behind a bicycle, 'I'm sure a young chap like Grahame's friend, a young chap, won't have too much trouble.'

He waited until the car had headed over Waterloo Bridge and then hesitated on the steps. His whole life depended on the next few minutes, but Din's voice, her face, had somehow got in the way of the scene that was to come. He would go through the doors and lose himself. Later he would find himself back outside the doors. Nothing would have happened. There would be merely Din, and merely the Colonel, to carry him away again. He glanced up to the windows in the massive block, and could see figures, silhouettes, and each one was Cranton, watching down and waiting for him, to tell him his destiny.

He had come into the divine orbit. He ran forward up the stairs, to enter its centre.

She was the one, of course, to tell Colonel Rones. He clambered into the back and waited for her to explain. He was suspended until she spoke, and then strangely exalted. He couldn't meet the Colonel's eye for fear that the exaltation should show.

'I'm sorry, old chap. Very sorry.' He moved jerkily off into the traffic, waved his gauntlet at a taxi-driver (under the impression that forking fingers were some kind of civilian salute) and spoke once again, for the last time before Mallows. 'Thought things might have advanced a little. But they never do.' After that there was silence except for the creaking of the frame and the barking of the engine, although Dianah turned around often, her eyes awash with sympathy, to smile at him, and offer him rugs for his knees.

He was drawn forward to the landing by the low voices underneath. Even the Colonel's silence rose to him, through Din's low murmur, Aunt Mary's staccato questioning. The voices stopped and were followed by decisive actions. He crept back, opened the door of his room, and shut it. Then walked towards the stairs, and was just about to go down when the light in the hall went on. Aunt Mary stood at the bottom, staring up.

'Grahame, my dear?' She scanned the upper landing. 'Are you there?'

'Yes, Aunt Mary,' he whispered, gazing down at her in astonishment. He had never seen her so clearly—the lines around her eyes, the stretching of flesh beneath her raised chin. She was old and looked bewildered.

'Where, my dear?'

'Here, Aunt Mary.'

She focused her gaze a few feet from him. 'Death is a dreadful shock,' she explained to the bulk of a long-silent grandfather clock. 'Are you all right, dear?'

He slithered along, caught his foot against a corner of the bookcase, and pitched quietly forward.

'Grahame? Have you fallen?'

He crouched beneath the clock and stared through the railings. From this position he could see only the rear curls of her grey head.

'Yes, Aunt Mary,' he whispered, as he fought down the rising waves. He concentrated on the problem of getting to his feet, in order not to concentrate on the image of himself as furry, behind bars, shooting out a deadly paw.

'Have you hurt yourself, my dear?'

'No, Aunt Mary.'

'Well,' she stepped back and peered up, baffled. 'Don't come down unless you want to, dear.'

A mad voice muttered in his ear and caused him to snort out.

'What, my dear?'

'Thank you, Aunt Mary,' he whispered. 'Thank you.'

He sat on his bed until dinner-time. Then he went down and ate a little, not nearly enough, in fact, for he was very hungry. During the rest of the evening he was silent and remote. He walked to chairs stiffly and left them. He picked up magazines and put them down with a sigh. He was aware, as he went out of the living-room, of their eyes upon him. For a time he sat on his bed again, gazing emptily across the room. 'Cranton is dead,' he said experimentally. 'Michael is dead. I would have died for *him*. Dead. Dead,' and so didn't hear his sister until she had come into the room. She sat down beside him, put her hand on his arm and studied him compassionately; and as he stared back into her pale, serene face, he wished he could be downstairs listening to the wireless, or in the old nursery, working on his thirty-page life of Rimbaud, currently in rhythmic prose. 'Poor Dodie.' She slid her arm up around his shoulder. And miraculously he began to cry.

'Of course, you don't have to go.' House Master put the letter down on the desk and stared out of the window. He made it clear, by angling his head and shrouding the upper part of his body in smoke, that he had abstracted himself morally from the room, and the dilemma in it.

'Sir.'

'It's *your* decision, Thwaite. Entirely, old chap.'

'Yes, sir.' Hope flared. A little courage, a movement of the tongue and a shake of the head, and he would be free.

But despair, engendered somehow by the frayed bottom of House Master's jacket, the exposed hip-pocket of House Master's flannels, the judicious popping of House Master's pipe, followed at once.

Nevertheless the excuses tumbled to his lips—there was his work, sir. His cold (nose blocked, sir, head aching), his conviction that no good would come of it (Cranton himself said she was mad, sir)—and froze there. Other words slipped past.

'It's the right thing, Thwaite.'

He lowered his eyes. 'Sir.'

'After all,' he blew out an extra large cloud, and gave him a level if watery gaze, 'after all, he was one of us, you know.'

'Sir.'

Only a serious illness could help him. His forehead burnt, his body trembled, and his knees were on the point of buckling under him. He kept passing his hand over his eyes, held his head during class and in the library, and worked up, without any effort, an eerie, whistling cough.

'You should see Matron,' Aprilson said, on being invited to guess at his temperature for the sixth time. He dabbed some dubbin on to his boots and examined the face, red and wet, that pleaded up at him from the pillows. 'It's probably hay fever or polio.'

'Yes.' He coughed dreadfully. 'I don't feel too well.'

That evening he went to the corridor that led to the infirmary and found himself face to face with House Master.

'Everything all right, Thwaite?'

'Sir.'

'Got a bit of a cold?'

'A little bit, sir.'

His voice was so faint that House Master had difficulty

hearing it. But Thwaite's rosy cheeks and sparkling eyes were in themselves evidence of excellent health.

'That's it, that's it.' And went popping and puffing up the passage.

He watched House Master go, looked towards the Matron's room, and returned, finally, to the Upper Common. That night he lay awake, staring into the darkness. He listened to the noises of Aprilson asleep, and hated him. But at least his throat did seem to burn and his head to throb a little; although too late.

But once he'd set out on his journey it never occurred to him not to arrive. He sat on the train to London with his hands folded into his lap, his eyes closed; he consulted at Paddington the instructions House Master had copied from the letter, and caught the tube to Wembley Park. He walked inevitably to the right street and found instantly the right house. His only hope was to remain in a vacuum, as he did at the dentist's, until the afternoon had ended and he was himself again.

And yet there was enough of him present to be surprised by the size of Cranton's house. He had had no idea of what it would be like in detail, but he had responded to its atmosphere as he had responded to the atmosphere of houses in novels. It would be large, dark, for the widow Cranton to rage through, in her weeds and grief. In her accusations.

Through the gauze curtains he could make out the shadows of neat furniture and the warmth of chintz, as background to a round, smiling face. He stared away from the face as if he hadn't seen it, wagged his head, gave his whistling cough, and went towards the door, which was already opening to receive him. He was a sixteen-year-old smiling public schoolboy, with excellent manners—everyone in Morton said so.

They sat in armchairs decorated with yellow roses and green shoots, a tea-table between them. There was a silver pot on a silver tray on a lacquered table, and a plate of iced cakes, and two cups so thin that the brown liquid showed through. In one corner of the room was a small television set; in another corner, by the window, was a glass case full of guppies. Everywhere else, too, there was furniture— bookstands that held gardening magazines, little tables that supported an ornament or two of a pastoral nature, a sideboard on which a porcelain shepherdess tended porcelain sheep, a mantelpiece with swans on it and a wild goose in flight above it. Mrs. Cranton was plump, with a round pink face, curly grey hair that was blonde in patches, a small mouth that never stopped smiling, and brown, protuberant eyes that never stopped staring.

'No,' he said. 'I'm jolly glad I could come.'

'Please help yourself to cakes, when you want one.' She handed him a cup and the sugar tongs. 'Michael hated tea. He was funny that way.'

'I like tea.'

'And cakes?'

'Yes. And these are jolly nice. Oh gosh, thanks.'

He felt very large, dominating the room with his legs, his shoulders, his loud voice. His head still hurt, the tea stung his throat, but the evening light fell through the net curtains and lay over the porcelain figures on the sideboard and Mrs. Cranton was very nice, and he was safe.

'The hall was white,' Mrs. Cranton said, 'with an altar. He lay in a coffin behind the table. The coffin was on rails, and when the service was finished it slid forward, Grahame, through the door in the wall. And it was done.'

He lowered his eyes respectfully. 'If only I'd known where to go.' He picked up a yellow cake and removed the shiny paper at its base. He saw it sliding through a door in the wall. His head was pounding now and his throat was fire.

'You have a brother or a sister, Grahame?'

'I have a sister, actually.'

'And you are very close?'

'Yes. Jolly close.' Would there be a door in the wall for Aunt Mary? And Din? And Colonel Rones? What had Cranton looked like when the door had opened, and what was she saying now, that her smile had changed and her eyes impossibly enlarged themselves?

'. . . in a blue over-night bag I gave him for his operation.' She rose and picked up a plastic envelope from the table beside her. She went to the window and shook the envelope over the guppies. They swirled into each other, became clotted, separated. 'I didn't know', she said, 'that Windhoven boys wrote such letters.'

He wagged his head and gave his whistling cough.

'Did Michael write to you, Grahame?'

He coughed again. 'They were jolly interesting, his letters.' But he knew, without looking up, that her eyes would be on him, and that she would be smiling. He looked up, and her eyes were on him, and she was smiling. Then she moved to the sideboard, to adjust a figure. She picked up her cup and saucer from beside the chair, and put it on the silver tray. She circled a little bookstand and straightened its rubber wheels. Each movement brought her closer to him, in roundabout ways, and closer.

'Tell me everything,' she said. 'Because it's too late for anger.'

'I'm very sorry,' he whispered, staring down. 'I think I'm——'

She bent suddenly; her breath rumpled his hair. 'You wanted him to forgive you for the cloisters. What was it?'

'Nothing, Mrs. Cranton.'

'Did you do something? Oh, Grahame, something dirty to him?'

He whispered a sentence pertaining to his health.

'Dirty, Grahame? Are you a dirty boy?'

'Nothing. Nothing. Honestly, Mrs. Cranton. Honestly.'

Which was correct. Because it had been difficult to fit himself over Cranton's long, bony body and at the same time to keep his balance. It had been difficult to arrange his feet between Cranton's, and to hold his head so that it rested on Cranton's shoulder. But it had been less difficult than thinking about why he worried about all these things. The thickening mass of wall around them closed them in, but there were little slits high up that let in light, like eyes, and at any moment House Master would come to chapel and trap him. He nearly fell, and would have swung out an arm to protect himself if an arm had been free, but one was caught under Cranton's belt. So his legs had bowed, his neck arched and he aimed a blow at Cranton's sighing mouth. He struck again and again, until his heels jarred against the stone and he was free. Through the darkness he saw the thin figure straightening slowly on the slab, a corpse raised up. He ran off, down one of the side cloisters, where there was another bench. He adjusted his clothing and sat there, waiting for Cranton to find him. He was trembling, his body itched and his mouth was dry, but it would be all right because they had done nothing. He waited, shaking with the cold, his forehead burning. Hoarse sounds leapt out of his throat, that were half coughs. The bright objects in the darkening room shone into his eyes. He stared at the television set and then at the guppies, which were specks of frolicking blackness.

'Please.' She thrust into his lap a brown paper package, tied with string, that he thought in his fever were sandwiches for a picnic. 'Please get out of my house.'

He rose on liquid legs. He paused before each door, waiting for it to slam in his face. 'I'm very sorry,' he said, over and over, until finally, on the doorstep and remembering his manners, he thanked her for a lovely tea.

He didn't know precisely how it would happen, but it would probably start with House Master. Then he would be sent to the Head Master. Mrs. Cranton would come and sit beside the Head Master on the dais in Assembly. The stool would be there, with the stick against it. Aunt Mary and Colonel Basil Rones, D.S.O., Old Windhoven, would fetch him home.

He walked from the library to the classroom, from the classroom to the House, with his gaze lowered. He could meet no one's eyes, and answer no one's call. Aprilson gave him a look. The others stared and smirked and gossiped. The masters circled around him in the cloisters on the way to chapel, and put their hands behind their gowns and their heads together, and talked of his dirtiness, which rose from him to fill the Upper Common, the classrooms, the library. It billowed out of the cloisters and leaked into the chapel, where, through 'Oh Lord, our Help in Ages Past', he screeched words out of his ragged throat for mercy.

It was Cranton's fault.

'Thwaite?'

'Sir?' The cough came. The head wagged.

'Are you ill, Thwaite?'

'Sir.'

'Can you make it, George?' An arm went around his shoulder; a tweedy side pressed protectively against his; friendly smoke filled his nostrils and the world skidded. 'I'm sorry,' he cried, 'I'm sorry, sir, but it was Cranton's——'

'Someone give me a hand. He's fainted.'

At last, he thought. 'Fault.' he cried.

He would come out of a sleep, stare hotly around at the white walls, stare hotly down at the brass knobs, and retreat. He was outside himself, away from his prickling body, his twitching limbs. But however far he went, Cranton would follow and catch him. Cranton was everywhere, springing from the slab in the darkness, running after him up the steps to the library, hiding behind the pews in chapel; laughing at him; waving his thin hands; pointing to a blonde cluster between his legs. There was only peace when Din came, to tell him it was Cranton's fault and that Cranton would be punished.

'Feeling better?'

'Sir.'

'Soon be out and about. Mind if I light up?'

'No, sir.'

'Good show, George.'

'Thank you, sir.' He made a slow fall back to the pillow. He could protract his delirium, become a trifle mad for House Master, whose eyes were compassion. 'But why does he call me George?' he wondered.

There were two long letters from Din. She knew what he was going through, and mentioned Cranton and grief.

The Matron said it was a cold that had turned to 'flu, and that he ought never have gone to Wembley Park to see that poor lady. He had given them all a turn, she said. Yes, what had he been thinking of, not to tell House Master he was ill.

So there was indulgence from every side and he was safe. But in his box under his bed in the dorm was the brown paper package. He visualized Aprilson opening it, and struggled to rise.

As soon as he was allowed out he took the package from the box, and hiding it under his coat, went for a walk past the playing fields, around the pavilion, to a small, stagnant pond. He wedged a stone between the string and the paper, and threw the bundle out into the water. The stone and the papers disappeared, as one by one the letters drifted up to the surface. But he waited calmly as the floating pages merged with the scum on the water and sank back into the darkness. Then he went off through a copse, up a nearby hill, and along the sides of the pitches to where the First were playing Eton. He joined the crowd on the lines, and urged, in an increasingly strident voice, the school to victory. Afterwards he hung about for Aprilson, who had played gamely through the second half with a bruised hip and scored a goal. They walked together back to Arnold's, and that night he slept well. He was free.

For the rest of the year he returned to the path that had first been indicated by Mrs. Holydrake and Mr. Victor. He found a place at one of the side tables in the main library and spent all his spare time working. He rose before Morning Callers and worked; he hurried away after lunch, during Footers and worked; he stayed at night until the library lights were clicked off, and worked. He had always done well in class, and come first, but now he outstripped the others completely. His essays were twice the length they needed to be; he read the set texts three times, and he made a point of cultivating little areas (like the Existentialists, to whom Cranton had introduced him) outside the syllabus. He flowered, in fact, so magnificently that Mr. Keel, senior history master, made a special point of examining the plant himself. Mr. Keel groaned occasionally as he studied the leaves, and groaned again, on a different note, when he finally turned over the last. He had a horror of prolixity—he called it waste—but he could recognize a scholarship candidate when he saw one. Thwaite had application and energy, had a rapid mind to match his rapid pen, and would be susceptible to discipline—Mr. Keel called it order, or in a facetious mood, harmony. But whatever he called it, it was his particular skill that he could provide it, as long as the material was there. He made Thwaite a member of his scholarship team; convinced, as he did so, that he would one day wear him as yet another feather in his already multi-plumed cap. For if it was true that the world at large knew of Windhoven only through the playing fields, it was also true that a number of Oxford and Cambridge colleges were beginning to learn a thing or two about Windhoven through their examinations. In the four years that Mr. Keel had spent in the school he had sent three boys to Trinity, Cambridge; one to Peterhouse, Cambridge; two to Christ Church, Oxford; two to Magdalene, Oxford; and only one (unstable from the beginning) to a rest home in Shropshire; and in so doing, had significantly increased Windhoven representation at each of these institutions.

But then Mr. Keel had himself been a Fellow of an Oxford college. He once said to his team that he'd come to Windhoven to get away from *there*, back to where he belonged—a characteristic joke, the point of which lay in his team's almost but not quite grasping the irony implicit in their own fates—that Mr. Keel had only come back far enough to send them forward in his place. In fact, his spirit was more conspicuously abroad in the Courts of Oxford two years after he had abandoned them, than when he had been physically present. Whether he was himself a gifted academic was debatable, but he knew what appealed to the academically gifted. After all, fifteen years earlier he had set a kind of record in his own papers, had portended brilliance so brilliantly that his later failure to produce anything distinctive had only been the more perplexingly tragic.

The first thing he taught his team was the proper tone— 'it would seem', 'it could be said', 'it might be argued', instead of the 'I think', 'I feel', 'I believe', which the History Fifth Master had preferred. The History Fifth Master was a tired old Romantic (as the team realized soon after they had begun their grooming) who only *enjoyed* the past, and whose favourite historians were Gibbon and Macaulay, because of their prose styles and the broad sweep of their minds, with H. A. L. Fisher in third place—'the one modern who is truly, truly a classic. Apart, of course, from Churchill at his most majestic.' But Mr. Keel explained to his team what modern history—the exploration of small possibilities through the examination of small details—really was. He also taught them what to think of H. A. L. Fisher ('Adore old Winston. Worship—in your civilized ways—the *genius* of Macaulay and Gibbon, but nothing more. Snub Fisher. He's only worth mentioning as a way of showing that you're above mentioning him.') just as he taught them the titles to memorize (along with fastidious content-summaries—'Naughty. But where would we be without me.') and how to window-dress. 'Range of reference makes the General Paper man. N'oubliez pas, mes enfants. And get up little titbits on the side. Hornsey goes strong on the medieval philosophers because he's a Catholic. Thwaite seems to have Kafka, Kierkegaard, Sartre, about his mental person, for reasons unknown. You can't go wrong on those, *ces jours-là*. And never, never, never, forget the novel. I shall give you some Notes on some Names, before the day itself.' Mr. Keel was a tall, tapery man, with white cheeks, damp black hair, and a mystery under his bottom lip that might have been baby to a beard. He hardly ever smiled, but he laughed a great deal.

'. . . it could be said that the world, to Kafka, is an insoluble problem that man is ordered to try and solve; for Dostoievsky a congregation in pursuit of a church; to Camus a moral agony,' Grahame wrote, in his General Paper essay on 'The Modern Paradox'. The question might actually have been designed for him, it was so pertinent to his cultivated area (and he had used exactly the same phrase in a weekly paper for Mr. Keel), but he suspected that he was so well prepared that he would have deployed it to convincing effect if the question had been on Nineteenth-Century Landscape Painting. His history papers were good enough to win him an Exhibition. The General Paper made that up to a Scholarship. He was a particularly luxuriant feather in Mr. Keel's cap, as he was the first Keelite to break through and into that particular college.

'Didn't know the old place went in for it,' Colonel Rones commented, as a means of bringing his congratulations to an end. He looked at the tall eighteen-year-old who was standing in the centre of the Mallows' living-room with a symbolic book, or a book on symbolism, in his hand; and then looked at Mary Medway, who was seated on the sofa, ceremonially pouring sherry. 'In my day it didn't.'

'Brains are important, too, Basil,' Mary Medway replied. She passed a small blue glass, a quarter full, to Grahame; and a small blue glass, an eighth full, to Din, who that very afternoon had learnt that she'd been accepted into Portsmouth's best secretarial college. 'Times have changed. Haven't they, Grahame?'

'Yes, Aunt Mary,' he said politely. He licked his drink down and wondered how he could get back upstairs, away from her awkward idiocies, away from the Colonel's idiot awkwardnesses, away from Din's perpetual smiles; away from them all, and back to his books.

'And what will you do when you're there, old chap?' the Colonel worried.

Do? Why he would do as he had done. He would work. He would work and work. He would get more scholarships. He would do so well that there would be a fog around him whenever the Colonel looked at him. In particular he would do so well that Din would stop borrowing his Namier and his Tawney and would accept the fact that brilliance was brilliance, and sisters were sisters, merely.

'I don't know,' he mumbled shyly. 'I haven't really thought about it.'

The Colonel looked at him again and noted to himself that the old place was still the old place to this extent, at least; that he'd never yet met a conceited Windhoven. And hoped he never would. And hoped he never would.

'He'll know what to do when the time comes,' Aunt Mary said. But she was a trifle surprised at the way her tall, broad, brainy nephew had swilled his sherry down.

'Would you like mine, Dodie?' Din passed him her glass. 'I can't get used to the taste.'

He accepted it, brainily.

BOOK TWO

Hardles, a mathematical genius, was perhaps the nicest person Grahame had ever come across. He had round pink cheeks, a mop of moppet's hair, and the smile of one who believed that everyone was as pleasant as himself. He dropped in on Grahame several times a week, with a cake his mother had sent, or a bottle of sherry from an uncle. He would cut up the cake, pour out the sherry, and chat about all the jolly good films he'd seen recently, or the jolly incredible article he'd read in *Varsity* about drug addicts and free love, and when Grahame indicated that he had essays to write, he'd go across the street (in the first year) or up the stairs (in the second year) with the cake and sherry for a chat with Endfer about the same things. Endfer was similar to Hardles, without the genius and with a fraction less of the pinkness and freshness, and was the second nicest person Grahame had ever come across. He was tall, dark haired, unnoticeably good-looking, and had some money. He did a bit of everything, in a two-two way—played squash, got beaten at chess, joined any society that wanted him, gave mulled wine parties every three weeks, went abroad with five friends in a truck, and was quite prepared to become a solicitor like his father, in his father's firm in Reigate. He liked Grahame and Hardles awfully and the three of them were friends.

So Grahame's first two years consisted, socially speaking, of Hardles and Endfer, and a few others of the same kind that he saw less often. Nothing special happened—still socially speaking—until Din came down at the end of his third term, to visit him in his shabby digs in the retired postman's house on the edge of town. In his room (the view from which was of another small red house, with the slate roof of a needle factory rising above it) he had a squat desk covered with coffee stains, a red leather couch with tufts of horse hair sticking out at one end, and three hard chairs whose pads came extremely close to fitting. The iron bed dipped in the middle, it was impossible to distinguish the patches from the pattern of the curtain and a smell of bacon and eggs hung over from breakfast to breakfast. The retired postman patrolled the hall until two in the morning, and his wife had a scalp ailment, the symptoms of which floated in Grahame's tea or formed a kind of sparse nest for his unevenly fried egg. Din thought it all quite romantic, of course.

He'd told Hardles and Endfer that she was 'in publishing' in Portsmouth and as he hadn't seen her for nearly a year, he came to expect the sort of girl the phrase conjured up—an illusion which would probably have vanished if he had remembered that the firm specialized in gardening manuals. Inevitably she turned out to be only the old Din, shy and peaky. She was awed by everything, by the college, by Cambridge, by his friends—particularly by his friends. She stood tensely, a glass of unsipped sherry in her hand, almost dumb. She failed to laugh at Henry Borning's famous story about the bedder, and later she got herself trapped in a corner with John Hardles, whose radiant desire to please made her shrink away.

He *had* to say *something*, of course.

'Oh, I'd forgotten him. Why, Dodie?'

'Oh, nothing, just that I got the impression that you didn't care for him. Or for David Endfer either.'

'I don't know.' She smiled weakly. 'He's a little frightening, though.'

'Frightening? He's not at all frightening. Nor is David. Quite the opposite. So is David, Dianah.'

She bent about in the room, first of all tugging at the horsehair as if determined to hollow the sofa, then straightening the books (which he always kept neatly), and finally collecting the glasses.

'Was I rude to him, then?' she asked suddenly, in a low voice.

'Of course not.' He laughed at a thought so ridiculous (in its impertinence). 'But they seemed to make you nervous.'

She faced him, hunched to keep the glasses pressed safely against her stomach. He wondered, as he smiled at her bowed head, what she was like in the publishing office, where presumably some life went on, some intelligent conversations took place—and remembered at last about the gardening manuals. He wondered why she had to wear such a baggy skirt, as if she had dressed out of Aunt Mary's winter wardrobe; but did her hair in a truncated pigtail, as if she were still at school. 'They both told me stories, well, the same story actually,' and she crouched a little lower, to catch a slipping glass or in preparation for total self-abasement, 'the same story I think it was, Dodie, about a bedder. And I don't know what a bedder is, you see.'

He strolled over to the window to conceal his irritation. 'A bedder, oh, *you* know what a bedder is, Dianah. Din.'

Her scattered phrases clearly constituted some kind of guess. So he grilled her harder, and got it out.

'My God, Dianah, Din, do you really think John or David would tell *my* sister a story about'—and he went on to explain precisely—'just an old woman who makes the college beds in the morning, that's all'—so that she would respond to the comedy the next time she heard the joke.

The following morning found them in Endfer's room for mulled wine. Din spent twenty minutes with Hardles and ten with Endfer, and was just as awkward. He could tell she was only trying because she knew he was watching.

He was a bit cool with Hardles and Endfer after she had gone. He fancied a slight change in attitude on their part, as a consequence of their having met her. But eventually he decided that he had misjudged them, because he heard through someone else that Hardles had said that Grahame Thwaite had a 'super sister. Fantastically pretty'. Which he could now see that she was—in her way. Even so he was relieved when she took a job in Cardiff as private secretary to a professional writer who was doing a B.B.C. series about Welsh slums. His social life resumed its former even-ness—Hardles and Endfer, dinner in Hall, coffee after it, the occasional film, and a great deal of work.

He had done as well as Aunt Mary had prophesied, for all her ignorance; as well as he himself had hoped, for all his wariness. He got a First in Prelims, which didn't count for much, but at least showed that his scholarship was no acci-dent; another First in Part One, which was a positive step. During his first term he had been worried that Mr. Keel's General Paper Man might prove inadequate to the more complex challenges, but he had soon discovered, from his supervisor's reactions to his weekly essays, that the General Paper Man, once brought to his peak, could run for ever. His manner in Prelims and Part One had been almost the same as in the Scholarship Paper, and had met with the same result. Hard work within defined limits, and the proper tone. A First. It was true that his supervisor had said, 'Yes, you've got the trick, but couldn't you, just once, take a risk? Between friends, and in safety.' But he'd replied that well, there *were* certain lines he hadn't been able to explore, for lack of space, and left it at that. That particular supervisor was anyway a Marxist, who always took the same risk, and hadn't been of much use from the examina-tion point of view. His other supervisors, and his Director of Studies, were all agreed that his papers were dead right.

When he came back from Mallows at the beginning of his last year, it was to a room in Great Court. Large, oak-panelled, handsomely furnished, with a good desk (mahogany) and three brown leather armchairs arranged around a wide fireplace. Hardles and Endfer had rooms in college as well, but Endfer was given an obscure set on the other side of the river in a new residence (because of his two-two) and Hardles, in spite of his Starred First, had chosen East Court—perhaps because, although his genius deserved the best accommodation in the land, the rest of him was more at home in humbler quarters. Hardles wasn't really a clever chap (as Grahame frequently pointed out to Endfer), except in his limited field.

He was pleased to be back from the shallows of Morton —from Aunt Mary's meaningless attack on the new Butlin's camp; Colonel Rones's grisly inquiries about the boat race (as if *he* knew). As soon as he had unpacked, arranged his books in the welcoming shelves, placed his notes near his desk, and spread out the pages of his current essay, he settled at one of the window seats and gazed down into the court. He followed with ambitious eyes the elected that strolled across the grass, and dreamt of the day when he would accept his fellowship, and walk beside them. He had only to work, and work, and work. The day would come and the pastures would be opened. In the soft autumnal sunlight his future seemed, literally, to glow up at him, and that evening he hurried away from Hall after an extremely quick coffee with Borning (a friend of Hardles, as who was not?), partly to continue with his essay, really for the pleasure of his new estates. Eventually he settled on the window seat again, with the curtains pushed aside, and watched the night mists as they curled around the edges of the stone, listened to the footsteps that echoed along the paths, the raised or hushed voices of his destiny. Once or twice he imagined how he must appear from below, framed against the lighted window in his self-containment.

The knock sounded on his door just as the bells were ringing, and five minutes later he was standing uneasily between two Japanese screens, calculating the best method of negotiating them, to the safety of a chair. The screens were covered with naked boys playing under oriental trees with dogs that seemed, in their shiny pinkness, to be naked also. In a bid to reassure himself, and perhaps to gain a little time, he bent to examine the texture of the screens more closely. He pressed a finger against the surface of one of the panels, thus causing the whole structure to sway rustlingly. As he straightened he thought he heard an exclamation, but when he peered over the top he could see that Hazings, his back to the door, was still busy with the whisky bottle.

Hazings' room, directly above his own and therefore identical to it in its essentials, was unlike it in every decorative detail. The floor was covered with a thick Persian carpet, wall to wall; there were several pieces of doubtless very fine furniture—a regency desk, a cottage diner, a spinet—all arranged with a carelessness that exquisitely gave the impression that any mislaid article could be replaced by something surprisingly different and yet its equal in charm. The bookcases that lined the walls contained both privately bound volumes and those American paper backs that have to be brought especially across the ocean. By the fire were three black and swivel armchairs, and facing the aisle formed by the screens was a Queen Anne writing table, above which hung a portrait. The portrait, in greys and blacks, was of a slimly elegant boy of about fourteen, seated on a kitchen stool with his legs crossed. His face was long and pointed, with wide hazel eyes, a small nose, and a small, full mouth, and he was beautiful. But then the adult version, now standing carelessly under the picture and pouring the Scotch, with a cheeroot sticking out of one side of his mouth and smoke pouring out of the other, wearing tight white jeans (craftily stained and neatly frayed), high brown boots, and a checked flannel shirt, was also beautiful. Certainly too beautiful to be friendly.

Until five minutes before, Grahame had known Hazings only by sight and by reputation. He had often seen him around the college courts or on Trinity Street, usually in the company of Craley, a burly man who seemed to wear, every day of his life, a sloppy boiler suit; and Stafford, a thin, neat little person with close-cut red hair, a sauntering walk and a studied smile. The three of them, so contradictory in their individual appearance, made up a kind of clique, managed somehow to seem glamorous, and were therefore famous in a university way. Other undergraduates were slightly afraid of them, but Grahame himself had always made a point of scowling whenever they passed. At first he had assumed that they were merely moneyed and nasty (Craley's grubbiness being an affectation). Then, when the Prelims and Part One results had come out, he had been forced into a new assessment. They were moneyed, nasty *and* clever. Which made them nastier, as far as he was concerned. So when Hazings had knocked on his door and invited him up for a drink, his first impulse had been to say, 'No, he had too much work.' Instead, he had found himself on his feet, apologizing for something, thanking Hazings profusely, and following him up the stairs. These pretentious screens were exactly the kind of thing he now saw he ought to have been on his guard against.

Hazings turned, at last, and stared around the room. 'Oh, *there* you are. Come in. Come in. It may make you feel sick, old chap, but it *is* gorgeous. Don't you think?' His smile was also beautiful, and completely friendly. He stubbed out his cheroot on his way to one of the black swivel chairs by the fireplace, and sat down with a swish of cloth. 'For a minute, anyway. Do come. Do come and tell me frankly and fearlessly, what you think of it.'

He scanned the room authoritatively and then moved delicately forward. He was broader than Hazings, and both his shoulders brushed against the tautened silk. He was sure that if he continued he would send one of them over with friction; he was equally sure that if he turned sideways, he would knock one of them over with his elbow. 'Yes, I like the whole *style*,' he said, and advancing a few steps more, slid deftly sideways and knocked the screen with his elbow. He spun around, but Hazings, who had apparently been anticipating *gaucheries*, came skidding across the room and caught the frame with one hand. The only damage was some Scotch on Grahame's O.W. tie. But he walked to a chair with the feeling that he was going to crash through the floorboards, or splinter the spinet with an elephant foot.

'Does doing that sort of thing bother you?' Hazings' smile was now as sympathetic as it was beautiful—more beautiful *because* it was sympathetic. 'For God's sake don't worry. It's only a trap I put up for a friend of mine. He's large, much larger than you. Broad, broader than you. Dirty, dirtier than you could imagine. And, Christ, much cleverer than me. That's why I try to make him knock things over. To remind him that at least he's clumsy. To remind him of mortality.' He sat down, slid one boot over the other, and shook his head in self-contempt. 'One of those school competition things.'

'Well,' he said, in tones he hoped were sufficiently light, 'I hope I'm not stupid, as well as clumsy. What school, by the way?' He knew it was a foolish question. He never asked people what schools they went to, from the innate assumption that it didn't matter because Windhoven was good enough.

'Oh.' Hazings hesitated. 'God. Winchester, as a matter of fact.' He glanced at his guest's tie, to which the scotch had contributed an extra sheen, to make two of the crowns look almost varnished. 'Is that a Lancing business?'

'Windhoven, actually.'

'Windhoven.' He leaned forward, concerned. 'Was it *very* distressing?'

'It was all right. A bit Philistine, footbally, you know. But all right.' He had never made these qualifications before, and was amazed that he had been able to find them with so little warning.

'Ah. Well, you're lucky. Winchester keeps us little boys for ever. The Crab, the Staff and I, we'll behave like this,' he pointed to the screens, 'until we're finished.'

'The Crab and the . . . ?'

'Staff, Craley and Stafford. Have you met them? You must. You'll like them. Of course we won't be finished for years, thank God, because little boys are excellent at looking after themselves. Now I think that's important, extremely,' he spun his chair in a half arc, 'extremely, to look after yourself, don't you? By the way,' he swung the chair back again, brushed his hand through his dark hair, and smiled, 'I hope you don't mind my talking like this. I'm excited, you see. I've no idea what I'm saying, but I'm always excited when I've just introduced myself to someone very new. Aren't you?'

'Yes,' he said. 'I know what you mean.' Although in fact he was wondering how so much simplicity could be made to sound so sophisticated. He took a sip of Scotch and laughed, to put himself more at his ease. 'Nerves, I suppose.'

'Or animal fear. Don't you think?' He did another half-revolution, so that for a second he was smiling into the empty half of the room and away from his guest; then another half revolution, which brought them face to face again. 'You know, like those scenes in Lawrence.'

'Yes.'

'My God,' Hazings touched his brow, 'he's a great writer. No?'

'Yes.'

'A very great writer. A genius.'

Grahame could have spoken for approximately five minutes on each of Lawrence's major novels, if Hazings meant D.H., and about ten on the *Seven Pillars of Wisdom*, if Hazings meant T.E. But he could see, by Hazings' change of expression, from negligent but paradoxically enthusiastic courtesy to negligent but paradoxically enthusiastic reverence, that the distinction was crucial. So he sipped more Scotch, and nodded ambiguously. 'In a sense', he said, 'he's a great writer. Yes.'

'But, my God, how small he makes one feel. Don't you think. How mean. I always wonder what the Hell I'm doing in a place like this when I'm pondering, pondering, oh,' he sighed, 'take anything. Take *Women in Love*.'

'D.H. then,' he thought. But why all this about Lawrence unless Hazings were being nasty in a Winchester, moneyed and clever way? Or testing him, to find out what his capacities were? So he remained silent, keeping himself back and waiting.

'I hope you don't mind.' Hazings leaned forward, intently; then rose to his boots and strode swiftly along the line of his bookshelves. 'I hope you don't mind. The Crab always says that I'm the most appalling, egoistical little bastard, and of course he's quite right. He always is.' He plucked a book from the shelves with a neat and mystical movement of the wrist, rather as if extricating a flower from danger. 'I can't leave Lawrence alone, you see. And I can't leave anyone else alone *about* Lawrence. It's probably just a post-adolescent crush, don't you think?' He came back, his head bent over the book, his fingers caressing through the pages. 'When I get too boring, you will say? You will. I know you will.'

'No. I like talking about Lawrence.' He crossed his legs and nursed his drink, elaborately.

Hazings gave him a strange, swift look. 'Do you? Good for you, old chap. Do you talk about him often?'

He thought of Hardles and Endfer, with whom he talked about many small things very often; and banished them. Even as points of negative reference they were inadequate to his present situation. 'Yes,' he said, and was just on the edge of mentioning an old school friend who had shared his literary tastes when Hazings, cutting politely and rapidly through, began. He talked fluently and at length, with a fine passion and an uplifted head, and his lecture was only fleetingly marred when, towards the end, he let out a laugh of modulated self-derision in which Grahame unfortunately and quite unintentionally joined. 'No, no, I mean it,' Hazings said sharply. 'He does give us hope. *That's* the triumph. Hope.' And held the book out, as if assisting it to take a bow.

For a minute he couldn't think of anything to say, and then, without knowing that he had started, he was in the middle of a sentence about perspective and subjective judgement. He said that Hazings had been offering feeling as if it possessed objective validity, but that the real meaning of an art-work depended on its context. Words like hope, while permissible in conversation (this with a rough approximation to a Hazings smile) weren't useful because they concentrated too much attention on the ('let's face it') speaker; not enough on the intricate but actual causes. His real purpose in saying this was to get away from *Women in Love* itself, but he felt pleased with these arguments, that had come from him without strain, and were similar to his

125

frequently deployed objections to the romantic historians. He had, he knew, kept his end up.

'Do you think,' Hazings reached down and scratched the sides of his boots, 'now do you think that having feelings is a little business? That friend of yours? The one I've seen you having dinner with in Hall?'

'John Hardles?'

'Something. Does *he* have feelings? *Does* he? Perhaps he does.' But whatever feelings Hardles had, they couldn't have been good enough, for Hazings was knocking them away with polite wags of the whisky bottle; from which he then topped up Grahame's glass. 'Well, you'd know about him, I expect, old chap.'

The whisky and the comparison with Hardles, the splendid room, the sudden image of himself confidently and intimately debating with one of the most envied undergraduates in Cambridge—all these elements combined, in fact, brought a smile to his lips. Of course he didn't want to smile, for he didn't want Hazings to see how much he was admiring them both. 'No.' He took a gulp from his glass, to conceal his smile. 'No, he probably doesn't. He's very nice, but scarcely responsive, I'm afraid. But that's not the point. The point, you see,' and for a hideous second, under the impact of victory, he blacked out. 'Life', he heard himself repeating, 'life', 'life', 'life'—and then, '*history* is life'.

'What?'

'Life.'

'What is?'

'History.'

'I see. Well, yes, it is. And so are, oh, pimples and dusters and Leonardo and Verdi and *Women in Love*. Read it, anyway.'

'I've read it actually. At school.'

'You're not at school now. Read it again.'

126

'I haven't got time,' he said. 'I really haven't.'

'Haven't got *what*?' And for some reason pointed backwards, over his shoulder, at his own portrait. 'Old chap.'

For the first time in his life he got a little drunk that night. When he finally got to his feet, the copy of *Women in Love* in his hand, he was swaying slightly; and when he left the room he knocked over one of the screens again. But it didn't matter; not at all. For Hazings, although he claimed to be 'absolutely stinking', was still quick enough to reach the screen before it hit the ground.

'I've enjoyed this evening, my God I have,' Hazings said, as he righted the screen with one hand and squeezed Grahame's arm with the other. 'I've learnt a lot. Masses.'

'So have I,' Grahame mumbled, returning the squeeze. 'So have I.'

And in the morning, and even with a slight hang-over, he knew one thing. He'd started life in Great Court, and found someone who was Tops.

'Renewed.' He used the word several times to Hazings, who shot similar words—'delivered', 'grasped', 'captured', back at him.

'You sound like St. Paul confronting himself on a bad afternoon, just for the practice. Or two salesmen in a competition.' During most of the conversation Craley had been slumped into one of the swivel chairs, tugging at the back hair that curled over the collar of his boiler suit, biting at his finger-nails, yawning. Sometimes he lifted his heavy, unshaven face in theatrical bewilderment, and then let it drop forward on to his chest, as if he had been pole-axed by an invisible assailant. All such mimings were clearly part of a game—or so Grahame deduced from Hazings' lack of concern. But once, for a long moment, he felt Craley's small blue eyes fixed upon him, as if measuring the spread of his shoulder or interpreting the play of his features.

127

'Oh, Staff,' Craley whispered, pretending to grind the palms of his hands into his ears, 'oh, Staff, please tell them we're not interested. Do something. Throw a bomb, or fall asleep. Please.'

'But, Crab,' Stafford raised his eyebrows and tilted his head, 'they're talking about life, you see.' He had been sitting on one of the window seats, with his hands slotted into his jeans' pockets and his face as carefully still as Craley's was ostentatiously on the move. Mainly his lips were pursed in a silent whistle, and mainly his black, steady eyes were focused on the picture opposite him, as if he and the fourteen-year-old Hazings were brothers, or at least made a pair. This was the first time he had spoken, and his voice was so light that Grahame could only just make out the words.

'Wee Staff, they don't know anything about life. All they know about is dark urges, male pride, Lawrence stuff. Life goes on in details, Staff. It does, really.'

'Goes on in details does it, Crab. I see. Thanks. I'd been wondering how it went on.' And tilting his head back, went on with his noiseless whistling.

Hazings picked up a fresh bottle of Scotch. 'It goes on in details,' he aimed the neck of the bottle at Craley, 'because *he's* a botanist. The poor bugger's a botanist, and that's all he is. Except that he's also a poor bugger, wouldn't you say, Staff?'

Craley heaved his body upwards and held out his glass. 'More Scotch, Hazers, my little flirt. More Scotch, please. It's your role, to be the provider, and you aren't providing. Sexy wriggles and hot talk and flirting are not enough. By no means.'

Grahame, grinning towards Craley, wished that he had kept himself under closer restraint. He certainly wouldn't have spoken so loudly about Lawrence, and with such fiery confidence, if Hazings hadn't trapped him into it by introducing his two friends with a wheeling and patronizing motion of the hand, and then moved into a stream of questions about his reactions to *Women in Love*. He'd assumed that they stood in about the same relation to Hazings as Endfer and Hardles did to himself. But now, in the light of this strange passage, he realized that Craley's satirical gesturing and Stafford's dreamy silence both concealed independent attitudes, and thus, just possibly, powers of contempt.

'There's no doubt about it. You have to watch our frisky Hazers every second.' Craley was still holding his glass out. 'Which is, of course, what he wants. To be watched every second. Hazers, where's my Scotch? That's why he does it.'

'Does what?' he insouciantly wondered, now chuckling towards Hazings. Who didn't chuckle back. Who, in fact, stood glaring, his slender face quite pale except for some purplish lines that had suddenly appeared along his cheeks.

'Buy', he said at last, in a high, spitting voice, 'your own fucking Scotch.'

'Mmm.' Craley rapped his empty glass against his forehead. 'Now, Staff, I thought it was Lawrence he was being today, didn't you? Tender flames, visions, loins. But it's only our usual lady novelist, after all.'

'Better than a butch scholarship girlie.' Hazings poured some Scotch into his own glass and drained it down. 'A picker-up of inconsiderate triflers.'

'Oh, Christ.' Stafford uncurled himself neatly, and strolled towards the gap of the Japanese screens. 'Oh, good Christ. You two.'

'*And* you.' Craley, following Stafford with eyes suddenly alert, pointed dramatically, either at one of the sportive creatures on the screen, or at the small and impassive face that just showed above its top.

'Well, come on then,' Stafford commanded mildly.

There was a little pause, during which the four young

men held their positions exactly. Hazings, standing with one long hand on a slim hip, staring at Craley; Craley sprawled forward, his face wearing an expression that might have been a smile and might have been a scowl, but was probably a combination of the two; Stafford gazing coolly over the screen, as if at boring adults; and Grahame pretending to be lost in a particularly vital passage of *Women in Love*. Then Hazings, with a laugh, restored vitality. He sauntered across the room, poured some whisky into Craley's glass, and whispered something into Craley's ear. Craley shrugged sloppily, and kept his glass extended until the whisky ran down its outside edges, on to his knees; Stafford emerged from between the screens and wandered, smiling, back to his window seat; and Grahame turned over another page of *Women in Love* busily.

'Don't worry,' the bottle was aimed at Grahame now. 'Happens all the time, Thwaggers. Among friends.'

'Among us, anyway,' Stafford suggested.

'And to hell with Lawrence,' Craley said.

'With us, as well,' Stafford suggested.

'Friends.' Craley darted his tongue into his whisky. 'Friends.'

'Thank God,' Hazings exclaimed, as he moved to the centre of the room, where a patch of sunlight brought his eyes to brilliant points, 'thank *God* we all adore each other.'

Craley had got a Starred First in Part One Botany, and had read extensively in philosophy, literature and history, and would have got a First—Starred—(Hazings told Grahame) in virtually any subject. His mind (Hazings explained) was not only absorbing, it was absorbent; and had the texture of genius. His parents were poor, his father a draper—which accounted for his deliberate and rebellious dirtiness, didn't Grahame think?—but he knew exactly what he wanted from everything—from his friends, from university, from life, yes, from life itself. Which was why, didn't Grahame see, he would end up very famous. 'Not just a mere botanist, of course, but God knows what. He did have his weaknesses though. Didn't Grahame think?

Grahame did; and waited to notice them.

Stafford, on the other hand, was a Classicist, a Major Scholar in his college and the best First of his year. Eventually he would get a Fellowship, just like that—should he want one, which Hazings doubted. 'He's incredibly ambitious, and supremely, I mean it, supremely gifted.' He had a great deal in common with Grahame in that he, too, was an orphan, with parents unknown. He was vaguely French on his mother's side; vaguely but fantastically well-connected on his father's. 'He's not interested, though. I remember once in our last year at school the Crab and I tried to find out. We went to Somerset House and I got to know his lawyer through my uncle' (a judge), 'but there was blankness, blankness, just blankness. His guardian is a superb old lady, a retired head mistress who knows everything about the Staff, *and* his parents. But she won't tell, or *he* won't ask. She lives in Kidderminster, or Reading, that sort of place, and looks after him and his money. The Staff says she's conventional, like an old-fashioned doll, but extremely *nice*. I think it's important that there should be people like that. Don't you?'

He did; and cited his aunt, Mary Medway of Mallows, Morton, as another example of the same type.

But however hard Grahame tried to see the three of them through his own eyes, he couldn't, during the early weeks of friendship, penetrate through the magical net that Hazings had cast over them. Perhaps they wouldn't have seemed unusual to anyone who had known them at Winchester, and from the age of thirteen, but in comparison with Hardles, Endfer and Bornings, they were richly in-

131

comprehensible. In fact, if Grahame's ordinary friends formed a set because they were identical in their ordinariness, his Winchester friends formed a set (a little circle, Hazings called it) because they were so distinct in everything but superiority. But superiority made for the closest of bonds, to a community of language, even. They could talk about books, films, and particularly music, in a kind of code; they went together down to magnificent parties in London and analysed the guests in half-sentences and three adjectives when they had returned to college; they had jokes about each other that went back eight years; they had so subtle a control over each other that they could demolish themselves with a phrase, and raise themselves up again after a short silence. All in all, they belonged to a whole that was infinitely more mysterious than its sufficiently mysterious parts. And Grahame came to see that he himself, although accepted when he was present, was never allowed to come close to the living centre. He was their historian, and a First (naturally) and what he had to say was listened to and commented on, but the concern and the intimacy were always slightly thinner about his person. When Craley insulted him he did so with a reserve that was the real hurt in the insult, and when Hazings flattered him it was with an expansiveness that left too much out of account. And Stafford's stare at him, friendly and yet detached, told him nothing about anything. So he, for his part, learnt to keep his distance and measure out (at least in front of them) his admiration. After his one attempt at assertion—he invited them all downstairs for a drink of his Scotch, which he had got in especially for the occasion; an invitation that was emphasized by a sudden hush, and then lost in a sudden flow of conversation—he understood that he hadn't grasped even the cruder rules of the relationship. So although he went upstairs every night, where he was expected, and laughed and drank and joked and began to smoke, he went on looking at them with the entranced eyes of a privileged guest. Which was presumably, to them, his particular charm; for when he had left or was unavoidably absent, the circle would become diminished to itself, and frequently fall into a torpor. They were at their best, and at their most subtly interrelated, when defined by an alien presence.

Just as Hazings was often at his best when clarifying Grahame's confusions.

'Because of *you*, old chap.'

'Me?'

'Yes. Because you were there. You brought it to the boiling point, you see, and made it all spill over.'

'Well—brought what?'

'Oh, I've forgotten. We've all forgotten. We always do. But I think the Staff took offence at something.'

'Stafford!'

'I expect so. Don't you? I mean, he's usually the cause.'

'But he hardly says anything.'

'Exactly. At least out loud.'

'I see.'

'He's a bit of a poet, of course. Although he doesn't let anyone see what he does. But I expect his stuff is super. Don't you think the Staff's poems would be?'

He did.

'Did you write things at that school of yours? I'm sure you did.'

'Well, only the usual.'

'There *is* no usual', Hazings explained, 'from people like the Staff.'

Or from people like himself.

Of course he didn't give up his history. He worked, worked, worked at his history, as he had always done. He went to lectures in the morning, sketched out the neat lines of his weekly essay in the afternoons, and filled in the detailed arguments in the early evening and after Hall. He continued to impress his supervisors with his enclosed fluency and his orderly mind, and his reputation stood as high with his Director of Studies as it had done during his first term. But at night, after a couple of hours with Hazings, Craley and Stafford, he would put all his texts and notebooks on the floor in a careful line so that they could be quickly reassembled in the morning, cleared his desk of trivia (invitations to Endfer's mulled wine parties, etc.), spread out some blank pages, and set forth. In two hours he would cover ten sheets and go to bed exalted. His only problem lay in what he thought of as 'continuity'. However high he soared before sleep, he could never resume his flight during the next session. In three weeks he had amassed some ten pieces that amounted to a total of a hundred pages, with only his characteristic tone to organize them into a whole. It was as if the habit of weekly essay writing had become a habit of his imagination, as if Mr. Keel's discipline and harmony controlled his creative self also. But when, after he had refined his language and eliminated awkwardnesses, he read one of the pieces aloud; when he listened to the rhythms of his own voice so exactly attuned to the rhythms of his own prose; then he would be transported. He saw that the limitations that confined him were really the expression of his instinct for perfection. He was an artist, as Stafford was. And like Stafford he would keep his art to himself. He would not face public examination, however flattering, until he had made his masterpiece, which would be of at least twenty pages.

He sat coolly at his desk and tried to see around a book, which he held close to his face. Then he put the book down, settled sideways in one of his armchairs, and watched casually. Finally he turned around completely, and with his hands on his knees, studied Hazings openly. But Hazings' face, usually mobile even in repose, remained a fine, narrow blank. He made scribbles in the margins, tapped his pencil against the heels of his new boots (black) and was unaware of any anxious presence. His magnificent eyes were hooded against scrutiny.

But he finished at last. He sighed, shuffled the papers together, and nodded. 'Yes,' he said. 'Yes, yes. Brilliant, of course. Brilliant.'

He rose to his feet and blundered about the room. 'Is it? Well, it's not. No, the problem is to go on from there, without, well, coming to a halt.' He came to a halt anyway, by his bookcase, and waited. He knew more praise was coming. Hazings' impatient smile told him so—and he was open-eared, to catch its every inflexion. 'So you really like it?' He hung his head.

Hazings, too, got up. He strode about the room, more swiftly and easily than Grahame had done. His boots crackled and creased with every elegant step. 'You have a genuine, an absolute genuine gift. I'd call it genius.' He circled the desk and made for the window. He lifted the curtain. 'For pastiche.' And peered compassionately out across the darkened court. 'What did you say?'

'Nothing.'

'Oh. Sorry. I thought you spoke.'

'No.' And he hadn't. He had merely made a small noise at the back of his throat.

'God!' Hazings saluted a figure in the farthest shadows. 'You're not angry.'

'No.' He laughed. 'Angry! Of course not. Why should I be angry?' He stared at Hazings's tailored back, his gracefully tilted head, and saw them for the first time. Hazings was screeney. 'Why should I be?'

'And you *do* want me to tell you what I think? Without

cosiness? You asked me to be frank, and you meant it. I know you did.'

'Yes, I did. I do.' For it was necessary, in the face of criticism that was making him spoil with rage, to remain calm and curious. He knew that. In the same way he knew that his desire to make reference to Hazings' boots and gestures, and then to smash him down with his own boots, and with accompanying gestures, had at all costs to be over-come. So, sinking his hands into his pockets and chuckling a little, he wondered in a voice he couldn't prevent from being a trifle icy, whether Hazings could be more specific. Which Hazings, who had made notes entirely for that pur-pose, then was.

'The Crab and the Staff are coming in tomorrow,' he said as he left. 'You'll be there of course?'

But he wasn't. For the next few days he made a point of being out at the times Hazings looked in to invite him up; or if he was caught, said that he had a lot of work to do, for an essay. His fictional pieces he put aside for a short while.

'You're not giving us up, old chap? No, of course you're not? You couldn't be, could you?'

'Of course not.' But he couldn't meet Hazings' eye. He had pictured to himself the scene in which Craley and Stafford were given an account of his story; of Craley's devastating contempt, and most particularly of Stafford's ironic indifference. So he worked hard at his weekly essays, thought about his future Fellowship, and when Hazings dropped in to flatter him from the door, felt humiliated, shook his head, and had too much work.

Not too much work for Hardles, however. He hadn't dropped his ordinary friends after making his extraordinary friendships, but he had come to see that he had never had much to say to Hardles, and that first evening in Hazings's room had diminished further his stock of conventional responses. Hardles, however, seemed to enjoy silence almost as much as conversation. He continued to plop amiably into one of Grahame's chairs, grin his good-natured, pleasantly meaningless grin, and wait for an observation or a joke. Then he brought up all the topics he was at home with—what his tutor was like, how his bedder was behaving, the jolly good this and that he'd read, heard or seen lately. His mother had taken to sending him fudge rather than cake, but he stuck firmly to his principle of equal distribution—a quarter for Grahame, a quarter for Endfer, half for himself. He was delighted at being in Grahame's room—his smile made that clear, just as it made clear that he would have been delighted at being in most other places, short of a concentration camp. Sometimes in his own room he would be visited by other chaps as like himself as they were different from Grahame. They were mathematicians, historians, theologians, anthropologists, architects, footballers, physicians, rowers, boxers, even foreigners; but to Grahame they were essentially twins to Hardles, whose names he couldn't remember, whose ambitions were insignificant, whose attitudes were negative; men who knew their worth in the scale of things, and were well-adjusted. Of the second category, in the second class, as the Tripos would doubtless show. They looked on Grahame with an awe that wasn't the less flattering for being without envy —looked on him as a major scholar in History, a sure First in Part Two, who mixed with famous intellectuals like Hazings and Craley, and that small, red-haired chap; and had opinions on films, plays, novels, politics and people—on all serious matters.

And certainly he had opinions. They had developed in him during his intimacy with Hazings and his group, and now achieved maturity in the company of Hardles and his group. He was particularly authoritative on anything they'd enjoyed. He had insights on films they mentioned—'Oh, I haven't actually *seen* it,' was his opening formula, 'but from the reviews and what *you* say about it'; and savaged novels and spoke with resonance about Lawrence. A mind so active could hardly be expected to rest on anything as uninteresting as an attentive face, and a twin of Hardles. Which was perhaps fortunate for all concerned.

'Gosh!' Hardles said one evening, as he lifted the top off a new box of fudge and began to divide with a knife. 'Gosh, Grahame, I don't see why you haven't been doing things for the magazines. I should think you'd be breaking out all over Cambridge. In print, I mean.' He slipped Grahame's portion on to a plate and carried it tactfully to Grahame's food cupboard.

He made no actual decision. He walked to the desk, took one of the stapled manuscripts out of the bottom drawer, and pushed it into Hardles's now empty hands.

'What's this?' Hardles stared down, as if the plate of fudge had reappeared, hideously transformed.

'Just a little thing of mine. I'd be interested to hear what you make of it.' And he was so relaxed that he began to hum; interrupting himself only to thank Hardles for his rations.

Hardles glanced down at the manuscript again, in alarm; glanced towards the confidently humming figure in the chair, in embarrassment; and glanced towards the door, with nostalgia. Then he sat down and read. He came to the end of each page reluctantly, started a new one as if he feared it might be the last, and worked through the last one as if it were in assorted foreign languages. When he had finished he sat staring into his lap. 'I don't know—I mean, I can't judge things like this. But it's—*I think* it's terrific.'

The humming stopped. 'Do you? Do you now? You don't find it a bit facile, perhaps?'

'Facile?'

'Slick?'

'Slick?' He shook his head in bewilderment. 'It's very easy to read.'

'Exactly. That's it. Oh, I have *that* talent, of course.' He laughed at himself, in despair for having it. 'But can I *write*? *Really* write? Explore.'

'Oh!' Hardles picked up the sheets again. 'Can you explore?' He nodded. 'I don't know.'

'Neither do I, John, neither do I.'

And when he next held court in Hardles's room he was asked how his novel was going, and whether he'd consent to have it published. Endfer, who was playing a ninth clown or something in a college production of Shakespeare, and was consequently among them in a dunce's cap and rouge, wondered why he didn't turn his hand to the drama. 'John says your dialogue is absolutely brilliant.'

'Well, you see, David, the modern drama . . .' he explained.

He took his drink and walked to the window. 'And my talent for pastiche?'

'But I said your story was *super*. I said that too.'

'To us,' Craley said. 'He said it was super, and only that.'

'Well, it was. In its way.'

'In its way.' Craley shook his hair out of his eyes and raised the glass to his lips. 'Hazers was only teasing, you see.'

'But we don't want to be cosy with each other. That's what I said to him.' Hazings sat down with a joking flounce. 'We don't believe in cosiness.'

'Don't we, Hazers? Well then, what *do* we believe in. *You* tell us.'

He watched them with a satirical smile. His absence of a week had brought him back strengthened and quick. He had established his reputation in the rest of the college, and he was prepared at last to deal with any subtleties of talk and silence. Above all he had shown that he could hold himself aloof from Hazings until Hazings had come positively begging for his company. He was independent, and an equal. He would speak when he felt like it and taunt when he pleased. 'Well,' he turned to Stafford and indicated Craley with a laconic motion of the hand, 'what does the Crab believe in?'

'He believes in being, let's see,' Hazings skimmed the chair around, and stopped opposite Craley with a crack of heels, 'in being scientific. He doesn't go further than that.'

'There *is* nothing further than that,' Craley explained, with a grin at Stafford.

'Isn't there?' And Hazings slid off his chair to his knees and began to whisper to Craley—presumably to tell him that there *was* something further than that, and to describe it to him.

'How's your writing going, Staff?'

'Writing?'

'I thought you wrote poems. Somebody said.'

'Somebody.' Stafford shifted his eyes to where Hazings was murmuring up into Craley's face in imitation of an Edwardian wooer; and Craley was nibbling at the end of a large thumb and smiling around it, in imitation of a Mafia gangster. 'Him, you mean?'

'Well, yes, it might have been Hazers. So you don't write poems?' But the ironic control was leaking away from him. There was something more than mere pantomime going on in the centre of the room; there was something more than mere amusement in Stafford's steady smile. It occurred to him that he had never exchanged a sentence with Stafford in isolation before, and that of the three mysteries, Stafford was easily the most mysterious. He tried to return Stafford's smile with a smile of his own, but the round, delicate face remained impassive. Stafford's smile was decoration, and his eyes, unwinking, dreamed out at him.

'Don't you write poems then?'

'Not as I imagine you write prose.' He shifted his feet slightly, so that the soles of his canvas shoes were resting against Grahame's thighs. 'Not in your way.'

'I see.' He would have laughed if he hadn't checked himself with a constriction of his chest. He struggled casually up and turned. 'What way *do* you write them in?'

Stafford stirred beneath him. 'Can't you guess?' His voice was very low and private, as if deliberately.

He braced himself, stopped another laugh, and spoke. He didn't really know what he was saying. All he knew was that there were things to be said between Stafford and himself, and that any moment there would be an interruption and his chance would be gone. There were things to be said, that would bring out the sudden excitement in him that he had, at all costs, to suppress. 'You're very close to Craley. Close to Hazers too, but closer to Craley. The Crab,' he whispered.

'Close to Jonathan? I see. Do you think we're too close? Does it worry you that we're always together?' Stafford moved again, languidly, and stared up at the face above him, that was turned away from him. 'Does it', he said distinctly, 'make you feel neglected?'

'Neglected? No, of course not. No.' He wanted to look down directly, into the dark, unashamed eyes, but the murmurs from the other side of the room reached his ears, warningly. He leant towards the window and pretended to inspect some figures in the court below. 'I mean, you've known each other for years, haven't you?' he whispered. 'And I suppose I'm only a well, don't know any of you. Not even Hazers, really.' He forced his eyes down. 'Not any of you.'

'What the hell do you want?' And now Stafford, too, was whispering. But it was a whisper that had nothing to do with embarrassment, or the fear of being heard. 'Are you *propositioning* me?'

141

Something very cold happened to his cheeks.

'Don't you know then, Thwaggers?'

He shook his head.

'Oh, I expect you do. Even if you've never said it, or felt it.'

'What?' And terribly, he laughed. 'No.'

'Not propositioning me? Or don't know what there is between us?'

He held himself in suspense. 'Between *us*?'

'Between Jonathan and me.'

'Oh, between, I see, the Crab.' And terribly, laughed again. The sound he made now wasn't quite a laugh but it was as noisy. 'The Crab.'

'And me.'

'Yes,' he said. 'No, I don't understand, actually.'

'Well, then it doesn't matter, does it? Especially as you're not propositioning me. Although you probably wouldn't know if you were. Would you, Thwaggers?'

It was as if there were a hand on him, of ambivalent intention. 'The thing is,' he began, with no ending in sight, and into a complete silence. He turned back in alarm and stared into the intruding face. The eyes were much smaller than he'd remembered, and the whole expression more dangerous.

'The thing is, I'm taking him off now.'

He nodded; and laughed.

Stafford, half blocked off by Craley, got up. 'Where, my dear?'

'I thought,' Craley was still peering into the laughing, disclaiming, apologetic face, 'I thought you wanted your weakly treat.'

'Oh, I do.' Stafford passed calmly towards the screens. 'Yes, please, and goody.'

'Baddy,' Craley said. 'Very baddy, Thwaggers.' And turning, went after his friend. But he caught one of the screens with his shoulder, and fell into Hazings' Winchester trap at last. Not, however, that it appeared to matter, for although the screen swayed and then crashed to the ground behind him, he went on towards the door and out of the room. His footsteps on the stairs sounded through Hazings' high laughter, but where they went to was a mystery, at least to Grahame, who had hurried back to the window, to watch the couple cross the court. There was only one person in his vision, and that was Endfer, dressed in clown's gear and smiling to the world at large.

'You have to be careful with those two, old chap,' Hazings said, as he arranged the screens to leave a slightly narrower channel. 'Very careful.'

'Careful.' He stepped away from the window and stood negligently by Craley's chair. 'What of?'

'Well, you see, the Staff's fantastically clever. That's what we adore in him. He's much cleverer than the Crab, at the thing that matters.'

'The thing that matters?'

'Oh, at catching people like the Crab. And poor Jonathan is always frightened,' he drifted around the room, arms extended, 'that he's less clever at keeping them, Grahame. The Staff's fancies worry him.'

'I see,' he said. 'I see.'

'Do you really? Do you? I said you did.'

But he really didn't; at least completely. He saw that there was something between Craley and Stafford that he didn't see; and he saw that Hazings knew about it and probably had a part in it; he saw also that he had been warned, by each of them in different ways. But what he wanted to see was what there might be between Stafford and himself, the thing that he had felt so strongly when talking to Stafford, and that Stafford had appeared to hint at, when talking to him. He wanted to see it so much that he was unable to concentrate on his history, and had that week to hand in an essay that was incomplete.

143

'I can scarcely believe it,' said the Marxist supervisor to whom he had had to return for two weeks. 'Are you having a go, then, and *actually* taking a risk?'

'Yes,' he replied politely. 'There *were* a lot of problems. I thought I'd better go into them carefully, before committing myself.'

But he had no chance to commit himself. Whenever Craley saw him moving towards Stafford on the window seat he would begin to talk in a loud, emphatic voice; while Hazings would advance fluently with his whisky bottle; and in the resulting confusion of badinage and intimacies, the opportunity would be gone. Hazings often referred to their little circle, but to Grahame he seemed very good at making it a large one, all surface contact, all noise and jokes and quick retorts, and no conversations. Finally he began to suspect that Hazings shared Craley's determination to keep Stafford and himself apart, and despaired. Stafford's face and voice still rose before him when he was downstairs struggling with his work; but the face was averted and the voice still when he was upstairs, anxious to observe and to listen.

'You're coming up tonight,' Hazings said one evening before Hall. 'We've got a surprise on. You'll enjoy it.'

'He's bound to come,' Craley stared scornfully. He had had his hair cut and was wearing a dark suit, in honour of some convention known only to himself. 'Does he ever not?'

Grahame glanced quickly towards Stafford; who reclined indifferently, his lips pursed.

He went to his room and stayed there, struggling against his desire to climb the stairs. Twice he got up from his desk, and for long periods stared out of the window, across the Court. From above came the sounds of laughter, that had started shortly after he had closed the door on them; then the strains of a Mozart symphony leaked down, and the noise of voices raised against each other through it.

In the end he went out and hovered on the landing. He went up three stairs, revolved fiercely around, and went down and out across the Court, to Hall. He found a place next to Endfer, who was delighted to see him. But Endfer's bland ignorance was a torment, and throughout each course he was being tugged back to Hazings' room, or to his own room where, in an insinuating way and from below, he could make his absence felt.

After Hall he stood in the Court and looked up. The curtains were undrawn and there was no light—only the flickering glow of the coal fire. But he could make out the shadows to the sides of the windows, and could feel them, in his very nerves, standing in the rosy darkness and staring down at him. He went up the stairs and stood outside his room. He waited for a few minutes that grew to twenty for the noise of feet, but although he heard sounds they were soft and furtive. He tiptoed up the next flight and listened outside the door. Again he could make out faint sounds, rustles and whispers and suppressed laughter. He tiptoed down the stairs and into his room. He sat at his desk, his books spread, his eyes prickling, his whole being directed to the ceiling and its insults. They knew what he was going through, and were alert to every tremor of self-pity in him. He pushed his books away and got up. He walked around the room, picked up a letter from Din, and dropped it to the floor. Then he went softly out and crept up. Still there were no voices; just the infinitely louder sounds of people being quiet. He ran downstairs and out on to the path that led to the river.

About an hour later he stood by the fountain and looked at the various rooms, some darkened completely, some showing a light through chinks. He watched Hazings' room, and saw a slim silhouette, Stafford's, passing from

145

curtain edge to curtain edge. He went back to his room, rearranged his books, picked up his pen and began to work.

The knock he had been waiting for, to be indifferent to, sounded on his door just after breakfast.

'My God, we spent hours waiting for you. We were going to take you to a party in London.' Hazings was looking tousled and tired, and thus fractionally more glamorous than usual. 'Did you forget about our surprise?'

He controlled instantly the relief that flooded through him. 'Well, I had some work to do.'

'Work! But, God, you missed a superb party.'

'Did I?' He smiled pleasantly. 'Oh, yes? What a shame.'

'*Any*way, we got hold of some girls, if you like that sort of thing. And I must say *I* do. One's from London and sweet, and the other's from Newnham. She's smashing.'

'Really?' He stroked his hand over some pages and remembered his decision, made on the banks of the Cam in the lonely night. 'I'd better finish this.'

'Oh, God, Thwaggers, you must come,' Hazings hesitated. 'The thing is, the Crab thought you'd taken offence at something he said, but I knew you hadn't. You *couldn't* have, I said.'

'Taken offence.' He threw back his head and laughed. 'Taken offence? Whatever at?'

'The poor old Crab.' Hazings laughed back. 'He gets sensitive, you see.'

'He must do.'

'He does.'

But he stayed at his desk after Hazings had left until he had hardened his determination not to go up to Hastings's room that night, or ever again.

The smashing girl from Newnham was pale and plump,

146

had tangled dark hair that fell to her shoulders, and large green eyes that she preferred to keep half-shut. She wore tapered flannel trousers, a thick blue shirt, and boots that were both shorter than Hazings' and a great deal dirtier. She sat on the floor in front of the fire, with her ankles crossed, a cigarette hanging negligently from her lips, giving the impression that she had sat in a similar way in front of more sophisticated fires every evening of the week. She also gave the impression that she knew the reputations of everyone in the room, that they were impressive reputations, and that she wasn't at all impressed. She had large breasts that swung when she yawned, an infrequent smile, and an unabashed stare. She could make almost anyone feel awkward.

The person she was immediately engaged in making feel awkward was tall and slim, with a helmet of dark hair, bright brown eyes, and a bright, embarrassed smile. Jennie Haverstock was prettier than Sylvie Wasserman, and more fashionably dressed; she was evidently nicer than Sylvie Wasserman—she looked at people when they spoke to her, and demonstrated a positive interest in what they said; she was probably more talented than Sylvie Wasserman—she organized children's charity parties, and recited poetry at them, and was a gifted amateur painter; and she had more distinguished connections than Sylvie Wasserman, with an uncle who was Master of one of Cambridge's theological colleges, and a stepfather who was a Conservative M.P. for a fashionable constituency in the West Country. In fact she was better at everything than Sylvie Wasserman, except at being noticeable to Grahame, when someone like Sylvie Wasserman was in the same room with her.

'Yes, I like it.' Her eyes focused on Sylvie Wasserman with the intensity that goes with either profound calculation or inhibitions overcome, then moved to Hazings, who was standing between them with his hands in his pockets and his head cocked. 'I suppose I'm jolly lucky to have got it, really.'

'I'm sure you weren't,' Hazings contradicted. 'You're being modest, that's all. How *did* you get it?'

'Because of her voice.' Craley was sitting on the window seat, so close to Stafford that parts of them overlapped. He was staring at the two girls as if he were on the other side of the panes and eager to pass on. 'Because she's got a *preety* voice.'

'Well,' Jennie Haverstock stroked the tops of her silk-clad knees and laughed shyly around the room. 'I had to take some tests. To make sure I wouldn't frighten the children, probably.'

'Oh, I'm sure *you* wouldn't frighten children,' Sylvie Wasserman said from around her cigarette. She puffed smoke expertly down her nostrils and hunched her shoulders, method fashion. 'I have a friend who's played the guitar on television. I expect *he* frightens the children all right. He frightens most people.'

'Does he frighten you?' Craley asked, with a roll of his small blue eyes.

'Hardly.'

'Really? Why does he frighten most people then? Is he very nasty?'

Sylvie Wasserman, by way of response, studied him sarcastically; and was studied sarcastically back. Stafford, his hands clasped behind his own head and one elbow almost under Craley's, meditated serenely; and Hazings poured more drinks.

'He only does television for the money,' Sylvie explained eventually, to the fire. 'He's a pusher.'

'Pusher?' Craley frowned. 'That's a kind of peddler, isn't it?'

'Of course *you* like music?' Hazings revolved gracefully

148

around, darting a sharp glance at Craley *en route*, and finishing with a laugh that shared itself between the two girls. 'You must do.'

'Yes,' cried Jennie Haverstock, in the tone of one accepting an invitation. 'Love it.'

'Jazz,' said Sylvie Wasserman, in the tone of one refusing an invitation. 'Only.'

'Oh, God, no. Not jazz.' Hazings flung out his arms, appalled. 'Oh, God, no.' And as he patrolled the room with supple strides, and dismembered the cult of jazz; as he talked and walked and gestured and conferred, the expression of imperious boredom departed from Sylvie's face; the innocent stare and guileless smile of Jennie Haverstock turned into a speculative blankness. And from the window seat, where he accidentally cuddled Stafford, Craley grinned derisively; and from the same window seat, where he allowed himself to be cuddled, Stafford dreamed his dreams, which probably excluded Craley definitively; and from his hard-backed chair in front of the screens, with his head tilted forward so that it shouldn't rest against either the sportive dogs or the naked boys, Grahame watched closely. He was preparing himself.

And when the moment came (a fraction before, in fact, for Hazings was still rounding off an argument and bestowing a smile) he got to his feet and trod intelligently about, in defence of jazz. He ransacked his memory for Cranton's anecdotes about early deaths and Harlem violence, and if his facts were confused and his history ridiculous, he still managed to flourish his sentences off with an air of conviction that Hardles, at least, would have found convincing. It was thus some time before he noticed that the two girls were finding Hazings, static and gracefully listening, more rewarding than himself in emphatic flow.

'You don't know anything about jazz,' Craley informed

149

him, when he had come to a meaningless halt. 'So you might as well stop.'

'How do *you* know he doesn't?' Hazings turned, aflame, towards Sylvie Wasserman, who hadn't spoken. 'How does *he* know he doesn't?'

'I've never heard of Earl Buckley,' Sylvie said.

'By what he says,' Craley explained, 'he doesn't even know what it is.'

'But he doesn't have to know, to be articulate. Grahame's *always* articulate, even when he's ignorant. I think he's super. Don't you?'

Sylvie frowned; Jennie beamed; at Hazings' own superness.

'Anyway, it's time to go to dinner.' Craley rose in such a manner that Stafford was forced to rise with him. 'If we want to get to that Chink place.'

'Of course you're coming,' Hazings insisted to Sylvie Wasserman, who showed no sign of being likely to refuse. 'We can't have dinner without *you*.'

But they could have had dinner without *him*. He soon realized that. Their conversation ranged from one interesting Cambridge personality to the other, all of whom they seemed to have known for at least ten years; and it ranged mainly between Hazings and Sylvie Wasserman, with Jennie included for minor confirmations. He tried to engage Jennie in separate talk, but he couldn't distract himself from the sound of Hazings' voice, or the sight of Sylvie's face. Anyway, his careful aphorisms seemed to be completely wasted on Jennie, whose smiles and 'Ohs?' and unrelated laughs reminded him of Din with Hardles and Endfer, and finally he turned back to Hazings and Sylvie and attempted once again to break through. He stormed critically in ('Of course, I haven't seen it, but from what Hazers says . . .') on a film that they had, as it turned out, finished discussing; or fell into a sensitive trance when they talked of Cambridge writers, only to discover that there were other, prodigious talents at work in the colleges. Altogether they had no room, in their intimate exchange of preferences, for his dialectical displays or his unfashionable modesty. So he leant across Jennie, thus depriving her of the chance to be seen before being ignored, to Craley and Stafford, who were whispering about a man called Timmy that they had met in London. And he wondered, as he forced out an inopportune word here and an inconsequential anecdote there, what it was he had found exciting in Stafford and frightening in Craley. Their condescending manners were merely irritating. Everything was irritating. The four Chinese waiters, the food, the wine; particularly the company. Finally he turned away from Craley and Stafford and, lolling back in his chair, exposed his irritation to whomever might be polite enough to glance in his direction.

'Thwaggers, have some more wine. Pass Thwaggers the rice. He's not eating anything.' Hazings surrounded him with bowls of rice and sweet and sour, jugs of water and bottles of wine. And barricaded him off for good.

'I don't want anything,' he hissed, rather more loudly than he intended. But even so Hazings, leaning confidentially towards Sylvie Wasserman and offering to pop a crispie noodle into her mouth, pretended not to have heard. Although Grahame knew he had.

Hazings had got himself between the two of them, thus forcing him to walk on the extreme outside edge, in the gutter. But he held fast, for the alternative was either to walk just behind, by himself; or twenty yards behind, with Craley and Stafford.

'Well, how shall we do it?' Hazings slipped a hand under each of their arms and swung them playfully around.

He too swung around, although not playfully, and almost stumbled under the wheels of a bus.

'Are you all right, old chap?' And Jennie gave a little scream.

'Perfectly all right.' He stood facing them, with the chill of fear still on his cheeks. 'Do what?'

'See everyone home. Who should see whom where?'

The girls walked away to investigate the contents of a shop window. For a second they almost made a pair—the tall, elegant Jennie; the plump, sexual Sylvie—drawn together by their determination to have nothing to do with the discussion. For they both wanted the same thing, and were letting it be known by their refusal to negotiate.

He stared at the backs of their heads, stared into Hazings' face and explained down at the pavement that actually he had some work to do. 'I mean, if that's all right.'

Oh, it was, yes. Perfectly. Everyone else was going the same way. But it would have been. Perfectly. Even if they weren't. He could work *that* out. As he strode off down the street he could work out a number of other things, too. He could work out, for instance, that he had behaved appallingly. He could work out, also, that there was only one solution. He must see less of Hazings, and less, until Hazings had disappeared altogether.

He went straight back to his room and took out his books. He began to write, and to study passages, and to mark off a bibliography, and all the time he listened for the sounds of Hazings on the stairs. He would make Hazings feel, through the oak itself, the intensity of his dissociation. Hazings was over and done with. The little circle had lost its audience.

'Weren't they super?' Hazings cried, from the threshold. He hadn't bothered to knock; which was fortunate for him, as the sound would have fallen on deaf ears. 'Isn't *she* super?'

'She's all right.' He indicated his books with his hand. 'Look, I'm afraid——'

'*All right?*' Hazings advanced into the room until he was directly under a light that would expose the patch of red on one of his narrow cheeks. 'She's gorgeous. And the other one's very interesting too, in her way. Didn't you think?'

'She's very quiet. She seemed shy to me.' He eyed the triumphant cheek. 'Look, I really must——'

'Oh, she was probably frightened of you. All that jazz of hers. God, what a marvellous evening.' He stood grinning under the light, clicking the heels of his boots together and soundlessly clapping his hands, while Grahame worked out one other thing. That he had misunderstood the situation entirely.

'Well,' he said finally, and trying not to let anything show. 'The Crab and the Staff didn't seem to enjoy them much.'

'I should hope not, indeed. They were busy enjoying each other. And between you and me, the Crab was delighted that you were interested in the Wasserman.'

'Interested?' He denied it with his expression, his gesture towards his books.

'Well, I thought you were, from the way you were behaving. Playing it cool, in the Wasserman's idiom. That's why I kept bringing you together.'

He saw her as in dreams, hunted softly around her, wrote novels and made public speeches for her benefit; humiliated Hazings in a battle of wits (that concluded in fisticuffs) and had it out with Stafford and Craley that they were what they were, the screeney wankers. He directed a film, and conducted an opera; was the most famous young man in England. He did everything he could to win her except send her a letter or go around to Newnham to see her. For

L   153

a week or so he hoped that they would bump into each other on the street, and consequently spent a great deal of his time drifting poetically along the pavements. But when he did see her she was with a small man with a crew-cut, a long, pale face and an air of inscrutable suffering. She recognized him though, and acknowledged his indifferent nod with an indifferent frown. So in the end he did his best to usher her disdainfully out of his consciousness, and get on with his work.

Hazings, on the other hand, turned his pursuit of Jennie Haverstock into a public spectacle. He rang her up every evening, sometimes went down to London to take her out —Delbario's and a ballet—and persuaded her to come to Cambridge to visit her uncle at week-ends. He wrote her letters, parts of which he read out in the evening, and in other ways made her a by-proxy member of the little circle. When he let slip—a gay indiscretion that caused her cheeks to flame sweetly—that they were sleeping together, Grahame realized that no, she didn't fascinate him, but he would give anything to fascinate someone like her, in the Hazings' manner, in lieu of Sylvie Wasserman. So he did his best to usher *her* out of his consciousness, and get on with his work. But he seemed to have ushered so much out of his consciousness that he had nothing left to work with. He approached his desk from a sense of duty, plodded mechanically through his books and produced his little essays, that were only a trifle less perfect than before for being a trifle more mechanical. He knew that he had got the examination trick, and that all he had to do was to feed himself the right amount of information. But he no longer took pleasure in his mastery. Thus if he had no fears, he also had no interests. He had only his intellectual habits and his desires, and too much time. He went more and more to the films in the early evening, before Hall, usually by himself, sometimes with Hardles and Endfer, and he

154

hungered. Once he tried to write a short piece about Cranton, but he gave it up. He felt he made Cranton seem dead. Which, of course, he was.

All the other girls had pink complexions, wore brightly coloured party dresses, and talked in loud voices. Sylvie Wasserman was wearing tapered flannel trousers, black boots, a grey polo-necked sweater, and wasn't talking at all. She was leaning against the wall near the door, staring with bold boredom over the shoulder of her host. Who was clutching a glass of sherry, from which he took hurried sips, gazing desperately into her immobile face, and laughing. Apparently—at least this was Grahame's interpretation of Hardles's account—Borning had met Sylvie at a party in London, got on with her like a house on fire, and had decided to repeat the conflagration before witnesses. Well, as Grahame chuckled to Hardles, Borning was certainly making a *spectacle* of himself, though the only flames were in his cheeks. Surely no man, even of the long-toothed, small-eyed, chinless variety, had ever laughed so much and looked so miserable. ('But I thought you *liked* Borning,' Hardles said.)

Borning would probably have stood laughing until the last guest had gone home (although he would have gone reluctantly, with a mental shaking of the fists) if he hadn't jerked the contents of his glass down the front of his cream sports jacket. A girl from a nearby group, who had been studying him with eyes at once compassionate and vindictive (a neighbour from Hampstead Garden Suburb, Hardles communicated) came to his aid. She positioned herself directly in front of Sylvie Wasserman, to eliminate her temporarily from the party, and mopped at Borning with her handkerchief. Then she led him by the hand to another corner of the room, and flirtatiously forced him to remove his jacket for further attention. Sylvie

Wasserman, restored to the party but abandoned, widened her plump lips, rapped her glass against her thigh, and let her eyes rest on a supercilious face that was peering discreetly at her from behind many shoulders. She identified the face—presumably from a previous context; and possibly its expression from her previous experience. She had only to raise her glass and nod. She did so.

The supercilious face withdrew, reappeared, withdrew. The mind behind it blurred. The heart beneath it sank.

'But what about old Borning?' Hardles wondered, as he observed his dearest friend with innocent eyes. But a glance in Borning's direction was enough to establish that he had come ablaze somewhere else. He was in his shirt-sleeves, doing something comical with his striped braces.

He took her glass and lingered over the drinks table, mixing a little from any bottle that came to hand with the quarter of an inch of dregs that were already there; and hoped that reinforcements would arrive while his back was turned. But she was still by herself. Somehow more by herself than ever. The room was crowded except for the space around her.

He stepped into the arena and prayed for inspiration.

It came. His first remark, that Borning ('known in the college as Boring') gave more parties than people could be bothered to go to, provoked an accomplice's smile. His next, that life in Cambridge would be tolerable if it weren't for the tolerance, moved her to agreement. 'Check.' From there, with no hesitations and a diminishing nervousness, he proceeded to a kind of analysis that two minutes earlier he had believed himself incapable of. He was satirical about the men, their clothes, voices, intellectual capacities. 'John Hardles, Old Johnnie, is charming, don't you think? Do you know him? Well, he is. Very. No, no, I mean it. Although', he made a movement with his cigarette, part of his plunder from Hardles's London-based uncle, 'he's really just a mathematical gland with a smile on top. Borning's main talent is for being ignored. He and Endfer —have you met him? You must. As a *type*. He and Bornings are always having coffee with friends. The sort of people no one minds having around, but no one would dream of 'phoning up.'

'So they 'phone each other up?'

'Well, they have each other around.'

'You really hate them.' She frowned into her glass—as well she might. Even for her, who had drunk much life to its dregs, the mixture was enterprising. Vodka, gin, tonic water, sweet sherry and cidrax. 'God, you *mix* a drink. Really hate them, don't you?'

'You like my brew? So glad. No, I adore them, actually. In a way.' He groped within his bag of treasures and found another aphorism that dispatched the Hampstead Garden Suburb girl into limbo, and then one more that polished Hazings—who wasn't at the party—off the face of the earth. After a time he could take in the effect they were having on the party as a whole. Out of the corner of his eye, as he went on in his devastating new manner, he could detect people looking at him out of the corners of their eyes. He was sure that their conversation was providing conversation for all the other couples in the room. In fact, to himself, he went further—there *were* no other couples. Only paired spectators.

But though small dreams began to unfurl, he couldn't look at her; in case the desire should show, and the dreams be blighted. He exited finally on a mordant pun that cloaked a timid invitation.

'Who?' He'd been sitting stiffly at his desk, forcing his mind off the next hour.

'Sylvie. She *is* interesting, isn't she? Did I tell you Jennie and I met her on the train after *Swaggers Laggers*?

'No, you didn't. Anyway I'm only seeing her for lunch.'

'Marvellous. Yes, she was telling us about that jazz man. Of course she could hardly keep off him, under the circumstances. I think it's very touching. Don't you?'

'What?'

'Her knowing so much about jazz. I find it moving, really. Yes, moving.'

'Why?'

'Because of Toby Moss, of course.'

'Toby Moss.' He shook away, with a twist of his head, a vision of the crew-cut man with the suffering face. 'What Toby Moss?'

'Oh, God. The man who was sent down for smoking reefers in King's Chapel last term.'

'Sent down?'

'Yes. They said he wasn't happy here. Anyway you're much better for her than Toby Moss.' He went to the door. 'Look—good luck, old chap.'

'What for?'

But Hazings had gone.

She told him about Toby Moss over lunch in a coffee bar in King's Parade. She spoke calmly, in her low, nasal voice, but she smoked heavily and smiled bitterly. Smoked and smiled, not at Toby Moss, not quite at herself. At, oh Christ, the way things went.

For she had been very innocent, kind of thing. She had slept with Toby, why? Because he had told her that people in Cambridge, men and women, women and women, men and men, slept with each other. Except for the drags. (Besides, he had acted with such speed, such mumbling eloquence, along with a bout of tears and a horrifying tantrum, that she had felt it her duty.) 'It was a funny thing about Toby,' she smiled and exhaled, 'everything *he* wanted to do was *my*, I don't know, duty? Because I'm a woman?

But, Christ, he could be charming. Toby was a charmer.'
This was the refrain. Through the long account of Toby's
addictions (he had prepared himself for the second assault
with a stick of weed) emotional somersaults (and thus not
been able to go through with it) unfortunate paralyses of
will—'Clever? Not First clever, examination clever. But
the cleverest, no, you know, most *intelligent* man I've ever
met? And on the *trumpet*"—he remained simply, charming.
Like a baby. Crying himself to sleep on her breasts (which
stirred reminiscently) buying her presents, was, oh Jeee-
zuz, charming. Know what she meant? (He did. He said so.)
But Toby thought *everyone* was a drag, except a few friends
in London. 'He would have thought', with a wry puff of
smoke into his face, 'that *you* were a drag. Just because of
meeting me in a dark suit and polished boots and—is that
really an old school tie?' Oh (she toyed with her coffee
spoon), she was glad she'd told him all this. It was the first
time, to anyone. *Any*one. ('So', he thought, 'Hazings lied.')
And perhaps, if anything should, know what she meant?
Start? Well, she was *conventional* (the smile on her lips, the
shaking of her blouse, refuted her).

His fingers, which had prevaricated between his cup, his
spoon and the sugar-bowl, scampered sideways and settled
like a friendly toad on the back of her wrist. A swift movement, as with a couple table-wrestling, and their hands
were locked together. 'Yes,' he said hoarsely, 'we can start
afresh.'

'Check.'

Well, not actually quite, as it turned out, afresh. If Toby
Moss never appeared, he continued to hover in an oddly
persistent way in the background. He wrote letters and
even at intervals sent cables, the yellow envelopes of which
she would display, but the precise contents of which she
couldn't reveal. She wondered several times an evening
where he had gone, what he was doing, and whether he

really missed her as much as he claimed. But if his presence was a tantalizing mystery, his past was soon an open book. She took Grahame over it many times during the next week —from the first enchanted encounter in the blues and smoked-filled room in Corpus, when he had been sick; to the final, agonizing parting in the Waffle, when he had been very tearful—she piled on the details and elaborated the theme.

He envied Toby Moss, for having put her through so much. He hated Toby Moss for continuing to put her through so much. But really he was convinced that his own sympathy would in the end be more appealing than Toby Moss's extravagances, and that he himself would contribute a new, possibly the definitive, chapter to her saga. Oh, oh, he would soon possess her future as he now, indirectly but intensely, possessed her past. And the way she buried her large, pale face in his shoulder when they walked together; or offered her hand when they talked together, encouraged him to believe that their time was nearly come. For one thing she whispered that she couldn't well, imagine her life without him? For another, she no longer apologized for boring him with her confessions—went straight into them without preamble. For a last thing, everyone else— Hazings, Craley, Stafford; Hardles and Endfer—all showed in their different ways that they knew a great passion was unfolding itself behind his oak door.

Thus he listened to Sylvie's intimate documentations with patient sympathy, and refused to wonder whether so much information might not be getting in the way of a deeper knowledge. He bided his time.

Until he could abide it no longer. For Sylvie, who had succumbed convulsively to Toby, gave the impression of hanging back a little with Grahame. She seemed never to be at ease until she had got down to the main purpose of their meeting. After a fortnight he was as familiar with the twists and turns of the Moss affair as she was herself—he could, occasionally, have limited an exaggeration or pointed out a contradiction—and it began to dawn on him, even in his loyal adoration, that he was merely the means of enriching her old relationship. When she wasn't looking he would go on little excursions of his own—over the line of plump thigh in her trousers, down the drooping curves of her breasts against her shirts, across the swell of her belly —and to himself he made unambiguous gestures. 'Tomorrow', a Lawrence voice said within him, as he escorted her back to the Newnham gates, 'I'll do *some*thing,' and he would gaze through the iron railings, across the black space, to the row of lights that marked the bedrooms.

But the next day there was always some detail, some sharp fragment of unnecessary reality, like the coffee mugs, or the angles at which they sat to each other, or the bells that tolled curfew, to make an impetuously life-enhancing approach impossible.

He sprang forward, indifferent to the splash of coffee on to his trousers, or the splintering of pottery immediately after. He flung an arm around her shoulder, as if to prevent himself from falling to his death, and crammed his nose and mouth against her cheek.

There was a moment of heavy breathing, of amazed tussling; before she erupted through his clutch and went wheeling across the room. He stood for a second, babbling apologies, and drawing breath. Then he was on her again, pantherine.

She stood sedately still as he plunged his tongue towards her sealed mouth, and pummelled his hands against her tautened buttocks. He was on the edge of ecstasy.

'I thought,' she said, forcing her face away from his, 'that you cared for me.'

'Care for you?' he whispered. 'Care for you? Oh, Sylvie.'

161

She slapped his arms away. 'Thought at least,' and blew a tendril of hair out of the corner of her mouth, 'thought at least you *under*stood.'

'Understand? Oh, Sylvie.'

'But you just want what *Toby* wanted. Oh, *no*.'

'What Toby wanted?' He took three steps backwards and raised a hand to his chest. 'I'm not Toby, Sylvie.' Which, as every passing second showed, he certainly wasn't.

She came towards him slowly, rubbing her hands down the seams of her trousers. 'Did I misunderstand? Did I?'

'Yes,' he said, grasping at the straw that would drown him. 'I just wanted to comfort you. I couldn't hurt *you*. Oh, Sylvie.'

She touched him searingly on the cheek. 'Couldn't you?'

'No, Sylvie, no.'

And smiled. 'Check.'

So, and fortunately, within five minutes they had developed a new relationship, based on sensitivity and respect for each other. He was so understanding (her compliment) so compassionate (her compliment), so piffling, piddling, pathetic (his compliments).

The next evening she came tragically through the door and stood with her back to it, her expression sacrificial. He saw at once that he was about to be rejected, but before he could pour out another stream of promises and accusations, she came flowing towards him, to collapse, all sweet smells (except for a hint of hamburger which she had heated on her gas-ring and eaten for her supper) against him. They sat on the window seat that evening with their arms around each other, talking again in trembling voices of the incident that had nearly driven them apart but had, in fact, brought them closer together. He was, she said, so intelligent about people.

A few evenings later she permitted him to fumble her

out of her blouse. Three evenings after that, out of her trousers. Their times followed the old pattern, but with a coda added. The knickers and bra never came off, naturally, although they figured in the ever-expanding revelations about Toby, who after all had removed them with consequences that if sometimes blissful were mainly ghastly. 'I hurt and hurt and bled? You know? I couldn't go through that again—and Toby was a, well,' (grimly exhaling) 'expert.'

She would stretch out on the window seat and lower the bra an inch or two. The great white breasts were there for the stroking, if you were Toby Moss. The tailored white knickers could be peeled down rolling hips, suave thighs; if you were Toby Moss.

'Oh, Sylvie,' sighed Grahame Thwaite.

'I love it when you cuddle me,' she sighed back. 'Love it.'

He paid no attention to the stuffiness in his nostrils, his itching skin, or his headache. He scrambled up on to his altar and worshipped the mysteries.

A doctor, just qualified, if he wanted to know. She had met him at Hammersmith during the Jewish holiday. He was, yes, a friend of her cousin's. She'd only asked him to come up from politeness.

'But do you have to spend the whole day with him?'

Jeesus, she could hardly send him away. Now could she?

'The evening, *too*?'

Well, she'd have to look after him until he got his train. Now wouldn't she?

'But you've never once let *me* in your room in Newnham. You said it was forbidden.'

Yes, but he had a room—just look at his room! There was no *point* in asking him to her room, was there? Now was there? 'Check?'

She didn't come around the following night either. Her note said she'd had to go to Hammersmith for something Jewish. She would see him when she got back. Wouldn't she?

Check.

No, Grahame. Not tonight. She didn't know, well, she had a headache, and her nose was blocked. She thought, from the way her skin itched, that she had 'flu coming on. She didn't want to give *him* 'flu. Now did she? So she'd just go home and see him soon—'check?'

Check.

She had been, oh Jesus, dreading this scene. Dreading the thought of hurting him. 'No, Grahame, don't. No, darling Grahame, it's no *good*.'

'It's that medical student. Isn't it?'

Doctor actually. Anyway she hadn't see him more than a few—what?—well, if it was any of his business, four times. But it wasn't him. No, it was simply that she realized there was no hope, somehow no hope, no don't, no, I know, dear Grahame, I know. But she had to tell the truth. She had been thinking about it all the time. She hated pain.

'You'll see *him* again though. Won't you?'

Grahame. She must be free to live her own life. Mustn't she? Now mustn't she?

'But I love you. Oh Sylvie, oh Sylvie, oh . . .'

She burst into tears.

And so he comforted her through the ordeal of her confession and walked her back to Newnham through the poignant darkness. He held her hand as they walked and tried to think of words that would describe his feelings. But no words came. He saw as in a vision the doctor who had won her, and knew him to be a very fine man. What chance had *he*, what chance had he *ever*, with a girl like Sylvie?

He did see her a couple of times, but it was only to have the same conversation with the same conclusion. She met her doctor most week-ends in her home in Hammersmith, and stopped coming to his room. So check to Grahame; and mate, the following September, to Nathan Hornstein, M.D.

Even Hardles was capable of being hurt. 'Well, I *was* with you when you met her.'

He went to the window and stared out across the Court to where the fountain sparkled in the sunlight. 'As a matter of fact,' he said formally, 'we're not seeing each other at the moment. We thought it would be better.' He put his hands behind his back, and then slipped one of them into his pocket, to touch the crumpled note asking him not to write again, for Nathan's sake. 'Just at the moment.' He fixed on Hardles a look that warned against further questioning, but Hardles, patting his moppet's mop and studying his snub-nosed shoes, had no need to be warned.

'I'm sorry,' he mumbled, as if at the news of a death. 'I didn't know.'

He turned mannishly around. 'Between you and me, John,' he said, 'she was becoming a bit of a drag.'

'Drag? I see.' And a few minutes later was in Endfer's room. 'David, what does that word, drag, mean?'

Which was how, with Hardles and Endfer, and through them with the college as a whole, he enhanced his reputation. From being a man who had been having an affair with Sylvie Wasserman, who had an affair with the notorious Toby Moss ('He tried to make out it was incense, but they found the reefers in his pocket') he became the man who had broken off an affair with Sylvie Wasserman because she was a bit of a drag.

'Do you think so? I must say, *I* don't. I thought she was a smashing girl, in her way. Perhaps she's afraid of you, because you're—you're too many things, Thwaggers. Now this Nathan chap, is he a Jew? Of course Jews stick together, don't you think?' But you're very attractive too, you know. Jennie said so, and the Staff.'

'What do you mean?'

'Nothing, only well, we met her on the train again the other night and she said she felt sorry—but probably she was just putting a good face on it. Nathan certainly looked Jewish. Sensitive and tough. Jennie thought he was gorgeous. He bought us some gins and was pretty sharp with Sylvie about something. Jennie says they're sleeping together. It sticks out a mile, to a woman. *Is* he a Jew?'

'Sleeping together?' His voice cracked contemptuously through the room, to startle a seventy-six-year-old German lady who was touring in the Court below. 'He's welcome. She's terrible in bed.'

Craley bought a Monopoly set, and they played for hour after hour. They had small bets on the game, which added to its excitement. Grahame always lost, five shillings, seven shillings and sixpence, once or twice as much as a pound. But it was worth it. The concentration and tension created by every roll of the dice obliterated his boredom. He went to the cinemas before Hall, did very little work, and had dreams.

It took him many nights, though, to get the girl tied to the post. The first few times she managed to break free, perhaps reading the intention in his eyes, or noticing the coils of rope that hung out of his pockets. But on this occasion there was a blank line between approaching her on the beach, beneath the swooping Haglers that were really gulls, and looping the cord around her wrists. Yes, she was completely and exactly tethered, but happily very gymnastic—sometimes presenting him with her narrow back (although she was plump), sometimes with her neat, protected breasts before which her fair hair wavered. But he was strong and swift, and gentle and good, and only bound her and gagged her to teach her his love; and later he took her to his room in College, folded pleasantly double by ropes in a sack, and chained her to the ends of his bed. She begged him to let her go, although deeply she wanted to stay chained to his bed, being loved and punished by him. So she stayed, stayed tethered and loving, bound and beautiful, stayed spreadeagled and adored until he expelled her with a sigh of shame, the screeney wanker; and there was only the Cambridge morning breaking around his head and the despair of another day.

'Isn't there *anyone* called Sylvie? Perhaps he was teasing me.'

'*You* know Endfer.' He passed her the sugar. 'One of those Cambridge things. Anyway we're not seeing each other any more.'

'Oh, what a shame, Dodie. She sounded very nice.' She sat waiting for more, but with a shrug and a laugh he consigned Sylvie to the cupboard of finished business, along with all the other Cambridge things; and thus made Din, in spite of her new stylishness in clothes (a tight grey dress and black stockings) and hair-do (swept back to emphasize the high brow and the neat features), look deprived and gauche.

Nevertheless she demonstrated at Hardles's party that evening that she had found a public manner to go with her unlikely elegance. They were in different corners of the room, but from his fleeting glimpses he could see that she was finding lots of people to talk to, lots of jokes to laugh at, and perhaps even one or two to tell. She had changed. But he didn't find out how much, for it never occurred to

167

him to ask. Besides, he had Endfer and Borning in front of him, to destroy with his irony; and glass after glass of sherry in his hand to help exalt him.

He was, in fact, exalted into an abrupt and astonishing confession. 'Yes,' he said, as they walked to the station, 'that part of it was fine. I suppose *that's* what held us together. We had *that*, kind of, between us,' he glanced at her, but her cool smile told him nothing. He remembered, though, how she had animatedly laid a hand on Endfer's shoulder, and later taken a piece of grit out of Hardles's eye. 'Then there came a point when it wasn't enough. Nothing.' He bent his head sorrowfully. A phrase, read somewhere, heard somewhere—perhaps from Sylvie herself, about Toby Moss—sprang into his mind and out of his mouth. 'We went round and round and round, in sexual circles, Din.' His eyes swivelled towards her, in alarm, but still she walked impassively beside him. He recalled what she had said of her script-writing boss, and the increase in sophistication it implied, and her silence goaded him into a more pungent analysis of the ghastly situation he had hungered for. If he had spent many evenings futilely contemplating the defence around Sylvie's loins, the tantalizing mesh at her breasts, if then he had fallen back in awe before such seductive prohibitions—now, now in the agony of his remorse he was able to rip them sadistically off. 'I must have been mad, mad, mad,' he shrilled. 'I had no respect for her. Every night, Din. *Every* night, the same.'

She stopped. Her narrow face, turned directly towards his, was tinted a weird yellow by the glare of an overhanging sodium light. 'Where did you do it?'

'What?'

'Did you', she asked coldly, 'do it in your room in College. The one *I* was in?'

'Well,' he threw out his hand to disclaim everything, and perhaps accidentally gave the impression that he was indicating a spot near by, a private garden or the gutter. '*You* know how these things are, Din? What you were saying about that man Larry? *You* know?'

'I said Larry was sordid.' She started up the street.

'It *was* sordid,' he admitted, when he caught her up. 'I know that now.'

She walked steadily on, staring ahead towards the bulk of the station. Her heels clicked smartly on the pavement, her handbag swung indifferently between them, and she would not see that he was lonely, and needed her sympathy. But on the platform, just before getting into the train, she looked at him. She examined him with her small clear eyes, and then with a sound that was like a sob, she put her arms around him and pressed her cheek against his.

He went back to the College, forgiven.

He lay curled in bed in the mornings with his sheets pulled over his eyes to fend the daylight off; or bunched over himself at night, his wrist pumping out his favourite dreams. But other dreams intruded. Mr. Burnlow, his hands bound and a pink handkerchief gagged into his mouth, floated by in a coffin. Cranton chained to a bench in the cloisters. House Master popping smoke out of his flies. He could not trust his dreams.

He missed his lectures, spent about an hour in the library (most of it having coffee in the canteen), bluffed his supervisors with talk of solitary revisions, and waited for the cinemas to open. He would settle into the lapping darkness, and light up a cigarette. Around him would be the other single shapes, middle-aged men with coughs, old ladies who made whistling noises between their teeth, a few housewives who crackled the paper on their boiled sweets and whispered across the rows. The sound of any close presence brought him irritably back to where he was, and eventually he would have to move to the front, in isolation.

Then he could be comfortable, with his cigarettes and his matches on his lap, and from two to four hours of self-negation before him. He was particularly fond of Westerns, thrillers, pirate adventures or horror films; any in which girls were victims and captives, bound and gagged, lashed, locked, tethered by leather. Some Saturdays he went up to London especially to see a film, the gaudy advertisements or hostile reviews of which seemed promising.

He would hurry back after a drink in a pub, or have a quick dinner in Hall, and then saunter up to Hazings' room, for Monopoly. The intricate commerce of the little circle was no longer magic to him. He understood at last that the only sophistication had been his own, which he had brought to it in his confusion, from his Windhoven and Morton background. There was no mystery except that of habit. They were friends, all of them, and needed each other. But their gestures and language had coarsened with the gambling, which gave them opportunity only to make remarks about each other's play, exchange compliments and contrast tempers. Hazings lost gracefully or disgracefully, as the mood took him—flinging his papers across the table and swearing, or congratulating the winner on his properties. 'Superb. Brilliant. I wish I had *your* luck.' Jennie played on Saturday evenings and there would be scenes between them. 'For Christ's sake, why didn't you buy it? You'd have stopped him getting the yellows. Look at those hotels. Just look at them.' It was part of their baffling public manner that Jennie didn't mind, and anyway a second later and with a smile, Hazings would make it up, and even somehow use his rudeness to do credit to both of them. It was feverish, a waste of time. They were turning into ridiculous little addicts—as Craley said, as Hazings said, as Grahame said. And as even Stafford, the consistent winner, said.

But then Stafford and Craley worked hard in the mornings, and Hazings laboured far into the night. They were all men with two Firsts, who were determined to get one more. This was the principal bond between them, their ambition and superiority. So Grahame knew that they would despise him if they guessed what he did during the day, and to prevent their doing so he made jokes at their expense that showed he had their measure and despised them back. He tried to avoid Hardles and Endfer, but they would still drop in, generally after lunch. To them he remained the critic and intellectual, a Major Scholar in History, a Master Mind. And for their benefit, and from a fear that they too would see through him, he played the role. He sucked on Hardles's mother's fudge and allowed his powers full rein. There wasn't a book or a film, not a College celebrity (including and especially Hazings), that he didn't arrow with his wit. But in the evenings, after Monopoly, he would go for a walk, around the Courts, through the Cloisters, to the river. There, on a little bridge that linked the banks, with the Cam moving silently beneath him, and the lights from the ancient buildings faint in the gathered mists, he faced up to what he had become; and determined to purge himself. He would begin again. Tomorrow he would begin again. Tomorrow. Shoulders braced, he strode back to purity tomorrow.

That Easter the winds swept across the Morton beaches and the rains fell continuously. Tarred gulls were sunk into the sands, then tugged back by the hungry tides. A rowing-boat overturned and two hoteliers were drowned. The Admiral, his shrouded finger jammed between his teeth, took the definitive step into madness; Bella left for London after a gruesome exchange with her employer about some missing brandy; Mrs. Holydrake issued quietly out of sleep and into death; and in Brighton Miss Hagler was put on probation for shoplifting.

171

'What does he do then?' the Colonel wondered. 'Up there all day?'

'My dear Basil, *I* don't know what he does.' Recently she had been plagued by headaches which neither Dr. Blander nor common sense could dispel. 'I expect he's working for his exams. Far away in a world of his own.'

The second of these suppositions was correct. He was at that very moment lurching up and down in his bed, a gagged maiden concealed behind his eyelids. But he was only a screeney wanker in his own room. In the nursery he wrote to Hazings and Hardles, trenchant indictments of the former to the latter, and violent manifestos against the stagnancy of Morton to both. The rest of the time he held himself aloof, in brainy dignity; or turned the pages of a set text with listless fingers.

One night there was a storm. The wind collapsed the empty chicken coop, and the rain washed at the roots of the apple tree, then swirled through the garden into the rising marsh; while inside Mallows a pale face pressed against a window-pane, and shamed eyes yearned towards the cleansing sea. Tomorrow he would begin again. To-morrow.

She was sitting perched on a stool with the knees of her long legs (encased in white jeans) pressed together, rather as if she had just caught an invisible object in her lap. Her wide mouth was smiling politely, perhaps out of respect to the soft music that gushed from boxes on the walls, or to the many voices whispering around her. Occasionally she adjusted the black rubber raincoat, her dearest possession, that hung from her shoulders like a cape, then tugged at the neck of her black sweater (new, and bought on borrowed money). She had dark, closely-cut hair, and large, slanting green eyes, and would probably have been the prettiest girl in the pub even if she hadn't been the only girl in the pub.

His heart leapt in despair—at her, because she sat so near, and yet had nothing to do with him; at himself, because he sat so far away, and was so helpless. He took a sip of his Scotch and gazed across the room to where two delicate men in blouses and woollen trousers appeared to be exchanging telephone numbers, then eased himself back, by way of a particular scene in *Prey of Dracula*, to his essay. He lingered there an instant, before his eyes started forth again. Yes, her small buttocks bulged firmly against the white cloth, and would be warm against the false red leather of the stool. She had been led through the dungeons by a rope around her neck, wrists lashed; bound to a table, feet tethered by thongs, shirt ripped, skirt sliced; Dracula Thwaite, teeth protruding, ran his hands suavely, grinned, kissed. Dracula Thwaite tied her, lashed her, tethered her.

The mouth was wide and gagged. The green eyes suppli-
cated. He was boss.

The green eyes moved and stared directly into his. The
wide mouth parted. He tried to crouch quickly back into
himself, to conceal the rope that was burgeoning damply.
'Six-fifteen actually.'

'Fifteen?'

'Or a minute or two fast.'

'Thank you.'

'Not at all. I'm sure I'm right.' He leaned forward and
spoke a sentence, the meaning of which was swept away by
a sudden gust of violins.

'What?' She swung about and stared solemnly into his
face—his courteous, civilized Cambridge face. 'Sorry.
What?'

'No, I was just wondering if you were waiting for somebody actually.' And gesturing ridiculously, prepared an
apology.

'This friend', she said, 'is a bit strong. I *mean*, he arranges
to meet me in queer pubs, which is typical, and then doesn't
turn up.'

'A queer pub, is it?' His eyes rolled humorously about
and fell on the two woollen-trousered men, who were now
trying on each other's rings.

'How droll,' he added.

'Yes, well he likes queers because he says their colours
are so lovely. Of their clothes, see. He's a painter and he's
good at conning drinks.'

He rose immediately. 'What will you have?'

'No.' She shook her head. 'It's all right, it wasn't a hint,
honestly.'

'No, you must. I insist. I insist.'

'No, honestly. Well,' she cut her age to fourteen with a
smile, 'except perhaps a small gin would be nice. I'm still
a month or two under, and it can be tricky, that.'

'I'm more than a month or two over,' he said neatly, and went to the bar.

He was glad to get there. He needed time to find a manner for this situation, or to find an excuse that would extricate him from it. He leant negligently against the imitation wood, and studied her in the mirror above the bottles. She was staring around her with a frank, open grin, as if now she had a proper invitation and could enjoy herself a little. Her face was so pretty that it was only safe from a distance and by reflection, but also so young that in this context of shine and sham it seemed almost unformed. He, polished up by his educations, was much older than she was by more than the years that separated them; and consequently very sure of himself. 'Gin and lime, please,' he called for the fourth time, to the gossiping barmen. It was an *interesting* thing to do, to introduce himself to girls in homosexual places; to buy them drinks; to smooth them over; to rough them—he called out again for the gin and lime, and five minutes later went back with it, followed by many estimating eyes that stripped him naked, sucked him dry, and threw him on to the pile of murdered fantasies.

'Vile music,' he said. 'Vile. What do you do, actually?'

'Oh, I'm just', she shrugged, 'nothing really. At an art school. That's all.'

'Is that nice?' He lifted a sardonic lip. 'Do you enjoy that?'

'Oh, it's all right. I mean, I live at Wimbledon, so the school's something else, isn't it? And then Donal, my friend, he has this room near Covent Garden he lets me use.'

'A drag.' He sipped from his fourth Scotch. 'But it seemed the choice to make. Old buildings, old rivers, old men. Jee-sus, I hate it.'

'Donal knew someone there. He got thrown out for smoking reefers.'

'Really? Must have been Toby. Toby Moss. We shared a girl. In a way.'

'. . . cries a lot.' She stroked the surface of her third gin with her tongue. 'I know it's all very sad and that, because she loved it, whatever *that* word means, as Donal says, but it was disgusting, how it used to crap over the carpets. And I couldn't slouch about looking sad all the time because of a dog. So I had to get out tonight, if you see?'

'Know *exactly* what you mean. Real grief isn't actable. It's a state of awareness. The rest's a joke.'

'Is it like that with you, then? Grief, and everything?'

'I had a friend,' he said. 'He died.'

'I don't know anything about, well, death.' She looked down humbly, waiting to hear.

'It doesn't matter.' He smiled into his glass as if into the great mystery itself. 'Nothing to know.' Although he said a few things anyway.

'I expect it's not very good.'

'You want me to be frank, though? Without cosiness?'

'Oh, I do, yes, although I don't know whether Donal would.'

He studied the poem, six lines in pencil on the fly-leaf of a novel by Burroughs. He had known what to say about it before he had uncrumpled it. It therefore didn't matter that he couldn't make out a word. 'Pastiche.'

'Pas——?'

'Cribbed. You know?'

'Poor Donal.'

'Listen', he deciphered a line, 'to this. Pure Yeats. And to this. Unadulterated . . .'

By the time he had attributed the last line (to Coleridge) it was quite obvious that Donal wasn't going to come. It was equally obvious, from her explanations, from the way she glanced towards the glass doors, that she no longer wanted him to come. Finally, she re-crumpled the poem and stuffed it (along with its efficiently de-glamourized author) back into her raincoat pocket. 'I mean he's just been left out, like a battered cat. That's why he has this thing wrong with him all over, on his skin.'

He caught the implications of her tone, the sudden apprehension that Donal, the fraudulent poet (and by extension, fraudulent painter) was shameful to herself; that worked against her probable habit of parading him as a rebel living on the edge of danger.

'Self-destruction', he explained, karate-style, 'is a temptation like any other. I know what you mean, or what you think you mean. But——' and with his foot on Donal's neck he proceeded, in a few husky and moving sentences, to throw up a picture of his own experiences—more terrible than those of his slaughtered foe, less frequently boasted of. 'Dostoievsky,' he murmured, 'got it all in *The Brothers*, and Lawrence in *Women*.' Oh, he had been where Donal could never go. *And* emerged.

'Poor Donal.'

'*Lucky* Donal.' He stood up and smiled. It was a smile that mourned Donal's emptiness and took her in his charge. 'Shall we go?'

They walked slowly up Charing Cross Road and then into Leicester Square. They passed the poster for *Prey of Dracula*, and he made an amusing comment. Yes, he walked nonchalantly at her frail side and spoke eloquently on the major problems, but he halted sometimes to evoke a silence that was itself a significant communication. 'I study history at Cambridge and have two Firsts. I'm thought to be clever, but I have no idea of what I am, what the world is, or whether I care. Even my humility is a kind of hypocrisy, don't you think?'

'I know. It's awful, isn't it? I'm the same way, I mean I'm

177

always worried what the other person is thinking about me. I suppose it's because I haven't, well, ever had a', she drew a breath, 'proper experience. Not a *real* one.'

'Oh?' He toyed with a florin in his trouser pocket, that had become slippery with his excitement. 'You're free, are you?'

She stared down at the pavement, then towards the traffic. Her eyes, when she finally lifted them to his face, were shiny in the hard lights. 'Yes,' she whispered, 'really.'

'It's funny, if you like that sort of thing.' And he began to tell her a little more about Sylvie. 'Sexual circles, round and round.' He laughed bitterly into the noise of Piccadilly, then steered her casually up an alley that lay behind one of the cinemas. 'The Wasserman was a bitch, and I hated her guts. It was quite amusing, though, because I *do* like that sort of thing.'

'Ooh, she sounds squalid. I mean, hamburger in her hair.'

'She was merely beautiful.' And pulled her to him. There was no fear in him that she wouldn't submit. She had submitted all evening. She had shown her submission in her looks, her yapping laughs, her ignorance and her cockney accent. But for a second he was afraid. Policemen everywhere, and Nathan Hornstein's derision, and what he had said to Din. But her mouth was turned up and her eyes were wide with yearning. One cheek reflected the blue of a nearby neon.

'God,' he stepped back, cool as a cucumber, 'I wish there was somewhere we could go. For a real, you know, talk?'

She moved into a patch of darkness, as if to hide herself. 'Donal won't be at his place and he'd let me. I mean, he must have gone to Guilford for one of his weed parties.' She retreated another step, and then another, until the wall

178

was against her back. 'I've got a key and we could go there if you want to,' she whispered. 'But it's a bit, well——'

But no. He was afraid not. There was a game of Monopoly in Hazings' room, and his books, and his tripos.

Donal's place was in Little Side, which ran behind Covent Garden at the farther end of Garrick Street and Long Acre. It was a dirty street, and narrow. In the half-light most of the shops seemed to sell strange, worn pieces from wireless and television sets, lumps of metal, coils of spring, and hooded tubes. There were also a few magazine shops illuminated from the back. The Paris Exchange, The Little Side Book Mart, Continental Magazines, Inc. The covers of the magazines were indistinct, but an occasional form, unnaturally tinted, would leap into his vision. *A History of Bondage.* He could not speak as he walked. He could not look at the girl. He was concentrating on the fact that there was a train in an hour which he must absolutely catch, or the Monopoly would begin without him. She stole along beside him, dark and mute.

Number 32 was a tall house between one of the book-shops and one of the spare parts shops. Its garage-like door was open, presumably to let in scraps of paper and dry orange peel from the street. He followed her, when she went through it, with no intention of going in; and climbed the stairs that were covered with rags of linoleum, with no intention of going up. They went very high, and turned many corners, before they reached another door. She knocked sharply, her back to him, her face close to the peeling wood. She knocked again, and then, still keeping her face attentively to the panels, she took a key out of her raincoat pocket, fumbled it into the lock, and opened the door. She turned on a naked overhead light.

There were cushions everywhere, all of them stained and most of them torn. There were glasses everywhere, which

179

had recently contained alcohol and now contained thick lumps of brown paper; there was a drum in one corner, with a rent in it from which a bottle protruded; and in another corner, beneath the ledge of a blurred window, was an electric fire with two of the three bars broken and hanging. On the iron bed in the centre of the room was a pair of rumpled sheets and a pillow without a case. A sour pall of nicotine, drink and bodies, was stirred by their entrance.

'Oh, Christ,' she flung her rubber raincoat over a chair and stood staring around the room. 'Donal is a little filthy.'

The train left in fifty minutes; which, allowing twenty minutes to get to the station, meant that he would be off in fifteen minutes. In ten minutes, therefore, he would have to tell her.

'It's a sort of kitchen, through the door.' She went towards it. 'And a toilet place just off.'

He walked across the room and perched on the corner of the rumpled bed. He took out a cigarette and lit it. His hand trembled slightly. But it would be all right, he knew that, once he was out of this repulsive room, out and away on a tube that would take him to a train that would take him to Cambridge, and Monopoly. Or the one after that, if he had, from politeness, to linger a little.

What was he doing here?

Who was she, anyway?

From behind the door by the bed he heard a noise that was like a laugh. The noise of a door shutting was followed by a complete silence. He got to his feet and was just about to look for her when another door slammed violently. A window slid down, with an ugly scraping sound, and outside a woman screamed or an animal died in agony. The hairs on the back of his neck buzzed upright as he realized that he had been lured into a trap.

She came back into the room. He noticed the flush to her

cheeks, the jerky briskness of her movements. 'Of course, I expect the place is too disgusting, and you'd like to go, I expect.'

'Good heavens, no,' he said, as a preliminary to his explanation about the train. 'Can I help?'

She looked at him, with the glasses clasped into her waist in a manner that reminded him of another girl in a proper world a long time ago. She shook her head. 'If you'd like to open the window?'

He went over to the window and struggled with it. It came up eventually, and the foul night air leaked in to mingle with the foul room air. Opposite, a few feet away, there was the mass of a house wall, but by craning out and peering upwards he could enjoy a small section of the London darkness, with a star lodged in it. He fixed his attention on the star as he rehearsed the simple phrases that would lead to his departure.

It took her nearly a quarter of an hour to clean up. She cleared away all the glasses, shoved the broken drum deeper into the corner, swept up the floor with a pan and a brush produced from underneath the bed, and exchanged the soiled sheets for fresh ones kept in the bottom of a green carton. He watched her every movement whenever she couldn't see him—watched the way she moved her legs, turned her head, kept tugging her sweater down over the tops of her jeans. He lit a new cigarette from the stub of his old one, puffed deeply, and watched her. He wondered now and then where he was and who he was. But he wouldn't know that until he was clear away, back in Hazings' room and teasing Craley. Craley the Crab.

'Look,' he said, turning regretfully around a second after she had run out of the room.

She came back almost at once, with two glasses of Nescafe, and a blotch of dust on her nose.

'Sorry? What? I mean did you say something?'

'Nothing, nothing. No, I was just', he sauntered from the window and sat down on the bed, 'thinking. You know. About what I was saying about Sylvie.'

'Oh?' She handed him his Nescafe, looked vaguely about her, then, with each gesture separate in itself, sat down beside him. 'That girl with the hamburgery hair?' She clamped her legs together and rested her glass on her knees. 'That one?'

'Yes. Dear old Sylvie. And about this friend of mine called Hazings.' He shifted away a fraction, frowning thoughtfully. 'He's very brilliant, in a way. Did I mention him?'

'No.' She shook her head. 'No.' She took a sip from her glass. 'You didn't.'

So he told her about Hazings and his brilliance in a way. And as he talked he felt some of his own brilliance returning, and enough inspiration to glide away from Hazings— 'he fascinates me. People like that always do. Know what I mean? I see him as a kind of spiritual mirror to myself. A thinner, more elegant, Jeezus, soul, if you like?'—away from Hazings and on to Craley the Crab—'Oh, yes, a genius all right. Have you ever been adored by a genius?'

'No. Well, I know Donal isn't a genius. Not really.'

'A genius is *all* Craley is. He exhausts me.' And from there to Stafford the Staff. 'The quietest person I ever met. And the most beautiful. Everyone wants him, and none of us knows why.' And by the time the first train left he had covered Stafford the Staff, and also Hardles the Hardles and Endfer the Endfer and even Borning the Boring. He would have gone on to Din the Din and Thwaite the Thwaite, for he had no intention of stopping until she was prostrate with admiration and he was heading back to all those he was encompassing with his phrases and enlarging with his insights, but suddenly he felt her thigh pressing against his and a new observation died on his lips.

182

'Sorry.' She fumbled in the deep, tight pocket of her jeans and drew out a crumpled package. 'Sorry. Fag?'

He looked into his glass, down at the residue of his Nescafe, which was scum, and shook his head.

'Sorry,' she said again. She got up and stood before him, her legs spread, one hand holding the broken cigarette to her lips, the other shaking out a lighted match. 'I've never been to Hampstead Garden Suburb, but if it's like Wimbledon? Is it that sort of place?' She puffed smoke. 'Is his name *really* Boring? Honestly?'

He laughed hoarsely, shuffled his feet as if testing ice, and stayed where he was. 'Borning.' He spelt it out. 'With an N. But I call him'—he raised the glass to his lips, and failed to prevent his eyes from fixing on her stomach. Her sweater had ridden up from her search for cigarettes, and half the whorl of a navel was exposed in the taut flesh of her belly. 'Boring.' He drained the scum down his throat and forced his gaze to her face. Her wide green eyes stared shinily down at him, shinily. He was magic to her, in his insouciance. 'A college joke, sort of thing.'

'Oh, I know. At College we've got lots of names like that. There's old clitoris for Clithero, because of the way he fancies you and his trousers go in. He's the assistant principal. And——'

And he wasn't, in fact, listening. He was, in fact, rising, and moving towards her, his glass held out like a torch.

She took it from him, very nearly. For the second time in his experience of women he heard the smash of crockery.

'It doesn't matter, honest. Donal doesn't care what he drinks out of. His shoes, even.' She squatted over the pieces and piled them into the cup of her hand; and he went back to the bed, where he stayed, smiling redly.

When she had got rid of the shards she came back into the room and wandered indirectly to her old place, beside him.

'Clitoris,' he said. 'Old Clithero. You were saying?'

'No, it doesn't matter.' She was up again, delving into her pocket for her fags. 'They're not names like yours. The ones you were telling me about. There's no one at College, really. Where are my matches, then?'

He groped beside him and found the box. He rose towards her and suddenly, before he knew how, his arms were around her and he was drawing her hard against himself. He began a sentence that ended in a laugh, and then they fell backwards on to the bed, slowly, like a couple wrestling in diving suits. He was vaguely aware, as he buried his face in her neck, that she was spitting out tatters of paper and tobacco, some of which went into his hair.

Finally, as a climax to their rapid, jerking movements, he was standing with his tie under his ear and his trousers hitched almost to his chest; and she was lying on the bed, her sweater rolled above her black bra, and her jeans pulled below her hips. She was staring up at him, without expression, and he noticed that on one of her cheeks there was a yellow lump that must have come from her cigarette. He bent down to pluck it off, and she winced slightly, away from him.

'Please.' He shifted his hand to the coarse wool of her sweater. 'Please.'

She turned her head to the wall.

'Please.'

She said something that made him crouch lower, to hear it.

'Do you really want to?' she whispered into a gap in the plaster. 'Honest?'

He shut his eyes. 'Yes.'

'Honest?'

'Yes.'

'I mean', she whispered, 'it's not because of that hamburger girl?'

'No.' His hands went sideways, to knock Sylvie out of the room and back into the arms of Nathan Hornstein, M.D.; where she could stay for ever, as far as he cared. 'I promise. It's because of'—he opened his eyes on the swell of her buttocks—'you.'

'Me?'

'Yes.' He slid his hand off wool and on to skin. 'Honest.'

She lay there and said nothing, but it was half a minute before he dared move. Then he edged along the bed on his knees and pulled on the ankles of her jeans; at first as if to rouse her; and then, when he met with no resistance, to get them off. And though she kept her face averted, she began finally, with leverings from her hands and rolls of her hips, to help him.

Her pants were small, tight, white. The mystic pants that encircled, and drove mad. He had them off, and there was the nest of hair he couldn't look at, but the last trains had hurtled into the night and left him there. Even so he would have stepped back with a rush of pleading followed by a rush to the door, but she was herself unclipping the bra, and there was nowhere to go, and he was caught at last with what he wanted, and was afraid.

But as he undressed he glared around the room and saw that it was squalid and secret, and that he was safe. No one anywhere could stop him now. His penis jabbed out, hot and damp, and he was free.

They lay on their sides, back to back on the narrow bed. He was on the outside, facing the room, and he stared forth at the broken drum and the lopsided table and the green carton and the trail of clothes, as if searching for the clue to a large, melancholy puzzle. Once he shifted slightly, to straighten his legs, which he had drawn up to his stomach, and another time his shoulders jerked convulsively. But mainly he was still.

N 185

Her head was resting close to his shoulder, and her legs, stretched out, were pressing gently against his. She was breathing audibly and he wished she would stop.

'You're not to feel humiliated and that,' she said into his armpit. 'See?'

He inched his legs to the side, away from her.

'It's just that we haven't had much practice,' she went on ticklingly. 'It was that you didn't know, well,' she lifted her face, 'forgot, I mean, and it's difficult when you forget. To find, even. It doesn't matter about Donal's blankets. He does much worse things, and——'

'I didn't know what I was doing.'

'No, that's what I mean, but I . . .' and her voice died away so that her offer to show him something was nearly lost.

'I mean the whole thing.' He chopped sideways with his right arm, he didn't know why, and hit her somewhere. She gave a little gasp.

'The whole thing?'

'Yes.'

They lapsed back into silence.

A few minutes later his right leg kicked sideways and struck bone. 'Sorry,' he said. 'Sorry.' Then, 'We'd better go.' He rolled over to face her, his mordant wit struck down, and every aphorism entombed. Consequently, for the first time in a year, his expression was charming, if a trifle embarrassed. 'We'd better go,' he said.

She stared into his helpless eyes and saw the truth. 'All right.' She propped herself up, looked down the length of her body, then raised a hand and let it hover above herself. It floated shaking towards him and hung there, in promise. He lay watching, unable to move as it fell softly down and settled on his stomach. 'We'd better go.'

'Yes, well Mum might certainly be wondering and worrying, because I expect she's buried the dog or Dad has and she'll start thinking about me.' She made a sudden movement and caught him. His body jerked, and he cried out for shame and beggingly, but she held fast as she detailed, in terms meaningless to both, those elements of ignorance, suspicion and insight that coexisted within her mother's make-up.

'Because I get men to strip me and fuck me, you mean. Is that why I'm wise?'

He laughed. It was the first time he had laughed since entering his cluttered little kingdom. In fact, as his shoulders heaved and his head bumped up and down against her belly, it seemed to him that he laughed for the first time in his life.

'Is she pretty?'

'Well, not the way you're pretty.' He studied her with acquisitive eyes. 'She's got fair hair and she's very neat.'

'Is she clever?'

'*Quite* clever.'

'Not as clever as you, though.'

'Hardly.'

'And is she wise, like me?'

'Hardly.'

'You don't have to ask. Ever. Ever. Honestly.'

'It's my education. I was brought up to be polite.' For with his lifting pride, his wit, too, was on the rise. 'It's my curse.'

She made a joke that Donal, although he would have understood it better than Grahame, could scarcely have appreciated as much.

They had dinner in a steak house in Leicester Square. He was very tired—it was as if some vibrant tissue, on which his energy depended,—had been removed. He was hungry, but eating was nearly as difficult as conversation. Only the bottle of red wine produced any effect on his system. It blurred all the outlines, to create the sensation of a warm underwater world in which the waiters, the girl opposite, the other diners, were human-faced fish.

But she wasn't at all tired. She talked little only in order to eat much, and at great speed. Even in his listlessness he registered that her manners, while in keeping with a girl who would behave as she had done in bed, weren't those he would have expected from the daughter of a shop manager. Not that she was ignorant of the niceties, but rather that she had learnt to cut through them as through a thicket of irrelevances. Her small face dramatized in its every part—the eyes, the cheek muscles, even the forehead—her involvement in her food. Occasionally she flashed out a hand and wrapped it around the stem of a wine glass. The wine itself she poured into a mouth already full.

He began to wish, through the fog of his gratitude and physical self-wonder, that she would eat more slowly. He began to wish that she was wearing slightly more ordinary clothes. Her sweater and jeans, so right for the queer pub and the small room, were out of place in a clinical restaurant serviced by waiters with judging eyes. A woman two tables down, with purple hair and silver-framed spectacles, was staring in their direction; and one of the waiters was saying something to another of the waiters.

'I've made a pig of myself.' Her voice was out of place, too. It was loud.

'I expect', politely, 'that you were hungry.'

She picked up a piece of celery and crackled it into her mouth. Then she gestured with another piece of celery at the woman with purple hair. 'I can eat perfectly when I have to. Mum's seen to that, all right.'

'Can you?' He raised and lowered his eyebrows pointedly.

'It's just that places like this give me the creeps.'

He leant over the table against the voice of another kind of manners, and shook his head at her rather as if it were his fist.

Her cheeks flamed. 'I'm sorry,' she mumbled. 'I'm sorry.'

'No, oh no. No. *I* don't mind about things like that. People like this.' He darted contempt at the waiter's back. 'I was merely thinking that perhaps I'd better get back to Cambridge tonight after all. I haven't got a leave or anything, and I wouldn't want to get caught climbing over the gates.'

She looked away, blinking. 'It's probably best, then. I mean it doesn't matter my having 'phoned Mum about staying with Jennifer. I can just say I changed my mind.' She wiped her mouth and her eyes only accidentally. 'Because people shouldn't stay the night with people if they think, you know.'

His own eyes began to blink. 'I'll get the early train tomorrow.'

'No. No. You mustn't. Honestly. Not if you don't fancy me any more.'

She was curled on the floor between the fire and the chair. She had taken off her jeans and sweater and was lying on her raincoat, close to the one functioning bar, with her back to him. He sat on the edge of the bed, studying each detail that made her herself, and his. Then he rose and went over. He bent down, slipped a hand under her head, the other under her legs.

'I'm sorry. Sorry about the restaurant and that. I only talk so much because I'm a little frightened.'

'What of?' he whispered.

'Of you. I've never had anything to do with, well, someone like you before.'

He boarded the train next morning with aristocratic languor. He sparkled his eyes at the other passengers and helped a pretty girl get her bag on to the rack. He was a lord, who smiled on life. And also on the pretty girl, whom once or twice, between Bishop's Stortford and Audley End, he addressed on the state of the weather.

He was as free as eagles are.

'Well, what do you *do* in London, every week-end?'

'He's got a sweetie,' Craley explained, 'and he shacks up with her. Don't you, Thwaggers?'

Stafford rolled the dice. 'Twelve. I start. With the shoe if you don't mind.'

'You always have the shoe. *Have* you got a girl?'

'In a way,' he said. 'A sort of girl. I'd like the ship, please.'

'Hard cheese, Thwaggers.' Craley pointed to his nine. 'I get the ship. You have the top hat for taking your sweetie out in.'

'Well, why don't you bring her up here. Can she play Monopoly? I'd teach her.' He threw eleven. '*I'll* take the ship, Crab, thank you very much. Unless Jennie wants it?'

Jennie didn't. She already had everything worth wanting —sitting beside her in white, calf-length boots; white jeans; black shirt and a fresh shampoo—and was perfectly willing to accept the miniature whisky bottle as her emblem. So placing it on GO she raised demure eyes to Grahame, and checked on all those symptoms that, the week-end before, had stuck out a mile. They were there multiplied, and out to a mile and a half.

But that evening was the last for Monopoly. At the end of the game Craley rose by way of Stafford's shoulder, and said, 'We can't play again until after the tripos, of course.'

The tripos, of course. He shook his head, to shake the

tripos out of it. He succeeded so well that an hour later he was posting a letter to Little Side. It was a long letter, that showed all the intellectual brightness, the gift for allusion and connection, that had made him Mr. Keel's favourite pupil, and a Senior Scholar in History with a special talent for the General Paper.

He received a telegram from Din on the morning of the first exam. He could hardly bear to read it, she was so confident on his behalf. It was only after he had thrown it on his desk, among a pile of feverishly ransacked notes, that he realized it didn't matter about the tripos. He had outgrown it, and no longer cared.

He didn't care during the five days of the exams. What he had read in the previous terms, when he had been a dead man, remained in the tomb; the live man could not dig it up. The long tables were laid out, the stools placed, the sheets of paper and of rubrics arranged, and all around him undergraduates shook with fear or were ice-cold with confidence. He himself, with his senses wandering, merely went through the motions. He went through them with an industrious wrist. He wrote on every question; he wrote complete nonsense on every question. He sat on the stool, his head bent, his gown bunched under his buttocks, his pen flying; and in the evenings went to the cinema and longed for Little Side.

But when he walked out of the Hall for the last time he carried with him a vision of what he had done. The lost opportunity was a present pain, that obliterated everything but itself. He tried to concentrate on Little Side, where he would be the next morning, where his real life went on; but his eye caught Din's telegram, open on the desk. He sat down on his window seat and gazed firmly out, across the court. To where Endfer, prominent in a group of three, was holding out a question paper and disclaiming anything but modest hopes for a third. Although he probably knew he had scraped a two-two.

Endfer. Even Endfer would have done better than the College Scholar in History.

He got up, away from the spectacle of mediocrity ascendent, and sat down by the empty fireplace. His head began to wag, despairingly.

He took the lid off the shoe box and peered in, as if viewing some insects he kept there. He spoke.

'Oh?' She turned over the left shoe and frowningly examined its heel. Then she stared about the room and sniffed. There was still the odour, in every crevice of the flat, of a party Donal had given three days before, and the light that came through the small window facing the wall was thin and grey, as if it had passed through layers of dirty gauze. But she was seeing and smelling nothing. She moved her head and wrinkled her nose and tried to look nonchalant, and was dazed. Finally she swung around and looked at him.

It was a face that he understood, every expression of it, every movement. But he had never seen it before, it was an alien face that had been formed in a world he could never enter. He shut his eyes, partly from the intensity of his conviction, partly to block her out. 'Married,' he said again. When he glanced up she was still staring straight at him, her slanting eyes cloudy with an ancient and appraising wisdom. Then she smiled. Her eyes filled with tears and she touched him on the cheek.

He leapt to his feet and strode about the room. He gestured, radiant, as he explained how he had always known, from the first moment in the pub six weeks before, that they would end up married. His gaze, as he spoke, flitted scornfully across the lumps and tatters of Donal's life.

'Of course,' she hesitated, 'of course someone'll have to

tell my parents because I'm under age and that. If you don't mind.'

'Mind!' He did a graceful quick-step and jammed his toe into Donal's drum. 'I'm looking forward to meeting them.'

But for the rest of the day she did things nervously, hardly spoke, and suddenly, just as they were about to go out for dinner, she sat down on the edge of the bed and burst into tears. She cried silently, in some forlorn and un-comprehending misery that seemed in no way related to him. He crouched beside her, filled with a grief of his own.

Eventually she stopped. She sat stiffly, her cheeks damp, her eyes red, waiting.

'I love you,' he whispered.

She surged up and flung her arms about his neck. She kissed him, soft wet kisses that fell everywhere, against his nose, against his lips, against his eyes. Then she held him tight, with her arms around his neck. The rubber of her raincoat was against his cheek, he could smell the pungent, rubbery smell of it. It seemed to cover the whole of his face, to block his nostrils and suffocate him. She was saying something over and over that sounded like 'always'.

That night he knew he had taken his step and moved into his future. He had liberated himself at last, from his old habits and his old fears. He lay in her arms after they made love and he cried. He cried for her uncertainty and her longing, her love for him; he cried for himself, for all that he had been and done, for the waste of his years, for the deprivation of love everywhere. He even cried a bit for Din, who had no one.

She held him tight, with his head against her breasts, and sometimes she kissed him with a vast care, as if he were a baby.

Later, when he felt emptied and clean, he turned on the light and began to tell her everything. He had been afraid that she would find him out, see through the deceptions of education and manners, the advantages of age, the mysteries of his difference. Of course he could not, quite, tell her that. Instead he told her more about sex with Sylvie, and about Cranton inasmuch as he cared to remember it. She sat cross-legged, her mouth open with greed. She was complacent in her possession of him, he could see it, and jealous of everything that was him. She was not only on his side, but living in the glamour of his new past. His confessions were magic to her.

'I thought it was wrong, although he begged me. He wanted me to, before his death, and I loved him. In a way.' He raised a hand to his forehead and looked back to a junior self who was magic to *him* as well. 'I always want to be brave, from now on.'

'Yes', she reached for him, 'from now on you *are* brave.'

He woke up once in the night, with no idea of where he was, and tried to climb out of bed. But her arm around his neck held him fast. He peered down at the still circle of her face, and then moved his hands over her breasts, down her body. They were movements without desire, movements of discovery and possession, that made her his wife. And she was with him in her sleep, murmuring, her body pressing against his for protection. He slipped a hand underneath her, around her buttocks and then between her legs. They opened to receive him, and then clamped together to trap him there. He could feel the stickiness of her hairs from their love making, and it seemed even the pulsing of her blood within the damp folds. She was his. His wife. He had found someone, at last; someone to love.

There was nothing much to do but go to parties, visit his tutor, and see the year and his academic career through to its dismal conclusion. His room was a foreign place. The books on the shelves, the desk, the window seats—they were no longer his. There were some examination papers on the floor, and his gown lay across the arm of one of his chairs, where he had thrown it that Friday evening.

He cleared his desk and sat down to write a letter to Din. From the moment he had spoken words of marriage in Little Side to the moment when he had said good-bye at Liverpool Street Station, Din had only entered his mind for pity. But from Bishop's Stortford on she occupied it entirely, and in a different role. He saw that he would have to bring them together, future sisters-in-law, and he had a sense, suddenly, of imponderables and embarrassments.

The opening sentences of his first letter were unsatisfactory. Read in one way they gave the impression that he was asking permission; read in another, that he was acting in defiance of permission inevitably withheld. His second attempt, at direct honesty, had a confessional shrillness; his third was inexplicably spiteful. In the end he scribbled a short note asking her up for the week-end, as he had something to tell her that was 'on the whole quite important'. When they were face to face he would take a sophisticated attitude to the whole thing. He was 'in love, my dear Din, and might as well get married. Don't you think?'

After he had posted the letter he went upstairs and knocked on the familiar door. But Hazings wasn't there. His books were piled into boxes, his furniture removed, and his screens folded and propped against a wall. Only the table was left, isolated in the stripped room. 'Chance' and 'Community Chest' were spread over it, and the properties, with their coloured tops, were organized around its edges. If he had an odd twinge of dismay at the realization that the evenings in Hazings' room were over for ever, it was accompanied by a greater sensation of relief. He wanted Hazings gone, and Craley and Stafford. And even Hardles and Endfer. All of them gone. He could take his step more jauntily unwatched.

Of course they hadn't gone quite yet. Hazings and Jennie

were off to Greece at the end of the week, and Craley and
Stafford were going to Hamburg to stay with a Fellow of
the College who was doing research there. Naturally they
all expected to be back the following year, to do research
themselves, although they were superstitiously pessimistic
about their chances. It was a game, and he had to play it
with them, in double bluff. It superseded Monopoly for a
few evenings although it was similar to it in its assortment
of winners and its one big loser. But there wasn't much
opportunity for the little circle to reform in its old, hermetic
way. There were parties all the time—every evening, most
afternoons, and a few that began with breakfast. At one
party he got drunk and told Hardles or Endfer or Borning
—afterwards he forgot which, for most of the mediocres
seemed to him even more interchangeable than usual—that
he had a girl in London. They were sitting on the Trinity
Backs at midnight, sharing a bottle of champagne that had
come through someone's uncle (which later made him
think it must have been Hardles). She was a lovely little—
well, terrific little—well, marvellous at *you* know, he said.
Whoever it was, Hardles or Endfer or Borning, wondered
why he hadn't brought her up for the May Ball, then? 'Oh,
she's not the type,' he explained, 'for May Balls in Cambridge. She's very London.' Then Endfer or Borning or
Hardles said that *he* had a girl, too, in Hampstead Garden
Suburb (so it must have been Borning, after all) and once
they'd almost gone, you know? the whole way.

So he had lots of advice to give. His voice throbbed with
the enlargement of Borning's possibilities, and Borning's
face shone back at him, enlarged, in the May river lights.
They were very close for an hour or so, Grahame and
Borning. If it *was* Borning.

Then the parties were over and everyone said good-bye.
He told Hazings that he might go to France for the vac. to
work on a novel, although he didn't mean it or believe it

except when he was actually saying it. He was anxious, however, to account for himself in the general exchange of addresses and holiday information, something in keeping with trips to Greece and Hamburg and Newfoundland (where Hardles was going, on a university expedition), and returns to do research. Hazings said to be sure to send his address—he and Jennie would be honeymooning in Paris for a week before the end of the summer; and he said yes, naturally he would. And Hazings said, by the way Crab and the Staff sent their love and would see him soon; and he sent his love back, and was looking forward to being seen soon. So he stood, a twenty-two-year-old graduate, his hands in his pockets and his educated young head tilted to one side, chatting here and chatting there, an integral part of the farewell scene. He had been allowed to keep his room for a while, a concession that he knew would end in humiliating apologies with the publication of the tripos results, but it didn't seem to matter. He had thrown so much dust into so many eyes that he had blinded himself a little. Besides, for the first time he was beginning to feel a tender affection for the college, and for the university as a whole. He wrote an elegant letter to Little Side in which he said he didn't know whether he had been happy in Cambridge, but he was ready to indulge in a kind of preliminary nostalgia, for the happiness he would come to believe in. Then, on her advice, he wrote another letter to her home address as a way of forewarning her parents, and settled back to wait for Din: who had written to say that she had been intending to come to Cambridge anyway, as she had some news for him. He wished he could find some method of forewarning *her*, too; but he didn't worry about it much. He was at peace, or in a dream.

He found himself staring at a large bracelet, apparently made up of smooth, golden pennies, that was extravagantly out of place on her slim wrist, and disturbingly noisy. He kept expecting her to take it off, with some explanation about trying it on merely as a humorous experiment. On the other hand he could see that it did go, in a way, with her new dress, which was dark grey, tight around her trim hips and small breasts; and with her black stockings, which might almost have been a pair from Little Side. She had changed her hair again, so that it hung loose down each side of her face and brought an expression of soft surprise to her neat features. He remembered her as she'd been on her first visit, to the postman's house on the other side of the town—baggy, bowed and staid—and he marvelled at her transformation. He wished, though, that she would stop walking about. His neck was growing tired with the effort of turning his head to follow her, and his ecstatic monosyllables had become tedious to his own ears. Finally, with the grunt of one who wishes to interrupt a stream of large revelations in order to insert a larger one of his own, he stood up. Immediately, with a chink of her glittering coins, she sat down. She crossed her legs with a swish and smiled at him. It was a smile so triumphant, so conceited, that it forced him back into his chair.

'You see, Dodie, the Academy's got heaps of possibilities.'

'How marvellous,' he said for the fifth time; although

really, however heaped, he still couldn't see them as anything but the possibilities of any secretary. Din, with her blonde hair swinging stylishly over a typewriter; Din with a pad on her black-stockinged knee. Endlessly typing; endlessly taking dictation. What else could a secretary do, even at an Academy? 'How marvellous,' he said again, ashamed.

'Yes, and our both being in Cambridge—that is, if you decide to stay on?'

'Well, Din,' and the moment had come. 'Well.' And he went into an explanation, that led to an explanation, that culminated in an explanation that was half an apology. '*Complete* mess of it,' he said. 'Complete mess, Din.'

'I see.' She sat opposite him, calmly seeing. 'Everyone always says that, Dodie.'

'No, Din.' And he did his turn again, with details from one of the papers and a few quotations thrown convincingly in.

'But they can't! Because of one paper!' She shook her head in moral scorn. 'After your First last year, and your scholarship. They won't!'

'Ah!' He was very wise about life, its lack of generosity to the losers. 'No,' he said, smiling valiantly, 'no, Din. I'm on my own now.' He flung his hand around the room, 'completely on my own.' Then saw the link, and eagerly took it up. 'Well, perhaps not *quite* on my own. He got up from his chair and paced across to the window. He stood looking out over the grass towards the fountain, and felt the dryness mount from his stomach to his throat. He put his hands behind his back, nonchalantly. 'The thing is, Din,' with a shrug and an unexpected laugh, 'not at all on my own There's something I haven't mentioned, you see. Something else.'

'Oh?'

'You're the first person to know.'

'But, Dodie, what? I don't know anything, yet.'

199

'No. Well the truth is, I'm going to get,' he stared out of the window, into the court, where not even an Endfer was in view, 'married,' he said.

There was another pause, which ended with the sudden chinking of her bracelet. 'To Sylvie, Dodie?'

'Sylvie? Sylvie! Oh, no. No, no. Not to *her*,' he shook his head. 'Not to *Sylvie*, Din.'

'Oh?'

'No, not Sylvie. It's a girl, you don't know about her, I met in London. She's an artist. Studying at a school. A College of Art? I don't know if you've heard of it. One of the best.'

'I see.' He heard her rise. He heard her take a few chinking steps across the room. 'Well, that's wonderful, Dodie. Wonderful. How old is she? Where did you meet her? Tell me about her.'

'I met her in London.' He opened his mouth to say more, but couldn't think what.

'Well, not in a pub, I suppose.' She chinked out another step.

He closed his eyes, to re-create the scene that might have taken place if he hadn't met her in a pub. 'At a party at Borning's. Do you remember Borning? In Hampstead Garden Suburb. She's, oh, quite young. Younger than me, a little. She's, let see.' It was horrible, an explosion of shame that posed as laughter. 'Nigh seventeen,' he gurgled. 'Yes, seventeen. Not', he gesticulated, laughing, 'that that matters. Four years. Five.'

'Six, if she's only nigh.'

'Six.' He knew he must stop those laughs, that were like a madness. 'Actually.'

'Six.'

'Yes. But the important thing is that we want to get married. Din, I——' Turned. She was standing a little away from the chair, gazing down at something in the

200

grate. Most of her face was covered by the swing of her hair; in fact, he could only see the tip of her small, straight nose and the curve of her small, round cheek. At the same time he saw more of her than he had ever seen in his life. He saw the swell of her breasts, the line of her waist, the slight mound of her buttocks against the tight cloth of her unsuitable dress. She stood absolutely still, in profile for him; and behind the fan of her hair, where his eyes couldn't reach, he knew she would be smiling strangely. He began to walk towards her.

She waited until he was close, then chinked to her chair, and picked up her handbag.

'You're not going?'

'Going?' She looked up at him, smiling, concerned and Din again. He felt a throb of relief that was only in a very confused way a throb of disappointment. 'Why should I be going, Dodie?'

'Well, that's what I wanted to tell you.' He stood swaying on his feet and as if about to whistle. 'That I love Janice.'

She looked down at the bracelet of golden pennies, slid it off, unclasped her handbag, slipped the bracelet in, and snapped the bag shut. It was a small green bag with a large metal clasp, and a chain instead of a strap. 'Janice?'

'Yes, Janice.'

'Janice . . . ?'

'Janice', he said, 'Trullope.'

'Janice Trullope?'

'Yes.'

'Janice Trullope.'

'Isn't it a terrible name?' He raised a fist. 'I call her Jan, of course.'

'Of course.'

'And as for Trullope,' he joked, 'well, that's going to be . . .' he bent almost double, incapable of speech.

'Changed,' she said. 'I know.'

He straightened himself with a 'But seriously, Din'. Then, when he could bear her seriousness no longer: 'Her father is manager of one of those large shops that sells linen.'

'Linen. I see. That must be very interesting.'

'Yes. Very responsible position. One of the top jobs of its kind, I should think. And', he smiled, 'they dwell in Wimbledon.' He walked over to her chair to exchange gestures and words of final understanding, but she was engrossed in a detail about her person. She was swinging her leg gently up and down, picking at her stocking just below the line of her dress; which was hiked up a little.

'Well,' he waited. 'Well.' And when she continued to slide one nail across the dark mesh, 'That's it, sister mine.' Which must have been another joke, because he followed it with another snort.

She got up suddenly. She stood in front of him, she looked at him, she rose on tiptoe and kissed him on the cheek. He put an arm around her shoulder but she stood with such meticulous awkwardness that only through violence could he have managed more than the peck on the top of her head.

She stepped back. 'I'm going to take you out to dinner, to celebrate our news. I get expenses, you know,' she added, as she walked to the door, 'for coming up.'

'Jolly good,' he cried, his brotherly self again. But the words were lost as the oak swung mysteriously behind her to shut him in for a moment; and it was impossible to repeat them for somehow, on the way to the restaurant, she was always that little step ahead. But at least this gave him time to decide that he must tell her more. If there was anything lacking in her attitude so far, then a display of his actual emotions, untainted by freakish outbursts of laughter, would help her to understand. He would be intimate over dinner, and intense; and thereby blanket out his previous gaucheries.

He began circularly with anecdotes about Hardles and Endfer and others that she'd met; and about Hazings, Craley and Stafford, and others that she hadn't met (touching, too, on Jennie and *that* forthcoming marriage) in the hope eventually he would find himself in the middle of a movingly personal sentence. But there seemed such an immense distance between them, the table was so large, although designed specifically for two, and all the objects on it—the wine bottle, the glasses, the pepper and salt— were so obstructive to confidences, and the waiters so solicitously present, and altogether his anecdotes so expanded and trailed and guttered and finally Janice's name seemed so idiot on his tongue, and most of all Din seemed so impenetrably poised, that the sentence never came. He laughed a great deal, however, and his gestures became extravagant; and he drank too much wine, and was easily the most communicative person in the restaurant, in a way. By the time he came to his brandy he was a trifle drunk, which probably accounted for the surge of emotion with which he first stared into the oily eye that flickered up from the brandy's golden surface, then swayed his balloon across the table. 'You'll like her, Din. Come on, Din, a toast. I know you'll like her.'

She glanced her own glass delicately off his and sipped some water from it. 'I want you to be very happy, Dodie. That's the main thing.'

The tears rushed to his eyes and coursed down his cheeks. He mumbled through them that he knew she did, knew she always had. Always would. Him, too. Wanted *her* to be— he put out his hand and patted the prong of a fork, which somersaulted to the floor.

'Everything's going to be all right,' she said, smiling to

203

him through the rising mists, 'because you're such a loved man. Besides I've got a plan.'

After that he rolled into dimness; and was unable to take in the details of her plan, although he chuckled and swayed and nodded to the hypnotic rhythms of her voice, and sometimes exclaimed that she was a nifty little genius, his old Din. Finally she had to take him back to the college in a taxi, and also had to tip the driver a lot of money after a quarrel about something or other that had happened to one of his seats.

He registered her talk politely, but really he was concerned with shielding his eyes from the sun and with wondering if his head would ever stop its slow heavy pulsing.

'Yes, he's very keen to meet you, Dodie. I 'phoned him this morning and he said to be sure to bring you, sometime. If you'd come.'

'What's he like, this Mr. Spill?' Although he didn't at all want to know.

'Oh.' She studied her bracelet, back on her wrist and noisier, shinier and more disturbing than before. 'Oh, he's a bit awful, I suppose. Until you get used to him. He's a snob, and he's got an odd sense of humour, but he's, well, interesting. Aunt Mary would say that he's an energetic little person, although he's not so little. He's as tall as you.'

'Energetic? At his age?'

'His age?' She stared intently out of the window. 'He's not old, either.'

'Good,' he said. 'God, this bus.' *And* her voice, actually, and her bracelet, actually, both of which rattled continuously, to keep his headache at its peak.

'Have you heard anything at all about his Academy, Dodie? In Cambridge?'

He lowered the lids of his eyes protectively. 'The Spill

Academy? No. Well, David Endfer took out a girl once—
Dutch. Dutch girl, I mean. Din, would you mind lowering
your hand a little, that money cuff or whatever it is, very
pretty, but for some reason the coins, see. They're very noisy.
Thanks.' He clutched at the rail in front of him as the bus
juddered around a corner and up Station Road. 'She was
a little indignant about the fees. God, this driver must be
drunk.'

'Oh, yes, but then you see, Dodie, he's trying to raise
the Academy above the grubby little places in the back
streets. He really *believes* in teaching English to foreigners.
That's why he charges so much. And that's why', she
added, getting to her feet, 'he hopes to meet you.'

'I suppose I *will* need to think about a job,' he agreed,
following her down the platform to the train. They had
just had a cup of coffee in the buffet, and there were some
small signs that his hangover was at last in retreat. 'But a
teacher at the Spill Academy! For foreigners!'

'Oh, I know. But it might be useful, while you, while
you and——'

'Janice.'

'Look around. Last night, at dinner, you were quite
keen. Don't you remember? You said we'd make a wonderful team, me as secretary, you as a teacher.'

'Yes, yes,' he said. 'Did I?' He stopped, to let his stomach
settle from its recollection of the dinner. 'Yes. Wonderful.'

'After all,' she leaned out of the window, 'you're such a
loved man.'

'You've said that before.'

'Because it's true.' She withdrew her head as the whistle
sounded and blew him kisses as the train carried her away.
The last thing he noticed was that the bracelet had vanished
from her wrist. And among the muddled things he thought,

as he wandered queasily back to the college, was that, yes, Din had changed.

But then and after all, so had he. For he was such a loved man. And now he knew it, even in his queasiness.

And that was why, at first, he didn't see her. He saw only the blotches of many faces, humanly level with each other; and the confusing muddle of bodies and arms, shopping-bags, and brief-cases. There was no magnificence anywhere to match and greet the magnificence of such a loved man. Then he made out the slim jeaned figure to the side of the barrier, and her wide and childish grin.

She took his arm and she began at once. It seemed to him that in the first five minutes, as they walked to the Underground, she made every single remark she had ever made before; and that each one struck some of the magnificence out of him. He, who had so much love to give, had only chattering familiarity to give it to. His disappointment fixed itself on small things—the inevitability of her rain-coat, for instance, that had once been a cloak of mysteries. Why was she the only girl in London to be wearing a rain-coat? At the very least she must be uncomfortable, it was only affectation, people were staring at them, at *him*, because of her raincoat. And her short hair. And her jeans. Must she wear them so often? He compared her, with secret movements of his eyes, to the girls they passed, girls in summer frocks who had shoulder-length hair or lady-like curls and spoke in low, modest tones. There was one, a small blonde girl in a white skirt and blouse, who sat opposite them in the Tube, and flicked amused grey eyes over them, and whispered something to her companion. He couldn't hear what she said, because during the journey to Covent Garden he heard nothing but Janice Trullope's voice, her cockney accent riding crudely over the inaudible criticisms from the other passengers. Her hissed jokes

206

('Do you think that monk's a nun in drag?' 'Oh, Grahame, it must be, I mean! A man's falsie, see?'), her chokes of laughter followed by a hiccoughing gasp and more jokes, made him whip his head from side to side as if searching for a part of himself that was deaf. His grin of compliance was a matter of straining cheek muscles; and good manners, of course.

On the street she ambled confidently beside him, one hand impertinently in the hip pocket of his trousers. And he went on tightly grinning, replying monosyllabically, until he could bear it, no, not one second longer. He took an abrupt stride forward, from some idea of giving everyone, including himself, the impression that he had no connection with the girl holding him by his trousers. But her hand was thrust deep, and the unexpected jerk of his hip brought her skewing around. She detached her hand and he hurried off.

She had to run to catch him up. 'What's the matter?'

'Nothing. Nothing, Jan.' As he hared towards the burrow of Little Side.

She pattered behind him, silent, until they were in the room at last. Then she sat on the bed and stared down at the tops of her wrinkled blue knees. 'I'm sorry,' she mumbled to her knees. 'I'm sorry, Grahame.'

'Sorry? What are you sorry for, Jan?' He was elaborately folding his jacket and whistling a little, preoccupied. When he had finished, and there was nothing else he could do except possibly wrap his jacket up and post it, he turned around and doled her out a puzzled, friendly smile.

She didn't look up. She continued, in a strange, mumbling voice to address her knee-caps. 'I can't help it, see. It's just that when I first see you every time I'm a bit nervous and,' the last words came out in a whispered rush, 'and I'm frightened, see? Of, you know, well, boring you and not being what you want and that.'

207

'Not being what I want?' He whirled over to her, took her in his arms and clutched her to him. He held her very tight, very close, to squeeze such ideas out of her. And then, when he could find the nerve to look down into her small, satisfied face, so much simple love shone back at him that he shrivelled in hatred of his treachery. At last, in his words, with his hands, with all his heart, he was able to confer his love upon her. Besides, in that room, with that bed under them, away from the eyes of people who did not understand, he was safe. He wanted her. It was a marvellous security, to want her so badly. He gazed into her eyes with almost as much defiant nobility as love, and began to undo the buttons of her shirt.

The rest of the week-end wasn't spoilt by any further displays on his part; for they spent most of it in Little Side, where it was easy to be Antony and lose the world.

He had wanted the meeting to take place in London, from a feeling that Janice would be more at home there. But as he looked tensely at her across the table, he could see that she felt perfectly at home where she was, in the Cambridge restaurant in which Din had treated him to the celebration dinner. Besides their last two days together had restored her confidence—aided by some trenchant analyses of Din from himself. And though she had said several times that she was nervous, he was glad to see that she wasn't.

'Nothing', he insisted for the third time, 'to be nervous about. Not at all. We'll just have this pleasant introducing lunch together, and then go.'

During the further quarter of an hour during which they waited, he kept up a discreet scrutiny. He pretended to glance around at the other tables, mostly empty, or to stare expectantly towards the door; but this was only to induce in himself a kind of blankness, so that when he turned back to her he would see her fresh, as others, more austere than himself, might see her. Clothes, he knew, would be very important on an occasion like this. They were, of course, only important on a first impression; but then Din's was going to be a first impression. He wanted the impression to be impressive.

She was wearing a dark suit and a white blouse and dark stockings. Very nice, yes. They made her look very nice. Also her face was slightly made up, which was, yes, a good thing. A touch of lipstick on the wide lips; a little shading around the slanting green eyes. She had known what she was doing, had taken precautions. In her woman's wisdom she had aimed for a *soupçon*, rather than an excess, of sophistication.

'Well, am I all right, then? Do I look smart enough?'

'Lovely,' he said, with a *soupçon* of his own. 'Lovely, lovely, lovely. Yes.'

'Yes, I do, in fact. I look very sharp. I know that.' She touched the top of her dark short hair. 'But will your sister?'

'Yes. Of course she will. She always looks smart, these days.'

'No.' She let out a yap of laughter. 'I mean, will *she* think I look sharp? Will she, Grahame?'

'Of course she will.'

'Will what, Dodie?'

He had a glimpse, as he rose, of a cool pale face in front of him, a pink, grinning one beneath him; he sensed a scuffle of movement that indicated people rising and people sitting. When he had concluded a series of spacious but deprecatory gestures that accidentally brought a waiter to the table, and was able to see reasonably about him again, he found that Din had sat down in the chair next to his, and that Janice was standing opposite him, clutching a napkin in one hand and Din's green handbag, with its metal chains and clasps, in the other.

'Why don't you sit down, Jan?' he explained, as he rose.

But they couldn't sit down until they had completed a series of embarrassments over the handbag. It passed from Janice to the waiter, who made off with it. It was brought back again by a yap of laughter from Janice, a cold signal from Din. It then went from the waiter, a laconic man with freckled cheeks and a gold tooth, to Janice, who went around the table and virtually tumbled it into Din's lap. *Then* they could sit down.

A few minutes later they were calmly sipping sherry, and smiling. Din was also talking. She was talking of this and she was talking of that, and there was not a word of it that he, nodding and bobbing, grimacing and chuckling, could understand.

When he finally came to consciousness, with an assurance from himself that everything was swimming along swimmingly, his sister was looking directly across the table. 'Dodie's told me all about you.'

'Dodie?'

'Well, this one.' She tapped him playfully on the shoulder. 'I'm Dodie.'

'Haven't *you* got a nickname, Janice?'

'Well, only Jan. That's what Grahame calls me.'

'And Dianah's', he said, 'is Din.'

'But at school, Janice?'

'At the college, you mean. Well, it's a bit awkward, see. I mean, embarrassing, actually, because of my last name.'

'Trullope? Isn't it Trullope?' She gave him a perplexed smile; and he gave Janice an encouraging one, while jabbing at the underneath of the table with a concealed finger. There was a splinter of wood there that could cause him pain if he worked on it.

'Trullope? What could they make of that?'

Janice, invited to be herself at last, was; and told her.

As he threw back his head and stabbed out one laugh, he still couldn't believe that she had actually and actually spoken those words. He had, of course, known she was going to speak them, but he had drawn a bubble of blood from his finger as a tribute that would prevent her. So he studied the side of his sister's faintly smiling face; then, with the same clinical intensity, studied the front of Janice's blushing, yapping face. And laughed towards her to silence her for ever.

He was partly successful. Their melons were consumed in a deathly lull, and only the clatter of their knives and forks marked their journey through the fish. But with the arrival of the meat, and the Beaujolais, Din began again. This time he found himself capable of listening to every word and of watching every expression. He was therefore strongly placed to notice how her wit and her air of composure seemed almost an embarrassment to her. But it was perhaps the triumph of her recently achieved elegance that she was able to overcome the awkwardness she was creating by shining her kindness through it. She addressed herself exclusively to her prospective sister-in-law, and even when talking on subjects that only her brother could have understood—the topography of Morton and the recent Butlin's invasion—she made a point of inviting Janice to have a go. Unfortunately she was always obliged to accept these invitations herself, although Janice did say 'Honestly?' and 'Oooh' quite often.

She moved by a sequence of steps too intricate for him to follow, to the Hornsey College of Art. 'You must be so much freer there,' she said, as she sliced through her cold tongue, 'from what Dodie tells me.' And she added with self-effacing irony that the only advantage of a secretarial course was that people fell over themselves to get you. He couldn't tell whether this was a deliberate trap. He only knew that Janice, dropping her knife with a clatter and gulping down a piece of meat, was anxious to fall into it. This time, however, he raised his glass stoically to his lips and made no attempt to cover her laugh. He took five sips from the instant of her first yap to the instant when she subsided into a pink and staring silence.

'I mean, of course,' Din apologized, 'for different jobs.'

'Honestly?'

'Which reminds me——' she took a pad and pencil out of her handbag and made a brief note in shorthand. 'Something I have to do for Mr. Spill.' She poked the pad and pencil away, took out the bracelet, slipped it around her wrist, and leaned across the table once more. 'Do you . . . ?' she began.

He didn't trail the question through to its end and therefore never found out why Janice's reply should have involved her in a demonstration with a fork. But it was clearly unimportant. It wasn't referred to after the waiter had mopped up the wine with three clean napkins.

She stood smiling down at them as she had done when she had first entered, but now he found in her slightly averted eyes a different gleam. There was compassion for him and an understanding of his tragedy. There was mercy. She who had become so mysteriously urbane on her own account, had not lost the power to suffer on his. She could have no part in his monstrous folly, he saw that; but she could stand by, in civilized grief, to help him face the consequences.

This time, at least, the monstrous folly (held in check by his sudden glare) did not struggle to rise. Instead she sat grinning vacantly at the wine bottle as if receiving from its stained label some message, doubtless bawdy. He couldn't look directly at her when he spoke, lest his despair show, but even so, every little gesture she might make, every

trifling change of feature, registered itself on his person—
even the soles of his feet, which were damp with humiliation.

'When will I see you?' he begged upwards.

'Well, when will you be back from visiting Janice's
parents? Mr. Spill wants me here until Sunday night, probably.'

'I'm not quite sure.' He knew that the eyes of the monstrous folly were on him, in suspense.

'Well, Dodie, don't for goodness' sake rush back.' She
suavely bent and charitably placed a kiss on the cheek of the
monstrous folly; who blundered back a dreadful peck no
one could be blamed for flinching from.

'Have a lovely time in Cricklewood.'

'Wimbledon.'

'Wimbledon.'

'Thank you,' Janice whispered, to no one in particular.
'Thank you.'

'Lovely to meet you, Janice.' And walked swiftly, and
only slightly chinkingly, across the floor of the restaurant.
On the way she stopped the waiter and paid the bill.

She held his hand for a minute in the carriage until he
had snuffled and coughed enough to warrant the production of a handkerchief. Then by degrees he was able to
retreat behind a newspaper, and leave her to her corner
where she sat, shoulders hunched, staring out of the
window. From behind his camouflage of print he wished
she would stop whatever she was doing as it was getting
on his nerves; and wondered why, if she was going to be
cowed and silent, she couldn't do it on another train, with
someone else.

But the sight of the room was worse. He stood at the
door glaring into its squalor.

'They had one of their parties,' she said, glancing at his

face and then away again, 'that I heard about. It was filthy, I expect. I know how you are about filth.'

'Donal?'

'What?'

He followed her inside. 'Was it one of that—Donal's parties?'

'Oh well, it's his room, so I expect he was there.' She smiled, unhappy.

'Well, I don't want to hear about him.'

She looked down at the floor. 'You asked me, that's all.'

'It doesn't matter.'

'No, well I don't mind,' she said humbly. 'Honestly.'

But her helplessness enraged him further. He wanted to have it out between them that she was sordid and uneducated and not up to him. He wanted her to protest and argue, so that he could protest and argue her into oblivion. He wanted anything but her abject submission.

'*I* do,' he said, although by this time he didn't know what it was that he did.

'But, what do you mind?'

His hand swung in her direction, performed a contemptuous circle away from her, and ended up in his pocket. 'Him.'

'Oh.' She went over to the bed and sat down. He observed the way she somehow bundled herself further into herself, as if she had been hit, or knew she was going to be. He hated her for it. 'Oh,' she said again. She looked down at her clasped hands. 'Didn't your sister like me, then?'

'My *sister*? *Din*? What's she got to do with it?'

'Well, I mean . . .' she shook her head. 'I'm very sorry, Grahame,' she humble-mumbled. 'Sorry.'

There was a long pause. Then slowly he took off his jacket; and walked to the bed; and sat down with a sigh. 'Of course she likes you. I'm sure she does.' He lifted his

214

hand and dropped it among hers. 'It's just that I'm very tired. I had too much wine, probably.'

She made a small noise that he refused to identify as a sob; and he sat beside her, his hand sprawled loosely over hers, gazing straight ahead, at the broken fire. Finally he turned and put an arm around her shoulder. 'That's all it is,' he said. 'That's all. See?'

It was the first time he'd ever noticed the smell. It rose from her, the smell of her body, like a corruption. He withdrew with a jerk and tried to curl into a clean corner of the bed, his knees up to his chin. The sight of those gluey patches, the stink that rose from her loins, the damp itch between his thighs—he would never be clean again. Never. He would have given anything, including the First he hadn't got, to stir without touching her body.

She lay quite still, carefully away from him, as if the slightest movement would put her in danger. Then she whispered something.

'What?'

'Have you got a hangover?'

'No.'

'Are you unhappy, then?'

'No.'

She slipped an arm under his neck and caught his head in its crook. He made no attempt to free himself. He knew that if he did he would become violent. She turned her face until they were staring directly into each other's eyes. Her face was warm and soft with fear. He touched her on the face, just to the side of her lips, smiling his love at her. But it was a terrible love, born out of his shame for her, and the stench of her sex.

'Oh, Grahame,' she said, 'oh, Grahame, I love you so.'

They made love again the next morning. And again, as

soon as he was spent, he sought a cool place, free of her. But again there was the stench that found him wherever he squirmed.

He got out of bed and almost ran into the kitchen. As he sluiced his pubic hair he invented excuses for returning to Cambridge straight away and by himself. He saw now that it would be grotesque to meet her parents. The Trullopes! 'I think', he called, 'I'll just go out and buy a paper, Jan.' And left without looking to where she would be lying, supine and stenching, on the bed.

He walked down Little Side in the ten o'clock sun, past the magazine shops, past the spare parts shops, and found a telephone booth near Leicester Square. He counted the coins in his pocket, the sixpences and shillings. He didn't know whom he was going to call, though, until he had asked enquiries for the hotel in Cambridge.

The reception desk got hold of her immediately. Her voice was bright and intimate, a thousand miles away, in a world where decent life went on and there was pity, only pity, for brothers.

'Ted?'

'Who, Din?'

'Oh, Dodie. How are you, Dodie?'

'Very well. Extremely well, thanks. Fine, really.'

'Where are you? Wimbledon?'

'No. Oh, no. We stayed with some friends, last night. In the centre.'

'Oh? Which friends? Of yours?'

'No. Actually Janice's cousins actually. Very charming.'

'Oh?'

'Yes. *Very* charming.'

'Good.'

'I just, well, 'phoned to thank you for the lunch and everything. I mean, for coming to the lunch. I didn't mean you to pay for it.'

216

'Oh, I can get it on expenses. Mr. Spill won't mind.'

'Janice', he said, 'enjoyed it too.'

There was a silence.

'Are you there?'

'Yes. Oh, yes, I am. Yes, Dodie?'

'Ah. Well, I mustn't keep you. I just wanted a', he laughed, 'word, Din.' Just a word. Merely a word. A word, Din. 'You're probably very busy.'

'Well, I *am* expecting Mr. Spill to 'phone. I thought you were him.'

'No.' He laughed. 'No, I'm not Mr. Spill.'

'No.'

Another silence.

'Listen, Dodie, perhaps we'd better——' but mercifully there were the pips and a scramble of money into the slots.

'Din,' he clutched the 'phone. The thing he desperately wanted to ask he no longer needed to ask. He put his mouth close to the receiver, to whisper it, and fixed his eyes on the instructions to telephone users, so that he could not hear himself.

'Dodie, is there anything I can do?'

'Do? For me? Of course not, Din. I just wanted a word. You know?'

'Well, if there isn't . . . ?'

'No.'

'Well, have a good time at Wimbledon.'

'Thanks.'

'And my,' mysteriously her voice, which had been so clear, faded.

'What?'

'To Janice,' she said. 'Good-bye.' And hung up.

He bought a paper, went into a nearby café, and ordered a cup of coffee and a cheese sandwich. It seemed to him that he had never enjoyed the simple act of reading a news-paper so much. It was luxurious, something he could only do by sneaking out of his real life, into a private world of public events. Murders, cricket matches, a wild-cat strike, he participated in every item. When he had finished he went out and bought another, but this time he came back with the *Telegraph*, which had a forthcoming marriages column to keep his eyes off. Respectable names, an assumption of responsible lives. Hetherton-Peteres, Wilfton-Gray, Norton, Hascombe, Denweaver. He thought suddenly of Hazings and Jennie, and what their marriage would be to their relatives and friends, to Hazings' uncle, the judge. And then of Thwaite and Trullope, and what *that* would be to Aunt Mary and Colonel Rones. Aunt Mary and Janice, in the living-room of Mallows. The Trullopes. He put the paper down and went back to Little Side, to his little room that was an everywhere. In the window of one of the shops his eye caught *A History of Bondage*. On the cover was a lithe, blonde girl, her wrists manacled together, and those manacles linked to a chain at her waist, from which other chains reached to her ankles. There was no suffering on her face—painted lips pouting open to admit a metal gag; wide blue eyes, as guileless as Jennie's; small neat breasts, with nipples around which there were no spots or pimples. Her legs, clamped by the fastenings, conveyed no suggestion of pubic hair. No smells. She looked so clean and remote, so pure and loved, in her bondage.

She was sitting on the bed in her underwear, with her hands clutched to her stomach; as if she had just finished a prayer, or been sick. He looked at her anxiously to conceal his distaste. 'What's the matter, Jan?'

'I thought you'd been run over by a bus or something, you were so long?' Her smile was nerves. 'I was a bit worried, I expect.'

'Oh, Jan.' He screwed up his eyes and opened his mouth and tenderly laughed.

She came over to him and gave him a kiss—a kiss on the cheek, because at the last second, obeying shrill orders from within, he turned his head away. She went back to her clothes and he followed her. He took her by the shoulders and, turning her around, kissed her on the mouth.

'We'd better hurry,' he said, holding her close, 'if we're to have lunch and everything first. Before—you know——'

She did. The Trullopes.

She stepped into her shoes, with her slender back to him. 'Are we coming back here, then? Donal says we can have it all week-end, as his wedding present.' She plucked meaninglessly at a suspender. 'Or what?'

'Of course we are. If they'll let you.'

'Oh, now we're going to be—well, they won't care. As long as you tell her some lies, that she can believe if she wants to. You know, the way I do. See?'

'Well, *you'd* better do it, then,' he said. 'I'm very bad at lying.'

'It's horrible, I know.' She had been quiet all the way to Wimbledon, but now, sitting in the corner of the grapes and vines sofa (purplish on greenish) her knees pressed together and her hands sunk into the satin-covered pastilles on her either side, she was anxious and critical. He could see that she was attempting to dissociate herself from the world she sensed he must be judging, and her evident realization of the impossibilities made him at last feel compassion. It was not her fault that she had been born into Heaslop Avenue, just as it was not his that he couldn't marry into it. His case against the Trullopes and their daughter surrounded him—in the glass-topped tables, the varnished and independent bookstands, a large new television set, the perfectly tailored, floral curtains; and most particularly

219

in the souvenir ashtrays, with the badges of different countries inset. It was a room, the total effect of which was ghastlier than the sum of its ghastly details. He was grateful.

'Oh, no,' he said, from his dominating armchair (which, he was glad to see, was mounted on high rubber studs, and hooded in plastic), 'it's smashing, in its way.'

'I mean,' she laughed at the television set and the Van Gogh reproduction that actually did hang above it, 'it's so, well, you know, empty.'

'I wouldn't call it *empty*, Jan.'

'Yes, I know it's got lots of *things* in it, but——' she was interrupted by sharp, rapping noises, of perhaps pictures (more reproductions of Van Gogh, he hoped) being hung. Then there was the sound of something like a Hoover being run over bare boards, and the beginning of a monologue in a female voice.

'They always do stuff like that,' she pointed a desperate face up to the ceiling. 'They weren't expecting us till five— I mean, it's what they do after lunch on Saturdays.'

'How thoughtless of us', he said, 'to inconvenience them.' And looked towards the door just as a round head, with a very little grey hair combed neatly back, appeared at it. It was a modestly anonymous head, the kind of head that was probably more accustomed to withdrawing from rooms inch by inch, than to thrusting brazenly into them. 'Oh, hellow, hellow, hellow there, Jannie. We won't be a minute!' The worried eyes skirmished towards the tall, politely nodding young man in 'Mother's chair'; who was noting that Mr. Trullope's accent was fractionally worse than his daughter's. 'Hellow, old chap.' The eyes skirmished away. 'We're just doing the weekly tidy-up, in the top of the mansion.'

'Please, not to worry on our account.' He toyed with a 'sir', and let a suspicion of it leak out.

Mr. Trullope puzzled at his lips with his tongue, as if

to trick them into an appropriate expression. 'See you in a minute, then?' he said, unable to suppress a suspicion of a sir himself. 'Old chap,' and withdrew. He could be heard whistling 'On Ilkley moor bah tat' as he went up some stairs. Then there came more rapping and something unnervingly loud but indistinct from the female voice. 'Yes, my dear, they are,' he called. There were three more taps before the female voice issued a command. 'Yes, my dear, I will,' he called. This was followed by a wistful last tap and the clump of feet on the floor.

'You can hear everything in this place,' she whispered, picking up one of the satin pastilles and putting it on her knees. 'That's another thing. You know, once I brought Donal back and we had to have the TV on to—well, it all went straight up to them. Mum told me what I said afterwards. And what Donal said.' She smiled scornfully past him at a pumpkin head and thus drew his attention to it. He also noticed that her cheeks were still red and that she couldn't look at him, and from a strange charity that he knew was indirectly putting him in the right, he explained again that it was a smashing room. Just as he'd imagined.

'There's another in the kitchen, with the cakes and salmon sandwiches,' Mrs. Trullope said into the silver milk jug with the curlicued handles. She was bent very low over a very low tea trolley. 'Jan.'

'All right, Mum.'

He was on his feet and would have made a move to help, but Janice with her 'All right, Mum,' had slipped around the corner of the tea trolley. He smiled at Mrs. Trullope as the words went through his mind. 'All right, Mum, all right, Mum, all right, Mum.' She had been struggling to establish a common understanding against the life of the room, but she had put herself back into it with a phrase and a movement.

Mr. Trullope made his entrance before the second trolley had appeared. He was wearing a dark suit, a white shirt and a red tie—all of which he had put on since first glancing around the door—and had thus brought his natural anonymity to a natty completeness. Mrs. Trullope, with her curly grey hair and in her patterned summer frock, talked incessantly as if to make up for the drabness that hung at her side. She had a manner and an accent that reminded him of Matron when he had been sick in infirm.

'Well,' Mr. Trullope leant over a corner of the trolley, 'we meet again. Hah. It's a pleasure to, er——'

Mrs. Trullope watched her husband shake hands with her future son-in-law over the sugar cubes. 'We've heard so much about you, Grahame. I think you can get by to the throne, Arnold.'

Arnold Trullope made his way around the back of the sofa to a recently studded leather armchair in the darkest corner of the room. 'Learning names is a trick, I always——'

Mrs. Trullope shifted the trolley to a new angle, thus causing the wheels to scream. 'Oh, Mr. Trullope couldn't even remember the name of our dog, Grahame, could you, Arnold? Although we had it for ten years.'

Which was how she introduced the topic of the dog, which lasted them through the bread and butter, the scones, the salmon sandwiches, the Lyons's sponge cake and three cups of tea. It had been called Weckles.

'It was always yapping and messing up the carpet.' She had been staring down into her cup during the most inventive parts of the conversation. 'He had disgusting habits.'

'Oh, but one does get very fond of them, Jan,' he said, with a reproving smile.

'She's a bit like her dad. Not so fond of animals.'

'Oh, yes, my dear, excuse me, I do like——'

'Bullfights, *you* pretend to like, my dear.'

222

Mr. Trullope pushed his head forward, out of the darkness, and coughed. 'Now I've never been to——'

'Spain even. Have some more tea, Grahame.'

'Corridor, I only meant, only nobody ever listens to poor old Dad when he's at——'

Which was probably the truth, as no one was listening to him now. Not even his future son-in-law, who was giving everything he had in the way of smiles and nods to Mrs. Trullope, who was elaborating on a truism and combining it with a cliché.

'But I mean, they're bound to go in the end, aren't they?' Janice stared at her fiancé intently, to remind him that she was his and not theirs; and he smiled blandly back at her and waited on Mrs. Trullope's next formulation.

'So is everything else, Jannie,' she said, in a tone of religiose satisfaction. 'We're all human.'

'. . . much time with Jennifer and her cousins in Kentish Town that we knew there must be someone.'

There was a pause, during which he dimly heard an unlistened to voice mutter that she was very young, another pause during which he smiled around the room and saw no one. Then he began.

He was modest and charming. He took feelings into account before they had been felt and answered objections before they had been raised. Although, on the whole, he stuck to sense, he could have talked gibberish if he'd preferred. For he knew that what was being listened to was not his explanation but the rhythms of his voice, its Windhoven rises and its Cambridge exactness. Of course the marriage he was discussing was quite unreal to him. He did not think about Janice Trullope, a few feet away from him and blushing; nor about his future, which was, as always, remote. All he thought about, all he cared about, was that he should be allowed, as a tribute to the superiorities conveyed by his tones, to marry the girl, whatever the colour of her cheeks; and make her a part of his future, however remote. 'You see,' he finished, after a short description of the kind of degree he expected ('A good third, or a reasonable two-two'), 'I don't want to spend the rest of my life loitering about the groves of Academe.' He made a point of addressing this to the head of the Heaslop Avenue household, who pondered it as if it were a fact in a lecture.

'I should think you wouldn't,' Mrs. Trullope agreed. 'It's not for the likes of you.' That she intended this as a compliment she made apparent by a proud smile towards her daughter. And her daughter responded with her first grin of the afternoon. Her eyes were fixed on a vision, who was now making modest disavowals.

So. He put his hands on his knees and looked easily around him once more. He knew that if he were to offer to set fire to the house there would be humble encouragements from all sides. And then, unfairly and just for a second, came the flash of different perspectives. He saw the room and its occupants as Din would have seen it, from her secretarial chair in the Spill Academy; or Hazings, with his Jennie, now staying with friends in, what was it? a villa outside Athens? Hazings, with *his* forthcoming engagement, to be announced over the sherry and through the *Telegraph*. Jennie, with her dark helmet of hair and her Roedean voice. He saw them all in this room, gazing around at it, from the smiling assessment of Mrs. Trullope, to the neat diffidence of Mr. Trullope, to the—to the—to the face of Janice Trullope. What *they* would make of it. What *they* would make of *him*, for being there. His second home, 'in Heaslop Avenue, Hazers, actually.' There would be jokes for Craley the Crab and Stafford the Staff.

But oh, no, he picked up his own thread smoothly. Not that kind of teacher in those particular groves. But he *was* considering, was *considering*, going into language teaching.

224

Hardly as a career; more as a way of gaining experience while he, so to speak, looked around? He hadn't yet made up his mind, but he did happen to know, through connections, that language teaching was the coming thing. Language teaching was——

'What, well, is language teaching, if an old ignorant——' Mr. Trullope, seizing the opportunity, as Mrs. Trullope rose to switch on three small bulbs arranged behind a green lace shade, next to Mr. Trullope's head.

Language teaching was the teaching of English, as a language, to foreign students. Foreign students came over to England to learn English as a language. He cuffed his knees. Yes, it was the coming thing.

Mr. Trullope dipped his head as if to get reverently underneath the coming thing lest it should smash into his face.

'You've certainly thought it all out,' said Mrs. Trullope, who hadn't.

'Isn't that what your sister, I mean Dianah, isn't she in that, didn't she say?' Janice was curled into her sofa corner, adoring.

Ah, yes, Jan. No, not quite. His sister, Dianah ('*You* must meet her, too') was an assistant to the principal of a very big language school that was really more a university. He himself would prefer to go into language teaching as a language teacher.

Mrs. Trullope, her voice shaking, confessed that he had *her* blessings.

'And mine.' The light from the three bulbs, although very close, reached Mr. Trullope as a kind of green gloom, through which the tip of his nose and the ring of his collar asserted themselves. 'And mine,' he repeated, grabbing double rations.

Yes. He thanked them. It was kind of them. Kind. And gave his impossible bride a plausible smile. After all he had put on his best display for her, a display of education and intelligence, of breeding and accent. She might not be good enough for him, but he had shown her how high, how ridiculously high, his standards were. She was being deceived by the best, who couldn't help it.

'We expect to be seeing a lot of your Grahame, from now on. As the other male member. Don't we, Arnold?'

'Oh, Mum!' And she grinned towards her father, whose face, even in the tinted darkness, was illumined by a smile of amazing affection. 'I always knew one wasn't enough, not this old—and well, as long as *you're* happy, Jannie.'

They were accompanied to the front door by Mrs. Trullope, with Mr. Trullope indistinctly behind.

'If it's a nice party, Jannie, and your 'varsity friend is putting it on especially for the happy couple——'

'Hazings is a very decent chap.' He opened the door, ready to place his well-bred feet on the pavement, when suddenly 'Grahame', Mrs. Trullope called, in a quite new voice.

He stopped and turned. Mrs. Trullope, brushing past her daughter, was coming rapidly at him. There was a weird, sideways smile on her face, and her blue eyes were moist, and he knew, with the utmost certainty, that he had been found out.

She laid a hand on his shoulder and she stared into his face. He would have recoiled, but he was a child, merely, subject to adult controls. He gave in passively.

His head was drawn down, something wet and soft pressed against the side of his lips, at the same time his hand was quickly clutched and quickly dropped. A voice mumbled to look after his girl, his Jannie. Another voice whispered lovingly, 'Oh, Arnold.'

He had no resources. He stared at the Trullopes, at their deferential, gentle faces, and his throat blocked up.

226

Mrs. Trullope drew her daughter against her breast. 'You bring him to Sunday dinner next week, and one thing is your dad will make sure you visit his shop, won't you, Arnold?'

'Oh, Mum. Oh, Mum.' She grinned through her tears. 'Oh, Dad.'

The trip back to Leicester Square was gay and relaxing. Janice, pink and bright-eyed, was become lovely to him again. The stares of the other passengers were part of his strength. He and his fiancée were admired.

'You were superb,' she whispered. 'I didn't know you could be superb like that.'

There was something he couldn't bear to think about, that he had just done, but that wasn't it. There was something that lay ahead of him, that was still to be done, but that wasn't it. There was his future, that never would be, and his marriage, that never could be, but neither of those was it. It a combination of all these things combined with something more, the something that made him heavy and listless, that made him want—not to dash out into the street, as during the morning—but, but just to lie down. To stay lying down for ever.

But he could see that she was triumphant. He had held her on the train, cuddled and kissed her when no one (except the other passengers) was looking, had beamed pride and devotion at her, for public endorsement. He was hers again. And so, as he drifted back into listless distaste, she began to flower in the confidence of his love for her; or at least, hers for him. She took off her coat and kicked off her shoes and enjoyed the privacy that was Donal's gift to them. Her grin was new in feeling, proprietary, justified by her parents' acquiescence.

'Come on, then. There's something I want to do.' She

took him by the arm, in one of their old games together, and led him across the room. He drifted beside her like a sick man, and will-less. She pushed him on to the bed and he sagged backwards.

She unlaced his shoes and took them off; and unbelted his trousers; and unbuttoned his shirt; and unknotted his tie. She prodded and pushed, and made lewd jokes and whistled between her teeth as workmen had often done to her; and he rolled to her touch, and helped her to do as she liked. He was giving himself up, in sacrifice. When he was naked she drew the covers over him, up to his chin, and stood back. 'Neat,' she said. 'Very, very neat.'

Quickly she undressed. She went through the movements with a deliberate provocativeness, for his sake. She twisted her shoulders when she unclipped her bra, threw out her legs when she unrolled her stockings, and generally did things that would have made old men burst.

But he was not an old man. He was simply himself. And he watched her in despair. Her body, as it emerged, her slender, tough young body, with its fine, full breasts, and its long slim legs; her face, brow furrowed in comic concentration; her slanted glistening eyes. *She*. He thought of the blonde nude on *A History of Bondage*, manacled and gagged; clean, virgin and subject. *She*, his Janice. He wanted to be sick. 'Yum, yum,' he said courteously.

She pattered over to the bed and flung the sheet back. She stood over him, legs apart, scowling.

'Child's play,' she said, which was her own version of one of Donal's favourite jokes. Then she went back to his trousers and drew from his pocket one of the cream-coloured tins, which she clipped open. She pulled out a furled tube and dropped it on his nose, and clambered on top of him.

He lay supine under her. 'This is the life,' he said.

Her hands worked, probing and stroking, and in spite

228

of himself, his hatred of her body, life jerked up between his legs. He possessed a malicious snake between his legs, that moved and hardened against his instincts.

The heaving of his body, when he eventually and dutifully pinned her under him, was in aggression and disgust. The snake lay limp, damp, satisfied.

And so was she, as far as he could tell. She sprawled back on the bed, her fingers resting under his enfeebled traitor. On her face, when he could bear to look at it, was a smile of imbecile sexuality. He smiled back at her as from the sheets there rose into his nostrils the poison of her love.

He was extremely gallant. He took her to an expensive restaurant and then to a film. He spent most of the dinner bending towards her, listening to some chatter about one of Donal's friends at college, a seventeen-year-old Negro who had been raped by a Lesbian. She stopped in embarrassment the first time she mentioned Donal's name, but he was glad to hear it, as evidence against her.

And all the evening he studied, listening to her speech, watching her movements. Even in the cinema he turned to study. He considered, in the darkness, the side of her face, how the swell of her cheek and the characterless button of her nose gave her away. He held her hand for a little, to feel the stubbiness of her fingers. He waited anxiously for her to speak, especially in the darkness, when he could follow undistracted the commonness of her syntax, her vocabulary, above all her accent.

But he smiled, but he talked, but he was amusing. He mentioned little details of their past, such as it was; and their future, such as it would be; and all the time, every second of his time with her, he wondered how he could have wanted to spend his life with this—this—*this*. Whose parents were Mr. and Mrs. Arnold Trullope, of Heaslop Avenue; whose conversation was grotesque; whose body reeked and whose knickers were probably stained with sex. He was extremely gallant to her. Extremely.

When he went back to Cambridge that evening the battle was over. He saw it then, in his new and hygienic morality, as a battle. He could think of himself as if he were a separate character, from a novel or a film. He had lost control of himself; he had regained control of himself. Now he could start again, start afresh, free from marshy pollution. He would be clean. He would be able to mix with everyone he knew, in his proper world of Din and Hazings, Hardles and the Crab and the Staff, and Aunt Mary, and Miss Hagler, and Din—if they would have him back.

Then he tried to imagine Janice, his Jan, as he had first known her. But he could see only spread legs and damp hairs and the puckered skins of an imbecile mouth. Still he tried to force away that sickening image, to be, in his new resolution, generous. But it was no good.

She had made *him* smell.

Although she was in Cambridge—she had told the desk she would be staying until Monday—she wasn't in her room. He left the hotel, haunted the steps for half an hour, and then made his way to the Backs. He knew, though, that he had been deserted. He needed to talk to her, to be helped by her, to re-establish the intimacy that he had put in jeopardy. To make sure that she, above all others, would have him back. But secretly he knew he had driven her away.

But at least there was also no Janice. The night air was cool, and the sparse lights from the colleges were tranquil. He was detached from all that he had been and had done, floating in a cleansing loneliness. About him there was a fragrance of violets, carried on the rustling evening breeze.

He walked in this rapture for an hour before, in a sudden burst of impatience, he ran to the hotel. She was still not back.

He went, desolate, to his room. Half-way up the stairs he saw a light under his door. And behind it, a book open on her lap and smiling calmly she was waiting, and was his beloved sister.

He went to the other chair, sat down, and stretched his legs. He let his head fall back against the leather and closed his eyes. He wanted, just for a moment, to bask in the safety she created for him.

'Had a tiring day, Dodie?'

He opened his eyes and looked across, straight into her pale, loving face. Then he smiled, ironically and easily, a smile to the person who knew him best in the world. 'Bit strange, Din.'

'Oh.' She nodded. 'The parents?'

'Yes.'

'Poor Dodie. Were they—were they——?'

He remembered a word from a long way back, that covered it perfectly. 'Gruesome. I'd say they were gruesome.'

'Poor Dodie.'

He cleared his throat. He lowered his eyes slightly. 'And so was everything else.'

'*Every*thing?'

'Yes.'

'Oh.' There was a long pause, while she did things to her wrist and snapped clasps on her bag. 'Did you settle it all, then?'

'Settle what?'

'Well, all that you had to see them about. The Trullopes.' He noticed that she said their name quickly to avoid prolonging his pain.

'Oh, yes. All settled. Her dad is going to let us visit his shop.' He stared down into the grate, comforted by the knowledge that her eyes were still on him. It was as if each stage of the conversation had been planned in advance, between the old two of them.

'I'm glad,' she said, bringing him gently into the next phase, 'that I met Janice.'

'Are you?'

'Of course.'

'And——?'

'I should think she's very sweet.'

'Think she's sweet.'

'And obviously mad about you.'

'Mad about me?'

'And delighted at the thought of, well, getting you.'

'Yes,' he said. 'She is.'

'So', she offered, as if it were biscuits, 'everything's all right?'

'Yes,' he said. 'Perhaps it is.' He was holding his hands in his lap in an unnatural position, the palms turned upwards and outwards. 'I don't know, Din,' he whispered. 'I don't know.'

The centres of his palms were touched, lightly, a finger drawn across each one. Then her hands clasped around his. 'Don't be unhappy, Dodie. Don't be.'

'It's terrible,' he whispered. 'I've made a terrible mess of everything.'

'Listen, my love,' she was kneeling now, in front of him, her head tilted back to show him her whole face, loosed from the curtain of hair. Her hands rubbed his. Her eyes were love. 'You can do whatever you want. You're free, Dodie. As free as I am. As free as you want to be. Isn't that true?'

He nodded.

'You must do what you want. What you really want.'

232

He nodded. He hesitated, then looking down into her eyes. 'It's the thought of telling her, Din. That's what I can't bear.'

She squeezed his hands, so hard that it almost hurt. 'Oh, Dodie, you're brave enough for *that*.'

'I'll have to be,' he whispered. 'Won't I?' And he knew that as long as she was there, kneeling before him; as long as he could depend on her to be there, kneeling before him; he was brave enough for anything. Even his freedom.

He had been nervous all the way from Cambridge, with pre-visions of Mrs. Trullope to one side, scolding and damning; Mr. Trullope to the other, drab and hurt. There would be gestures towards suicide and hints of court action. But as soon as he saw her properly through his mists of fear, saw her long neck, her short, dark hair; as soon as her large, uncertain eyes met his, and she made a familiar gesture of greeting, a reflex grin; as soon, in fact, as she was there in all her usualness, he knew that it would be all right. He was in full possession of his courage from that moment on. The pity that stirred in him was also a comfort—a luxury of feeling that would come at other times, in his musing solitude when he was free. He ordered a couple of sherries and sat over his, carefully cold.

She drank hers very quickly, with the slight gulping noises that he realized he had always detested, and then put the glass away from her, in the centre of the table.

'I expect you've really come', she said, 'to tell me that you don't want me any more.'

It was only instinct that enabled him to convert shock into opportunity. He made a movement with his hand, vague, deprecating, meaningless.

'Well,' she looked at her glass, 'it's obvious, isn't it? I've probably known for weeks. It's just been a matter of waiting, see.'

He made another, ambiguous gesture; and searched her face anxiously for symptoms of distress.

'Is that it, Grahame? Is that why you've come?'

This was his cue, then. He had not had to work around, to make preliminary excursions into the hypothetical. She had given him a chance to plunge straight in. So he reached coolly into his pocket and drew out a piece of paper on which he had already scrawled a few rough figures. He put the sheet of paper down in front of him and took out a pen.

'It's just that', he cleared his throat, 'it's just that, well, to tell you the truth, Jan, I haven't been quite honest with you. Or your parents, see. There are some things I, you know, ought to tell you? It wouldn't be fair not to. Not fair on anyone.'

'Oh, yes.' There was just the slightest relaxation in her tone, as if she had failed in an attempt to stop herself from hoping. 'What, then?'

'Well, mainly about money. I've been thinking about money and our, the future.'

'*Money?*'

'Yes. You see, it's like this.' He glanced up. Her eyes were fixed on his face and were incredulous. She gave the impression that she was repeating the word over and over to herself, to examine meanings she had never encountered before. He shook his head, lowered it over the paper, and doggedly began. He mumbled numbers and made strokes of the pen beside the calculations he had prepared on the train. She didn't listen to what he said, nor to the precise sums he reeled off, nor to how he proved, logically and inevitably, that existence for two would end in starvation for at least one. He paused only to exclaim over the pen, which had run dry. She offered him a pencil, the tip of which he broke; and then a drawing stylo, which wrote crudely, but served. When he had finished the paper was covered with scraps of arithmetic, and in the whole tissue of his deceit there wasn't one lie. He was sure of that.

He dared to stare up at her, at last. She opened her mouth to speak, and he handed her back the stylo. She picked up the empty sherry glass and he took it from her.

'All right.'

'I feel terrible,' he said. 'Terrible.'

'It's all right. You needn't worry.'

'But I do worry. I shall worry.'

'I don't expect', she said, 'that you will, for long.'

'Yes.' And to his amazement his voice began to tremble. 'Always. Always, Jan. Always.'

'Well, it doesn't matter.' She hoisted her black raincoat over her shoulders, and stood up. She slipped one hand into her jeans pocket. 'I'd better go, then.'

'Please, Jan. Please don't.' He looked around the restaurant, for help, perhaps, or perhaps from fear that they were being watched. 'Have lunch at least.'

She sat down again. 'Don't you know I can't help it, about fancying you and that. It's all over me, the thought of seeing you, and sometimes I think I'll, I don't know, if you don't come, or when you get moody. And when you do it to me like the other day, you think I'm deaf and blind or something, the way you scramble off and curl up and look at me with that look, all polite. So you can give me lunch, if you want, I don't care. I don't care about anything.'

'Jan.' He took her hand and squeezed the fingers he still found stubby. 'Because of the——' he flourished the paper at her. 'Because of this.'

'*That!* Oh, yes,' she nodded, 'I see why it's got to end, if that's what you mean. I see that, all right.'

'Because of the money.' It was a point of honour to get her to say it. 'The money.'

But her eyes were fixed unseeingly on the paper he kept

235

thrusting at her, for she was listening to, and repeating, other voices, the voices of her little experience. 'I expect this had to happen. I probably had to get this over with, like Donal said. I'll be able to deal with anyone from now on, see, Donal says. I'll manage all right, after a bit, and I suppose I should thank you. I mean, for what you've done, because it's told me all the things I had to know or something like that. I won't throw myself out of the window or take pills, or any of that stuff. I'm not the kind. Although I'll probably want to, for a time, see, because I loved you. I really did. Whatever the word means.'

He saw that tears were running down her cheeks and suspected that waiters were watching. He tried to think of something to say, something that would make her understand. 'I—I—I,' he stammered. 'I——' Then, 'What about *me*?' Tears began to form in his own eyes as he himself began to understand at last. 'What about *me*?'

'I don't know about you. I've never known. Because you're like I said, so polite. Like your sister.' She dropped her eyes. 'I thought when you told me about that boy at school, and wanting to be brave, it was because you loved me, but I couldn't tell.'

'I did. I did, Jan.'

'Well, that's all right, then. I mean, if you don't any more, that's all right. Now you've told me. As long as you've told me the truth for once.' She got up with her raincoat now hanging from one shoulder, sloppily. Her face was small and white, her eyes rimmed with red, as if she'd been a long time in the rain. 'But you could have done it,' she whispered in fury and despair at herself for giving in to it, 'without all those numbers and looking so, I don't know, important.' She turned away with a coughing noise and hurried through the restaurant to the street.

He left ten shillings on the table for the sherries and ran through the waiters' stares after her. But she wasn't hiding from him. She was walking slowly towards Charing Cross Road, and seemed willing to let him go with her, as far as he wanted. So he accompanied her to the underground at Tottenham Court Road and bought her ticket to Wimbledon and plodded along beside her to the platform. After they stood there for a few minutes he put an arm around her shoulder. She turned in to him, to clutch at him.

'You're the only person,' he whispered. 'Ever.'

She pressed her face against his chest.

'Ever,' he said, as his nose twitched with the smell of rubber from her raincoat. And even as his body recoiled, too, even as he knew that she was waiting for him to kiss her on the mouth and start them together again, and knew also that to save her life he couldn't have done it, even so he felt something for her that he finally knew he would never be able to forget, whatever happened to him from then on.

The train came into the station and he stepped away. He said something, and she said something, and he said something else that had the word 'write' in it. She reached up and touched him on the cheek, then walked to a compartment.

She sat with her back to the window, but just before she was carried past him she stood and turned. She pressed her hand flat against the glass and they stared for an infinity that was less than a second straight at each other. Then she was gone.

He wandered about London for a while and felt nothing. He went to a film, parts of which he enjoyed, and after that went back to Cambridge. By the time he got to his room he knew that he was free at last, absolutely free.

BOOK THREE

The estate had originally been the Glenvale Rest Home and had accommodated elderly alcoholics (the East Wing) and young people with more complex addictions (the West Wing) between their bouts with life. It had flourished quietly, as such institutions must if they are to flourish at all, until a scandal had devalued it late in the summer of 1956. Either one of the patients had attacked one of the nurses with a croquet mallet, or one of the nurses had attacked one of the patients with a croquet hoop (it was to become one of Mr. Spill's jokes that he confused both the victims and the weapons) and the Glenvale had rapidly begun to develop the symptoms of an institution on the decline. Nurses came and went, patients were withdrawn, at least the kind the Glenvale wanted, and others, the kind that the better institutions hadn't wanted, were delivered in their place. Dr. Gander's vacations grew longer, and on one occasion he had had to refuse to answer questions put to him by a crusading Sunday paper. Nevertheless a photograph had become public, of Dr. Gander departing for somewhere in a car that shadows or ingenious printing made seem official. Two months later the Glenvale had been put up for sale. It had stayed on the agent's books for over a year, while the paint on the central and elegant building had peeled, and the lawns turned to weeds. And it would certainly have become one of Cambridge's notorious white elephants if Mr. Spill hadn't come up from London (with his mother's money, that he had multiplied) and converted it, with a few presidential commands and at great expense, into his own institution.

Although the Academy had no connection with the university, many tourists who came across it on the town's outskirts took it for one of the remoter colleges. At first Mr. Spill had encouraged this illusion, for he suspected that nothing so enhanced the reputation of his kind of Academy than the assumption of academic status. There was a rumour in the Combination Rooms that in those early days Mr. Spill had also asked all his teachers to wear B.A. gowns and to call him Master. The rumour went on to the effect that both the gowns and the title had had to be abandoned. In the last analysis, a painful affair, some of the teachers were found to have less right to the gowns that they had originally led their principal to believe; and the students, quick to misunderstand the intricacies of English tradition, had referred their many problems, financial and emotional, to 'Master Spill'. So there had been a purge, a number of silver (and in one or two flagrant cases of misrepresentation, copper) handshakes, and new appointments had been made. The Academy closed down for two months in order that it could begin again unblemished. When it reopened Mr. Spill was known to his staff by his Christian name, and no one was required to wear a gown, although by now everyone was entitled to do so. Mr. Spill had not made the same mistake twice. He had picked his men carefully, both for their academic records and for those spiritual qualities that would make them fit and permanent members of his institution. He knew, he told his mother (a widow, paralysed from the waist down and lodged in a little house on the other side of Cambridge), yes, he knew the types he wanted. After all, he had kept up their morale in a prison-of-war camp in Sicily.

Thus every teacher had passed through public school and then through either Oxford or Cambridge. And the one

242

part-time teacher, Mr. Meadle, had received the education appropriate to his half-and-half station. Mr. Meadle's grammar school was only partially concealed by his loud laugh and cheerful voice, and a provincial university was constantly advertised by the crest on his blue blazer. However much extra work he put in at the Academy, however often he applied for one of the vacancies, he could never permanently belong. Everyone at the Academy knew it except Mr. Meadle, who took up Mr. Spill's favourite hobby, *The Times* crossword puzzle, in a bid for notice. Mr. Spill enjoyed Mr. Meadle's help on the puzzle, admired his fund of classical knowledge, could scarcely credit his genius for anagram—but his next permanent was Philip Waybull, who had recently recovered from a nervous breakdown as a consequence of something that had happened to him, or something that he had done, while teaching in a prep school on the Isle of Wight. He was a thick-set man with glossy hair, a flushed face and dull eyes, youngly and Englishly handsome in the way that forty-five-year-old naval officers tend to be. Sometimes, especially when Mr. Spill teased him, his hands would tremble and he became quite dangerous; but he had been to Westminster and to St. Edward's Hall, Oxford, and his accent showed it. In spite of Mr. Waybull's appointment Mr. Meadle continued to work as hard as ever—not being on Permanent meant merely that he wasn't listed in the school brochure and couldn't be paid during the vacations—and continued to spend his coffee breaks on his feet, bending over Mr. Spill and feeding into his cocked ear the correct solutions. 'Thank you, Meadle, indeed I thank you,' said Mr. Spill, winking into his *Times* and writing rapidly with his golden biro. 'What, oh what would I do without you, irreplaceable Meadle?' But when he next gave a small buffet supper in honour of yet another Permanent—Simon Quine, who had a soft face and large hips and a narrow

243

waist; who fluttered his hands when he spoke and referred to the students as 'the children'; but had been to Charterhouse and Trinity—when Mr. Spill gave a small supper for Simon Quine, Mr. Meadle was found to be replaceable once again. No doubt Mr. Meadle would have been replaceable for the school lunches, that the staff took in the refectory with the students (but raised up from them by a platform) if he hadn't been so useful in some presidential *jeux d'esprit*. Amidst general hilarity (Mr. Meadle's apprehensive snorts sounding loudest) Mr. Spill would stalk to the end chair with a bowl of potatoes or a jug of grapefruit juice. He had only to bend solicitously over Mr. Meadle's crinkled head to reverse the crossword tableau and effect a neat little satire on the proper order of things.

The Permanents, then, weren't like Mr. Meadle. They weren't even like each other except in the way in which they weren't like Mr. Meadle, and in a shared poverty of morale (where again they differed from Mr. Meadle, whose morale was always high; or rising). Apart from the two recent additions—Philip Waybull, from the Isle of Wight; and Simon Quine, who even in his first week at the Academy was to be glimpsed in various nooks of the corridors gossiping about grammar with young foreign aristocracy—there was Jeremy Peaslow, a small round man (Repton and Christ Church), thirty-five and balding, with a talent for puns. Mr. Spill called him 'our Mr. Punch' and sometimes, to keep him up to the mark, complicated his puns with the air of someone hoping to be topped. But he never was. Mr. Peaslow, faced with presidential badinage, would be afflicted with a stammer that had lain dormant since childhood. There was also Mr. Winder (Lancing and Trinity House) who had taken a good second in Scandinavian languages and was the Academy's chief intellectual. He was a bachelor, tall, with large teeth, and in discussion had the voice of a cultured madman. He read all the latest novels, saw all the latest films, admired them before Mr. Spill had heard of them, and began to see through them just as Mr. Spill was getting to admire them. And finally there was Mr. Bloomington, the only survivor of the original purge, and thus the staff-room's oldest resident. Everything about him, from his slow speech to his almost somnambulistic walk, suggested withdrawal. Twenty years before he had been the prettiest boy at St. Paul's, and fourteen years before, one of the most enchanting undergraduates at Clare. Now he spent hours in an armchair, his feet up, his long, womanly face turned to the ceiling, dreaming back on old triumphs. He sometimes hinted at a disappointment with the world and its noises, and would be sharp with Mr. Meadle about his energy. 'Bustle, bustle, bustle. Why don't you relax, man?' With such a team (and with only one more Permanent to find) Mr. Spill could afford to be as presidential as he wished.

So one mid-afternoon in July (the month of vacations, for it came between the end of the summer term and the beginning of the autumn term) he stood between the opened iron gates of his Academy, facing his green estate. From the back and from the distance, in his dark suit and black shoes, with his white collar gleaming above the round of his jacket, and the rims of his spectacles glittering like golden threads behind his ears, he might have been taken for the manager of a large hotel, with something of the idealist mixed tastefully in. But from the front and from closer to he looked more like a clever schoolboy who had been elongated and thickened and then magically waxed against the corruptions of the world. His eyes behind the lenses were round and winking blue, the skin of his small face was unmarked, and his short black hair was pasted close to his scalp by a softened paraffin. He smelt so pungently of after-shave lotions that the flowers he held in his

245

left hand might have been waxed as well, for all the chance he gave their scents.

When at last he heard the tell-tale chinks approaching up the drive he made a small movement of his lips, to confirm that his dentures were secure (they were; they always were; they had been fitted by an expert, in possession of the most advanced techniques), put away an image, blonde and calm, that his mind had been toying with, and turning quickly around, prepared to concentrate a welcoming joke on the young man, in order to delay concentrating his hungry blue gaze on the young man's sister.

'I was wondering', he said, as he shook hands, 'whether you existed. But I see you do, in your plenitude. Did you know Dianah loves to tease? Did you know that, Grahame?'

Grahame didn't. Nor did he believe it. He stood looking away from his animated host and thinking that the sun was very hot, that the exchange now taking place was incomprehensible, and that Mr. Spill had a shiny face, and a shinier smile. Mr. Spill, glaring comically, was demanding that Din check her pretty little memory for an Academy rule he had whispered to her on her last visit.

'Oh, I'm sorry.' A pale smile showed on her calm face. 'Ted, I mean.'

'Ted, you do and must mean, and ever more shall be so. So. So now you and your sibling, my good lady, have a stroll through the grounds. I snipped these for the cottage, as *sans doute* and *sin dudad*, you'll have guessed. Because of flowers for the sweet? They'll brighten it up until you come to brighten it up yourself.'

Din took the flowers with a sketch of a curtsy. 'They're gorgeous.'

'Not as——' Mr. Spill's head trembled, either with the effort of keeping good jokes in, or of forcing good compliments out. 'Now go. And brighten.'

In fact the cottage needed no brightening. It was one of two across from the main lawn at the back, small and compact and only recently built. It contained a sitting-room, a kitchen-dining-room, and up a short flight of stairs, a bedroom with a double bed and a bathroom. It was well-serviced—hot water ran immediately from the right taps, the fridge hummed efficiently unto itself, and the kitchen cupboards contained a dozen plates, cups and saucers, all with 'Spill Academy' flourished around a black representation of an ancient spire. There were two square grey armchairs in the sitting-room and some plastic (but removable) logs in the grate. It was neat; and only nasty in little corners.

'Well, Dodie,' she arranged the flowers in a blue jug that was itself emblemed with the Academy, and put them on the table. She stroked her hands together with a chinking of coins. 'What do you think?'

He looked out of the window to avoid his own embarrassment. 'He seems very nice.' He hesitated. 'But I see what you mean about those three years in a prison-of-war camp, how it must have affected him.'

There was a little pause.

'No, I meant the cottage.'

'Oh, very,' he waved, 'with a little, you know, imagination.'

'Yes.' She sat down, pushed the wings of hair back from the sides of her face, and eyed the plastic logs, which had been designed to glow as if from fire; then stood up and walked towards the window. 'Just look at the grounds. They're enormous.'

'Yes. I suppose they are.' He stood beside her and felt, for a number of reasons—not one of which he could work out—awkward. 'What's that stuff sparkling on the edge of the lawn, behind the rose beds?'

'Barbed wire, I think. It's a little odd—there's lots of it, all over the place. I suppose it's to keep the hooligans out.'

247

She turned around. 'Anyway, I can always have the logs taken away.'

'Yes,' he said, 'without the logs it'll be comfortable. What hooligans?'

'I don't know, Dodie. There are always hooligans, probably. Even in Cambridge. Perhaps we'd better go over now and look at the main building?'

'But I've never heard', he said, as he followed her out of the door, 'of putting up barbed wire against hooligans.'

There were french windows everywhere, so that the sun streamed through the classrooms, and down the corridors and converted the libraries, the staffroom, the two-tiered lunch hall, even the lavatories, into temples of light. All the floors were carpeted and all the walls showed off engaging lithographs of the grounds. In the staffroom, which opened sumptuously on to one of the lawns, there were two oil paintings of the whole estate that might have been worked up from helicopter photographs, but had, in fact, been done by one of Glenvale's first patients, as therapy. There were many armchairs, too, deep and comfortable.

Everything was comfortable. Everyone was comfortable. Mr. Spill himself said so as he served tea in his study (off which, as it happened, was the one room that wasn't comfortable; and thus not on view. A long, windowless cupboard which contained a camp-bed; a knapsack full of clean underwear; a gas ring and a vacuum flask. This was Mr. Spill's base, when he couldn't face returning to his paralysed mother). He had had the tea arranged on his desk, around which he had placed two swivel seats and a low armchair. He himself sat in the armchair and thus reduced his presence to such an extent that his smooth, smiling face only just showed above the top of the desk. He adjusted the perspective, however, by talking a great deal and being mother.

Throughout the talk and the proffering of plates Grahame sat stiffly, fondling his cup and attentively an applicant. But even so he was sure that he had never heard so many bad jokes in as short a time before; and had never seen his sister so easily amused. She fixed her grey eyes on Mr. Spill's face, which admittedly was all there was of him to concentrate on, as if finding in his expression other jokes, quite independent of those issuing so compulsively from his mouth. Her laughter was as steady as running water.

'Do you like the French?' He pushed a plate of chocolate biscuits across the table. 'They're very intelligent, *n'est-ce-pas*? Dianah, my goodness, why are you giggling? It doesn't do to make fun of the French. At least out loud.'

The laughter, like running water, could be turned off; and was.

'So *do* you like the French? Grahame, my solemn chap?'

He said he did.

'And find them intelligent?'

He said he did.

'All my men agree. People talk a lot of nonsense about national characteristics. Utter Thomas rot. The Italians are emotional, the Dutch are phlegmatic. The Scandinavians are depressing—ooops—Dianah, you're off with your giggles again. Mustn't slander the Scans. We've a man here, good enough for a university post, calls himself Winder. He's our expert on the Scans. Talks all their languages like six of them tied together. Or however many it is. And agrees that they're depressed. The Spanish are proud as parsnips, poor as potatoes, and the Germans whom I know well—having been a little wartime captive—and admire hugely,' and went into a pantomime of embarrassment, eyes rolling, finger-nails scratching at his cheeks, shoulders hunched, at what people said about the Germans. 'Utter and malicious, Thomas and Harold rot. And do you know, it's all true. And I love them for it.'

The tap was turned on again. 'How lovely!'

The head swivelled towards the other side of the desk. 'Don't *you* think so?'

'Yes,' he said, eagerly laughing; and eagerly wishing that Mr. Spill wouldn't stare at him.

Mr. Spill considered him intently for a moment, then rose and walked to the window. 'Of course,' slicing down at the green lawns that rolled beneath him, 'the grounds were large when we took them over, but we've already moved our barbed wire out a little. There's a field we're dabbling in, Grahame, and with a trickle of luck and a torrent of the other stuff, I spy a swimming pool or some such. However,' he turned, 'that's all beside the point. Although not for your sis, who is *very* quick, bless her. I've never known a girl with such a head on her shoulders.' He glanced swiftly towards the girl, to make sure that the head, blonde and calm, was still there, and then put his hands behind his back and began some presidential negotiating. 'The point for you is the teaching point. That's what you'd be interested in? No? Or no denied?'

No denied. So he nodded his head and bent forward to ask the kind of question that applicants ought to ask, but before he could phrase it Mr. Spill indicated, with a raised finger, that he had the answer. And explained why it was that the Academy, while seemingly prosperous, and *in fact* prosperous, was, just at the moment, committed to what *might* appear to be at first sight, not a terribly high, although not of course, not a terribly *low*, salary so to speak scale? But then there were the free lunches, yes? and the other cheap little cottage (handy for the resident secretary, if the resident secretary was also a sister) that would go to the next single man taken on Permanent. So that all in all living expenses—depending on the style of living, what one was used to? would be negligible. What did he think of that for plainish speaking?

He thought it, he said, very fair. 'Very fair, under the circumstances.'

'It *was*—just for my staff records—Windhoven?'

'Yes.'

'Good. Good enough. And Cambridge we already know about. Most distinguished college. The best there is, bar two.' He came back to the desk, poured himself a cup of tea, shook the biscuits into a new pattern on the plate, and sat down on the edge of the desk. He tilted his head to one side, and patted his hair. 'We'd love to have you. If you'd love to come. And I bet your sis is pleased.'

His sis said she was. And cut Mr. Spill a slice of lemon for his tea. 'Have you decided about Mr. Mead, Ted?' she wondered, in the pause that followed Grahame's stammered thanks.

'Dell. Meadle, my dear. The poor fellow was after the Permanency that's just gone to this one here, you know. So I think he'll have to wait his turn, once more. No, honestly, longer than that. I fear that Meadle is best off where he is. Which is nowhere. A dear fellow,' he swayed his cup towards Grahame, 'but not quite what we're after, you see.'

'I see.'

'We want', he puckered his mouth, to keep the lemon from leaking between his gums and his teeth, and doing damage, 'chaps like you.'

But before he could say proper thanks again, Mr. Spill, mixing jokes with diplomacy, was off on an anecdote that must have been very funny; from the gestures with which he accompanied it, and from the laughter which Din, and now her brother also, poured through it.

Before taking up their respective appointments at the Spill Academy they went back to Morton for a week of summer rest. They walked on the beaches and swam in the

251

cold waters, made each other cups of tea, and sat in deck-chairs in the garden after lunch, drowsily. Aunt Mary, whose headaches had become less frequent—they had been replaced by dizzy spells—sometimes sat with them although on the other side of the french windows. She was a little uneasy in the sun, especially when the sounds of the Butlin's builders could reach her.

'I don't quite understand,' she called, opening her desk drawer with three little clicks and pretending not to be surprised by its emptiness—for if the papers relating to Morton's old and infirm were not there, where could they be but somewhere else equally sensible? (As, for instance, the base of the old grandfather clock on the landing.) 'Don't quite understand what it is you'll both be doing there.'

'It's a new educational scheme,' came from behind her. Colonel Rones, from sympathy, had also developed a preference for shadows. 'Dianah's in charge of the office and Grahame——'

'Can speak for himself, Basil.'

'Teaching,' he called, resting his head against the wooden bar from which faded canvas stretched, and turning his face up to the sun's full glare. 'Usual sort of thing. You know. That one does in a school if one isn't a pupil.'

'Teaching what?' But she forgot her question immediately. She was sure she smelt smoke and was inspecting the Colonel. 'Is that tobacco?'

'I've just put out a fag,' came from the garden. 'Didn't know you disapproved, Aunt M.'

If she *had* disapproved, she ceased to do so on the spot. 'Aunt M,' she exclaimed shyly. 'Well, well.'

'Very well, thank you, Aunt M.'

And they all laughed aloud, two in the sun, two in the shade; a family united.

It was Grahame's holiday, really. He had developed an

252

easy way with the old people, a teasing charm that came, perhaps, from having seen a bit of life as it really was.

'To think', he said to Din, when they had Mallows to themselves that midnight, 'we used to be afraid of them. Aunt Mary and the old Colonel. They're so sweet, don't you think? Quite smashing, really.' He put his cup down on Aunt Mary's desk, which (he didn't notice) was, for the first time in twenty years, completely clear of documents. 'Absolutely gorgeous. In their way.' And stretched out his legs, that had walked through a bit of life as it really was. 'Are you writing to him *again*, for God's sake, Din?'

She looked up from her pad, perched professionally on her tanned knee. Then she put down her pen and felt at her hair, which she had arranged for the first time in her life on the top of her head. 'I'm meant to be on duty,' she said, with the smile of one anticipating a joke back. 'And my present duty is to remind him that *you'll* be getting the other cottage.'

'That's it. Tell him he'll have to make me comfortable if he wants to keep me.' He folded into his lap the hands that had grappled with a bit of life as it really was. 'We'll show the old virgin who's boss.'

They worked out the details over coffee, after a lunch in which Mr. Spill had been in brilliant form.

'Dianah Thwaite to dress me up,' he said, smiling at his newest permanent. 'She'll pack me about with paper, to plumpen me and make sure nothing sticks out.'

'Sounds wonderful,' insisted Mr. Meadle.

'Then I waddle swiftly across the garden. Dianah Thwaite,' he said, smiling again at his newest permanent, 'to assist me out of the window. Because of my false bulk. What does Mr. Dozey think?'

Mr. Dozey (alias Bloomington) blinked, focused his eyes and went through some small movements usually associated with consciousness. 'Wouldn't it be easier', he wondered finally, 'to come through the door?'

'Easier, Mr. Dozey? Eas-i-er? Doubtless for *some* it would be, yes.'

The window', Mr. Meadle glossed, 'is better.'

'Why?' asked Mr. Waybull. He had been jotting down notes on graph paper and drawing in arrows that clarified as a means, perhaps, of forgetting the poster COME TO THE ISLE OF WIGHT that he had passed on his way to the Academy that morning. 'I don't quite grasp that, I'm afraid. But then I know I'm pretty thick.' His voice rose slightly and his pencil wagged. 'But not too thick to understand, if someone would explain.'

Mr. Meadle, who always took Mr. Waybull's hysteriae as challenges to his own powers of lucidity, adjusted his shoulders under his blazer pads and obliged. 'They won't', he enunciated slowly, 'be expecting anyone to come through the windows, if you see. People expect people to come through doors. Not through windows. Windows——'

Mr. Peaslow's eyes twinkled around the table. 'We could get a French student to come in through the french windows,' he said. 'As a kind of joke, Ted?'

'Visual gag,' Mr. Winder took him up. He was currently working his way through the films of Godard, mastering the jargon so that when he finally saw through them it would be from the other side. 'Would they get it, though? Visual gags demand a certain literary and let's face it, linguistic power of connection.'

'No.' Mr. Peaslow shook his head. 'I mean, just as a *joke*, Ted.'

It would have got a poor reception if it got anything like the reception Ted gave it now. 'Jokey-wokies, Mr. Punch? Is that what we're here for, think you, sir?'

'The crucial thing,' said Mr. Quine, averting his eyes compassionately from Mr. Peaslow's face, and shifting his soft hips against the surface of the wooden chair, and covering with his hand the sketch of an Italian count in his elementary grammar class that he had doodled, unawares, on to the pad in front of him. 'The crucial thing is whether they have a natural sense of the theatre. Most young people have it, especially at Christmas time.'

Mr. Winder made a swift but noisy comparison with Finnish Christmas traditions, to which Mr. Spill listened with ill-concealed impatience.

'Be that as it may,' Mr. Meadle had noted the expression on the presidential face. 'What we're concerned with, Windy old chap, is an English Christmas here,' he slammed his hand on the table and caused the coffee cups to jump, 'here in this Academy.'

Mr. Spill, recalling that a technical college had once offered Mr. Winder an assistant lectureship, decided in favour of conciliation. 'We can't *completely* see the point of a Finnish Christmas, Geoffrey, in an English language school in England.'

'It would finish them off.' From Mr. Peaslow, twinkling desperately. 'Ted?'

And won a laugh from Ted; and from Mr. Meadle, who aimed his across the table into Mr. Winder's face.

No, Mr. Winder explained, no. That what he meant was simply that there were interesting analogies to be made. If anyone had seen the over-rated films of Ingmar Bergman? But Mr. Spill, no longer concealing his impatience, interrupted to ask who would undo the catch of the french window, on which his effective entry depended. 'One maestro to usher me in. Another maestro to make a little speech about Father Christmas, as I come plumply through.' And the meaning of the smile he directed at his newest Permanent was commandingly unambiguous.

'Oh, of course, if there's anything *I* can do.' He spooned out his fourth of sugar crystals and sucked in his stomach.

255

He had had a big lunch and was a trifle uncomfortable. 'Couldn't make a speech, though, I'm afraid.'

'Couldn't. Shouldn't. Mustn't. Can't. Won't. What are these negatives, that sing all about mine ears, Mr. Sugar Lover.' Remembered, perhaps, whose brother he was addressing, and tacked off presidentially, towards generosity. 'No, no, we mustn't push a new man into new situations.'

'*I* could.'

'What?' asked Mr. Winder contemptuously. 'What could you do?'

'I can make speeches.' Mr. Meadle faced into Mr. Winder's scornful eyes. 'I've done it at Wicksteed—the college. Of course I couldn't do it in Finnish.'

'What is all this about Finnish? Now, I know I'm still being thick about everything but I'm trying to keep a check on these suggestions on my graph and it's no good——'

'Our Mr. Fix-it's in a fix, dear me. Now, Philip, not to worry. It's all——'

Fixed, as everyone agreed, which was the cue for the newest permanent to rise and slip rapidly towards the door. But Mr. Spill caught him in the corridor and whispered that he *had* been hoping that he *might* have been persuaded —'Meadle's a dear chap, but he's only a temporary. And there's a matter of style, is there not, or no again?'

'Oh, but Fred has style, don't you think?'

'Of course he has. Of course he has. Although it's an unusual——' then with a quick shake of his head, 'Is his first name Fred? He told me it was Francis, naughty fellow.'

'Meadle's to make the speech. I'm to unfasten the windows. And you're to put the rolls of paper around him to plumpen him up.'

'Yes. He told me.'

'You're also to help him out of the window. Because of his bulk.'

'Yes. He told me that, too.'

'You're very loyal to him. Aren't you, Din?'

She looked down into her cup. 'I work for him,' she explained. 'I couldn't work for him if I didn't feel loyal to him.'

'And you couldn't put paper around him if you didn't feel loyal to him. Could you, Din?'

She got to her feet. 'I'd better get back now, Dodie. He said he'd drop in this evening with some accounts he wants me to go through.' She opened the door. 'He does want it to be a success, you know.'

'And I'm sure it will be,' he conceded generously, to hide his irritation at her early departure. 'Let's hope so, anyway.'

Most of the students arrived for dinner at 7.45, a quarter of an hour before the announced time. They stood about the staffroom in small groups, perfectly at ease with themselves in their *smokings* or their expensively simple, knee-length dresses; and were consequently immediately distinguishable from the staff, who were visibly not at ease with themselves, and who wore, to a man, evening suits that had been handed on by fathers and uncles who were either taller or shorter than they. But it was the staff's duty to mix with the students, to make sure that they were having a good time, to keep them supplied with fruit cup or potato crisps, and to explain a thing or two ('But don't give the game away,' Mr. Spill had warned) about traditional English Christmases; and this, in their own ways, they were all doing. Mr. Peaslow was expounding a joke to three quick-eyed French boys who were finding great possibilities in it, although judging from a sudden burst of Mr. Peaslow's stammer, and from the way their laughter rang out at different intervals from his own, they weren't the possibilities that he himself found. Mr. Winder was among the Scandinavians, ferociously debating a point that none of the wondering, long-limbed Swedish girls, or the scowling Danish boys, appeared to have disputed; Mr. Bloomington, his pallor emphasized by the blackness of his suit and the weary ghastliness of his smile, was mute before a voluble, and from her gestures, extremely angry Italian girl with a club foot; Mr. Quine was laying hands discreetly, and resting eyes greedily, on a young man with a large brown face and small black eyes; Mr. Waybull was hunched into a corner, ticking names off on a list and occasionally throwing his pencil angrily into the air; and the newest permanent was by himself in another corner, where he had found a large bowl of cashew nuts and an unguarded jug of fruit cup, and was reminding himself that he mustn't spoil his appetite.

At ten minutes past eight Mr. Spill entered with his secretary close behind him. He looked most impressive in a brand new evening suit, but only a spectacular red rose in his buttonhole hinted at the extravagances to come. His secretary, in a white dress that was tight to the waist, and then full to just above the knees, might have been a hostess introducing a guest of international repute. Together they made a slow circuit of the room, Mr. Spill shaking hands quite often, his secretary having hers, beneath its chinking golden cuff, kissed once or twice. From his corner of the room, where he was now wedged between two Greeks, the newest permanent was able to observe the serene confidence of his sister's movements, the graceful manner in which she inclined her blonde head (hair down to her shoulders, grown out over months), or allowed her fingers to be raised to smiling lips. He scooped up a handful of nuts, poured them into his mouth, and marvelled at her manner.

When the couple had gone around the room a second time, Mr. Meadle, sweating noticeably (he had had, after all, to transport some seventy coats down the hall to one of the reading rooms), appeared at the door. He was wearing a blue serge suit, a tie that, with its excess of stripes and crowns, indicated the insignificance of the institution that had educated him, and a spectacular red rose in his buttonhole. He stared around the room, his hands on his hips, until catching Mr. Spill's eye, he drew attention to himself

by thumbing the rose and beaming at coincidence. Mr.
Spill acknowledged him with a hard blue stare from his
winking spectacles, and motioned with his hand towards
the door. Mr. Meadle left the room to reappear a few
minutes later without the rose, which he had dropped down
one of the staff lavatories. Again Mr. Spill stared at him,
and again Mr. Meadle would have left the room if the
secretary hadn't hurried around many groups and come to
his side. Her whispered instructions returned the beam to
Mr. Meadle's face. He clapped his hands. He threw up his
arms. 'Ladies and gentlemen,' he cried, 'foreigners. Dinner
is served. Be our guests. On behalf of Ted Spill and his
merry men, I invite you . . .' Mr. Spill's expression, as Mr.
Meadle pursued his tactless introduction to its tasteless
end, was a study in conflicting responses. He smiled with
his mouth at the students, and glared with his eyes at Mr.
Meadle; who, happily, caught only the smile, and was ele-
vated by it.

Dinner was served in the usual dining-room, with, as
usual, the staff on the stage above, and the students in the
large space below. There were crackers and ribbons and
false hats and bubbling pear cider. There was turkey and
there was ham, and, of course, there was Christmas pud-
ding, followed by mice pies. There was a tangerine and a
cup full of nuts for everyone, and for each of the students
there were two chocolates, one hard-centred, one soft.
There were even small bottles of peach brandy sent up
from Pepard by one of Mr. Spill's aunts; and best of all
there was absolutely no doubt that the students enjoyed
themselves. They liked the turkey and ham so much that
several of them wondered why there wasn't enough; they
drank their two allotted glasses of pear cider and guessed
at the chemicals from which it had been fabricated; they
squabbled humorously, and in some cases erotically, over

the chocolates, and they flicked nuts at each other, as no nut-crackers had been provided. A Portuguese girl sitting at the end of the table nearest the stage turned pale and clutched at her stomach.

There was almost as much gaiety above, for this was the staff's night, too, Mr. Spill reminded them. 'Let there be no doubt about it,' he said, Christmas was Christmas. 'Oh, I wish', he cried towards the end of the meal, as he mulled his peach brandy over the flame of a candle with one hand, and cocked his paper pirate's hat over the lens of his spectacles with the other, 'that one of my crew knew some Christmas verses. Oh, avaunt, ye lubbers.'

Mr. Meadle, his face suffused, soared up in answer, and was therefore best placed to get to the Portuguese girl, who swayed to her feet at precisely the same instant.

'Oh, faithful Meadle,' Mr. Spill whispered to his secretary, who sat graciously on his right; and 'Isn't Fred-alias-Francis wonderful?' he whispered to his newest permanent, who sat eating rapidly but impassively on his left.

'Here!' Mr. Meadle jerked the curtain out of his hand and let it fall back. 'Not even I,' he touched himself on the chest, 'not even I, am meant to pull the curtains, until the exact second by the clock.'

'But isn't it raining?'

Mr. Meadle laughed contemptuously. 'Look, just let me look after it. Eh?'

'Well, I expect', he agreed, 'that you're in charge of it, Fred, as you're making the speech of welcome. I hope it's as good as your invitation to dinner. Shall I open the window now?'

'Can't you leave it alone?' Mr. Meadle sawed his arm in exasperation. 'That's right. And my name is Francis, *if* you don't mind.' Several students swung their eyes in his direction, and he began to rock on his feet and grin abstractedly, as if concealing a corpse at the policeman's ball. Behind him the rapping increased, sharp and insistent against the panes.

'It's getting worse, Fred. Francis.'

'What is?'

'The rain.'

'Rain! Bit of rain won't stop Ted.'

Efficient fingers had packed cotton wool under the belt of his pantaloons, and stuffed a pillow under the flaps of his tunic. Gently they had sealed the beard in place; and pasted the moustache across the upper lip without provoking the nervy line of his gums. A slim hand had assisted him out of the window, a delicate arm had sped him on his way. He could have sworn that light had sparkled from the cuff around the wrist as the catch of the window was pushed into place. He remembered then that the staffroom clock was always slow. But not to worry. The faithful Meadle would have remembered, too.

A few yards more and the rain had started torrentially. But not to worry. He had only to race plumply across the grass to the staffroom windows, and tumble merrily in amongst his guests, the foreigners. He did get a little wet on the way, of course, but not to worry.

He got wetter during the two minutes that marked his first signals on the glass. The tappity-tap-tap-tap that only a fool like the faithful Meadle would have failed to hear.

But not to worry. He wheeled neatly around and hared towards the distant brightness that must surely be the ledge of another window; and only turned out to be barbed wire after he had smashed plumply into it. He left on the barbs, as he fought his way free, a few shreds of pantaloons and a little shred of skin. Also some lumps of cotton wool, from his beard and his moustache. But not to worry. To get back to where he had started from and call the whole thing off.

262

He blundered plumply through the darkness and over several prize rose bushes before he found the place. Now tears were mingling with the rain and confusing his vision, and as he stood swaying in front of the window he had for an instant the conviction that in the black emptiness there were five identical images, pale and calm, shimmering at a ghostly door. His cry of thanks and for help escaped his lips just as the ghostly door closed on the five identical images, and left him there.

He rolled back across the grass, skidding once to lacerated knees, and another time tangling his feet among the flapping tatters of his pantaloons. Again he began his staccato rapping, which he concluded by drawing back his fist, with the intention of driving it through the pane and into any part of Meadle that happened to be directly in line behind the curtain; then, in a spasm of presidential control, raised it to his mouth and jammed it between his false teeth, to block a sob. Not to worry, worry, worry. He pressed flat under a sloping wooden shelf that projected a few inches above the windows. The rain drove slantingly in on him, continuing to soak the front surface of his person and washing cotton wool into his mouth; it poured smoothly over the slanting shelf, on to the cone of his beret, and continued to soak the back surface of his person, and the sack of Woolworth presents that a lovely thumb had fastened over his shoulder. But no, no, no, not to worry. He would stand where he was and entertain his drowning mind with thoughts of what he would do to Meadle, when the clock struck and the windows opened at last.

She came into the crowded room, smiling. But when she had taken in the scene before her—of students gathered in impatient groups, of teachers eyeing the clock and comparing it with their watches, of her brother standing urbanely in a corner, picking out soft-centred chocolates from a saucer and avoiding her eyes, she began to worry, a little.

'What?'

'Where is he?' she repeated, refusing the chocolates with a chinking motion of her hand.

'Who?'

'Ted.'

'Ted? Oh,' he shook his head and crammed a strawberry cup in between his twitching lips. 'Meadle said he was with you.'

'But he climbed out five minutes ago. I thought *you* were meant to let him in.'

'No, Meadle said to leave the whole thing to him. Anyway, there's nothing to worry about. He can't be far away, Din—probably outside in the garden.'

'Outside?'

'Well, he can't get in until Meadle lets him,' he reasoned, 'can he?' And pointed to Meadle, who at that very second was stepping away from the window with the edge of the curtain in his hands.

'Surprise, surprise, oh, Christmas surprise.' Mr. Meadle undid the catch and flourished the curtain back with a double twist of his wrists. 'Guess what we have here.' He turned, with spread arms, to usher in from the streaming night a figure that caused him to jerk his arms higher, in dreadful surrender, and higher.

The Christmas surprise limped marshily across the staff-room, sobbing only slightly; through the aisle of students formed in preparation by the teachers; and out of the door that Mr. Bloomington had already, with somnambulistic courtesy, opened for him.

'He's taken it', she said late that night, 'very well.'

'Good for him.'

'He's decided not to blame anyone at all.'

'Not even for the rain? How decent.'

'Not even Meadle.'

'He's very tolerant, this leader of men.' And he turned his head away as another laugh exploded from him.

'I don't,' she said, 'I don't really think it's funny. He only wanted to give everyone pleasure.'

'*And* he did. Did you see their faces when he left?'

'I still don't think it's funny.'

'But, Din, but Din,' he brought himself under control at last. 'I thought you wanted me to be happy here,' he banged his fist on the table, and made the Horlicks mugs jump, 'here in this Academy.'

She stared coldly at him for a long moment; and then she smiled; and finally, and obviously against her will and plans, she began to laugh.

She was grinning, of course, and her knees were pressed together. She threw some of the furled tubes into the air, and he leapt snapping up at them, playing the faithful dog in one of their games. He noticed as if for the first time the little scar on her cheek, where Weckles had bitten her, and then noticed that she had become naked, was lolling back with legs astraddle, waiting; and that her damp lips smiled open to his investigating eyes; and that her nipples were small and hard, the halo of pimples distinct. He stared into the nest of her hair, rose to plug her smile, and there was the smell that made him sick. It was the smell of his desire.

He overcame it with five sausages, half a pound of bacon, two pieces of French toast, and coffee. Followed by pancakes with strawberry jam, an apricot yoghourt, and a cup of coffee into which he dropped a handful of sugar cubes. He rounded himself off with a dose of brandy and another coffee, sat for a time, smiling at the plastic logs in his grate, then rose and sauntered heavily out into the cool night air. Far up in the Academy a small light shone, like a glinting eye. He wandered towards it with lazy exhalations of sausage, jam and brandy, that mingled with the many scents of the roses that bloomed beside the barbed wire. He was at ease in the pastoral compound for he knew that underneath the glinting eye she would be putting papers away at last; perhaps even now coming towards him along one of the paths, to take him in her charge. They would have a Horlicks nightcap together, with a few of the Cadbury's chocolate biscuits he had got in especially—or if he'd already finished them, a little savoury of some kind. He had discovered cheese on toast with a grilled tomato resting on it.

But no slim figure discovered him there, and the light shone upwards, perpetually, and in the end he went through the french windows of the staffroom and blundered softly up the stairs. Her voice came to him, along the carpeted halls and down the carpeted stairs, met only occasionally by presidential qualifications that carried the more authority for the laughter that greeted them. He loomed discreetly towards the door, and then, as a burp arose, loomed discreetly away. He caught another burp against the back of his hand, tautened his stomach muscles, and slid his head into the room. It was empty.

But a long, narrow cupboard that opened off it was not. His sister was standing just inside it, carrying some files under her arm and studying something in what looked like a small blue box she was holding in her hand. Behind her an elongated shadow hovered.

'Din.'

She must have heard him, for she raised her eyes frowningly; but she couldn't have seen him, for she turned away and put the folders on the desk. Then she went back into the cupboard, presumably still unaware that half a face was offering itself to her from the door, and that a whole eye was attempting to catch her attention.

He let himself be found in the staffroom, sitting in Mr. Bloomington's chair with his feet on a stool. He let himself be quizzed, too, about what he was doing there in the darkness and all by himself; although he answered at first in monosyllables that only gradually stretched into a complaint.

'Ulcers! Dodie, hadn't you better see a doctor?'

'No, I'll be all right.'

'But haven't you eaten *anything* tonight?'

'Only a sausage or so. Quite enough, though.'

'Could you face some cheese on toast?' She stood behind him, worriedly rumpling his hair. 'You must eat properly.'

'I might be able to. A couple of pieces, no more.' He reached up and caught her right wrist in his hand. 'I thought you wore this on your left one.'

'I do, as well.' And bent her head over his, red and calm. 'Now they match.' She stepped out of his clutch, as if to move away from him, backwards and out of the room, but in fact she came around the side of the chair over which he wasn't foolishly hanging. 'I couldn't resist them.' She waited for him to lever himself back again and then stood, with her wrists clamped together to show him how perfectly the cuffs, from which money dangled, made a pair.

Something stirred in him that must have been hunger. 'Delicious,' he said, turning his eyes away, and getting to his feet. 'Yes, a couple of pieces of cheese on toast with perhaps some tomatoes on top? What say you, sister mine?'

She cooked what he desired, with a quarter of a pound of mushrooms as well, and a mug of Horlicks for a nightcap. They made quite a little feast together, and he lectured her through it on getting what she had earned.

'Don't let our false-toothed friend exploit you, Din. Have you noticed that whenever money's mentioned he stops making jokes?'

267

'Well, I'm trying to make him remove the barbed wire.' She went into his kitchen and popped another slice of bread under the grill. 'And I think I've succeeded at last.'

She had. Although too late to prevent a young Turk from ripping his trousers and doing himself a serious injury when plucking a rose for a Danish girl.

He slipped into Mr. Spill's office, perched on the back of Mr. Spill's swivelling chair, and telephoned inquiries. He wrote the number down on a piece of paper and hurried to Din's cottage, where a Sunday lunch awaited him. But after he had swallowed down the last of her peppermint creams with a second cup of coffee, he made an excuse and went to his own cottage where he smoked cigarette after cigarette, and finally, driven by the smell, crossed the lawn and stole up the stairs.

'This is a friend of hers, actually.'

'I see. Yes?'

'Just calling up about the exhibition at the College.'

'Oh, yes?'

He turned his head away, to prevent a burp escaping down the line. 'Could I talk to her, please?'

'Well, you see—who is this, by the by?'

'George.'

'I see. Well, George, you see she isn't here. She spends most of her week-ends with a friend in London.'

During the silence that followed this he could tell that Mr. Trullope was breathing regularly and was therefore probably alive.

'Shall I tell her you 'phoned, George?'

'No, no. Oh, no. I'll 'phone another day. Not at all important.' But he couldn't put the 'phone down. It seemed to be glued to his hand at one end, to his ear at the other.

'Thank you for calling, George.'

'Well, thank you very much, sir.'

'Not at all. Good-bye.'

'Good-bye. And thank you very much, sir.'

'Not at all. Good-bye. Good-bye.'

'Good-bye, sir. Thank you, sir.'

'Good-bye, George.'

'Good-bye, sir.'

And pursued the smell to Din's cottage where, as a surprise for him, she was baking a chocolate cake, of which he got down three slices, each one accompanied by a cup of sweetened tea.

During the weekdays he gave his classes and did his marking and prepared a few lectures on literature, although he read very little. The novels of Lawrence occupied the place of honour on his cottage bookshelves, but he never picked them out. He had an instinct that they would stir feelings that were against the course of his life—would make shrill claims and be abusive. But he had developed a taste for thrillers, mainly American, and during breaks or while waiting for Din in the evening would lose himself in their pace and violence, their obliterating brutalities. Sometimes, if Din were working late (as she did more and more often) he went reluctantly into town to see a film. He had to avoid the better cinemas, where he might meet Hardles, for instance—back to do research and already on a Fellowship because of his astonishing gland, which had brought him a starred First. Or more importantly, Hazings, and Craley and Stafford, the Staff. He was sure that they knew where he was, and from tact were leaving him be. Sometimes he would visualize the scene in which he gave an account of his career at the Academy, of the Crab holding his jokes in check, of Hazings' enthusiasm. 'What a superb job it sounds. Doesn't it, Jennie? Fantastically worth while. In its way. Fantastically.' And the Staff's eyes, laconic with pity, assessing. He couldn't stand that. He could stand only his thrillers; and of course only and always Din, for evening chats and snacks and mugs of Horlicks. Occasionally he realized he was becoming inert, and aroused himself to displays of his old General Paper abilities, for her benefit. He would summon up memories of the early conversations with Hazings, and become intense about Lawrence again: and she would sit spellbound, intense with him, until he was reassured that the old powers were still there to be tapped when he wanted them.

In the classroom (hallowed by sunshine; airy and light even in the rain) he scrutinized the faces of the girls. A few were plain, many were pretty, two were beautiful. But there was only one face that he yearned to see, and in its absence all others, however classical or warm, were really blankly foreign. And they showed back at him merely a polite interest in his knowledge of English syntax; no knowledge of *him* and what he sought for, unendingly. He welcomed his escapes at break, for in the staffroom there were coffee and biscuits, and in his hip pocket his most recent thriller.

His colleagues themselves came to life only when he was in his cottage in the evening, replete and expansive, with the best audience in the world to encourage him. Then, with his wit and his sophisticated insights, and with a great deal of laughter, he conjured them up. One of his favourite pieces, reserved for the Horlicks and the cheese on toast, was a recreation of the Christmas party.

'Poor Ted,' she would say, giggling. 'He did look stupid.'

'He *is* stupid, Din, methinks.' And so was Meadle. Had she noticed how Meadle had given up his blazer and flannels for a dark suit? How Meadle came in on the mornings when he had no classes? How Meadle offered to do other people's hours for them if they had urgent marking? Or their marking if they had urgent hours? 'Infiltrating, you see. He's even got his own, special armchair, like Bloomington.'

'I know.' She giggled again. 'And Ted doesn't even see him. He simply expects Meadle to do two teachers' work on half a teacher's pay. If Meadle's idiot enough to do it, it's not Ted's fault.'

Well, what about Peaslow at lunch? Had she heard Ted's newest joke, reversing the letters of certain words, offering people 'bees and chiscuits' or 'a jass of gluice'. Heaslop had tried it, too, congratulating the cook on his delicious 'pabbage and cork', and Ted had pretended not to understand. He had made Heaslop repeat it five times. 'His stammer got so bad I thought he was going to cry.'

So he went through them, one after the other. He would rise to do imitations of Mr. Quine's swaying hips and soft, loving manner. 'Monsieur le vicomte kept dodging away, but Quine was octopedal, and managed to give him a hug of encouragement in the end.' He was satirical about Mr. Waybull's recent filing invention. 'Two cabinets, you see. There's the old one, where we put the sheets of prose and comprehension. Then one of the new ones, for putting the cards that refer to the sheets of prose and comprehension alphabetically. And the other new one, for keeping the slips that go on top of the cards that refer to the sheets of prose and comprehension numerically.'

'Yes.' She looked suddenly grave. 'Ted wants a word with him about that. Apparently he took one of the cabinets without his permission.'

And as for the bloody Winder—he would put down his knife and fork, protrude his teeth and raise his voice to a polemical yak. 'Theories about everything, Jap poetry, Scandinavian films, Dutch caps, Greek plays, French letters, everything except anything interesting or useful. The only person with sense is Bloomington, who remains unconscious all day.'

'Another piece, Dodie?' She put it, golden brown and topped with tomato, on his plate anyway. 'They're very sad, aren't they? I suppose it's because they've not made out as they wanted to, so they've settled into habits, to help them get by. It's very hard for people when they're failures.'

'Habits?' He sucked at his teeth to dislodge a string of cheese, and took a gulp from his special Horlicks mug. 'Habits? They're just *feeble*.'

'Yes, I know.' She slipped a coin from one bracelet under the band of the other, so that her wrists were joined. 'But perhaps they're lucky there's someone like Ted around to look after them.'

'Perhaps *I'm* lucky.' He cut away the tastiest corner of his snack, because he wanted to save it for last. '*Am I* lucky to have him around? What habits do *I* have, Din?'

'Oh, Dodie.' She raised her wrists, that were pinioned together, and averted her eyes. 'They're not like you.'

Well, if they were, he didn't want to know. He refrained, as a matter of digestive policy, from attributing independent life to them. If the space within their grotesque contours were filled with anything, it would be pain; or something worse. He refused to ponder the consequences of Mr. Waybull's tragedy or tragic behaviour in the Isle of Wight; found no time to consider the implications of Mr. Quine's increasingly flagrant advances to foreign nobility; put aside the possibility of a serious disorder as the root of Mr. Bloomington's slumbers; ignored the intellectual cravings that controlled Mr. Winder's analyses; noted Mr. Meadle's grovelling ambition, but not the panic in his eyes; listened to Mr. Heaslop's stammer only so that he could reproduce it faithfully; and in particular avoided conjuring up any image of Mr. Spill in his *stalag*. He didn't want to know. He gave his classes, did his marking, prepared a few lectures on literature; and didn't want to know. He was comfortable. Although it added to his comfort to say the reverse.

'But, Din, I've *got* to. You know I have.'

'I see.' She walked to his window, pulled aside the curtain and stared across the dark lawns. 'Have you been looking for anything?'

'Yes.' He went through the list of opportunities he had uncovered. 'This one's the best,' he concluded, handing her the advertisement to show he meant business.

'Kuala Lumpur?' She studied it carefully. 'It sounds a bit—well, this, what is it? Needing some experience of, and interest in, the problems of backward and deformed children? But at least,' she returned the fragment, 'at least you'd be able to feel it was a real challenge.'

'Exactly.' He unwrapped a toffee. 'Poor little devils.'

'And then perhaps Aunt Mary could help through one of her charities. Not that there'd be much competition, I shouldn't think.'

'My dear Din, Aunt Mary's charity begins at Mallows and ends at Morton. What would *she* know about the maimed and the starving. Besides,' he peeled the toffee paper away from the advertisement, to which it had become stuck, and chewed reflectively, 'besides, I wouldn't want to use family connections. *This* one I'm getting off my own bat.'

'I see.' She turned her head away. 'All right, Dodie.'

But as he didn't apply, it was doubtful whether even family connections would have helped. Instead he incorporated his morning surveys of 'appointments vacant' columns into their evenings together, and enjoyed the anxiety they caused almost as much as he enjoyed the Horlicks and the sardines (which had replaced the cheese) on toast.

He was comfortable.

Except when goaded by the smell into writing letters. One night he sent three; to which he received, of course, no replies.

'She was just a dirty little bitch', he reared up in bed

273

and reached out for the spam sandwich he had placed on the table beside him, for emergencies, 'and never cared about *me*.'

'Half a bottle of Scotch and a little chat with the twice of you.'

Actually he'd brought a quarter of a bottle, from which a small amount had already been extracted. 'A thimble for the faithful Meadle, forced to stay late and do some marking.' He hitched up his dark trousers, did something to his top teeth with his bottom teeth, and settled into his host's usual chair. 'What a cheerful little place! What a rustic paradise—ooops!' This last as his host lost his balance with the kitchen stool he was bringing in for himself, and ran forward with the seat held back like a shield and the legs thrust forward like weapons. Fortunately he just managed to steady up—another foot and Mr. Spill would have been crushed to paste—and to swivel smoothly around. 'I'll knock *you* about after the Scotch, my chap. *What* a cheerful place you've made of it.'

'I haven't done anything to it, actually.' He perched on the stool, which he had placed between the two occupied armchairs, and found the most comfortable position—feet spread far apart, but knees pressed together like little Jack Horner. 'Not a thing, Ted.'

In which case, Mr. Spill observed, it must always have been a cheerful little place. He poured whisky into the three glasses that had been passed to him, and handed two of them out. His eyes, as he did so, raced around the blank walls, and his mind made calculations. 'Would it brighten even more,' he wondered with presidential indirectness, 'to hang a few Academy prints in here?'

'Well, actually,' he sipped from his Scotch, 'there were some, but I took them down, Ted. I've put six in the cupboard under the stairs, and the other three are in my bed-

274

room. I thought', he sipped again, 'perhaps nine were a fraction too many?'

'Indeed? Certainly a fraction more than none. In your bedroom? How charming? Where?'

'In the cupboard,' he finished his drink a mere second or two before the others started theirs. 'Truth is, I like bare walls, don't know why, Ted. Just prefer them bare.'

'Because bare walls do not a prison make,' Ted explained. 'And if you bare walls do want, you bare walls must have, because we can't risk losing you.' (For, as had been pointed out to him a few days before, the Thwaites came in pairs; and to see one off to Kuala Lumpur, would be to see the other off to somewhere else.) 'The time has come for me to offer you what I call permanent—permanent, or Bloomington status. What do you say to that?'

'Well,' he jerked his mind away from the prints and from the fact that he had, quite accidentally, thrown the largest of them out with the rubbish, 'well, I must say that's very kind of you, Ted. That's jolly, well, generous, Ted.'

Mr. Spill held up the bottle and peered into it. 'Good heavens, it's all gone.' But he gave the impression, as he tilted it higher and higher, that he really wanted to peer through it, to make out the expression on his secretary's face. Not that it could have told him much, for it was merely brown (coloured by the glass) and savage (distorted by the glass). 'I'm too delighted to talk about duty and such gobbledegook. I sometimes talk of duty to Stan/Fred/ Francis Meadle, whatever name the poor fellow goes under these days, because he *will* apply for permanent, even when there are no vacancies, especially for him. But duty in your case,' he was now aiming the bottle as if it were a telescope at the top two buttons of his secretary's blouse, 'duty in, what? Oh, your case,' he steered the bottle away to neutral territory, before it should slip from his wet palm, and tried to put together some presidential sentences in his suddenly disordered mind. 'We all know you were a trifle unlucky in the tripos. I've made it common knowledge. No, I mean that you were worth more.' He lowered the bottle and his eyes, perhaps in sympathy, perhaps to avoid a calm, grey glare. 'All I mean is', he hurried, 'you've come in for a bit of a rise.' And praised himself double—for having got it out at last, this offer that was an affront to established policy; and for not following it with a little joke about his young friend having also come in for a bit of a swelling, around the chops and waist.

His secretary, noticing the state of her blouse and fumbling the buttons up with chinking wrists, smiled calm promises at him through her brother's stammered thanks.

And so, after Mr. Spill's visit and on thirty pounds a week (which was five more than Mr. Bloomington was getting; but then Mr. Bloomington was not himself on Bloomington status) he was even more comfortable. Whenever the smell besieged him he would grill himself some toast, or slip into his bed and pump out a counteracting smell of his own; and gave up writing letters.

Which was perhaps why, six weeks later, he received an answer at last.

That morning he laughed at all of Mr. Spill's jokes and at some of Mr. Peaslow's. He consulted Mr. Waybull about the filing cabinet ('I'm glad there's *one* man here who doesn't think me an absolute cretin') had a chat at break about a little Spanish count with Mr. Quine, and assisted Mr. Winder in the demolition of the films of Kirosawa. He couldn't fit Mr. Meadle in then, but that evening he stayed on in the staffroom to discuss the chances of a temporary becoming a permanent.

'There are times, Fred, when everything looks hopeless, but then something happens.' He leant forward to stroke the dark cloth of Mr. Meadle's sleeve, and there reverberated within him a profound chord of brotherhood. Tears started to his eyes. 'Things we need, desperately need, do turn out.'

'Yes, Ted and I get on very well. Do you know I'm working on a crossword puzzle of my own? I'll enjoy watching him struggle, it'll give us a laugh. What's more he's offered to let me do the invigilating and mark some of the exams.'

'Exactly, Fred. There you are. That's what I mean.'

'So you think,' Mr. Meadle looked down at the hand on his sleeve and edged his arm away, 'you think I've got a chance?'

'I know you have. Know you have. We all have.' And walked off, confident that he had done some good, and thus deposited a small amount in credit with the gods.

'Good night, Francis, good night,' he called from the door. 'Old chap.'

'So,' thought Mr. Meadle, watching him go, 'our fat friend's a pansy, is he? He'd better not sniff around *me* again, even if he *is* on permanent.'

But it was odd that, having mixed so eagerly with those about whom he didn't want to know, he should have spent the night avoiding his usual companion. He took the bus into Cambridge for an Indian dinner, went on to a film, and then drank Scotches and smoked cigarettes in a pub. When he got back he could tell from the fact that his curtains had been pulled and his dirty shirts collected, that she had been in during his absence, but he went upstairs to bed and read late. He was determined not to panic and to keep himself to himself.

The next evening he caught the bus to Cambridge again, and again he stayed late. This time, when he got back, the curtains were undisturbed, but the washed and ironed shirts had been left on the table for him. Once again he went to bed calmly, and settled for a long read that would release him from his tension. But when he had put the book down he lay staring feverishly at the ceiling, and in spite of two mugs of Horlicks it was almost morning before he got to sleep. He would probably have remained asleep, all through his early classes, if she hadn't let herself in and wakened him up. She turned on the hot tap so that he could shave quickly, grilled his bacon and made his coffee while he was shaving, and straightened his bedroom while he was wolfing down his breakfast.

'I had a feeling you wouldn't be up,' she said, as she followed him out of the door. 'Because something's been worrying you. Are you all right, Dodie?'

'Just a bout of insomnia.'

'Well,' she came to stand beside him, very close, 'I'll come in tonight and make sure you're eating enough.'

'Actually, Din,' he stared across the lawn to where the president, his face calm and still, was moving with his secateurs among the flower-beds, 'actually I have to go into town this evening.'

'Oh?' She waved a completely naked and thus totally silent wrist at the stooping figure. 'Why, Dodie?'

'To see an old friend—Hazings.'

'I see. Well, come to think of it,' she stepped away from him, towards the rose-bed, 'come to think of it, I did promise to stay late and go over some stuff with Ted.'

'Oh.' And he felt, ridiculously, a throb of disappointment.

He went to a cinema and left it. He went to a pub and left it. For a time he sat on the steps of a fountain in the market-place, smoking; then he walked down Trinity Street, between the old stones of the colleges, to the Cam; and from there went to Great Court. He had a bag of

278

toffees in his pocket, so that he could keep chewing, and another packet of cigarettes, so that he could keep smoking, for he knew that the important thing was to be occupied, and maintain the illusion that he was going somewhere definite. The images of his future, so vivid the night before, had blurred out of focus, but the tension of hope remained and was unbearable. He walked around the court, past the staircase where he had had his room, and looked up at the windows. The curtains of Hazings' were half-drawn, the light was on, and for a second he had a distinct vision of the table, the five of them up there with their properties laid out and their false money in their hands, negotiating. Craley scowling and scratching at his stubble; Hazings teasing Jennie; Stafford moving the shoe past 'GO' and collecting two hundred; himself a little on the outside, urbanely losing, wholly integrated. Among his friends. It was as if he could walk up the stairs and wittily into his old life. But suddenly the light went out, there came the slam of the oak door, and the sound of an usurper's steps on stone. He hurried off, out of the court, before he could be seen, even by someone who would not recognize him. For Hazings, married to his Jennie, wouldn't want to know.

Her cottage was dark and even the light above her front door was off. But he knew she was there. She was always there when he most wanted her. And there was something about the cottage, its tense compactness, that assured him of her waiting patience. He tiptoed through the hall, through the eloquent and welcoming silence.

'Din,' he whispered. 'Din, are you asleep?'

There was nothing. Yet her little house stirred around him, and was alive.

'Din,' he whispered again.

There was a sound, faint, despairing, above him.

279

He got to the stairs and moved softly up. The cries now were low, piercing, tender, calling him on, it was as if he were in a dream or mad, he could only follow, noiselessly, up the stairs, while the sounds rose to a mingled scream, and subsided.

He stood on the top step, before her closed bedroom door and faced at last the truth that he had already known for months.

So again she awoke him, earlier this time.

'You must be up to something in Cambridge,' she called, as she poured his coffee, 'that you come back exhausted each time.'

'Oh, I'm all right now.' He studied his face in the cabinet mirror. There was a small, brilliant cut at the side of his mouth where the razor had caught. 'I'm absolutely super, actually.'

And when he sat down he stared grinningly at her. She moved her face slightly, as if she found his grin a little strong, and was presenting him with the severe, delicate line of her profile to quell it.

'And what did he say?' she asked, after a long silence, broken only by the sounds of his breakfasting.

'Who?'

'Hazings, was it?'

'Oh.' He traced a buttery finger around the Academy grounds that had been stamped on the spoons, and then grinned at her again. 'I didn't see him after all. But I found out a few things.'

'Oh?'

'Yes. By the way, where are those bracelets you used to wear?'

'Bracelets.' He was pleased to note the flush on her cheeks. 'I wear them sometimes.'

'For special occasions, sort of thing?'

There was another silence, while he kept his grin and munched some toast; while she bowed her head and dusted at a speck on her blouse.

'You've been very good to me, Din,' he said suddenly, his grin becoming a laugh.

'What on earth do you mean, Dodie?' She looked up, looked down again.

He rose and went over to stand beside her. He could smell the crispness and freshness of her, the smell she always had, that mingled in his senses with a memory of the Morton seas. 'Oh, you have, Din. You've done a lot.'

'What have I done?'

'Now, Din, you know you've always been good to me. *That's* one of the things I found out last night.' He turned away. 'But we'd better go, or I'll be late.'

She didn't move. 'Will you be,' she hesitated, 'will you be in this evening?'

'Oh, yes,' he said. 'I'll be expecting you.'

And he was. The milk was already on when she arrived, and the Horlicks had been put into the mugs, and he was sitting comfortably in an armchair with his head thrown back so that he could grin at the ceiling until something funnier came along. She sat down opposite, in her usual chair, crossed her legs, and looked at him in a way that made it clear that she had decided to ignore his manner. 'You were in a funny mood this morning.'

'Was I?' He leapt to his feet and went into the kitchen. He brought in the milk and stirred it into the mugs. 'Everything seemed very strange to me, this morning.'

'Did it? Oh?'

'But it seems very simple, now.'

'Oh?'

'Yes.' He sat down and swung one leg over the other. There was an air of abandon in all his movements, and of jollity. 'I think, Din, I'll have a go at Janice again. Perhaps I was dreaming about that.'

She stirred her Horlicks, needlessly. 'I see.'

'But I don't expect, I really don't, that it'll amount to much. Things don't seem to, do they?' He swilled his Horlicks down with a flourish and went to the window. He stared out, to where the solitary light gleamed upwards. 'That is, if you depend on them.' Now he waited, and sure enough she too rose, and came to stand beside him. He looked down at the top of her blonde head, at the parting that showed a thin line of white scalp. 'Perhaps one should take everything as it comes, like, well, Ted does. Or you? Don't you do that, Din?'

She waited until his chuckle had ceased. Then, 'Why shouldn't it amount to anything, Dodie, between—between——'

'Janice? Janice Trullope.'

'And you. Why shouldn't it?'

He shrugged. 'Oh, I don't know. Perhaps it will, after all.'

They remained side by side without speaking, although he knew that she would speak soon, and that what she had to say he wouldn't be able to listen to. He felt her move slightly, so that her arm pressed against his. He heard her take a slight breath.

'Ah.' He pointed out of the window. 'It's time for you to go. The light's out over there.'

She stepped away from him and their eyes met. But whatever she expected to see on his face, there was only a bland, affectionate smile, the smile of a brother for a sister, or the smile of a young man who has become immensely fond of the confusions of the world. She turned as he opened the door and lifted her face to him to show him her tears, but with a chuckle and a playful shove he manœuvred her outside. When she stopped at the edge of the path and stared back, he raised his hand in jovial salute. But he continued to watch while she picked her way around his cottage, to the other, narrower path that led to her own. Then he went inside and scrambled himself some eggs.

'I wondered if you'd come,' she said across the darkness. 'I expected you would, though.'

He groped at the wall and found the switch in its remembered place. He turned it on and blinked towards the bed. 'Mmmm.' He smiled. 'Mmmm. I like the trousers.' They were white twist trousers and he did like them, although of course he had been expecting the jeans that had figured in his lonely nights. He also liked her blue singlet, her short leather jacket, and the little cap, suede and peaked, that she was wearing at a rakish angle on the back of her head. And said so with more 'Mmmmm's' and smiles.

'Are you coming inside?' She swung her legs off the bed. 'Or have you only got a minute?'

'Oh, lots of time.' But he stayed where he was, one hand holding the door open as if he were really intending to pass up the stairs and out through the loft. 'At your disposal, in fact.'

'Well, come in then.'

'Yes.' He stepped forward with a jerking movement that his easy laugh didn't quite smooth over and closed the door behind him. 'Thanks. Good. Well,' he rubbed his hands and gazed about him. 'All very different, toned up and sharpened.'

'Yes, I got some things in.'

The things she had got in were a number of new blankets and eiderdowns for the bed; a small table, with a black angle-poise on it; a wicker armchair that had probably spent many summers in a wet garden; a large piece of cardboard covered with bright red paint and harsh charcoal loops; and a new electric fire, with no bars broken. Under the bed was a carrier bag, from which the sleeve of a sweater hung out like the tongue of a dead animal. The drum, of course, had gone. In fact almost everything he remembered had gone, except the smell, that would linger there for ever, and would always be foul, and must be Donal's.

'*Very* smooth.' He concentrated on the painting. 'So, by God, is this. Whatever it is.'

'Oh, that. That was worked up from a memory of you.' She scrambled across the bed, tucking the blankets under the mattress, cuffing the ends of the pillow, tugging the sheets out at the top and folding them down. And from behind his urbane mask he watched her every movement with the intensity of a blind man whose sight has been restored.

When she had finished she knelt in the centre of the bed and watched him back. 'What are your plans, then?'

Oh, very good ones, Jan, it seemed to him. A little talk, say, first; a little drink, say, second; a little dinner afterwards, say, third; and then, all duties done and courtesies paid, together in bed, say, fourth. *Or* together in bed first and straight away; with the other activities trailing into the future, to add variation to night after night, so that he could be himself again in his virtuosity.

But it was difficult to explain these things to her directly while she was taking off her jacket and cap, and patting her hair, which was cut extremely short. So he stayed at one end of the room, silently teasing at her from under the spludged lampoon of himself; and she stayed at the other, on the bed they must soon occupy. Then, when she was ready, he walked swiftly towards her, his arms hanging loose for the embrace that would take her up again. On the last step he veered away to crouch by the fire. 'Let it come as it comes.'

'Well, what train are you getting?'

'The nine-thirty-six.' He spoke rapidly and positively, so that she would not underrate the commitments that he didn't have.

'Oh. Well, I've got something here, Donal left it specially because he said I'd be bound to need it.'

His shoulders jumped as if they had been touched and he whirled around. But she was nowhere near him—in fact she was kneeling with her back to him, and rooting about in the carrier bag from which she finally extracted a bottle of gin, about a quarter full. 'Like some?'

He said he would.

'Hadn't you better take your coat off, then?'

He said he had.

'Because you'll probably be getting a bit hot.'

He said he was. And sat negligently down in the wicker chair, which sagged under his weight.

'Oh, it suits you, fat does. Like me—my friends, they call me Dick. You know? Because Dick goes with my personality. And fat goes with yours.'

He pondered the name. 'No.' He shook his head. 'Not really you.'

'Well, fat *is* really you. And Dick *is* me. As I am now.'

His eyes shot down to the carelessly stretched legs. 'I've missed you, I have,' he said. 'Of course.'

'I missed you, too. But I expected I would.'

'Expected you would?' His heart quickened and his smile tightened. 'Has it been bad?'

'Not really. People come and go, don't they? And you hope they'll stay, or you make them go, depending on things. I was the one who wanted you to stay, so I always knew, I mean secretly, that you'd go off quite quickly.'

'And come back?' he reminded her. And transferring his glass to the other hand, he reached down and patted her on the head. Which swayed slightly, although she made no positive movement away from him. 'Yes, yes, I've thought about you all the time, Jan.'

She turned her face up to him. She stared at him frankly. It was a stare he knew from before, a stare that had filled his cottage and haunted his nights; and yet there was something new in it—an impersonal curiosity, as if she had stared at many other people in the same way since. 'Good of you,' she said, thus reducing him to the show of emotion that he had been saving up, like his spam sandwiches, for emergencies.

'Of course psychiatrists don't understand these things. I was, what? By myself, I suppose. Isolated.' Another gulp of gin mingled with his need, and exalted it. 'I think of it now as a sickness, a purging, too. And I couldn't get, oh, *you* involved. Not *you*, of all people.'

'Oh, yes. And how's your sister, then?'

'My sister?'

'Yes—what's her name—Deidre?'

'Dianah?'

'Yes. How is she?'

'I don't', he shook his head, 'really know.'

'But isn't she at that place? Where you wrote all those letters from?' She giggled suddenly. 'Sorry. It's the gin, it gets me like that. That place.'

'The Academy? Yes, she's there.'

'So you're living together?'

'Together? Of course not. I live by myself. In a cottage in the country.'

'A cottage? You lucky bastard.'

'Yes, it's pretty good.' He dropped his hand innocently and thus could not let himself notice that she shifted, casually, away from it. 'If you like rustic living, etc.'

'Does *she* have a cottage?'

His arm flopped against the chair. 'Yes.'

'Is it near yours?'

'Yes.' And he saw that the fact that he and Din lived so close to each other at the Academy had somehow put more inches between Janice and himself at Little Side. It was going to be difficult to touch her now. It was going to be difficult to do anything other than gaze into his empty glass and long to touch her, long to explain that he was offering himself back for ever. Then she shifted suddenly close to him and put a hand on his knee, and something in the angle of her head showed that suddenly she was aware of him. Gently he slid his hand down and gently he rested it around the curve of her shoulder. The cotton of her singlet was thin, her skin was warm beneath it, and he drained off his gin, for courage.

'Janice.'

'Why don't you call me Dick. I'm more used to it, see.

'I can't help it,' he said tautly. 'You're Jan, Janice to me. But I'll try and call you Dick, if you want.'

She let out a shout of laughter that was still, with whatever ears he listened, a kind of yap. 'Christ, I don't mind, honestly. It's just that I hate Janice. Except from Mum and Dad.'

He, too, laughed; mysteriously. 'I expect they think I behaved a trifle badly.'

'Oh, yes. She thinks you're an intellectual seducer, and very treacherous. A disgrace to your education, she said. I think she meant about your being at that school you went to and Cambridge. Anyway, I don't know because she never mentions you now. That was when I was crying a lot.'

'Crying a lot?'

'She cried, too, to keep me company. That's why I stopped. I couldn't bear her being all disappointed and sniffling around Wimbledon. Dad didn't mind so much. He says that people like you don't matter.'

'An intellectual seducer? So she knows, she knows, well,' he hesitated from sheer excitement, 'knows that we—that we——'

'Fucked? Yes, well that part of it's tricky. She can't really hate you unless you fucked me, but then she can't admit that I let you fuck me, see? She makes it all a matter of broken promises.'

'Oh.' He stroked his hand down her back. 'I'm sorry, Jan,' he whispered. 'I'm so sorry.'

'But, Christ, who cares?' She shifted again, until she was resting against his leg. 'Honestly, Grahame, *I* don't.' And her grin of reassurance drained the last of his hope out of him.

'Well, go on then. In what ways?'

'Oh, perhaps—I don't know, more—wiser?'

'Oh, yes, I'm that all right.'

'And—kinder?' he begged.

'No. I'm not. I'm nastier.'

'Of course you're not, Jan. That I don't believe.'

'Don't you? Well, I'm quite generous and everything. I'm generous to Donal and look after him, but I'm nastier when I think about people. I think about what they want, and why they do things, and all that stuff. How they think about me, for instance. *Now* I think about that.'

'But you always did.'

'No, I didn't. Not about,' she tugged at a lock of her hair, frowning, 'not about you. I mean, there you were, and I wanted you because of, well, the way we met, and the way you talked about things, D. H. Lawrence and that, and

289

the way you would go silent and strange. I really thought I loved you, I mean I could stand *every*thing about you, even the smell you made from fucking. Well, of course everyone makes that smell, but yours was very strong and put me off a bit until it was, you know, *you*. So when you broke it off by doing sums, at first I just withered. But like I said, I'd been expecting it because I couldn't get it out of my head that you were better than me. It wasn't until afterwards that I really thought about you. About everything—well, like that time you clasped your forehead over being a coward with some boy at school you fancied, the one who died on you. Even that seemed marvellous, because it was from *you*, see. But then I wondered what was so great about being a coward.'

'I'm not any more. That's why I've come here, Jan. To tell you that. And about that smell——'

'Aren't you? Well, perhaps you're not. Perhaps it was just a bad time in your life.'

'It was. Terrible.' He raised his hand towards his forehead, then remembered in time to chop it sideways in contemptuous dismissal of the person he'd been, and the bad time he'd gone through.

'But then perhaps you still are. That', she explained ,'is the way I think about people now.'

'Yes,' he pointed out huskily, 'but I've come back, haven't I, Jan?' He clutched downwards, the chair creaking and one or two of the wicker strands actually cracking from the change in balance; clutched downwards, at the floor, and would have crashed on to it if she hadn't steadied it with a foot from where she was now lying. When he righted himself and looked towards her she had scrambled another few yards and was sitting against the back of the bed.

'Oh, you've probably come back because you need a good fuck, Grahame, and you're used to doing it with me. Virgins are always like that, for a time.'

290

'No, Jan. No.' He pulled at the strands on the seat under him, and some came away in his hand. 'That's not it.'

'You don't want to fuck me then?'

'Yes, but not—but only because it's *you*.' He held the strands up in evidence.

'Me?' She sprawled across the floor and tilted her small face to the ceiling. Her eyes were shut, either from concentration or because she had finished a tumblerful of gin and was perfectly comfortable. 'Well, that's probably the same thing. I mean, after you left *I* thought it was all over, bed and men and everything. And then I found out that almost all the men I met, except Donal who's bent, want to fuck me. Because I'm pretty and sexy and that. I honestly am. I always *hoped* I was, before. But then I actually was. Men just can't lay off me, even the teachers at school. Before you it was fumbling around and a quick dip, and my being grateful that anyone wanted to. But after you it's quite different. Easy, really.'

'Easy? Easy?' And hope revived. For if it was easy to do it with *them*—why it was also easy to do it with him. He was as they were, whoever they were, and would get his share. Of course he didn't put it to himself in those terms. He merely made a moral gesture, in gratitude. 'That's wrong, Jan. To do it just like that.'

'Is it? I'm only telling you how nasty I've become. And also', she added, with a little yap that converted itself into a yawn, 'why I don't want you to fuck me.'

He sat perfectly still as she lowered her face, opened her eyes, and smiled at him.

'See?'

He shook his head.

'Well, if it's just fucking you want, then you don't want *me*. And if you do want me, then you can't have me because I don't want *you* any more, and just fucking's no good to you, is it? Because to me fucking is fucking. So it's better if you just treat me like, well, an old girl-friend and that crap.'

They sat in silence for a long time. Eventually Dick (who again gave him permission to call her Jan, as a tribute to their former relationship) said she was hungry and shouldn't they eat soon? Especially as he had to catch the 9.36, wasn't it?

During the first part of the meal all that he observed was that her appetite was unnaturally large, under the circumstances; and his own, naturally under the circumstances, larger. She, however, had a great deal to observe in the form of comments that carried him poignantly back to other meals together, taken in other moods. She remembered the waiter ('Certainly the same one. The frog with a wig on'; this accompanied with a regal nod to the waiter, who returned it with added meanings); investigated her fellow diners ('I bet he makes her wear a nightie with horsehair outside and a hole in the bottom, for himself to slip through when he's not looking'), and enjoyed her food. ('Steak and wine are just the sexiest. Aren't they?') But of course he wanted her to say all these things, and as many more as she liked, as long as she was saying them to him. The large fillet and the jacket potato and the glasses of Beaujolais were warming him into the conviction that she wouldn't behave in the old way in public if she wasn't going to behave in the old way in private. She showed it in all her familiar gestures—leaning over the table to rap his knuckles gently with her fork, for instance—and in her characteristic jokes. She *did* know him.

'What time have you got to be back in Wimbledon?' he wondered, bringing a shout of laughter to a snuffling end.

'Oh, I'll stay in the rathole. It's you you've got to worry about.'

'But can you stay there without—you know—your parents——?'

She cracked at the meringue surrounding her peach and scooped out the cream. 'Well, one good thing about that business with you is that Mum doesn't worry. She wants it that I'm suspicious of men and that rubbish, like one of those novelists she reads.'

They had Camembert and biscuits, two cups of coffee each and a saucer full of peppermint creams, compliments of the house; and there was nothing she could do, even to spilling her coffee and yapping with laughter, that didn't intensify his need for her. Her bulging mouth, her grunts of satisfaction—these, and most particularly her grins across the table—held him enslaved. And still he waited, waited for the moment when she would suddenly recognize him fully, and grant him the forgiveness he deserved because of the past they had had together, and the future they would share.

'Look, how much money have you got?' she whispered, as he took out his wallet to pay the bill. 'I mean, could you lend me a bit?' And as her green and slanted eyes met his, he saw at last what he had yearned for; the glistening of her desire. 'We'll be seeing each other again, won't we? So if you could, you know, for tomorrow if I have to stay in London and see some people?'

He whipped out a fiver and thrust it at her; rejoicing that something of himself had passed into her keeping at last.

She shoved the note into a little pocket-slit above and to the right of her pelvis, wiped coffee from her mouth, and went off to the lavatory. 'Won't be a minute. Be right back.'

He followed her with hungry attention; and thus noted that she turned down the corridor that led to the telephone, and that it was three minutes before she hurried past the opening and down the corridor that led to the lavatory. While he waited he unwrapped peppermint creams and popped them compulsively into his mouth. His appetite had flared again in her absence.

'Did you make a 'phone call?'

'Did I?' She frowned. 'Oh, yes. Had to talk to someone.' She stood above him, putting on her leather jacket. 'When did you say you were going? Was it the nine-thirty-six?'

'In about an hour. What about?'

'What?' She adjusted the peak of her cap.

'The 'phone call?'

'Oh, I don't know. Nothing. Somebody I'll probably drop in on tomorrow, that's all. Do I look all right?'

He unwrapped the last peppermint cream. 'Yes.'

'Come on, then. We can get half a bottle of something and have a quick drink before you rush off.'

'Yes,' he said impassively. 'We could do that. Half a bottle and back to Little Side.'

'It'd be much nicer guzzling it in the park.'

But he was too busy smiling good nights at the waiter to hear her.

He paid for half a bottle of brandy out of the last of his five-pound notes, and took her arm as they walked past the shop into which he was determined not to glance. But he did, an uncontrollable swing of the eyes that showed him she was still there, tinted by the back light, trapped in her chains and clamps and metal gag. He wondered aloud who bought rubbish like that. 'Those tubes and whatever those other things are. Radio bulbs?'

He studied it for about half a minute, hoping he was paling visibly rather than, as he suspected, reddening ridiculously. He slapped his cheek. 'Ohmigod. I forgot. It's Saturday.'

'Yes. It's Saturday.'

'There isn't,' he jabbed the time-table into his pocket, 'there isn't a nine-thirty-six on Saturday.'

'Isn't there?'

'No.'

'Well, you'll have to get a later one then. Won't you?'

'But that's it. That's the terrible thing. There isn't a later one.'

'Isn't there?'

'They've all gone.'

'Have they?'

'Yes.'

'If you say so.'

'What do you mean?'

'Well, if you say it's gone, I expect it's gone, is all I meant.' She clipped the top on the brandy bottle and made a strange movement of her shoulders, as if bracing herself for something. 'What are you going to do, then?'

'Well, I could go to a hotel, I suppose. For the night.'

'Yes.'

'Yes, but then', he explained, 'I haven't any money, unless of course you let me have that fiver back. That's probably the best thing, isn't it?'

She sighed at last. 'You'd better stay here.'

'Well, I don't want to put you out.'

'That's all right.'

'But are you *sure* you don't mind?'

'If you've got to, you've got to.'

Yes. Exactly. As he put his arm around her shoulder and drew her towards him, he felt like a man who has just begun to discover his own resources. And also like a man who has reached the end of an extremely difficult manœuvre with a fragile object. The possibility of failure was remote; and consequently intensely present. 'Oh,' he whispered, 'Janice. Darling.'

'Yes.'

'I've missed you so much.'

'I know.'

'How do you know?' He blew into her hair. 'Darling.'

'Well, mainly because you keep telling me.'

He strained out his finger-tips to press them against the swell of the singlet. 'Because now you can trust me. Now you know——' he kissed her on the cheek and scooped her into the side of his body. Then he kissed her on the mouth, which opened immediately to let his tongue enter. But it remained open, merely, and was nothing more than an entrance for tongues. He drew his head away. 'You know me now, don't you, Jan?'

'Oh, yes, I know you.'

'Will you,' he dropped his eyes, 'will you come to bed then?'

'Oh, all right.' And marvellously, she got up; and marvellously, humming, not looking at him, intent on what she was doing, she unclipped her trousers and slid them down her legs. Then she pulled off her singlet and unfastened her bra. Every movement of the slender and strange body, which was about to be his again, was full of miracles.

'You used to like seeing me strip, didn't you?'

'Seeing you', he explained, '*emerge*. For me.'

'I know what it's like. I mean must be.' She walked across the room in her black short knickers, and climbed into the bed. 'I saw a film once where this girl was made to strip. The man had a gun and I expect that's what got me, I mean her having to be a sort of toy for him or something. I'm very kinky like that.'

'So am I,' he boasted, as he strode, penis erect, towards her. 'I am, too.' He got in beside her and took her in his arms.

'What are you doing, then?' she asked, after a moment of swift activities from him. 'You won't get to sleep if you stir yourself up like that. Could you get up and turn out the light, please, and switch off the fire? I don't know how I'd get past you. You're so big. Fatter than I thought, even.'

He got out of bed, walked across the room, and turned out the light. He bent down and switched off the fire. As he did these things he prayed that her eyes were upon him, and that she would respond to his body as he had responded to hers. He turned lithely around, but the room was so dark that he could hardly see the bed. He walked delicately forward, until his knee struck the iron bedstead. He climbed in.

'Careful with your feet. They're cold. Good night.'

'Good night?' His body was, inevitably in the narrow bed, pressed against hers again, but she had rolled over to present him with her back. His penis prodded against the cloth of her knickers. 'Oh, Jan, I love you.'

She made a groaning sound.

'Love you,' he sighed. He pushed out his arms, encircled her body, and closed his hands around her breasts. Her nipples were soft against his palms.

'Oh, Jesus Christ, what are you up to? All that stuff about time-tables.'

He jerked his arms away.

'Just to fuck me. I mean——' she wriggled against the wall.

He lay rigid, staring into the darkness. 'I thought you'd understand,' he whispered.

'Understand *what*?'

'Everything. Me,' he whispered.

'Well, I expect I do. I certainly understand about people who can't get trains and have to stay the night. I know all about *them*. I've been through it once a week, it seems to me.'

'I'm not—I'm not like them. Not like them.'

U   297

'Well, it doesn't matter, because you can't have me. See. I *mean* it, Grahame, I really do.'

It was a great rage that welled from his very heart. '*You* know. *You* know,' he shouted. 'You're the only person in the whole world who *does* know. There's nobody else. In all my life, only just, just——' and he lurched up. 'God. God. Oh Jan, you can't forget me. Please. You can't. It's wrong. I *need* you. It's wrong.' At which point he pounded his fist on his knee, where he had hurt it against the bed, in order to cause a distracting pain. 'Please,' he whimpered.

'Is it wrong?' She was implacable and sounded even a little rehearsed. 'I don't know what's wrong, I honestly don't. What I did with you, and with Terry and old Clitheroe, and lots of others, well, Mum would think that's wrong. And if I don't do it with you, and with them, then that's wrong. But why *should* I? It's my body, isn't it?'

But it wasn't her body. He had had it once, owned it so completely that for a time it had possessed no magic. But he had left himself within it, and now he wanted himself back by being in it again, for a good fuck. How could it be her body when she made it so attractive to him, when she wore fashionable twist trousers and grinned at him, when she undressed in front of him and said she was kinky and lay down beside him. When she had done all the things he hadn't forgotten, and a few others he would never forget. She was his.

But he could say none of this. The rage had passed and he seemed to be alone with his smarting eyes and his bruised knee, staring down the passage of his future and seeing himself in his need, for ever abandoned.

'Yes,' he said at last, 'you're right. It's me. Me, me, me, always me. I can't help it. Nobody can. Millions of us, all of us the only ones. Demanding our rights, asking for help. When there aren't any rights, there's no one and nothing. Oh, we're all babies, all of us, wanting someone to take

298

charge. That's what I want. That's it.' He spoke as if to the world that he had known, explaining it to itself, its follies and rages and deprivations. He spoke to all the others everywhere, the ones he understood at last, from Fairwell in the showers to Mr. Spill in his prison camp. He had resolved the mystery and was peering in on himself, in his own jail.

She stirred. She turned her head so that her mouth was close to his ear. Her hand moved to touch him gently on the thigh. And the desire quickened in him again, and a certain wonder also. There was going to be a miracle after all, and he was to be given the rights he had denied.

'Yes,' he focused his eyes emptily ahead, every nerve in his body vibrant to her gentle hand, 'that's what I am. What we all are. Orphans. There's no one to take us and free us from ourselves. No one.'

Her hand moved up his thigh and rested on the bulge of his belly. His penis, treacherously confident and deaf to all philosophies, sprang upright; and forced him into further improvisation. 'We all want justice,' he throbbed, shifting his eyes to keep the miracle coming, and sweeping from his mind the intrusive image of Mr. Keel, for whom he had once written, 'It could be said that the problem of divine love and human justice. . . .'

'Grahame.' She whispered his name. 'Grahame.' And her hand slid down to enclose him. 'Poor Grahame, oh, poor Grahame.' And she began, with rhythmic pity, to stroke him. He remained still, to make it clear to her that the reactions of his flesh in no way diminished the stature of his newly discovered and tragic self. 'Please,' she whispered 'oh please, Grahame, please hold me.'

He rolled woodenly over and clamped his arms around her.

'Tight. Pull me tight, oh hold me, Grahame. Hold me.'

'Jan, my poor Jan,' he murmured, drawing her against him. 'My poor darling. Are you an orphan, too, Jan?'

'I am, I know I am, I know.' Her hand went softly, explosively on, and he fell slack against his will, and threw his head back, and spread his legs. 'We're all forlorn, Jan,' he crooned. 'All of us.' His hand slipped down to her knickers, then between her thighs to press triumphant against the damp cluster. 'Lost.'

'Yes,' she grieved, 'yes. Even old Clitheroe was, I know.'

But he was no longer listening, for the folds had opened to receive him.

But when he was on top of her, his whole self driving into *her*, his Jan who had been returned to him, she rode under him with a strange impersonality, as if soothing all the helpless traitors, the cowardly orphans in the world. And afterwards, when he was spent, crumpled on top of her, she responded to his blessings and gratitudes with only a monotonous moan, as if she were in a shock. She gave him in his time of complete dependence no name. His cry had been for the millions. On behalf of the millions she had taken him. But in his exhaustion he didn't much care. He went to sleep quickly, only dimly aware that she was still awake beside him, and that there was something he had left unsaid.

When he awoke she was standing, fully dressed, by the bed.

He moved his arm and groaned. 'It hurts.'

'I've been pinching it.' She went across the room and crouched by the fire. 'To wake you.'

He walked unsteadily into the kitchen and washed his face under the cold tap. Then he came back into the room and stood naked above her. She demonstrated how alive she was to his presence by not moving a muscle. He touched her stubble of hair; and she lowered her head.

300

They had breakfast in the same café to which he had once escaped to read the morning papers. He said nothing while they drank and ate, for he realized that what he had to tell her he could only say when she was in a mood to listen. There was something about her at the moment, the way she kept her eyes away from his, the way she seemed absorbed by the coffee or the two market porters at the next table, that indicated that she no longer shared his potent vision of the night. But he was untroubled, for neither did he. He glanced at her occasionally, and within himself he grinned.

They went to Leicester Square Underground where he telephoned the Academy. He hadn't decided what he was going to say to Din, but he knew that it would be something casual, something conspiratorial. He would find a phrase, either now or later, that would make her realize that he, too, was grown-up at last and no longer needed her interference. He would be gentle, though, now that he understood the mechanics of maturity.

But she wasn't there. Mr. Spill had been waiting in his office (after a white night on the camp-bed in the closet) to inform him that Aunt Mary was seriously ill and that Din had gone to Morton the day before. She was expecting him there.

Ah yes. He thanked Mr. Spill and hung up. It was, of course, something to be taken into account. Aunt Mary was ill and he would have to go to Morton, almost for Din's sake. He knew she wasn't lying, but he couldn't believe her really. It was one of her interventions, instinctive and inspired, and he was on his guard. He looked out of the booth at Janice, who was lolling against one of the ticket machines, her hands in her jacket pockets, yawning. He was proud of her for being so pretty. And he was quite sure of himself, in his freedom.

They went to Waterloo together. When he put his arm

around her shoulder, she leant negligently against him; and she didn't shrink away when he darted a playful tongue in her ear and whispered an endearment.

'Well, you got what you wanted, didn't you?' she said abruptly. 'You and your sobbings.'

'I'll just buy my ticket,' he said. And when he came back. 'Are you angry?'

She stared at him, her large, slanting eyes fixed on his face.

'Well,' he touched her on the scar, 'I'll see you when I get back.'

She shrugged.

'Sunday evening?'

'If you want.'

'And don't worry about the fiver. I've got lots.' He stepped forward to kiss her, but she moved her mouth away. So he gave her a friendly squeeze instead. 'Sunday then? Or something soon. O.K.?'

As she turned away, he wondered for a moment where she was going and why he'd forgotten to ask her. But he didn't call out. He watched her as she moved through the crowds to the escalators, then when she had been carried down and out of sight, he went to the platform and got into the Havant train. He sat in a corner of the first empty compartment, folded his arms across his chest, and stretched out his legs in the posture of a man who has a great deal to think about.

But ten minutes after the train had left the station he was asleep.

CHAPTER FOUR

A shaft of light shone directly across her face, thus giving
him the impression that she had been decapitated. Then she
was a white outline wavering towards him, calling his
name against the rushing wind and the heaving of the distant seas. He stood on the path, boggling and mouthing,
until suddenly human arms were around him and she was
proving (for the second time in a week) that she was only
flesh and blood like himself. For a second it almost didn't
matter that everything was well at Mallows and that at the
top of the house Aunt Mary would be sitting in bed,
fit as a fiddle, with her charity nonsense spread over the
covers.

'Oh, Dodie, Dodie.' She hugged him closer. 'Oh, Dodie.'

He detached himself with cynical tenderness and tried to
remember one of the sentences he had prepared before
falling asleep on the train.

'Just a little bit of independence', he began, 'is all I ask,
sister mine. You have your Ted and——' she was hurrying
ahead, towards the hall, and the wind was carrying his
words back into his face; so with a comic roll of the eyes he
followed her. Followed down the hall, and up the stairs,
to the bedroom door. And with another comic expression,
allowed himself to be ushered into his Aunt Mary's
presence.

Where he sat for about an hour, in polite silence, bent
attentively forward in his chair but actually looking down
at the floor. When he dared to raise his eyes to the bed at

last he saw only the gaunt, anxious face of an old woman who appeared to be waiting for some word—of affection, perhaps, or gratitude. He jerked his hand to his mouth in a kind of agony, but it was too late. The noise that came out was percussive, a pistol shot of laughter. 'I'm sorry,' he whispered, 'I'm sorry.'

In the end, when he could no longer trust her stillness— once the eyes had unshuttered, and once the hands had clenched deeper into the sheets—he went out on to the landing and paced up and down in front of the grandfather clock. From downstairs he could hear a steady, hiccough-ing sound, and the tread of military feet, precisely measured on the living-room floor. Later he heard Dr. Blander's consolation and Din's soft voice. He moved closer to the stairs, in the hope that his indistinct figure in some way matched the hiccoughing and marching; and tried not to notice his hunger.

She stood against the bedroom door, with her head tilted and her arms folded against her stomach.

'Oh Dodie, it was awful. She kept trying to get up, and suddenly her glasses dropped off and she fell out of the bed. She crawled across the room; Dodie, she was crying because of some documents she couldn't find. And then we got her back, Dr. Blander lifted her and she struggled and— and—' She held her hand out suddenly, illuminating the area around them with pathos. 'After he'd gone I did her hair.'

'I'm sorry,' he said, 'I'm sorry. I didn't know.'

She opened the door, to flash him a glimpse of the grey lump on the pillow, the neat shaping under the sheets. 'I had to do her hair, so Colonel Rones could go in. He's been downstairs. He's been sobbing for hours.'

'I didn't know. I'm sorry. I didn't know.'

'Didn't Ted tell you?'

'He said she was ill. That's all.'

'Oh.' She closed the door, and turned away. 'He probably couldn't bear to say anything. He's like that.'

He went up to his room, lay down, shut his eyes, and pressed his face into the pillow. He would be found in the morning, fully clothed, and in tears. He must be, to show that he too was human, as human as Colonel Rones and Din and Dr. Blander. He swung his legs off the bed and struck himself in the face. But before the tears could come he had sagged back against the wall, asleep.

When he awoke there was someone sitting at the foot of the bed, and a hand was on him somewhere. He crouched away with a defensive gesture.

'You were having a nightmare, Dodie.' She touched him on the foot. 'You cried out.'

'I'm sorry,' he began. 'I didn't know.'

She knelt beside him, and took him in her arms. 'Oh Dodie. Oh Dodie.' And miraculously he began to cry.

Later, while she made him coffee and ham sandwiches in the kitchen, she told him about the funeral. He looked at her while she talked, and made numerous offers to help. He wanted, desperately wanted, to be thanked for something.

And he was thanked, quite often; although there was nothing he could actually do.

For a time he sat staring at the Mipps football in the corner, and the cricket pad that lay beside it. Then he studied the shelf of books that had made him a Major Scholar in History with a special gift for the General Paper —Sabine's *History of Political Theory, The Meaning of History, The Idea of History, Six Existentialist Thinkers, Kafka and the Modern Predicament.* Beneath that was another shelf where he had kept his different books from Windhoven—two novels about bull-fighting, a history of jazz (unread), and the translations of Lorca that Cranton had given him on his fifteenth birthday. He reached towards the Lorca, but turned suddenly and instead to the memento of his one great sporting year. From a distance he could make out only a clouded line at the top, of faces merging; and a clouded line at the bottom, of merging knees. The middle was a long smudge of chests and laps and more faces. He walked over and peered among the identical spheres, until he had found himself in the centre of the standing row. The school phenomenon stared back at him, grave and dedicated.

In the living-room Din was going over some papers that had tumbled suddenly out of the base of the grandfather clock.

'But what were they doing there?'

'I don't know.' She folded them over with a secretary's speed and knowledge, but her smile was perplexed. 'She can't have *put* them there.'

'Unless they were the ones she was looking for.'

'Oh no. Aunt Mary always knew where everything was.'

'Yes she did, bless her? He went idly to the desk, and began to go through it. All the drawers were empty, except for the bottom one, which had jammed slightly. It contained a copy of *Great Expectations*, the cover of which had caught underneath the catch of the drawer above. He prised it free, ran the drawer back and forth, and was about to replace the book when he saw an edge of yellow protruding from the middle pages. It was the corner of a snapshot that had been taken in the garden about sixteen years before; of a little boy and a little girl standing under the apple tree. The little boy, dressed in singlet, shorts and sandals, stood aggressively—round face thrust out, shoulders drawn back, stocky legs planted. The little girl stood beside him, one thin arm raised so that her hand had been frozen just above his shoulder. Her blonde hair was combed neatly down each side of her face, and she was smiling. At least there was a formal, upward lift to her lips that was like a smile.

He looked at both, but particularly he looked at the little girl. Once he glanced from her to the young woman on the sofa, who was now shuffling the documents into separate piles. There was no point of comparison, apart from the slight smiles and perhaps the eyes. But even the eyes were an illusion, for when he checked the ones in the photograph again he saw that they were merely two blank spots that gave nothing away. He put the children back where they belonged, beneath the closing paragraph; leaving them to go with Pip and Estella down the years, to their revised happiness. Then he went through the french windows.

He walked around the hen-coop and out through the side gate to the Shore Road. He had no idea of going anywhere, and even when he had passed the Admiral's house and turned up Sea Lane, hurrying through the summer heat, indifferent to the Butlin's bicycles and the music from the new arcade, he was only dimly aware that the Slocum school lay ahead of him.

Four neat houses in a ruched cement that reminded him of Din's first bathing-costume, and behind them the lawns had been cut into sections to make four small gardens, with concrete paths and little areas of crazy pavement. He was still smiling at the fear that had driven him so purposelessly, when suddenly a corner of grass between the two houses opposite opened into a green perspective that shrunk him down. He waited on the pavement, helpless, as his nostrils filled with the odour of marsh and lemon, and a ghost gleamed towards him in the sunshine. And he stood trembling, long after the scent had been carried away and the ghost had become merely one of the many shadows that flitted and danced down the empty street.

Later he made his way to a deserted part of the beach, sat down against one of the banks, and stared out across the wet ridges to the first small waves of the sea. Eventually, and without Din to help him, he began to cry. They must have been cleansing tears, that marked the end of something or the beginning of something else, for when he returned to Mallows he felt quite free.

'God,' he said that night as they packed, 'I'll be glad to get back to Cambridge.'

'So will I,' she said, discreetly emptying his small case and refolding all his clothes so that they wouldn't become crumpled.